Destruction from Twins, and So It Must End….

ONE comes *swiftly* in the *morning*.
ONE *unknowing* moves in *haste*.
ONE *beloved* though *mighty* fallen.
ONE is *chosen* to *forget* her place.

ONE though *strong* must fall *forbidden*.
ONE made *low* shall *rise* again.
ONE must be as these *words* written,
Then will ONE *forever reign*.

CARROLL

LOR MANDELA

Destruction from Twins

L. CARROLL

2011 Re-Release
Published by
House on the Horizon Books
USA

CONTENTS

MANDELA PALACE
AND ADJACENT TERRITORIES

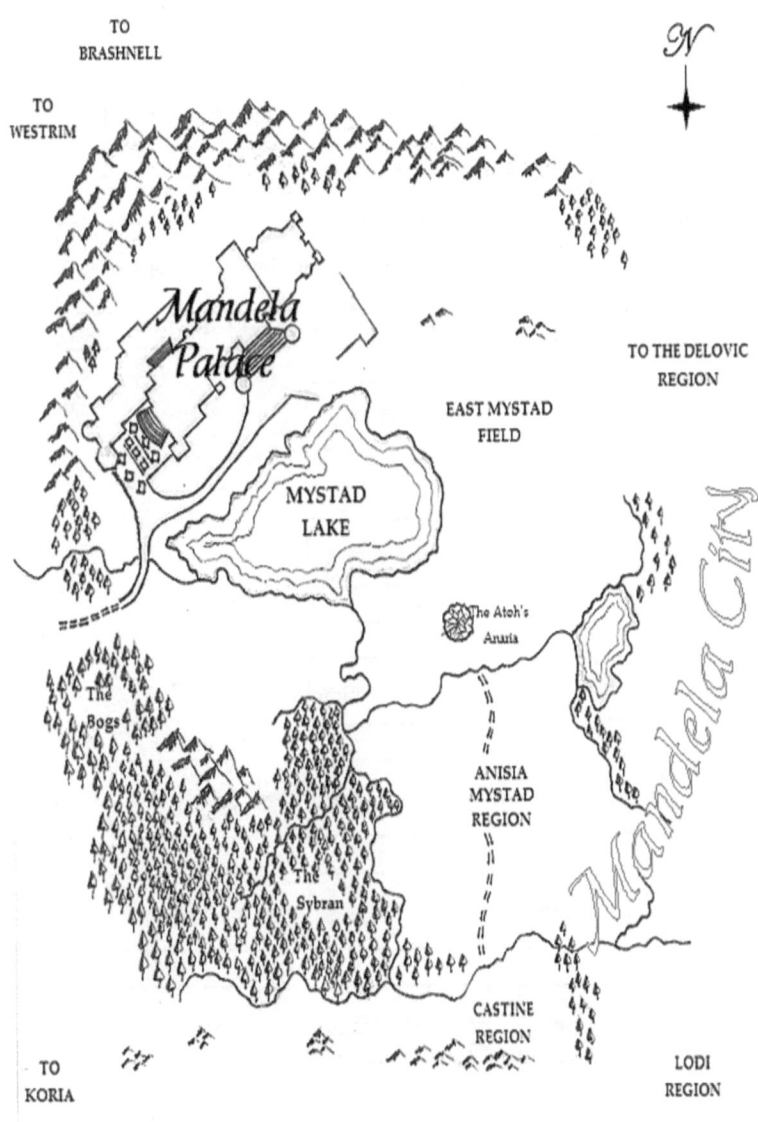

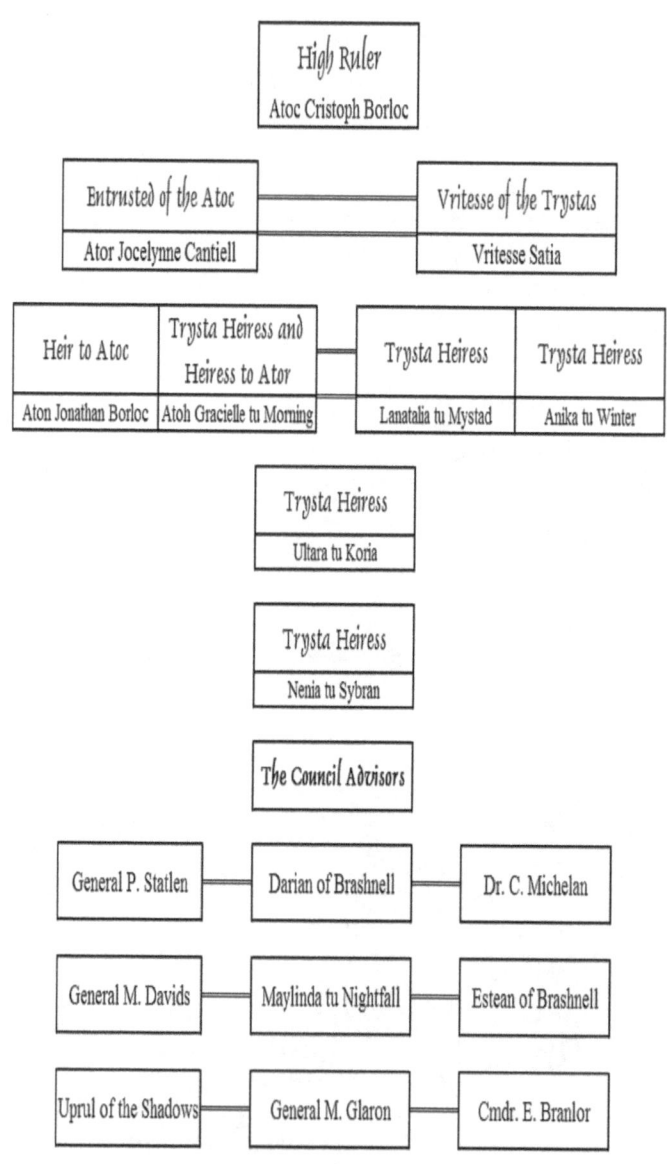

For my Fix-it Girl, Maggie's Twin,
The boy who discovered the Squanki,
Glogan, and Pooka.

And for the love of my life.
On to the next adventure...

Prologue

The alarm clock clicked from 6:04 to 6:05 a.m., and let out a sadistic buzz which jolted Maggie from a deep, comfortable sleep. With great effort and a disgusted moan, she reached out and smacked the top of the clock, hitting the snooze button for the first of three routine extra ten minutes. The room was quiet and almost completely dark; a faint cool breeze played with the sheer curtains that hung on the open window. In Maggie's estimation, these were the ideal sleeping conditions—a fact that only added to the cruelty of it being morning already.

Bzzzzz. Smack!

Wrapped in her favorite blanket and surrounded by a mountain of pillows, she wandered back and forth between awake and asleep—one moment aware of her surroundings, the next, slipping effortlessly into the beginnings of nonsensical dreams.

Bzzzzz. Smack!

She pulled herself upright and sat, still half asleep, on the edge of the bed. Her eyelids dropped, and her head bobbled around as she nodded back off; a sudden falling sensation brought her instantly back to life with a jolt. Her eyes popped open, but then, once again, blinked slowly shut.

She had just started to doze back off, when she realized that she had seen something in between blinks.

"What in the . . . ?" she mumbled as she forced herself to wake up. She rubbed the sleep from her eyes and squinted toward the other side of the room.

There, outside her second story window, two bright white lights—no bigger than a dime—darted around behind the fluttering curtains. They zipped to the right, stopped, and held still for a second, and then spiraled down together to the left. They made a faint but peculiar noise as they jumped from place to place, like a cross between static on a television and chirping crickets.

Maggie had been a little skittish since the break-in, but at this moment, curiosity was stronger than fear, so she stood and started toward the window. As she walked, the floorboards of the old house creaked ominously beneath her feet, causing her confidence in the situation to rapidly decline. By the time she was half way across the room, she was forcing herself to stay calm.

"C'mon, Maggs! Don't be such a wimp!" she scolded under her breath. "It's probably just lightning bugs!"

She reached the window and lifted her hand to pull back the curtain for a better look. All at once, two more little lights zipped up and joined the first. Maggie jumped and her breath caught in her chest. Her heart began to race as an uneasy feeling stirred—the feeling that she was being watched. She inched her way backwards.

"It's okay," she breathed. "They're just bugs."

The four tiny illuminations whizzed around in formation for a second or two, and then the lights started to multiply. Out of nowhere and everywhere all at once, hundreds and hundreds of bright, piercing, white orbs whirled and buzzed outside her open window, creating a riotous screech. Maggie slapped her hands over her ears as the volume of the bizarre noise grew...and grew...and grew. Blinding flashes, like bolts of lightning, burst in through the window and ricocheted around the room, creating a turbulent strobe effect. They crashed into the walls and the floor, making the whole room convulse violently.

Maggie's fear grew to sheer terror! She turned and tried to run, but as she did, the floor bumped hard, knocking her to her knees with a painful smack. She screamed, but her voice was drowned out by the horrendous buzzing of the chaotic little lights.

Horrified, she curled up into a ball on the floor—hands clasped tightly over her ears, eyes squeezed shut—and begged, "Oh please . . . oh please . . . oh please! Someone help me!"

Just then, her bedroom door swung open. Within a split second, the multitude of lights vanished; the quaking stopped, and the dreadful noise came to an abrupt halt. All was as it had been before....

Part One

Destruction from Twins

CHAPTER I

ANIKA

"**A**nika? Highness?" The booming deep voice of General Kort echoed through the evergreen-lined halls of Trysta Palace.

"Yes, Kort . . . come in."

Next to the general, the prickly emerald branches of a stately pine slowly swished downward, revealing an intricate carved stone doorway, which framed a room so ethereal, that it looked more like a wooded forest glade than someone's bed chambers. At the back of the room, a woman, short and petite, with long, dark, wavy hair, hurriedly flipped a silver satin cloth over the top of a stone table. She was almost elfish in appearance, and dreamily illuminated by the rays of bright sunlight streaming through the high glass-like ceiling overhead.

"I've been expecting you, General."

The general's brow furrowed. "You have?" He replied as he hunched over and ducked through the arch. He ducked, not because the arch was small—on the contrary—it was because General Kort was quite a tall man. As he entered, the leaf-covered floor crunched beneath his feet. The warm sunlight from above spilled over him, defining his strong, muscular physique with a bright white outline. "How'd you know I'd be coming?"

Anika started toward him. She seemed to float rather than walk; there was no crunching of leaves as she approached. She moved in complete silence, her olive-colored gown and silky brunette hair twisting and flowing hypnotically around her. She stopped close to Kort. There was such a contrast in their sizes that they looked rather odd standing beside each other.

"Honestly, Kort," she explained, "I knew you'd be here as soon as you heard that my mother was dead." She reached up and swirled her finger through a stray lock of auburn hair hanging on his forehead. "You've come to secure your connection with power—to make sure that when I am made the vritesse, you won't be left out somehow."

Kort cleared his throat. He seemed offended that he'd been so easily read. "That's a pretty bold statement, Anika," he snipped. "What makes you so sure it'll be you and not your sister?" He turned away in an attempt to hide his pride in such a bold comeback.

Anika was not amused. Without the slightest hesitation, she grabbed him by the shoulders and whirled him around as though he were nothing more than a small child. Her lavender eyes glowed eerily and as they did, Kort dropped to his knees, sending up a whirling of leaves.

"Aaaaaggghhh!" he screamed curling into a ball on the floor, writhing and groaning in agony, as a strong surge of electricity like thousands of needles stabbing into his skin simultaneously twisted through his body.

"My mother was not stupid, General!" Anika's normally silky smooth voice was now loud and coarse. "She's always known that I am the strong one! Not Lantalia . . . *me!*" She stepped back a bit and the glow in her eyes faded.

Kort gasped and strained for breath as he dragged himself back to his feet. "Forgive me, Anika. I was just . . ." he coughed, "just playing with you."

"Lantalia and I were born seconds apart, Kort. No one even thought to pay attention to which of us was first. I guess two at one time was just too much for their simple minds to process." She walked over to a large stone pillar on the other side of the room and leaned against it, her back facing the still gasping general. Lost in her thoughts she continued, "Lantalia is weak. She's never been able to lead anything. She's never . . . ." Her voice trailed off into nothingness as she stood silently staring for several seconds, but then spun back around.

Kort winced at her abrupt movement, fearing that she might attack him again with another energy surge. When he saw her face though, his eyes widened and his jaw dropped. "Anika? Wh . . . what's going on?" he asked. The skin on her face and the color of her eyes had suddenly, and very noticeably, darkened.

"There's nothing going on, Kort. Everything is perfect. You see, I will be vritesse! No one, not even my dead mother, can stop that!"

"But you're . . . ."

A bellowing voice, calling from somewhere outside the room, interrupted Kort's retaliation. *The Council of Lor Mandela will convene in two hours' time; the new vritesse will be called. All council members are required, without exception!"*

Anika smirked triumphantly. Her hair, skin and eyes all seemed to be getting darker by the second. "You were saying?"

Kort reached out and took her by the hand. "Listen to me, Anika. There's something happening to you—right now—right in front of me! Something's not right!" The changes in her were unnerving. He'd never seen anything like this before.

She grimaced condescendingly and replied, "What are you talking about? I'm fine! Honestly, Kort, you need not act so . . . well, dramatic."

"I have a right to be concerned!" he scolded. "I'm your entrusted! I'm supposed to care about you, aren't I?"

"Come on, Kort, you're just overreact . . . ."

"Anika," he interrupted, "look at yourself! Your eyes and skin just darkened right in front of me!"

With a huff and a roll of her eyes, she looked down patronizingly and gazed at her hands. "Hmm," she mumbled, turning them over and observing the change for herself. It was odd, but certainly didn't seem like anything worthy of such concern. "So what?" she replied. "Maybe it's just the vritesse powers finding me."

Kort frowned. "Listen, I know that you should be the vritesse, Anika. Everyone knows it!" He took a deep breath and added, "But if your mother did choose Lantalia, what can you . . . ."

"I've already told you, General!" she snapped. "I will be the vritesse! If Lantalia happens to get in my way . . . ."

"You'll what? Do something drastic? Like what? Like kill her? You're not a murderer, Anika!"

"Please, Kort . . . for goodness sake, who said anything about murder?"

"But the vritesse of Lor Mandela is only replaced at death. It's the law! You can't acquire the vritesse powers unless . . . ."

"Unless the vritesse dies, or wills it, or . . ." She stopped and studied Kort's eyes as though she was trying to convince herself that she could trust him. She hesitantly continued, "Unless her powers are, shall we say, taken?"

"Taken? Wait! You mean *stolen*? How?"

"There are ways," she mumbled.

"Anika, Listen to yourself! You are talking about interfering with some of the most powerful forces on Lor Mandela! This is insanity! You can't seriously be considering this as an option!" His voice had escalated into a roar. Normally, he didn't dare raise his voice to Anika, but he didn't care about being zapped again. She was planning something foolish—foolish and deadly—and he wasn't about to stand by and watch her get herself killed.

Anika just stared at him gaping. It was clear by his unrestrained reaction that she'd divulged too much. "Calm down, Kort. As usual, you're making a big deal out of nothing." She looked away and attempted to change the subject. "Shouldn't you be preparing for the council meeting?"

Kort acted as though he hadn't heard her. "I'm making a big deal out of nothing, Anika?" he argued. "What is going on in your head?"

Anika forced a smile and walked up to him. She leaned forward, and pulling him to her, kissed him on the cheek. "I don't want you to worry about it anymore, my love. I promise you . . . it will all be fine. I'm sure nothing, well, extraordinary, will even be necessary." She slipped around behind him and ran her hands across his broad, muscular shoulders, kneading the tension with her small yet magical hands. "At any rate, your, uh . . . position is secure. You and I both know that's all you really care about."

The general pulled away and turned to face her. He opened his mouth to speak, but Anika tilted her head to one side and looked at him as if to say, *don't push it.*

"Yeah, okay, Anika," he sighed, "it's not like I have a choice, do I? I guess I'll just see you at the meeting." He approached the doorway, looking despondent, and the branches of the tree drooped down. As he ducked out into the hall he muttered, "I *do* care you know, about you."

Anika nodded and rolled her eyes again. "Yes, Kort, I know," she groaned as she took a step back and impatiently waited for the tree door to reappear.

As soon as Kort was out of sight, she let out a relieved sigh. She rushed to the back of the room and pulled the silver cloth off of the flat rock table. Underneath, was a large tattered book. Anika glanced over her shoulder, and scooped up the old tome and began to study its yellowed pages. Poring over the words, she mumbled, "Elahk . . . Lor Mandela . . . Elahk . . . yes brilliant . . . frightening, but brilliant."

After a few minutes, she stopped reading and gazed out over the room. "Only one more step. If my mother . . . ." She turned toward a picture hanging on the vine covered wall across from her and gazed at the image of an aged, white-haired woman. "I hope you weren't foolish, Mother! I sincerely hope that you're not going to force me to do this."

CHAPTER II

THE NEW VRITESSE

A nika stared at her mother's portrait until it was time to leave for the council meeting. She glanced down at the book that she was still holding and gently folded it shut. After running her hand across its cracked cover, she placed it back on the cold rock table and spread the shimmering silver cloth over the top.

On the wall next to her, a rich purple cloak hung from a twig hook. She pulled it down, and draped it across her dainty shoulders then, with both anxiousness and anticipation, headed off toward the gathering that would decide her fate, as well as the fate of her twin sister, Lantalia.

She entered the Trysta Council Hall before anyone else, followed closely by a woman with straight, shoulder-length brown hair and magenta eyes. She didn't have to turn around to see who was there—Anika could always sense her sister's presence. "Hello Lantalia," she sighed.

"Good evening, Ani." Lantalia touched her warmly on the shoulder.

Though twins, there was not much of a resemblance between the sisters. Lantalia's features were feminine and soft; Anika's were defined and chiseled. Lantalia was tall and curvaceous; Anika was quite petite and nearly emaciated in appearance. They both had brown hair and violet eyes, but that was the limited extent of their similarities.

Anika strained to smile as she turned to face Lantalia.

It took less than a second for Lantalia to notice the changes in her, and she didn't hesitate to voice her concern. "Anika, what's the matter? Your skin's so dark! You look exhausted. Are you ill?"

"No, Tali. I'm fine . . . just worn down a bit."

"Oh, well, I guess that's to be expected," she frowned. "I suppose you've had a lot to deal with the last few days." She was far from convinced, but she could tell by Anika's aloof demeanor that it was pointless to persist; Anika never discussed anything that could be viewed as a weakness, and Lantalia knew that when she was stand-offish like this, any honest discussion was simply not going to happen. "Is there anything I can do?" she tried.

Anika just grimaced and shook her head.

"All right then," Lantalia replied grabbing her by the arm. "Let's go get settled in."

She escorted Anika across the room to where nine, round marble platforms sat—each topped with a heavily cushioned burgundy chair. Lantalia held out her hand to help Anika up to her seat.

"Will you stop fussing, Tali? I'm fine," she insisted. First Kort, now you? Honestly!"

"I'm sorry!" Lantalia snapped back as she stepped up onto her own platform. "It's just that you don't look yourself, that's all."

Slowly, their platforms rose into the air until they were high above the light polished stone floors below. Anika sought to avoid any further conversation by turning her back to Lantalia and staring out over the impressive room.

The grandeur of the Council Hall never ceased to amaze her. A huge stadium-like arena with chocolate brown walls lined with large, pure-white columns and huge displays of exotic, jewel-toned flowers in ornate silver urns, it was indeed her favorite room in Trysta Palace. Throughout the arena were hundreds of platforms similar to the ones occupied by her and Lantalia, but with less stately chairs, each cushioned in pale blue satin. Like all of the main rooms in the palace, the arena was lit by softly glowing sunlight. But rather than flooding through a ceiling of smooth plate glass—as was the case in Anika's chambers and most of the rest of the palace—the sun's rays filtered through a magnificent cut-crystal roof. The sunlight danced across the roof, filling the room with focused beams of direct light and small, muted ribbons of rainbows.

Anika watched from her elevated platform as the Lor Mandelan Council delegates began filing in, mingling amongst themselves as they entered. As each delegate took their respective seat, their platform rose into the air and stopped at the height corresponding to its occupant's political rank.

At last, when most of the seats were filled, there was a loud clunking as three doors at the far end of the arena slowly swung open. The delegates ceremoniously rose to their feet.

That is where I will enter from now on, Anika thought to herself, *Anika—Vritesse of the Trystas.* She pictured herself walking through one of the doors, dressed in the finest clothes, and covered in exotic jewelry. She imagined the entire council rising as she entered the room, and showing her the utmost respect as she gracefully crossed the hall. She smiled, and closed her amethyst eyes in an attempt to hold on to the image. Her reverie was suddenly interrupted, however, as an outburst of cheers and exclamations exploded throughout the hall.

The accolades were for a statuesque, black-haired, blue-eyed woman in her late forties or early fifties, who entered through one of the three doors. She stopped a few feet out and nodded graciously toward the members of the council. Her demeanor exuded absolute elegance, as did her stunning attire. Her long, black velvet gown was embroidered with elaborate silver leaves and randomly dotted with what appeared to be small sapphires. A wispy, flowing, midnight blue cloak was held at her shoulders by exquisite silver brooches, and draped in almost fluid layers down her back extending behind her in shimmering puddles. On her hands and arms were long white gloves, accented by thick, ornate silver bracelets on the right, and a large sparkling sapphire ring on the left. As the noise in the room died down, she lowered to one knee and bowed her head.

The applause again escalated to a roar as a debonair man with thick black hair and shockingly bright blue eyes entered the room through the door in the center. He held out his hand to the woman, who took it and rose to her feet. She looked him in the eyes and smiled lovingly.

Together, Atoc Cristoph and Ator Jocelynne started out across the floor of the arena. They embodied grace and confidence as they smiled and nodded at the delegates. All of the members of the council reverently lowered to their seats as the regal couple passed by.

When at last they reached their platforms, a voice from somewhere at the top of the room boomed, "Council members of Lor Mandela, prepare for the reading of the lineage."

The room fell silent.

The voice continued, "Our highest ruler, Cristoph Borloc . . . Atoc of Lor Mandela."

Atoc Cristoph stepped onto one of the red-chaired platforms and it rose almost to the crystalline ceiling. At present, it was the only chair higher than those of Anika and Lantalia.

"His entrusted, Jocelynne Cantiell . . . Ator of Lor Mandela."

Jocelynne moved onto her platform. It ascended to the top of the room, and stopped just below and to the left of Cristoph's.

"The vritesse of Lor Mandela, to be called."

A few gasps and whispers permeated the silence, as an empty platform climbed to the right of Ator Jocelynne's.

Anika fought back another smile. *Soon,* she thought, *all that delicious power will be mine.*

The voice continued, "Lantalia tu Mystad, and Anika tu Winter of the Trystas . . . daughters of our beloved, departed Vritesse Satia."

The sisters stood and exchanged glances.

"Jonathan Borloc, Aton of Lor Mandela."

Cristoph and Jocelynne's son Jonathan—who was the spitting image of his father—rose to his feet on the platform at Anika's left.

"His entrusted, Gracielle . . . by marriage, Atoh of Lor Mandela; by birth, Gracielle tu Morning of the Trystas . . . daughter of Lantalia."

Gracielle, a tall, slender, breathtakingly beautiful young woman, also with black hair and blue eyes, stood and nodded. Lantalia smiled proudly at her daughter.

"Ultara tu Koria of the Trystas . . . daughter of Anika."

Another stunning woman, this one with very long, wild auburn hair and pale golden eyes, rose on the platform just below Anika's.

"And concluding our noble and great succession, Nenia tu Sybran of the Trystas . . . daughter of Ultara."

Nenia—a spunky, eleven-year-old girl, stood and waved at the assembly, causing several of the council members to chuckle at her show of enthusiasm.

Once again the room filled with clapping and cheers until Atoc Cristoph took his seat, signaling to the other Nobles to do the same. He leaned forward and touched a small green button on the arm of his chair, and all at once, the room darkened, and his platform became engulfed in a deep blue glow; the atoc had the floor.

"My dear friends," he began, his soothing voice projecting through the Council Hall as though he were speaking into a microphone. "We convene at this difficult time of mourning to remember a great and powerful vritesse, and call—as she has dictated—her successor."

He paused and looked down at Anika and Lantalia. "As you all know, something miraculous took place on Lor Mandela when Satia gave birth to Anika and Lantalia. Two daughters were born to the vritesse within mere seconds of one another." Many of the council members nodded in remembrance as Cristoph went on. "Today, either of these wise and accomplished women would make an excellent successor." He nodded graciously toward the sisters. "As Satia's life was ending, she confided in me that this decision was more challenging than any other she'd ever made as vritesse. Today I am honored to read her calling to the Council."

The room fell silent, as though everyone was holding their breath in anticipation.

All at once, Anika's, Lantalia's, Gracielle's, Ultara's, and Nenia's platforms began to glow soft yellow.

Cristoph held a folded paper up in front of him; he cleared his throat as he opened the paper, and read: *"Atoc, Ator, daughters, and assembled delegates, I, Satia, Vritesse of the Trysta people, appoint and call my noble heir. My decision has been a difficult one. My daughters are both capable, each in their own way. If our laws permitted, I would call them both and rest confidently knowing that all was well. For a time, I even considered calling a descendant such as Ultara or Gracielle rather than having to choose between my daughters."* The delegates were clearly engrossed, hanging on every word Cristoph uttered.

"Anika is strong; she is courageous and powerful—all qualities a vritesse must possess."

Anika could not hide her smile this time.

"Nonetheless, as I ponder the needs of my people, and all of Lor Mandela, I know what I must do."

Anika's smile vanished in an instant and her face became tense. *What Mother? What must you do? You didn't . . . .* She glanced up pleadingly at Cristoph.

As Cristoph read the last lines of the note in his hand, an expression of surprise played across his face. He looked out over the crowd, cleared his throat and boomed, *"I call Lantalia! Daughter of Satia . . . Vritesse of the Trystas!"*

The room exploded in gasps, followed almost immediately by cheers and applause. Anika watched in a stunned daze as her sister's platform and the empty one at Jocelynne's right switched places.

Cristoph lowered the paper and commanded, "The vritesse of the Trystas! Rise and obtain all of the Trysta powers and keys, all authority and wisdom!"

Lantalia stood and looked out over the adoring congregation. She glanced down at Anika, fully expecting to see a dejected, disappointed face; but much to her surprise, Anika was applauding right along with the rest of the delegation.

Strange, she thought to herself.

At length, when the roar subsided, Cristoph reached down and handed her a small silver box. "Rule the Trystas well, Lantalia," he uttered.

Lantalia slowly opened the box. Anika seemed most captivated as she watched her sister lift the tiny box's lid. All at once, a blinding flash of white light exploded from it, filling the entire room. The light was so bright that everyone in the arena was forced to shield their eyes. After a moment though, the light dimmed, and spiraled its way back in, enveloping Lantalia, and hiding her from view. Pale wisps of different colors periodically drifted out of the light and floated down to the ground below. After a few minutes, the light dissipated, and Lantalia became visible again; a soft amber aura glowed around her and lingered for several seconds.

"Atoc Cristoph," she began in a new, formidable voice, "I have accepted the powers bestowed by my mother, Satia." She looked around the room at the many council members who all seemed delighted by her appointment. "I am Lantalia, Vritesse of the Trystas!" Again the room filled with applause, cheers and shouting.

"Council is hereby adjourned!" Cristoph bellowed over the din.

One by one, the delegates exited the room, chatting excitedly as they left. When most of them had gone, the platforms of the Nobles slowly lowered to the ground.

Anika wasted no time. She rushed to Lantalia and grabbed both of her hands. "Oh, Lantalia," she exclaimed, "I'm so happy for you!" She embraced her energetically.

Lantalia was more than a little shocked by the overwhelming show of support from her sister. She knew that Anika wanted to be the vritesse; indeed, this was not at all what she expected. "Thank you, Ani. Are you sure you're all right with this?"

"Of course, Tali," Anika assured, "you'll be a wonderful vritesse!" She smiled warmly. "Oh, I admit, I was disappointed at first, but you're my sister; I will support and help you however I can. I'm not going to be a scorned loser; that's not what our mother would have wanted." She hugged Lantalia again. As she backed away, she noticed General Kort standing across the room watching them.

"You will be my chief advisor, Ani, won't you?"

"Oh, Lantalia, thank you! I would be honored." Anika glanced over at Kort, who was eyeing her suspiciously, and shot him a disapproving scowl.

"What is it?" Lantalia asked, turning to see who Anika was grimacing at.

"Oh, er . . . it's just Kort. I hope you'll excuse me, Tali. It seems that I am . . ." She cleared her throat and raised her eyebrows. ". . . wanted."

Lantalia chuckled and brushed Anika's cheek with the back of her hand. "Of course, thank you, Anika."

Anika nodded respectfully and moved toward the door. She walked up to, and then right past Kort, and with an annoyed wave signaled for him to follow. She walked very quickly. Even with Kort's size advantage, he was practically running to keep up. *"You will be my chief advisor, Ani, won't you?"* she scowled,

Two

"Ghandentel!"

Once they were away from the council room—where no one would hear a male speaking disrespectfully to a Trysta female—Kort decided to test his limits. "Okay, Anika, what are you up to?"

Anika stopped. She whirled around, and stared angrily at him. "Listen to me, General." Kort took a small step backward, expecting to see that all too familiar glow creep into her eyes. "I owe you no explanation! I owe you no answers! I owe you nothing!"

"No, Anika, you don't." His tone was terse.

"So then why are you here?" she insisted. "Why aren't you pursuing my sister right now? She's the vritesse! She's where the power is! We both know that's what you want!"

General Kort looked poised to fire back, but all at once stopped. He shrugged his shoulders and admitted, "Okay, Anika. You're right. It's the power. I can't help it."

Anika raised one eyebrow. "You're obsessed with it, Kort. It's intoxicating to you." She seemed just a little disappointed. "So go ahead. If that's what you want. Go to Lantalia. I release you. Go!" She waved him off, trying not to show any emotion.

"I have no interest in Lantalia, my dear," Kort smirked. If I remember correctly . . ." He ran his hand down her arm. "Just a few hours ago, I was told that you would be the new vritesse . . . no matter what."

A mischievous smile grew across Anika's face.

He continued, "Why would I want to be the entrusted of a *temporary* vritesse?"

Anika slid up to him and reached her hand behind his head; she pulled him down and kissed him passionately. "Come with me," she whispered. "I have something I want to show you."

CHAPTER III
ELAHK E BER-A PLAN GONE WRONG

Anika led Kort back to her room and rushed directly to the rock table. She threw back the satin cover and lifted her grandmother's journal to her chest. "This is it, Kort!" she began. "It was here the whole time!"

"What was?" he asked, clearly frustrated that Anika's 'something to show him' was nothing more provocative than an old book.

"My great-grandmother's mother should have called *her*," Anika explained, "but she didn't! She called a self-righteous, power-hungry cousin instead. It was a plot—a scheme to overthrow the Borlocs. But Grandmother found a way to take the powers back . . . the powers that were rightfully hers to begin with."

"I see." Kort raised an eyebrow. "So that's what you're trying to do?"

"Lantalia can't do this, Kort! She's weak, and too good." Anika cringed. "Besides, Mother didn't give any reason at all! She said I was powerful! *Me!* Did you hear any mention of Lantalia's strengths in her calling?"

Kort plopped down onto a large, over-stuffed chair that looked as though it was made entirely of golden leaves. "So you're going to take the powers away from Lantalia? How do you propose to do that?" he asked.

Anika started slowly flipping through the journal; her darkening eyes studied each yellowed page before she turned to the next. "Do you know where the powers come from, Kort?"

Kort had heard the stories just like everyone else in the Trysta Empire. "Um, yeah. They come from the soul of Lor Mandela, right? Through the Koria Caverns?"

"Exactly," Anika answered, lowering down next to him. She held out the book and showed him a page covered with hand-drawn diagrams and sketches of caves and rocks. "All of the powers are gathered by the vritesse, and then harnessed in this." She pointed to a drawing of a small box at the bottom of the page.

"Hey, isn't that the box that the atoc gave to Lantalia?"

"Yes," she nodded, "there's nothing extraordinary about it; it's just a simple little box with the Trysta emblem scratched in the lid. But if I can get a hold of it . . . ."

"Wait," Kort frowned, "you just said the box has no significance."

"No, Kort. I said it wasn't extraordinary. It's very significant! You see, my love, it's not uncommon for the vritesse to periodically bring that silly little box to the caverns to renew her powers . . . you know, after a grueling battle or an illness or something."

"Yeah . . . uh-huh . . . so?" Kort mumbled distractedly. At the moment, he was only partially intrigued by the plan. Anika was sitting so close to him, so very confident and powerful. He was having difficulty concentrating.

Anika noticed his lack of focus and rose up out of the chair. He tried to follow, but she held up her hand signaling for him to stay put. "Will you try to pay attention?" she pleaded. "This is important. I have to convince the soul of Lor Mandela that I am Lantalia."

"And how, exactly do you do that?" he asked, resignedly dropping back down into the chair.

"I've already taken care of the hardest part," she bragged.

"Oh you have, have you?"

"Yes, I have." She looked supremely pleased with herself. "It was tricky," she explained. "There were a lot of steps involved, but one of my great-grandmother's powers was spirit-cloning and, as it turns out, I have that ability as well. I used it, along with my invasion powers to, um, borrow Lantalia's spirit while she was sleeping the other night."

"You borrowed her spirit?" Kort stood and moved toward her. He ran his hand down through her wavy hair, moving it from her neck, and leaned down to kiss her.

"Come on, General!" Anika whined. She pushed him off, causing him to lose his balance and fall back into the chair. "Try to control yourself."

"Fine," he snipped, "so you borrowed Lantalia's spirit. I get it. Wait! You did *what?"*

Anika smirked proudly. "I invaded my sister's body, borrowed her soul and made myself a copy of it. Now, I have a clone that I can use whenever I need." Kort looked at her like she'd gone completely mad, but she didn't really care. She continued as though this was the cleverest plan ever concocted. "Of course, I had to do it before she had the vritesse powers or she would have sensed me."

"Of course." Kort's skepticism was evident in his tone. "So, now what? You just take your little clone to the Caverns and say something like, 'Look, Lor Mandela! I'm Lantalia. I just had a bad cold. I need my powers refreshed'?"

Anika glared at him. "Nooo, it's a little more complicated than that, my dear." She floated across the room while she continued. "But if all goes as planned, the powers of the vritesse will leave Lantalia and come to me."

"Hold on a minute. Isn't that dangerous? What if you get caught?"

"It's not without risk, Kort, but I can do it. I'm not worried. I've studied this thing constantly for months." She glided back to where he was sitting and lowered down next to him.

"So then *poof!* You're the vritesse and Lantalia is powerless?"

"It will take some time for the powers to drain from her, as the powers I get from Lor Mandela will only be renewals. But, they'll be enough for me to draw the real powers away eventually."

Kort kissed her on the forehead and asked, "Won't people wonder when you all of a sudden have increased powers?"

"It won't be hard to convince the council that Lantalia is unfit to be vritesse, Kort . . . especially when her powers start failing. I just need to be discreet about using my new powers until I am called, of course."

"Of course." Kort traced over her cheek with his finger. "So, when does this little soul-swap take place?"

"In the morning," she answered. Her lilac eyes were dim and distant. "I wish you could come, my dear, but I have to go alone."

"What? Why?" Kort was tremendously disappointed that he wouldn't be able to watch such an important and powerful event.

"The soul of Lor Mandela will not allow any witnesses to a vritesse renewal. It would be fatal for you."

"Really?" he gulped.

Anika stood back up and held her hands out to him. He took her hands and she gently pulled him to his feet. "It's time for you to go now, General."

"What? But wait! No! You're serious? *Now?*" His displeasure was apparent.

"I need to get some rest tonight, Kort. I'll call for you when I get back from the Caverns." She kissed him goodnight and pointed toward the tree door. "I'll see you in the morning."

Kort sighed. "Fine . . . Good night, I guess." He pouted and grudgingly, ducked out into the hall, and disappeared behind the evergreen barrier.

Anika walked back to the chair and sunk down into it. "As if I could rest," she muttered to herself.

After a while, she got up and walked over near the door arch. The sun was setting, and the room was growing dark. She touched one of the tree branches, and a soft white glow illuminated the walls and ceiling. Once again, she picked up her great-grandmother's journal, and leafed through the pages, reading bits and pieces aloud. "Elahk E Ber . . . the balance of all . . . grant me. . . ." She stopped and looked out across the room. "Hold on," she whispered, "what exactly am I waiting for?" She gazed at the ground for a minute, collected her thoughts, and then rushed to where she'd thrown her cloak earlier. She snatched it up—still clutching the journal in her other arm, and headed for the door. "I need that box!" she breathed.

She was almost to the descending branches when she stopped short; a displeased scowl spread across her dark face. "I almost forgot," she seethed and turned back around. She floated over to where the picture of her mother hung. "Ghandentel, Mother!" she sneered, ripping down the portrait and hurling it across the room. It smashed into bits against the hard stone wall.

Without another word, she glided back across the room and out into the dimly lit, tree-lined halls. Quietly, she made her way through the corridors; the lower branches of the trees swayed gently as her cloak billowed through them. After floating down two long hallways, she came to a wide tunnel—the only part of Trysta Palace that wasn't tree-lined. At the end of the tunnel, shimmering in the few glints of moonlight coming through the clear glass ceiling above stood an ornate gold door. Anika took a deep breath and glanced nervously around. Confident that she was alone, she started toward the door and was within just a few feet of it when, without warning, it swung open and Lantalia appeared in the doorway.

"Lantalia?" she breathed restlessly, "I, uh . . . I . . . ." she stammered.

Lantalia was surprised to see her, too. "Anika? What's going on? Is everything okay? What are you doing here?"

"What do you mean?" Anika snipped. "I can't even come to see my own sister?"

Lantalia eyed her suspiciously. Just seconds before, she had a strange feeling—a sort of premonition. Something didn't seem right. Her new vritesse powers made her sensitive to such things. She sensed that someone was coming to harm her; it was disturbing indeed for her to open the door and find her own sister standing there.

"Aren't you going to ask me in?" Anika pried.

"Um, yes . . . of course. Please come in," Lantalia responded, eyeing Anika in a way that she had never seen before. It was a look of superiority—and of suspicion. In the few short hours since her calling, Lantalia had already become stronger and more in tune. "What can I do for you, Anika?"

Anika knew she'd have to be careful. She couldn't risk Lantalia reading her intentions. Fortunately for her, one of the many powers she possessed was the ability to lock her mind from outside influence. Normally, a mind block wouldn't work with the vritesse, but since Lantalia's powers weren't fully established it was worth a try.

"I couldn't sleep, Tali," she explained. "I have something to ask you."

Lantalia's expression softened—indicating that the mind lock was working. "What is it?" She asked. She glanced at the journal Anika had forgotten she was clutching in her arms. "And what's that?"

"Oh . . . um . . . this is?" she stuttered. "It's just our great-grandmother's old journal." She looked down at the book and an idea popped into her head.

With a new sense of confidence in her voice, she continued, "I was flipping through it earlier, Tali. Grandmother wrote about receiving her powers . . . that's what I wanted to ask you." She paused and smiled at her own cleverness. "What was it like when you opened the box? I mean, it must have been so incredible!"

Lantalia did exactly what Anika hoped she would. She walked across the room, picked up the small silver box, and brought it over to show her. "It *was* incredible. I can't describe it. It was a feeling of absolute power and control." She handed the diminutive box to her sister. "It isn't much," she observed, "but there's more to it than you see."

"Especially when it contains the powers, huh?"

"The powers are only part of it," Lantalia whispered. It's alive."

"The box?"

"Shhhhh," she scolded. "This doesn't leave this room, Ani!"

Anika lowered her voice to appease her sister. "So you're saying that this box is a living thing?"

She was having extreme difficulty holding on to her mind lock. Lantalia's powers were trying to penetrate it—and now, the opportunity of a lifetime had just been literally handed to her. *I don't have to steal the box,* she thought, *I just have to clone its soul!*

She turned her back to Lantalia, and pretending to examine the box, clanked it around loudly enough to hide a whisper. "Elahk E Ber silver box," she breathed quietly. She clapped her hands around the box to conceal the blue flash that zipped out from it, as a perfect little clone appeared in her palm.

"I would have never believed it myself," Lantalia continued oblivious to her sister's doings, "but the whole time the powers were being bestowed, it was instructing me."

Anika tucked the replica of the silver box into her cloak and turned back to face Lantalia. "Instructing you? What was it saying?" she asked as she handed the real box back to her trusting sister.

Lantalia ran her hand over the box's lid. "I . . . I probably shouldn't say."

Anika could feel her mind lock deteriorating fast. She realized that she had to get out of there now, or Lantalia would know everything.

"Whoa!" she groaned, slapping her hand onto her stomach.

"What is it? Are you all right?" Lantalia asked.

Anika fell back dramatically against the wall. "Whew! I, um . . . I'm sorry, Tali. I don't feel well all of a sudden. I'd better go-oh!" She clapped her hand over her mouth, and mumbled through her fingers, "Excuse me, Lantalia. I'll talk to you tomorrow!" She turned and quickly sped out the door.

"Do you need any help?" Lantalia called after her.

"No! I . . . I'm sure I'll be fine."

Lantalia leaned against the door frame and watched Anika practically sprint down the tunnel. "What was that all about?" she questioned aloud as she stepped back into her room and closed the door.

Meanwhile, Anika made her way out of the palace and headed for a large hill in the distance. She couldn't help but laugh out loud at her amazing good fortune.

"It's alive!" She mimicked her sister and sniggered, "I am the stupidest vritesse ever! Here, Anika, why don't I just tell you everything?" She was positively giddy. She continued until she was a safe distance from the palace, and then stopped in a large, grassy meadow. She knelt down, pulled the cloned box from her cloak and kissed it. "You are a beautiful little thing, aren't you?" She set it gently on the damp ground, stood, and then looked skyward and shouted, "Stoi Cantara . . . Lantalia!"

Slowly, a figure rippled up from the ground beside her, and within seconds, a perfect replica of Lantalia, with straight brown hair and magenta eyes stood at her right. The clone was glassy-eyed and seemed to be devoid of emotion.

"Nolta," she mumbled.

The clone reached its hand out toward her as another hand materialized at the end of her left arm. The clone took the phantom hand and pulled. Instantly, and in a flash of red, the spirit of Anika and the clone spirit of Lantalia traded places and Anika visibly became Lantalia. Her own soul stood glassy-eyed and emotionless beside her.

"Wait here," she commanded, in Lantalia's voice.

Her catatonic soul made an almost indiscernible nod.

Anika picked up the little box and continued up the hill, her dark silhouette rippling across the field. Within just a few minutes, she had reached the top where she paused for a moment to stare out at the intimidating landscape that stretched before her on the other side.

It was steep, and the trail was long, narrow, and seemed to lead down into an endless pit.

Anika's eyes glowed, lighting everything in front of her with a focused beam of intense pink. She drew in a deep breath and started in a run toward the trail. "The Caverns!" she shouted loudly.

Just as she was about to run right off the edge of the trail, there was a faint pop, and she vanished into thin air.

When she rematerialized, she was standing at the entrance to a massive black cave. She glanced back just to make sure that no one was around, and then scanned the cave with her glowing eyes.

Upon sufficient confirmation that she was alone, she proceeded cautiously into the cave, where the need for the additional light suddenly ceased. The Caverns at Koria were brightly lit and absolutely exquisite.

Throughout Lor Mandela it was common knowledge that the Caverns were among the most glorious places in existence. Huge, glowing, pastel-colored rock formations hung down from the high, glistening, crystal-encrusted ceilings; the vibrations of the planet bounced from formation to formation resonating in soft harmonious hums. Despite their location, far below the surface, the Caverns were well illuminated by a warm silvery glow, originating from an unknown source.

Although they were beautiful, the Caverns were also deadly. Inside, steep, sharply-winding paths bordered jagged cliffs—the walls of which were miles high. Over the years, even the tiniest errors in judgment had caused many to fall to their early deaths.

Anika didn't pause to take in the view, though. Tonight, she was on a mission. She nimbly maneuvered up the path until she reached a huge rock that jutted out over the cliffs like a giant platform. She stepped out onto it, held the cloned box in front of her and shouted skyward, "I am Lantalia, daughter of Satia, and Vritesse of Lor Mandela! Soul of Lor Mandela, grant me renewal! The balance of all powers from the beginning until the end!" A pillar of white light shot up through the center of the Caverns and bulleted toward Anika. It whirred and spattered and wrapped its way around her, completely enveloping her.

In the light, Anika heard a faint voice. It surged in and out. "Lantalia . . . Vritesse . . . you've only just received these powers. How is it that they are in need of renewal?"

Anika had anticipated that this might happen and had an answer prepared. "Wise spirit, my mother was very ill at her final renewal. I believe she was not able to fully gather all that you bestowed."

There was a pause before the voice answered. "Lantalia, Vritesse of the Trysta people, be ren . . . ."

Suddenly, the glowing white pillar lost its form. Violent shards of light shot through the air ricocheting off of the walls and rock formations. The voice boomed, "I am the soul of Lor Mandela! Lantalia . . . Vritesse . . . *twin!*"

Anika's stomach lurched. She had been discovered—or so it seemed.

The light bounced wildly throughout the Caverns but then, much to Anika's relief, it slowly gathered back into a straight column and the calm, rhythmic whir returned.

The voice spoke again, much more serenely than before, and the pillar of light shrank away. "Take your renewed powers, Vritesse . . . and go."

Anika felt strange. She tried to take a step backward but teetered awkwardly and collapsed, unconscious, into a heap on the rock platform; the hand holding the little silver box precariously flopped out over the edge.

It was several hours before she regained consciousness. She moaned softly, glanced around, and realized that the box was teetering near the end of her fingertips. She gasped and pulled it quickly toward her, hoping that nothing had escaped. A tiny sliver of white light peeked out from around the lid indicating that the powers were still inside. Anika sighed and rose groggily to her feet.

"That was more, um . . . physically demanding than anticipated," she breathed, as she dragged herself back down the path.

Upon exiting the Caverns, she realized that the sun was already rising. She would need to get back her own soul before it was discovered. She headed off at a furious pace. "Koria field!" she yelled skyward and was instantly transported back to the field on the opposite side of where she'd left her spirit.

The unresponsive soul was still standing across the meadow like a statue; luckily, no one was in sight.

She sprinted toward it and shouted, "Nolta!"

In response, her soul zipped toward her and dove aggressively into her, knocking her to the ground. Right when they hit, the cloned spirit of Lantalia burst out of her back and fell to the earth.

Anika looked like herself again except now there was no mistaking it. Her skin was very, very dark. "Strange," she mumbled as she rose to her feet and brushed herself off. She started off toward Trysta Palace, staring at her hands and arms as she went. She hadn't gone far when she remembered that her sister's cloned soul was still lying in the field behind her. She sniggered as she contemplated leaving it there for someone to find. "Erun cantara . . . Lantalia!" she commanded.

The spirit clone rippled and distorted. It wiggled around a bit, and then dissolved slowly into the ground and disappeared.

Anika glanced over her hands again and shook her head. "Very strange," she muttered, as she sped off again toward home.

Once she was safely back inside her room she wasted no time. She was very anxious to set her plan in motion. She lifted a small stick-like object from a bedside table and spoke into the end of it.

"Send for General Kort, immediately," she ordered.

A few minutes later, he was outside her door calling her name.

She rushed over and pulled him in, right through the branches that were still descending.

"Ouch! Anika," Kort exclaimed, brushing the pine needles from his shirt. "What's so urgent?" He picked a stray needle from his auburn curls and glanced at Anika, who was even darker than before. A look of concern spread across his rugged face. "Have you figured out what's causing this darkening yet? Is it because of the spirit cloning?" he asked, staring.

Anika didn't want to discuss that now. "Do you want to see this, or not?" she quizzed impatiently.

"See what?"

Anika smiled mischievously. "See the rightful vritesse receive her powers."

"What?" Kort gasped, "I thought I wasn't allowed to watch."

"No, Kort . . . you couldn't be with me in Koria, but I haven't done the power transfer yet," she explained. "Get ready, General. You're about to become the entrusted of the vritesse!" Her voice was sing-songy and playful.

Kort slowly lowered on to the bed and didn't say another word.

Anika lifted the silver box in front of her and removed the lid. A bright light surrounded her, and little wisps of color dreamily floated out of it.

Once again she heard a voice. Only this time it seemed almost sad. "Balance . . . balance is the key. Trysta . . . Borloc . . . balance."

"Balance," she repeated as the light wrapped tighter around her.

"The powers from Lor Mandela to . . ."

There was a long pause, and then the voice whispered, "Anika."

The light faded and Anika stood enveloped in a tawny glow for several minutes. She looked at Kort who was absolutely engrossed.

"Did you hear the voice?" she asked.

As the glow around her dissipated the most troubling change in her yet became evident. "Anika!" Kort gasped, "Your eyes!" The general appeared quite mortified.

"What about them?" She snapped and walked over and peered into a looking glass that was on the rock table near where the book had been before. Her eyes, which were usually a sultry purple, had changed to a dull, dark black. "That's strange," she whispered. "The journal didn't say anything about darkening. I wonder what's going on."

Kort gawked at her from across the room.

She started towards him, but had no sooner taken her first step when Kort bolted to his feet and flew toward her at an amazing speed!

In under a second, he was in front of her, wide-eyed and panting. "What was that?" he asked weakly.

Instantly, he rocketed into the air again, this time smacking against the wall with a loud *thud*.

Anika shrieked. "Kort! What are you doing? Are you okay?" She rushed over to where he lay in a crumpled heap on the floor. "What's going on?"

Kort shrunk back as she touched his arm.

"Don't!" he cried, sounding like a scared child.

Anika stepped back and stared at him.

"Can you get up, love? Are you hurt?" she asked.

"Please, Anika! Stop! Let me go," he pleaded.

"Kort!"

She wanted him to look at her but he kept his face turned into the wall. "I don't have a hold of you! I'm not even touching you!"

"Annnniiiikaaaa," he whined miserably, "noooooo!"

She leaned down and pulled him to his feet and a loud, mournful yelp issued from his lips.

"Kort," she demanded, "look at me!"

Slowly he turned his head toward her. His eyes were tightly shut. "Noooo, Anika. Please . . . I'm sorry . . . don't . . . please . . . ."

Tears streamed down his cheeks. "Stop! Pleeeease!"

"Kort!" she yelled. "Open your eyes!"

All at once his knees buckled and he went completely limp and slumped over into Anika's arms.

Anika lowered him to the ground and frantically tried to revive him. "Kort! Come on! What is it? Kort!"

After a few seconds, his eyes fluttered open; he looked up at Anika drowsily.

"Oh, Kort," she gasped, "are you all right?"

He shakily pulled himself to sitting and panted, "Anika, you've got to stop this! Something's wrong! Please end this now! I mean it! Something is *really* wrong."

CHAPTER IV
DESTRUCTION FROM TWINS

It didn't take long for Anika to realize that Kort was right. Something was terribly wrong. Although her powers were stronger, she had no control over them—no matter what she tried. In fact, they seemed to be controlling her—and Anika's powers weren't the only thing out of control.

As the days passed her skin became muddy gray and her hair, which looked wild and unkempt, darkened to nearly pure black.

Her eyes had remained black since the morning she had attacked Kort, but now even the whites of her eyes were a dull, murky gray. She had grown tired of the questions, and the whispers, and the stares, so she stayed confined to her room whenever possible.

As for Lantalia, her powers hadn't diminished in the slightest. In fact, since her calling to vritesse, she had been able to master almost every Trysta power imaginable and was well on her way to becoming the most powerful vritesse of all time.

Early one evening, Anika was once again alone in her room. She stood gazing at herself in a glass, wondering what was going on and if she'd ever be able to stop it, when Lantalia's voice blasted from the hall.

"Anika! You've finally gone too far!"

Anika spun around as the tree that normally guarded her door vanished entirely and her angry sister fumed in its place.

"This!" Lantalia hissed.

She moved across the room and shoved their great-grandmother's journal toward Anika. "So, this is what you've done?" she sneered, dropping the journal at Anika's feet.

"Where did you get that?" Anika's voice was scratchy and deep. "That's mine!"

Lantalia glared at her in disgust. "You left it in my room the night I was called! I was too busy to look at it . . . until last night." A fiery magenta glow rose in her eyes. "What made you think this would work, Anika?"

As the glow in Lantalia's eyes surged, a painful electrical charge twisted through Anika's body. She winced, but refused to give her sister the satisfaction of seeing her cower in pain.

"How dare you!" she growled, "Mother was foolish to choose you! You're nothing!"

Lantalia had to force herself to turn away and break her torturous hold. "I should have known you were lying, Anika," she sneered. "All of that, 'Oh, Lantalia! I'm so happy for you' and 'that's not what Mother would want' rubbish!" She whirled back around and faced her sister. "Now look at you! You're hideous and weak!"

Anika glowered at Lantalia for a moment, but then began cackling wildly. "No, my dear Lantalia! You're the weak one! I am becoming invincible!" She appeared positively mad as she shoved Lantalia hard and staggered across the room.

"Anika! You've gone too far!" Lantalia repeated, both anger and concern evident in her tone. "Do you have any idea? Do you even know the seriousness of what you've done?"

Anika scowled bitterly; her black eyes glared in disdain. She raised a dark arm and pointed it at her sister and the room began to shake violently. "Leave now, Lantalia," she seethed, "or I swear, I will kill you!" Her voice was evil and coarse.

"You can't kill me," Lantalia calmly responded. A quick wave of her hand and the shaking stopped. "We're twins, Anika. You kill me, and you'll die too."

Anika snarled like a caged animal and then charged toward Lantalia with every intention of attacking. All at once her black eyes rolled back in her head and she slowly rose into the air.

"Twin! Soon you will have no power over us!"

The voice was coming from Anika's mouth, but it wasn't Anika's. It was bizarre—a single voice, neither male nor female, and yet somehow both; the volume of the voice was earsplitting. "We made you, Lantalia, and we will destroy you!" Two powerful bolts of silvery electricity shot from Anika's eyes.

Lantalia spun out of the way, narrowly avoiding the bolts which crashed in an explosive shower of sparks against the wall behind her. She looked up at Anika, who was hanging in the air in a trance-like state. Lantalia closed her eyes and began to chant in a monotonous drone. "Reloia sa . . . reloia sa . . . reloia sa." As she breathed the strange chant over and over and over, a low hum surged in and out through the air. The hum grew stronger until the air itself began to vibrate in visible waves. The volume of Lantalia's chant rose to meet the volume of the hum.

The humming and chanting climaxed in a thunderous explosion which rippled throughout the entire palace, shaking the walls and floors violently. With her eyes still tightly shut, Lantalia raised her arm skyward and yelled, "RELOIA SA, RELOIA SA, RELOIA SA!" and made a flicking motion like she was throwing an invisible object at her sister.

Anika's shadowy body twitched and shook in the vibrating air; then, all at once, she fell hard to the floor, landing awkwardly on her right shoulder.

Lantalia rushed to her side and lifted her in her arms. "Anika? Anika! Wake up," she demanded gently slapping Anika's cheeks.

Anika's eyes blinked open. She groggily whispered, "Lantalia? Wh . . . what's happening to me?" Her mood was the polar opposite of what it had just been and her voice sounded normal.

"Anika," Lantalia blurted, "when you were receiving the powers, did you hear a voice?"

Anika nodded feebly. "Yes," she wheezed. She was getting weaker by the second.

"Stay with me, Anika!" Lantalia persisted, "What did the voice say?"

She took a few shallow breaths. "Balance . . ." she muttered. "It said something about balance."

"Balance?" Lantalia asked. "Anything else?"

"Yes . . . ." Anika's eyes slipped shut.

Lantalia shook her to keep her conscious. "Come on, Anika. Stay awake! We don't have much time! What else did it say?"

"It said . . . it was giving me . . . the powers."

Lantalia shook her again. "It said the 'powers to Anika', but from where? From where, Anika?"

Anika's head slumped onto her chest. "Fr . . . from . . . Lor Mandela," she gasped laboriously and then slipped into unconsciousness.

Lantalia lowered her sister to the ground and somberly rose to her feet. "From Lor Mandela?" she gasped. She slid down onto the edge of the bed and stared at Anika's limp body. "Oh, you fool! What were you thinking?"

Just then, Anika stirred. She moaned and rolled to the side.

Lantalia quickly sprang to her feet and raced for the door. She waved her arm and again, the branches of the tree disappeared and she darted from the room.

Anika struggled to lift herself from the floor and rubbed her aching shoulder. The tree branches rematerialized without her even noticing that they had been gone. "Oh, what now?" she questioned aloud, having no recollection of what had just taken place.

She took a few steps across the floor and stumbled on something. "What in the . . . ?"

There, at her feet, lay her great-grandmother's journal where Lantalia had dropped it. She reached down and picked it up.

"Where did this come from?" she asked. She couldn't remember when she had seen it last. She ran her hand over the faded burgundy cover and pulled it open. "Elahk E Ber," she sighed shaking her head, "what have you done to me?"

Meanwhile, outside Trysta Palace, Lantalia hurried toward Koria—for the Caverns. She knew what Anika had done, and why, but hoped that if she acted quickly the remaining consequences of her sister's stupid actions could be avoided. When she reached the cave, she headed directly for the rock platform; she had barely stepped out onto it when she shouted, "Stoi Cantara, Lor Mandela!"

A quiet voice seeped up out of the Caverns. "Only the vritesse can call on the spirit of Lor Mandela."

She took a deep breath. "Forgive me, kind and gracious one. I am Lantalia, daughter of Satia—and Vritesse of Lor Mandela."

The voice answered, a little stronger this time. "Vritesse Lantalia, or the twin? What is the blood in your veins? The soul has been corrupted."

"Yes," she whispered, "my sister has corrupted it. However, my soul is pure." She paused, and then added, "I invite you to determine."

The voice was slow to respond. "Vritesse Lantalia, are you aware of the danger?"

"I am," she answered, "but it's the only way for you to be safe, wise spirit."

"Very well," the voice replied.

A sudden breeze swirled throughout the Caverns, quickly escalating into a ferocious wind. Dust, leaves and even small rocks whizzed through the air.

Lantalia stood amid the debris and did not move. Her hair and clothes blew violently in the intense wind, but she maintained a statue-like stance. As the wind grew stronger and stronger, bright flashes of red light began slicing through the air, zipping and popping all around her, narrowly missing her. Had she flinched at all, the bolts would have cut through her like a sword and she knew it. She remained frozen in place for several seconds until the lights and the wind finally calmed, and eventually ceased.

The voice spoke again. "Lantalia . . . the true vritesse of the Trysta people . . . you have come to me to save your sister. Is it not so?"

"Yes," she replied.

"But why, Vritesse? She stole your spirit, did she not? Stole it, and then cloned it?"

Again she answered, "Yes."

"A twin spirit cannot be cloned," the voice scolded. "The clone will be corrupted and corrupt all that it contacts."

Lantalia nodded; her eyes filled with tears. "I'm afraid it has corrupted her and . . ." She paused as a tear escaped and rolled down her cheek. "It's also corrupted you, hasn't it?"

This time the voice replied, "Yes." After a long silence, it continued. "The corrupt part of my soul—the darkest portion—even now possesses your sister. She is dying, Lantalia, and I am dying because of her."

Although Lantalia knew this in her heart, the verbal confirmation pierced her to her core. "But surely there's a way to stop this! What can be done?" She feared what the answer might be—unfortunately, it was that exact answer that followed.

"She must die, Vritesse."

Lantalia dropped to her knees.

"And therefore, I am so sorry to say, beloved Lantalia, you must die as well."

Lantalia nodded mournfully. Tears streamed unchecked down her cheeks.

Again, there was silence.

After several agonizing seconds, she whispered almost inaudibly, "What about you? Our entire world is doomed then, isn't it?"

The spirit's voice was slow to respond. "There is a way," it whispered. "Perhaps . . . yessss, if balance is restored . . . yesss, that's it!" Again, the spirit of Lor Mandela seemed to gather strength. "You must go to your daughter," it advised. "You must go to Gracielle."

"Gracielle?" she asked. She couldn't imagine what *she* had to do with any of this.

"Yes, Gracielle," the voice of the soul replied. "Go to her quickly. Once you are with her, call on me, and I will show you both what can be done. There's not much time, Vritesse. Every moment is crucial. The process must be initiated immediately."

"Of course." She bowed reverently.

Suddenly, another voice echoed through the Caverns. "Vritesse! Vritesse, are you here?" It was General Kort, and he sounded frantic.

There was a rapid *swoosh* as the spirit of Lor Mandela retreated back down through the center of the Caverns.

Lantalia quickly tried to pull herself together. "Kort? I'm up here!" She stood, blotted her cheeks with the back of her hand, and brushed the dust from her knees.

Kort appeared at the bottom of the path, visibly agitated. Vritesse! Come quick! Hurry! It's Anika!"

CHAPTER V

THE ADVANTIERE

Lantalia didn't wait for an explanation. The details didn't matter. Anything that was happening with Anika right now was certainly not good. She rushed to Kort and the two of them took off at a full run back toward the palace.

Once they reached the gate, Kort tried to explain. "Ultara is with her . . . she just fell and started thrashing around. We couldn't get her to stop! And . . ." His eyes grew wide as he added, "She's totally black now!"

Lantalia touched Kort on the shoulder and nodded. She hurried off ahead of him toward Anika's room.

Ultara met her at the door. "Vritesse!" she blurted, "she's gone!"

"Wh . . . what do you mean? She's dead?" Lantalia tried to remain calm despite the panic twisting inside of her.

"No, Vritesse," Ultara explained, "she just vanished. She was jerking and convulsing for almost an hour. A few minutes ago she stopped. I thought she was coming out of it, but then she whispered something about Gracielle and disappeared."

"Oh no!" Lantalia gasped. "She knows!"

Without further explanation, Lantalia dashed down the hall and out of the palace. She ran through the doors and while in a full sprint shouted, "Mandela Palace!"

In a flash of blue, she vanished and reappeared again outside a sprawling cluster of grandiose white buildings, in the center of a large courtyard. She ran past rich emerald hedges and up a large stone staircase. As she approached the top, she waved her arm, and the set of tall etched glass doors leading into the palace foyer bolted open.

"Gracielle!" she shouted feverishly, "GRAAACIIIEELLE!" She sped through the elegant foyer, which was surrounded by stories-high stained glass and marble, and into one of the many tan hallways leading from it. The usually bustling palace was oddly silent. "GRACIELLE!" she shouted again as she maneuvered through the corridor.

Suddenly, there was a loud *bang* and a lot of commotion at the end of the hallway. Without hesitation, she flung her arm skyward, and one of the doors a few feet away blasted open. A thick, pewter fog billowed ominously through the open door.

The same strange voice that had possessed Anika in her room before oozed out from the fog. "Please, Gracielle. We need your help." The voice was eerie and hypnotic. "Just take our hand."

"No! DON'T!" Lantalia burst into the room. She was completely enveloped in a bright magenta light.

Gracielle was sitting on the floor in a cloud of black mist, held in a trance by Anika, who looked like nothing more than a black, three-dimensional shadow. She was standing above Gracielle—her scraggly black hair floating all around her head—with her hand outstretched to her niece.

A dazed Gracielle reached forward.

"No, Graci . . . don't!" Lantalia pleaded. Gracielle didn't respond.

Lantalia lowered her head and closed her glowing eyes.

The shadowy Anika sneered and growled and all at once, gasped sharply and bolted into the air. She flew across the room and crashed into a large window—shattering it into millions of pieces—before dropping like a rag doll to the ground.

Gracielle instantly snapped out of the trance. She jumped to her feet and dashed toward the door, not even realizing that her mother was there until she caught a glimpse of her out of the corner of her eye. "Mother!" she cried. "What's wrong with Anika?"

"There's no time to explain!" Lantalia yelled. She gestured toward the floor and a large section of it completely vanished, revealing an endless dark pit. "Stoi Cantara! Lor Mandela!" she commanded.

A hazy white light grew from deep within the pit, but then faded.

Once more she shouted, "Stoi Cantara! Lor Mandela!"

The light returned—a little stronger this time—but then went out again.

"STOI CANTARA! LOR MANDELA!" She literally screamed it this time.

A blinding flash blasted from the pit, knocking Gracielle and Lantalia to the ground. The heavy fog that had been consuming the room quickly dissipated, and the room became eerily silent.

Gracielle slowly rose to her feet. "Mother, are you all right?"

Lantalia was curled up in a motionless ball on the floor.

"Vritesse?" Gracielle tried again, cautiously moving toward her.

For a moment, Lantalia didn't respond but then, she suddenly pushed up onto all fours. Her back heaved up and down, and her breathing became heavy and labored. She lifted her face and stared wide-eyed at Gracielle.

Much to Gracielle's surprise, something—some sort of image—seemed to be materializing in her mother's lavender eyes. "It . . . it's Lor Mandela," she whispered as a revolving likeness of the planet came into focus in each eye.

Lantalia nodded. "Yessss, Atoh." Her voice was clearly not her own. It flowed from her mouth like a deep haunting song. "I am a portion of the spirit of Lor Mandela. The rest of me resides in Anika and we are both dying."

"What? But how . . . th . . . that would mean . . . ." Gracielle muttered.

Lantalia moved closer and locked Gracielle in her stare. Her lilac eyes glowed brightly with the now crystal clear images of Lor Mandela. As Gracielle watched, pools of large tears began to well up and flood out onto her lashes.

Just as they were about to spill from her eyes, they swiftly reversed their course, rolling back like waves—breaking violently against the glowing purple images. They swirled and twisted, swelling into torrential rapids that pounded buildings, swept away animals and people, and consumed everything in their destructive path. After a few seconds—and much to Gracielle's relief—the waters seemed to calm and finally recede.

She kept her gaze fixed on the images as somewhere far behind Lantalia's eyes, the sound of an eerie, distant rumbling started to build. The rumbling grew louder, and louder, and louder; the images of Lor Mandela shook and shuddered; and then—in a deafening explosion—they burst into billions of tiny pieces and disappeared in a haze of glowing purple dust.

Gracielle jumped. "No!" she cried. "Wh . . . what does this . . . Lor Mandela can't . . . I mean . . . what does this mean?"

"Yes, Atoh, Lor Mandela is doomed. But there is one way to save us," the voice explained. "This will be our fate unless balance is restored."

"What do you mean?"

"Balance has been destroyed—the balance that has kept Lor Mandela alive.

Suddenly, an evil, gravelly voice seethed from across the room. "NOOOOO," it screeched. The shadow of Anika had regained consciousness. She sprang to her feet and in a smoky, black blur, sped toward Gracielle.

Lantalia instantly threw herself between them, catching Anika completely off guard. She slammed into Lantalia and fell lifeless to the ground, but the blackness that had possessed her was no longer there. It was now inside Lantalia.

Lantalia's appearance was shocking and strange. Not quite half of her was a dark, inky shadow, while the other part of her glowed fiery purple. Her voice was distorted and strained. "Gracielle!" she shrieked, "Your daughter! She is the Child of Balance!" Her voice changed to a shrill, hissing screech, "Trysta mother . . . Borloc father . . . balance!" Lantalia struggled to continue. "The Child of Balance must . . . be . . . protected!"

All at once, the light around Lantalia intensified. She let out an ear-splitting scream and the black ripped out of her and flew directly back into Anika, who moaned and began to stir.

The voice of Lor Mandela's spirit burst from Lantalia's mouth again, speaking very loudly this time. "THIS IS THE ADVANTIERE OF THE TRYSTA LANTALIA! AT THE APPOINTED TIME, THE MESSAGE WILL BE UNDERSTOOD. ONLY THE CHILD OF BALANCE CAN SAVE OUR WORLD. SHE HAS ALL POWER, BUT CANNOT CALL ON IT ALONE.

THE RIDDLE MUST BE SOLVED FOR, OR BY HER. TWINS MUST LIVE STILL TO PLAY THEIR PARTS, HER FATHER'S HATRED DIE FOR LOVE TO GROW, AND BALANCE BE MAINTAINED FOR THE EXACT TIME BALANCE WAS MISSING. ANY OF THESE ELEMENTS MISSED, AND LOR MANDELA WILL CEASE."

The volume of the spirit's voice was so great that it seemed to have a density to it. With every booming syllable, the floor and ceiling and walls bumped wildly, causing them to crumble under the heaviness of the spirit's roaring proclamation. Chunks of plaster plummeted from the ceiling and gaping cracks ripped across the walls.

Oddly though, one wall in the room seemed completely undisturbed. As the soul of Lor Mandela spoke, a shower of red sparks sizzled across the wall, leaving behind the words of Lantalia's Advantiere:

Destruction from twins, and so it must end.
They are the lock, yet they are not friends.
The Child of Balance can only restore.
Her father the key and she is the door.
The riddle now told, the Advantiere presents,
healing begins following future events.

ONE comes swiftly in the morning
ONE unknowing moves in haste
ONE beloved though mighty fallen
ONE is chosen to forget her place
E lahk E Ber Lor Mandela!
ONE though strong must fall forbidden.
ONE made low shall rise again.
ONE must be as these words written
Then will ONE forever reign.
E lahk A Ber Lor Mandela!

With the final syllable, the spirit of Lor Mandela rocketed out of Lantalia's body, and retreated into the pit.

Lantalia fell limp to the floor.

Gracielle rushed to her side, but as she did, Anika—who had again become the dark, evil shadow—glided back toward her.

"I will have power," she seethed. "There will be no Child of Balance!"

Gracielle quickly scrambled backward and raised her hand in the air. The floor creaked and a wide crack zigzagged across it; a glowing, golden, needle-thin spike bolted out of it and raced toward Anika.

It sliced a deep gash across Anika's forearm.

"*Fool!*" she screeched, "Your powers are nothing! Do not attempt to cross me!" She pressed her hand against the wound which was bleeding an inky black. She slid one of her hands behind her and grabbed for something and then flicked her wrist like she was flinging an invisible object at Gracielle.

"Gracielle! MOVE!" A voice called out from across the room followed by a flash of gold ricocheting through the air. Gracielle fell to the ground and rolled just as a sharp, black object disintegrated less than an inch over her head. She looked up and saw Anika's daughter, Ultara, still glowing gold standing near the door.

Lantalia was back on her feet and shouted in her own voice, "Ultara! Get Gracielle out of here! Now!" She knew that Ultara would never disobey the vritesse.

Within a fraction of a second, Ultara was next to Gracielle. Her black cloak flew upward, swirled around them, and they disappeared.

The shadow of Anika didn't seem discouraged in the slightest by this little setback. She slinked her way over piles of broken glass and concrete to the door and set off through the palace in search of Gracielle.

Lantalia hurriedly followed.

"Anika! Stop this! You can not win!" she yelled as they reached the stained glass foyer.

Anika's shadowy silhouette headed for the large glass doors, seemingly oblivious to the fact that Lantalia was in pursuit.

"Little Atoh?" she cackled, "Where are you? Come out, dear little Gracielle!"

Lantalia flung her arm upward and Anika's dark shadowy form jerked abruptly, as though she had been hit by a large object.

She growled and turned to face Lantalia. "Forget about it, sister!" she sneered. "You cannot win against us!"

She raised her hand and a strange sound—like hailstones hitting glass—echoed outside the palace. All at once, hundreds of large wooden thorns broke through the walls and bulleted toward Lantalia at a startling speed.

Lantalia thrust both hands into the air and a pillar of crystal blue water—almost as wide as the foyer itself—rose from the ground. The thorns smacked into it and fell with loud clanks onto the marble floor.

"You cannot win!" Anika repeated. "I will find the Child of Balance and I will destroy her!" She pushed her hands forward and a crackling wall of black flames formed out of the air directly in front of her, sending an intensely hot wind blasting throughout the room. She opened her arms out to her sides and the dark fire surged and zipped toward Lantalia.

The vritesse made a pushing motion and the massive wall of water moved toward the flames. They collided in the center of the foyer, twisting and tangling together, forming a sizzling, spattering cyclone.

"Anika!" Lantalia yelled over the roar of the water and the loud snapping of the fire. "Stop now! Neither of us will survive this!"

"So be it!" Anika hissed. Her dark form walked through the center of the fire and water and they instantly disappeared.

She reached into her black cloak and produced a jagged charcoal dagger. "If we both must die, sister, I'll let you go first!" She hurled the dagger ferociously toward Lantalia. No sooner had it left her hand, than it vanished in thin air.

Lantalia hesitated for a moment, but then leaned to one side as the invisible dagger grazed past her head, narrowly missing as it raced through her hair. It whizzed past her, but then reversed its course and came at her again. She turned to face where she thought it was and dove sideways just as it raced by. Suddenly, she knew what she had to do. She waited for the dagger to come at her again and then ran, full-force, toward Anika. Just before the inevitable collision, she dove to the side and rolled across the floor.

The maneuver caught Anika so off guard she didn't have time to respond. With a loud gasp, she jerked violently and grabbed at her chest. In her hand, the shiny hilt of the dagger materialized; fully half of its blade was embedded in her coal black chest. Slowly, the blackness slid down her like thick tar seeping onto the floor. As her normal color returned, she looked pleadingly at Lantalia, and then sank to the ground. Anika was dead.

Lantalia crawled over to her just as Gracielle and Ultara ran in from one of the hallways. They stopped and glanced at each other and then raced to Lantalia's side.

The vritesse was choking and sputtering—trying frantically to get a full breath.

"Mother?" Gracielle pleaded. She knew that with Anika dead, it was only a matter of seconds before her own mother would be too.

Lantalia fought to lift her hand. "Protect her," she gasped, pointing at Gracielle's mid-section.

Gracielle put her hand to her stomach and nodded weakly.

Lantalia turned her gaze to Ultara and fumbled through her cloak while struggling to breathe. "Ultara . . . ."

Ultara knelt down beside her. "Yes, Vritesse. What is it?"

Lantalia held out her trembling hand and placed it in Ultara's. "Rule well," she sighed.

Ultara looked down in surprise. There, in her palm, was the little silver box.

The vritesse smiled, drew in one large gulp of air, and was gone.

CHAPTER VI

THEY ARE THE LOCK,
BUT THEY ARE NOT FRIENDS

After several quiet minutes in the palace foyer, Ultara's voice broke the heavy silence. "Come on, Graci," she whispered. "We should go. There's nothing more we can do here."

She stood and held out her hand.

Gracielle stared at their mothers' bodies for a few more seconds. A nauseating emptiness twisted in the pit of her stomach. Her mother was gone; it didn't seem real. Yet the evidence was right there, tragically staring her in the face. She looked up at Ultara, took her outstretched hand, and pulled herself to her feet. "I . . . I suppose you're right," she sighed.

Ultara put her arm around Gracielle's shoulder. "I'll walk you to your room, and then find someone to take care of the bodies," she offered in a cracking voice.

Gracielle fought back tears as they started across the foyer.

A nagging voice inside her head whispered over and over again, *the Advantiere . . . the Advantiere . . . the Advantiere.*

She ignored it, but it repeated. *The Advantiere . . . the Advantiere . . . the Advantiere.*

As they entered a hallway, the voice echoed in her mind again.

Gracielle stopped. "I . . . I'm sorry, Ultara," she said. "I just can't seem to shake this. I've got to go back to the Advantiere."

Ultara gaped in surprise. "You too?" She'd also heard a voice urging her back. "This doesn't really seem like the right time," she protested, "but, I don't think either of us is going to get any rest until we take a look at that thing. I'll get help from Koria first, and then meet you back in the room."

Gracielle nodded in agreement.

Ultara turned and walked quickly toward the main doors, intentionally refusing to look in the direction of her mother's body. Once outside, she ran down the palace steps and vanished in a flash of blue light.

Gracielle had to look again, just one more moment to be in the presence of the woman she loved and admired the most. She glanced over at her mother's motionless form and tears spilled in thick streams down her fair cheeks.

The Advantiere . . . the Advantiere . . . the Advantiere. The voice returned, louder and more demanding than before. *The Advantiere . . . the Advantiere . . . the Advantiere.*

She drew in a deep breath and started toward the corridor that housed the Advantiere room.

She had barely taken two steps into the hall, when Ultara returned looking very agitated. She informed Gracielle that a group of Trystas were on their way, and then stomped her foot and shouted skyward, "Yes! The Advantiere! I know! We're going!"

When they reached the room, Ultara waved her hand and the door flew open to reveal an overwhelming scene. Piles of broken glass, chunks of concrete, twisted metal, and splintered wood completely covered the once-marble floor. The only break in the mess was the huge, gaping chasm—the pit from which the spirit of Lor Mandela had come when it revealed to Gracielle that she was carrying the child responsible for saving their entire world. The very thought of it made her insides feel like they had been tied in tight knots.

Cautiously, they maneuvered through the rubble and around the hole in the floor to where the Advantiere glistened glittery-red on the wall. They stood and stared at it for several minutes.

Finally, Gracielle read aloud, "The Child of Balance can only restore." She placed her hand on her stomach and sighed. "You know? I just found out today. I haven't even told Jonathan yet."

Ultara touched her cousin warmly on the arm. "If it's any consolation," she tried, "it says, *'The riddle must be solved for or by her'*. I can only assume that means this isn't going to happen immediately. It's going to take some time."

She smiled at Gracielle, who was looking all at once pale and green.

"I'm sure she'll be remarkable, Graci. But I don't know of any infant who can solve a riddle."

Gracielle managed a weak chuckle. "No, of course," she replied.

She couldn't help but allow her mind to wander for a moment. She visualized a beautiful little girl with tight black ringlets, round porcelain cheeks and vivid blue eyes. She imagined her playing—happy and carefree—while hordes of people stood around, anxiously watching; waiting for her to do something miraculous to save them all from certain doom. She didn't want that for her baby. She didn't want her to have that kind of pressure. She forced her thoughts back to the present, stared at the Advantiere again and attempted to move on.

Unfortunately, the next line she read did little to calm her. "Twins must live still to play their parts. Wait!" she gasped. "How can that be? It's not possible! I mean . . . how are they . . . how are they supposed to . . . ? They're dead!" She looked pleadingly at Ultara. "Have we failed already?"

Ultara didn't respond right away. She seemed distant—lost in her thoughts. "Maybe they've already played their part," she tried.

"No," Gracielle answered, "it says that they must live *still*."

Ultara glanced away and began pacing.

"Then maybe it means the other set of twins," she muttered.

"What?" Gracielle pressed. "What *other* set of twins?"

Ultara plodded back and forth for several seconds before responding.

"Nobody, Graci, and I mean *nobody*, knows about this. It can not leave this room, understand?"

Gracielle nodded. "You have my word."

Ultara took a deep breath and explained, "Thirteen years ago, I gave birth to a son, remember?"

"Yes, of course."

Everyone knew about Ultara's son. It had been a great scandal. It was law among the Trysta people that the firstborn child of a woman in line to become vritesse had to be female. They believed that a first-born son was contrary to nature, and subsequently flawed.

Fortunately, nature itself usually took care of it. It was quite uncommon for a vritesse heiress to have a son first. But, if a son was born first, the law dictated that he would have to be put to death. In fact, it even stated that if twins were born and one or both were male, both were to be destroyed.

"Darian was so proud," Ultara continued. "There was no way he was going to allow anyone to kill his son!"

Darian, her former entrusted, was a very handsome, captivating, influential man. He was Chief Ruler of the Brashnellans—a race of people descended from the Trystas. The Brashnellans had divided from the Trystas nearly two hundred years earlier, due coincidentally, to the first-born son laws. With each passing generation their magical powers diminished; however, their civilization had continued to prosper and flourish. Over time, Brashnell had grown to encompass almost one quarter of Lor Mandela.

Ultara took another deep breath and continued. "When I gave birth, Atoh, I was alone. There were no witnesses."

"Really? Where was Darian?" Gracielle replied.

"He'd gone to Brashnell to meet with his father." She leaned against the wall. Her wavy auburn hair glowed red under the luminescent letters above. She lowered her voice and admitted, "The truth is, I gave birth to twins."

Gracielle's eyes grew wide. "What? How?" she replied. "I mean, I knew about your son, but what happened to the other one?"

"I was young and weak, Graci. I didn't want to kill my children."

She seemed almost ashamed of herself.

"A few minutes after the birth, I gathered as much strength as I could and created a hidden room next to mine in the palace. I placed my other child—a daughter—in that room and told Darian that I'd given birth to a son."

Gracielle could hardly believe what she was hearing.

"Brashnellans believe that a first-born son brings power," Ultara continued. "I knew Darian would never allow anyone to harm his son. Turns out I was right. I told Darian that he could have his son for two days, but at the end of them, the child would have to be put to death."

Gracielle was beginning to understand. "You knew he'd take him, didn't you?"

Ultara nodded.

"But, that doesn't explain what happened to your daughter."

Ultara thought for a moment and then asked, "Do you have the ability to alter, Gracielle?"

"No, of course not. There are only a handful of Trystas with that power."

Ultara smiled proudly. "Yes, and I am one of them."

Gracielle raised her eyebrows in surprise.

"I kept my daughter hidden until she was two years old. Then I altered myself so I would appear to be going through another pregnancy. When the time was right, I returned myself to normal and altered my daughter into an infant again."

"Nenia?" Gracielle breathed.

"Yes, Nenia. Now, Darian has my son and I have my daughter. They look two years apart, but they *are* twins," She smiled and added, "and there's nothing flawed about either of them."

Gracielle contemplated her words for a moment. "So then I guess that means that your children . . . they must be part of this Advantiere as well?"

"I guess so," she sighed. Suddenly, Ultara's expression grew deathly serious. "Listen, Gracielle, Darian can't know about this . . . nobody can . . . but especially not Darian. He hates me passionately. He's already tried to get to Nenia—for revenge, I suppose. He thinks that since I was willing to kill his son I don't deserve to have a child of my own. If he knew that she was his son's twin, he would hunt her like an animal. He would not rest until she was dead."

"I understand. I won't tell a soul," Gracielle agreed.

Ultara pointed at the Advantiere and asked, "So what do we do about this, then? Who do we tell?"

"I don't know," Gracielle answered. "It might be best if we just keep it to ourselves . . . at least until we've had a chance to think it over. I imagine we'll be busy with other things for the next day or so."

As her thoughts returned to her mother, she recalled her last moments and how she'd given Ultara the little silver box.

Ultara was still holding it in her hand.

"I guess you're the vritesse now, Ultara." Gracielle's voice quivered as she spoke.

Ultara looked at the box and sighed, "Yeah, I guess I am."

Gracielle glanced up at a large window that had somehow remained intact and noticed the sun sinking below it. "It's nearly time for me to meet Jonathan and his parents for dinner. I need to let them know what's happened. I expect they'll want to call a council meeting."

"I should get back to Koria, too. I want to inform the rest of my generals as soon as possible." Ultara responded.

They made their way out of the demolished room and agreed to seal it so that no one could accidentally stumble across the mess, or more importantly, the Advantiere. Once outside, Gracielle lifted her hand and a small yellow spark appeared in the bottom left hand corner of the door. It buzzed and zipped upward and sped around the door frame. By the time it reached the lower right side, the door had completely vanished.

"Thank you, Atoh," Ultara mumbled.

"Good night, Vritesse." Gracielle bowed and they went their separate ways.

Gracielle slowly made her way to the Grand Dining Hall where Jonathan was waiting for her outside the door. As soon as he saw her he moved to meet her; as he got closer a look of concern grew across his face. "Graci, what is it? What happened to you?" She was pale and covered in dust and dirt.

The reality of the day's events suddenly hit her hard. All at once she felt dizzy and sick. She tried to steady herself against a nearby wall but was still having difficulty standing. "It . . . It's the vritesse, Jonathan," she panted. "Anika attacked her. They're both . . ." Her knees buckled and she slumped over. "dead." Jonathan barely caught her before she hit the floor.

Her collapse was witnessed by Atoc Cristoph and Ator Jocelynne who had just come around the corner by the dining hall. "What's wrong?" Cristoph shouted as they hurried toward them.

Jonathan held Gracielle tightly. "She says that Anika attacked Lantalia and they've both been killed!"

Jocelynne gasped and both she and Cristoph froze in place.

Gracielle babbled, "Lantalia called Ultara . . . downstairs . . . sending for the bodies . . . the council will need to . . . ." Her eyes fluttered; she took a deep breath and seemed to regain a little of her strength.

Jonathan, who was still concerned, however, looked at his father and shouted, "Can you get the doctor? I'll take her to our room."

Cristoph nodded and he and Jocelynne rushed away.

Jonathan helped Gracielle down the hallway.

When they were almost at the end of it, he reached out to a beautifully carved wooden door and pushed it open. "Come on, Love, you need rest," he insisted as he led her towards the bed.

"I . . . I think I'm okay now, Jonathan," she assured. "A lot has happened today. I was just overwhelmed." She sat down on the bed, gazed into space, and then blurted matter-of-factly, "Oh, and Jonathan . . . I'm pregnant."

He stared at her for a few seconds and then mumbled a feeble, "What?"

She exhibited no emotion whatsoever. "We're going to have a baby."

Jonathan paced for a moment and then asked soberly, "And if it's a son?"

"It's not going to be a son, Jonathan. It's a girl," she replied.

"I understand it usually happens that way for Trysta Heiresses, but . . ."

Gracielle stopped him. "No, Jonathan, this has nothing to do with me being a Trysta Heiress. I've been told that it's a girl."

"Told? Who could've told you? Nobody would've. . . . "

Just then, there was a knock at the door.

"Come in," Gracielle answered, relieved that—at least for the moment—she wasn't going to have to give further details.

A tall, slender man entered the room with Atoc Cristoph.

"Oh hello, Doctor," Gracielle welcomed with a forced smile.

The doctor walked over and put his hand on her shoulder. "Good evening, Atoh. I'm so sorry to hear about your mother."

"Thank you, Michelan."

She leaned forward and gave him a hug.

"And thank you for coming, although I'm sure I'm all right now. It's just been a hard day; I let it get to me."

The doctor frowned. "Of course, but I would feel much better if you'd let me take a look. I'd like to make sure both you and the baby are okay."

Cristoph looked questioningly at Jonathan who smiled and shrugged his shoulders. "We'll be outside."

He put his arm around his father and led him out of the room.

Jocelynne came walking down the hall toward them. Her eyes were red and her cheeks were splotchy; she'd obviously been crying.

"They've taken them," she sighed.

Cristoph embraced his wife, and no one said anything for a few minutes.

Finally, it was Cristoph who broke the silence, "I think our son has something to tell us, Jocey."

Jocelynne sniffled and looked at Jonathan, who gently embraced her. "Gracielle and I are having a baby."

A knowing smile crept across Jocelynne's face. "Of course . . . I should have realized. She hasn't been herself lately."

She was giving Jonathan another squeeze as the door to the room opened and Dr. Michelan peered out. "We're all finished in here. Everything looks fine," he assured.

Jonathan sighed with relief and he, and his parents, stepped back into the room.

For the next couple of hours, Gracielle, Jonathan, Doctor Michelan, Jocelynne and Cristoph all sat in the room and talked. They spoke fondly of Lantalia and Anika and contemplated what Jonathan and Gracielle's child would be like. They discussed Ultara's appointment, and debated over when they should call the council together to make it official.

"Are you sure it's not too soon?" Jocelynne questioned, when Cristoph suggested that the council convene the following afternoon.

"Ultara has already been called," he answered. "She needs to receive the powers as soon as possible. It may be difficult, but I don't think we can put it off."

"But Ultara can go to the Caverns and get the powers herself," Gracielle argued. "The Council meeting is just a formality. Couldn't we hold the meeting after things have settled down?"

Cristoph leaned back in his chair. "Yes, my dear, I suppose we could. But I think that making these changes with minimal disruption to our traditions may help people feel more secure; it'll help them come to terms with this tragedy more quickly. Familiarity is comforting, you know."

Jonathan and Jocelynne nodded in agreement.

"I suppose that's true," Gracielle concurred.

"I'll make the arrangements and get the message out tonight," Jonathan offered.

Cristoph patted him on the back. "Thank you, son. I think we should go now. Your entrusted looks as though she could use some rest."

Doctor Michelan stood from the green wing chair in which he'd been sitting. "I believe you're right, Atoc," he agreed.

They said their goodbyes and the doctor, Cristoph, and Jocelynne all left.

"Will you be okay while I prepare for the council meeting, Graci?" Jonathan asked.

"Of course I will," she grimaced. "I'll probably just go to bed."

Jonathan kissed her on the cheek and headed toward the door. "Okay,

Love. I'll be back in awhile."

Gracielle changed into her pajamas and got ready for bed, but didn't feel much like sleep. She felt edgy and restless. There was no way she was going to be able to sleep with everything that was bouncing around in her head. She curled up in a large, dark green chair, and tried to read for a while but finally ended up just staring out the window at the reflection of the full moon sparkling on the surface of Mystad Lake. "Goodbye, beloved vritesse," she mumbled as tears welled in her eyes, and then flowed unchecked down her cheeks. "Goodbye, beloved mother,"

In the meantime, Jonathan had dispatched messengers to all of the chief council members telling them of the next day's meeting. He was updating Cristoph in a small, simply furnished sitting room, when there was a faint knock on the door.

A portly, young servant with a ruddy complexion and dishwater blond hair poked his head around the door. He cleared his throat and announced, "Atoc, Aton, Darian of Brashnell to see you, sirs."

"Thank you, Phillip," Cristoph replied. "Tell him to come in."

Phillip bowed as a charismatic man with strong, masculine features and long dark hair came through the door and confidently strode toward them. He lowered to one knee and humbly apologized for the intrusion.

"Good Evening Atoc . . . Aton, I would have never dreamed of disturbing you at this hour, but I have some very alarming news."

He looked up at Cristoph with eyes of pure black, except for the small orange, blue, and white fires that crackled where most people's pupils were.

Cristoph signaled for him to stand. "Alarming, Darian?" he questioned.

Darian rose from his knee. "Yes, Sire, I don't even know where to begin. I'm sure that it must seem bold of me to be bothering you in light of recent events, but I'm afraid that this cannot wait."

"What is it, Darian?" Cristoph glanced over at Jonathan who was glaring at their visitor. He had never gotten along with Darian of Brashnell.

Darian explained, "I'm sure that you know that Ultara and I are not on—shall we say—the best of terms."

Cristoph raised an eyebrow and tilted his head.

"Because of this unfortunate fact, I've found it helpful over these years to keep some close Trysta friends."

"Friends? You mean spies," Jonathan chimed in cynically.

"I suppose," Darian smiled as the fires in his eyes seemed to grow larger. "That would be one way of looking at it."

"And what alarming news have your *friends* brought you?" Cristoph asked.

"Sire, when Ultara and I were still together, we—I am ashamed to admit it now—but we were plotting to overthrow the government and rule Lor Mandela together. The plan was to wait until she became vritesse. With her ruling the Trystas and my position in Brashnell, we would be able to gain control over Mandela City easily."

"Why are you telling me this now, Darian?" Cristoph barked. Clearly, his level of irritation was rising.

Jonathan was beyond irritated and glared viciously at Darian.

"Atoc," Darian continued, "this was at least fifteen years ago. Please believe me. It is all in the past." He lowered his voice slightly and added, "At least it is for me."

"What do you mean?" Jonathan insisted.

Darian smiled condescendingly at Jonathan. "Well, Aton, my friend Omer, who is of course a Trysta, came to me just a few hours ago and said that he overheard Ultara talking to her advisor. She said that the waiting was over, and that the time had finally come for her to gain control of Lor Mandela. He informs me that she is planning some sort of attack, and very soon."

"Why should we believe you? Ultara has always been our friend!" Jonathan snipped.

"My dear, Aton," Darian's respect was clearly feigned. "I know that many people do not trust me. Indeed, you have no reason to trust or, in fact, to even like me, but as I see it, whether we care for each other or not, we are in this one together.

"Ultara is cunning and she loves power. If she sees a way to get it . . . well, let's just say that it doesn't matter who's in her way."

He turned his attention to Cristoph and continued. "Omer didn't know who the attack was going to be on, Atoc—just that it was either your family or mine." The flames in his eyes flickered wildly. "If we are ready—and help each other by keeping a watchful eye—it will surely benefit us both."

He shot Jonathan another contrived smile, then added, "Perhaps I have been misinformed, but if not, it behooves us all to be on our guard."

Cristoph nodded thoughtfully. "Of course. Thank you, Darian. Let us hope you were misinformed."

Darian bowed humbly and then strutted out of the room.

Jonathan barely waited for him to get out the door. "Well? What do you make of that?"

"I don't know," Cristoph answered. "Ultara has always been kind to us."

"And Darian is known for being . . . what's the word . . . um . . . deceitful?" Jonathan added. His tone was heavily bitter.

"Jonathan, this is not the first time I've been warned about Ultara."

Jonathan's surprise was apparent.

"Lantalia told me that Ultara should be watched carefully. It shocked me when I heard it. It shocked me tonight when Gracielle said that Lantalia had called *her* as the new vritesse." Cristoph looked his son squarely in the eye. "Darian's right, though. We need to be alert. Anything unusual is to be reported, understand?"

"Yes, sir," Jonathan replied. "I understand."

CHAPTER VII
THE GRASPING CURSE

When Jonathan finally returned to his room, he found Gracielle fast asleep in the big green chair. She looked so peaceful and beautiful lying there in her soft peach pajamas with her silky hair sweeping over one of her cheeks. He watched her sleeping and thought about the first time he saw her—*truly* saw her.

Actually, he had known Gracielle most of his life. They had played together as children. But it wasn't until two summers ago that he had really noticed her. At the time, she was seventeen and he was nineteen—and it was the first year she was old enough to attend the Celebration of Light. Gracielle was very excited about being able to go. She and her girl friends talked of nothing else when they were together. One time Jonathan happened to overhear her going on and on about it, and seized the opportunity—as he often did—to tease her.

"Oh yes," he mocked in a high, squeaky voice, "just look at me!" He thrust his hands onto his waist and puffed out his chest. "I'm a wooooman now!"

Gracielle, of course, slugged him hard in the arm and told him to go kiss a slarp.

But then, on the night of the Celebration, his eyes were finally opened. Gracielle arrived alone, wearing a flowing, pale blue gown that was the perfect shade to make her soft green eyes sparkle. Her straight, strawberry blonde hair that was normally pulled up in a messy, floppy ponytail was sleek, almost down to her waist and dotted with tiny blue jewels. Jonathan remembered how confident she looked, and how he was drawn to her like a moth to a flame. It was that night that he couldn't keep his eyes off of her. It was that night that he realized that he'd been in love with her for longer than he could remember, and it was that night—while they danced and laughed under the silvery summer stars—that he knew he wanted to spend forever with her. Two months later they were engaged. Six months after that, they became entrusted to one another.

Throughout the engagement, Gracielle worriedly anticipated the process referred to as The Exalting, when Jonathan would pledge his devotion to her by repeating an ancient vow. The vow—an ages-old spell—would change her, giving her the characteristics that on Lor Mandela, only Borlocs possess. Gracielle had never pictured herself with the Borloc features, but within hours of the ceremony, her hair turned to a rich, raven black and her eyes changed from green to bright cobalt—and although she was beautiful before, the contrast of her fair, slightly freckled complexion against these new, more dramatic attributes, made her even more stunning.

Jonathan walked over to where she slept, draped a lush white blanket over her, and whispered, "That did take you a bit to get used to." He kissed her on the cheek and then went to bed himself.

The sun had barely risen when there was a tapping at the door. Gracielle heard it first, and groggily staggered across the room to answer it.

Ultara stood behind the door in the hall. "Good Morning," she whispered. "I thought I would check in and see how you're doing today."

Gracielle pulled the door open wide and sleepily motioned for her to come in.

Ultara noticed Jonathan, who was staring at her glassy-eyed from across the room. His hair was wild and matted to his head on one side. "Oh, I'm sorry, Aton. Did I wake you? Should I come back later?" she asked.

Jonathan cleared his throat. "Uh hmm . . . of course not, Ultara. How lovely to see you . . . this early." He shot her a grumpy glare as he walked toward the changing room at the back of their chambers. "Excuse me . . . I'm gonna get dressed," he groaned.

"So," Ultara began, "how are you feeling?"

Gracielle, who was still trying to wake up, stifled a yawn. "Oh, I . . . I'm okay." She smoothed her pajamas and asked, "How are you?"

Ultara shrugged. "As well as can be expected." She glanced toward the changing room, and then took Gracielle by the arm and whispered anxiously, "I figured something out . . . something from the Advantiere."

Gracielle's interest was piqued. "Really, what?" she whispered in reply.

Just then, Jonathan came back into the room—fully dressed and looking quite put together for the short time he had been gone. "You two wanna go eat?" He was still a little grouchy. "You have to have something, Graci. You didn't get dinner last night." He spoke to Gracielle, but kept his eyes locked suspiciously on Ultara. Ultara and Gracielle both took notice.

"Um . . . actually dear, I think I'll just have something sent up from the kitchens. I'm still a bit drained." Gracielle made faces at him in an attempt to get him to stop glowering at Ultara, but he didn't blink.

The mood in the room was growing tenser by the minute. Even Ultara—who was not easily intimidated—was feeling uneasy about the mysterious stare-down. "Is there something wrong, Aton?" she finally asked.

"No," he snipped curtly.

"Um . . . all right then," she replied, "why don't I go to the kitchens and round something up for the three of us?" She didn't wait for an answer from either of them. She quickly backed out of the room, frowning at the aton as she went.

"What was that all about?" Gracielle demanded, as soon as Ultara was out of earshot.

"What?"

"WHAT?" she blurted. "You were eyeing her like she was some kind of criminal, Jonathan!"

"No, I wasn't," he insisted, "That's silly."

Gracielle gaped at him in disbelief. "What is wrong with you?" She threw her hands up in exasperation and stomped to the other side of the room.

"Okay," Jonathan sighed, "maybe I was giving her a look; but you have to understand, Graci."

"Understand what?" She turned to face him, folded her arms, and tilted her head to one side.

He explained, "Last night, I was meeting with father, when Darian . . . ."

"Darian?" Gracielle interrupted. She knew that if this had to do with both Darian and Ultara, it could not be good.

Jonathan continued, "Yes, Darian. He came to see us."

He told Gracielle all about Darian's visit, and how he'd warned that Ultara was planning an attack.

"Impossible!" Gracielle retorted. "He's just trying to stir things up! He can't stand the fact that she's more powerful than him now!" She couldn't believe that her entrusted would listen to a word Darian of Brashnell had to say.

Jonathan ran over to the door and peeked out into the hall. Ultara was nowhere in sight. "Graci, after Darian left Father confided that even your mother warned him about Ultara—told him that she needed to be watched."

"Oh, I see. So that's what you were doing, huh? Watching her?" Gracielle glared at him angrily and shook her head. "Honestly, Jonathan. You'd better check our food when she brings it back . . . make sure it's not poisoned!"

"Gracielle!" Jonathan snapped. "I'm just trying to protect you . . . and the baby!"

Gracielle, who was pacing irately, stopped in her tracks. She realized that her emotions were being stirred by events of which Jonathan wasn't even aware, and that he was only acting out of concern for her and their unborn child.

"You're right. I'm sorry," she sighed as she walked over to hug him. "You know, I saw Ultara do some pretty amazing things yesterday. She actually saved me and the baby from Anika." She embraced him tightly. "I don't think she would do anything to harm us."

"I know," Jonathan resigned. "I don't really think so either. It's just . . . I have to be careful."

He leaned down and kissed her on the cheek as there was a faint rap on the door and it slowly creaked open. Ultara strolled through the door pulling a cart full of food and holding a folded piece of paper in her hand. She smiled slyly at Jonathan. "I didn't know what you wanted, so I had them give me three of everything."

"Hey, Ultara, I'm sorry I was such a grump before," Jonathan apologized. "I guess I'm not very pleasant when I first wake up."

Ultara nodded as she unfolded the paper in her hand and started reading it. "Don't worry about it, Aton. We all have our . . ." Suddenly, she became quite engrossed in the letter. "Um . . . uh . . . forgive me," she stammered. "I . . . I have to . . . uh . . . I have to get back to the palace, this instant!"

"Is everything all right?" Gracielle asked.

Ultara shook her head and fumbled with the handle on the door. "I can't . . . I'll . . . I'll talk to you after the council meeting. I have to go!" She raced out of the room, slamming the door behind her.

"That was strange," Jonathan said.

"Yeah . . . I hope every thing's all right. I've never seen Ultara get ruffled like that."

"Oh, don't worry," Jonathan assured. "Whatever it is, she can handle it. I don't think there's much she can't."

Jonathan pushed the cart over to a small sitting area on one side of the room and patted the seat of the chair next to him, indicating to Gracielle that she should come and sit down. He lifted a silver dome from a tray full of fresh fruit and waved his hand over it like he was presenting it to her. "C'mon. Let's eat."

Gracielle smiled and joined him. "Still . . . I hope she's okay," she sighed, as they proceeded with breakfast.

Meanwhile, in one of the dining halls, Cristoph and Jocelynne were also sitting down to eat. The food had just been brought in to them by two female servants, when the same young man who had announced Darian's visit the night before, entered the room.

Cristoph stood and walked over to him. "Good morning, Phillip," he greeted warmly. Phillip smiled and bowed, then handed the Atoc a letter.

"Oh, thank you," Cristoph said.

Phillip bowed again. "Enjoy your breakfast Atoc . . . Ator."

"What is it, dear?" Jocelynne asked.

Cristoph turned the letter over and noticed a gold seal on the back. "Ah, it's a note from Ultara," he replied, as he strolled back toward the table to rejoin Jocelynne.

She smiled and began to eat.

Cristoph slid his finger beneath the seal. "Let's see what our new vritesse has to say." Gently, he pried the note open.

"I hope there's not a problem. You know, with the meeting this after . . . ." Jocelynne stopped abruptly.

As Cristoph unfolded the letter, a pair of black, smoky hands oozed slowly from the paper. He watched in awe for a moment, but then realized what was happening. "NO! JOCE! IT'S A GRASPING CURSE!"

He immediately hurled the paper onto the floor, grabbed a linen napkin from the table and threw it down on the note. He fell to his knees and tried to spread the napkin over the paper.

"WHAT?" Jocelynne exclaimed, seeing Cristoph's state of panic. "Cristoph! What is it?" She pushed her chair out and moved to stand.

"NO! Jocelynne! FREEZE!" Cristoph commanded, frantically jumping onto, and then across the long banquet table. He hurled himself through the air toward his entrusted.

"CRISTOPH! LOOK OUT!" she shrieked, as several more pairs of dripping black hands found their way out from underneath the napkin and sped toward Cristoph.

"NO! CRISTOPH!" Before she could say another word, the hands had a grip on him. Again, she started from her chair to try to help him.

"JOCELYNNE! DON'T MOVE!" He bellowed.

Slowly, she lowered back to sitting and held completely still, watching in horror as gnarled black hands started to rip and tear at him.

Two of them slid up and wrapped themselves firmly around his neck.

He tried to pry them off, but had no sooner reached up, when several heavy claws grabbed him around his hands and arms. He kicked and wrestled ferociously but was defenseless. A few seconds later, he let out a mournful moan, and then stopped moving.

"Cristoph?" Jocelynne sobbed. *"Please . . . no!"*

Another pair of fatal hands was now hypnotically weaving its way toward her. Still two more were heading toward Phillip who had just come in with more food.

Upon seeing Cristoph—bloodied and presumably dead on the floor—Phillip dropped his tray of food, and ran toward Jocelynne in a valiant effort to save her.

The hands responded though, and within a fraction of a second, he too was being ripped at and strangled by the oozing black hands.

Jocelynne was terrified. The claws moving toward her were now just inches away. She panted heavily, tears streaming down her cheeks. She couldn't think. She knew that if she moved she was dead, but she didn't see how holding still would save her either. In a desperate attempt to get help, she sat perfectly still and began to scream.

The hands that had mutilated Cristoph and Phillip now were twisting toward her slowly and ominously.

She screamed even louder, but didn't move anything but her mouth.

Two female servants burst into the room in reaction to the ator's screams.

"GET OUT! GET HELP!" she shrieked.

The servant closest to the door barely escaped back through it as two of the inky claws slammed against it, scratching wildly at the wooden surface in an effort to get her back.

The other girl panicked and tried to lunge out of the way as a set of hands viciously grabbed at her. Her death came quickly. The force of the hands hitting her as she dove, jerked her so violently that her neck snapped instantly.

The servant who had escaped was now wildly searching for someone to help. She ran down the corridor toward Jonathan and Gracielle's chambers screaming hysterically. Several guards appeared in the halls, responding to the commotion.

"HELP! The dining . . . Atoc . . . Ator . . . HELP!" She was panic-stricken and not making sense.

Jonathan and Gracielle heard the commotion and came to see what was going on.

"BLACK HANDS!" she screeched, "THEY'RE KILLING . . . THEY LOOKED DEAD!"

"A grasping curse!" Jonathan gasped.

He didn't wait for details. He sped down the hall towards the dining room, and Gracielle followed.

In the meantime, the first set of smoky hands had reached Jocelynne and had begun to wrap steadily around her throat. It squeezed just enough to squelch her sobs. She gasped for air, but the hands continued to tighten their deadly grip.

She knew that Cristoph was dead, and likely, that she was about to be.

In a final, hopeless effort, she tried to pull away. As soon as she moved though, the hands ensnared her and dragged her forcibly to the floor. She struggled and thrashed wildly, trying to get away—but there was nothing to be done. The curse was impossible to break free from once it had been unleashed.

A few seconds later, Jonathan burst through the door with Gracielle right behind him, but they were too late.

The scene was gruesome; blood, plates, linens, food and bodies were flung everywhere. Jonathan's parents and two of their servants were dead.

Though neither Jonathan nor Gracielle noticed, the fatal invitation was pulsating eerily underneath the napkin on the floor—the last traces of the deadly vapor disintegrating back into it.

Gracielle slapped her hand over her mouth; tears streamed down her cheeks.

Jonathan stood in the doorway in a state of shock.

"Mother . . . ."

It was all he could manage to utter. He sunk slowly to his knees and crawled over to where his mother's body lay.

"No . . . no . . . mother . . . NOOOOO!"

He lifted her gently into his arms and wailed uncontrollably.

Gracielle walked over to him and put her hand on his shoulder.

"Wha . . . how . . . who did this?" She mumbled through her tears.

Jonathan cradled his mother for some time, then laid her back down softly and stood and embraced Gracielle. They held each other tightly and cried.

By this time, a group of Palace Guards had arrived at the room and were already examining the scene.

The one who seemed to be in charge whispered to another, "Get news of this to General Statlen on the council."

The other guard nodded and hurried away.

Soon, the room was packed with guards—some who were busily cleaning up, and others who were investigating the scene.

Jonathan and Gracielle stood in the doorway, watching in despair as the bodies of the atoc and ator were loaded onto stretchers and covered with white sheets. As the sheet was laid over Jocelynne's face, Jonathan's breath caught sharply in his throat and he turned away.

"Aton?" The head guard walked up behind Jonathan and touched him on the shoulder.

"Yes, Falken," he muttered as he turned to face the guard.

"Sir . . . we found this." Falken held a piece of paper in his hand. It was the letter that had contained the curse.

Jonathan took it and examined it. It appeared slightly burnt on the edges, and smelled of sulfur. There were no words written on it at all. He turned it over to the back side. There, a slightly torn, bright gold seal gleamed about half-way down the page. "Ultara," he breathed.

"What?" Gracielle couldn't believe it. Jonathan shoved the paper at her.

"No," she gasped, "I . . . I . . . ." She couldn't say anything else. She stared at the paper and shook her head over and over again.

Jonathan looked at Falken. "Bring me Ultara," he seethed.

Falken bowed. He seemed very worried. Ultara was not someone he wanted to anger—but then again—neither was Aton Jonathan. He rose from the bow and walked out the door, feeling that the mission which had been thrust upon him was akin to suicide.

Gracielle's eyes were glassy. "What're you going to do, Jonathan?" she asked.

He didn't answer, but instead pointed to one of the guards and commanded. "When Captain Falken returns with Ultara, have him bring her to Court Four."

"Yes, sir," the guard replied.

Jonathan turned to walk away.

"Jonathan?" Gracielle called behind him.

He stopped and looked back at her. "I will take care of this, Graci. You go back to our chambers and *don't* leave them! I'm having Dr. Michelan come stay with you."

"What? Why?" she asked.

Jonathan approached her and put his hands on her shoulders. "It's for your own safety . . . and the baby's," he explained. "I don't know what's going on here, but for now, I have to assume that we're not safe. We can't take any chances." He looked her straight in the eyes. "Promise me you'll do as I say. Please. Don't leave the chambers until I get back!"

"But Jonathan," she pleaded, "I . . . ."

"Please, Gracielle!" He was adamant.

She studied his teary eyes for a second, and then reluctantly nodded. She turned and slowly headed toward the chambers, while Jonathan went to Court Four to wait for Falken and Ultara.

In the meantime at Trysta Palace, the members of the council were arriving for the meeting. News of the vritesse's death spread quickly, and everyone knew that they were gathering to witness the calling of Ultara, but when the time arrived for the meeting to commence, none of the Nobles were present. Jonathan, Gracielle and Nenia should have all been in their seats by now. With a loud *thunk,* the three doors at the far end of the room swung open. The delegates rose to their feet . . . and waited for Cristoph, Jocelynne and Ultara to enter.

The room was silent; nothing happened. Several minutes passed, and still nothing.

Suddenly, a Lor Mandela Palace Guard burst in through the middle door and shouted, "By order of Atoc Jonathan, the Council is in recess until further notice!"

All at once, confused conversations filled the room. None of the delegates could recall this ever happening before. Council Meetings just weren't spontaneously canceled. But perhaps the most bizarre thing was what the guard had said. "By order of *Atoc* Jonathan". It didn't make any sense. What was going on? Where were the Nobles? And why was Jonathan being referred to as atoc?

There was such a commotion, that no one noticed Darian—who was the only one not acting frantic. In fact, he stood calmly on his platform, not saying a word, grinning ear to ear with the flames in his eyes flaring maniacally. When his platform finally lowered to the ground, he nearly sprinted from the room and strode out of the palace to where an entourage of shiny silver vehicles waited. He stepped into one of them and told the driver to get him home . . . quickly! Within seconds the whole entourage was speeding noisily away. As the convoy raced toward Brashnell, he raised both arms in the air and smugly placed them behind his head. He stared out the window and chuckled, "This is perfect! Well done, my dear Ultara." The fires in his eyes intensified. "Very . . . well . . . done!"

CHAPTER VIII
THE LAST OF THE TWINS

In the days following the brutal deaths of Jocelynne and Cristoph, evidence began to surface that Lor Mandela itself was dying. Trees and plants withered; the water levels of streams, lakes and oceans receded; and one of the two moons that usually illuminated the night sky had gone completely dark. Throughout Lor Mandela earthquakes shook crumbling hills and mountains; violent storms raged; and volcanoes that had slept for centuries suddenly awakened with a fiery fury.

In Mandela City, tension was escalating. Unpredictable weather patterns and *un*-natural disasters kept everyone on edge, but as soon as news leaked out that Ultara had murdered the atoc and ator, a general sense of hostility, which had never before been present, arose between the Trystas and the Mandelans.

Ultara had gone into hiding, and a huge wall had been constructed around Trysta Palace. No one—unless they were Trysta—was allowed in, and even though Gracielle was a Trysta by birth, she was no longer welcome in Koria.

Now, another disturbing report regarding Ultara was being delivered to Jonathan. His personal guard—a gruff-looking, stocky, older gentleman named General Davids—brought him the news.

"What is it, Davids? Has Ultara been found?" Jonathan asked anxiously as the general approached.

"No, sir," Davids explained, "but it seems she had a good reason for rushin' out on you and the ator that morning. She got a troubling message about her daughter, Nenia."

"Nenia?" Jonathan questioned.

"Yes, sir. Apparently she's gone missin'.""

Jonathan's despise of Ultara was—for a moment—replaced by concern. "Missing?" he inquired. "What do you mean?"

"Well, Atoc," the general explained, "I heard that she and some other Trysta girls were out near the Sybran. Seems they were attacked by a rynolt. Nenia was carried off, and accordin' to what I've heard, she hasn't been seen since."

Jonathan bowed his head sadly. He cared about Nenia. She was such a pleasant, intelligent girl. "But wait!" he blurted suddenly. "A rynolt attack . . . during the day? Rynolts don't attack in daylight, and since when do they carry off their prey?"

Davids shrugged. "Sir, with all of the strange things goin' on, what with the plants and the moons and all, I've heard a lot of people sayin' their pets and livestock are actin' really strange lately. Maybe it's makin' the wild ones act up too."

"Perhaps," Jonathan replied, "I just wish I could figure out what's going on. It's like the whole planet's gone haywire."

Just then, Gracielle entered the room. "Hello, my dear . . . hello, General," she greeted warmly.

"Good Afternoon, Ator," Davids replied and bowed humbly.

"Graci," Jonathan began, "Davids has just told me the most remarkable thing. It's quite sad though."

"Sad?" she asked. "What is it?"

Jonathan repeated what Davids had told him about Nenia.

Gracielle's reaction to the news was far more extreme than Jonathan had anticipated. "Oh, no!" she wailed. "This is dreadful! She can't be missing!" She grabbed Jonathan by the front of his shirt and cried, "Oh, Jonathan . . . you have no idea how horrible this is!"

Jonathan was bewildered by her frantic outburst, but then assumed that her emotions were being affected by her pregnancy. "Graci, I understand. It is horrible. I'm sorry. Maybe I should have figured out a better way to tell you."

Gracielle shook her head. "No! It's just . . . . Oh, Jonathan," she whimpered as big tears began streaming down her cheeks, "what will we do now?"

Jonathan put his arms around her and held her to his chest. "I know, Love. She's part of your family. Shhh, it'll be okay," he soothed.

Slowly, she leaned away from his embrace and wiped her wet cheeks with the back of her hand. "No, Jonathan, you don't understand. Without Nenia . . . ." She paused for several thoughtful moments.

"Without Nenia, what?" He pressed. "What is it, Graci?"

Gracielle decided that she couldn't keep Ultara's secret any longer. Jonathan was the atoc, and he had to know. She nodded towards Davids, who'd been standing silently in a corner. "Please excuse us, General."

He bowed and backed out of the room.

She waited until he was out of sight, and then took Jonathan by the hand. "There's something I need to show you," she sighed.

With all of the mayhem surrounding the deaths of Lantalia, Anika and Jonathan's parents—and with her own new position as ator—Gracielle hadn't really found time to study the Advantiere or to figure out a way to tell Jonathan about it without divulging Ultara's secret. But now, one of the twins was gone. She didn't see how the Advantiere could possibly be fulfilled. Her only hope was to show it to him—ready or not—and see if he had any ideas.

As they approached the hall that housed the hidden Advantiere room, Jonathan asked, "What is it, Graci? What could be so important over here?" He had not been in this part of the palace for over a month. He had no need to come here—it was just old servant's quarters that were in the process of being renovated.

Gracielle stopped outside of where she'd sealed the demolished room almost two weeks earlier and stared at the blank wall. Slowly, she lifted her arm and a minuscule yellow spark jumped up near the floor. It buzzed and popped and gradually moved upward. Within a few seconds, the shape of a simple wooden door became visible. The little spark continued zipping across the top and down the other side of the door and then sputtered a few times and faded away.

"What's this?" Jonathan asked, taking a hold of the door handle and turning it.

"Wait!" Gracielle blurted. "I need to prepare you. This room will be a bit of a shock."

"Why?" he grimaced as he continued turning the handle. The latch clicked and he pushed on the door.

Gracielle grabbed his arm forcefully and held him from going any further. "Don't." Her voice and expression were very serious. "There're some things you need to know before we go in there."

Jonathan released the door handle. "Okay, so just tell me, then," he relented grudgingly.

"The reason all of these strange things are happening . . ." Gracielle's eyes were filling with tears again. "Is that Lor Mandela is dying."

"Wh . . . what do you mean?" He looked at her and half chuckled like it was some kind of joke.

"It all started when Anika tried to steal the vritesse powers from my mother," she explained. "Somehow the spirit of Lor Mandela became diseased by her actions."

"Anika diseased the planet?" He sounded skeptical.

"Yes. The spirit itself spoke to me through my mother. It told me that it is dying, and that the only way it can be saved is if certain events take place."

"Wait!" Jonathan blurted. "What are you talking about, Graci? The whole planet just can't die!" In his mind, this didn't seem logical—or at all possible. Unfortunately, he also knew that where Trysta magic was involved, logic was rarely a factor and the impossible often happened.

Gracielle didn't answer. She simply lifted her arm and the door slowly swung open.

Jonathan's jaw dropped. He stood in stunned awe of the scene before him. The room looked like it had been destroyed in a violent storm. Very few parts of it were even recognizable. There were piles of twisted debris and mangled furnishings everywhere, all surrounding a huge, gaping pit in the floor.

Gracielle stepped into the room and maneuvered around a large chunk of concrete that lay just inside the door.

Jonathan quietly followed. They scaled the piles of rubble, climbing over what they couldn't go around. Jonathan had just begun inching his way around the pit, when he noticed the Advantiere burning brightly on the wall in glittering red letters. "What's this? What's going on, Gracielle?" he asked.

She had already gone around the hole in the floor, and was standing near the Advantiere herself. "I'm sorry I kept this to myself."

"Oh, I'm sure you had a good reason for keeping something like this from the atoc," he barked indignantly.

"I did," she snapped back, "but I'm showing you now, so please . . . ." She didn't finish her sentence; she just stepped to the side and pointed to the glowing words on the wall. "These," she sighed, "are the events that must take place to save Lor Mandela."

Jonathan was already reading through the Advantiere. "You said that Anika diseased the planet?"

"Yes. She was trying to take over as vritesse."

"And that's what's causing the weather, and the animals, and . . . ."

"Yes." She couldn't tell if he was fully grasping the concept or not.

"Child of balance?" he mumbled, "Ours?"

She nodded.

"So, this is who told you we were having a girl?"

Gracielle nodded again.

"Twins must live," he sighed heavily. "Wait a second! So because Anika and Lantalia . . . ? Is this why you wouldn't tell me? Because the twins are gone? Did you honestly think I—the highest ruler in Lor Mandela—didn't need to know that we're all doomed!"

"That's not it, Jonathan!" she retorted loudly. "I didn't tell you because . . . ." She'd given her word to Ultara that she wouldn't tell her secret, but Jonathan was right. As the high ruler of Lor Mandela, he needed to know. "I didn't tell you because of the other twins."

"Other twins?" Jonathan's expression changed from angry back to skeptical. "There aren't any other twins. There haven't been other twins for over a hundred years."

"Yes, there are . . . or, at least, there were."

She took a deep breath and told Jonathan everything. She explained how Ultara had altered Nenia, and that Ryannon—Darian's son—was her twin brother. "Ultara made me promise not to tell anyone, but now, with Nenia gone, I don't know what we can do!"

At that moment, Jonathan realized why Gracielle had gotten so upset about Nenia's disappearance. Nenia had a part in the Advantiere, but was no longer around to carry out the role she had to play. He stared unresponsively at the words shining on the wall. "Maybe the answer is still in here somewhere," he mumbled, rubbing his forehead. "We'll need to get some of our best minds working on it right away."

Gracielle looked at him like he was out of his mind. "Jonathan! We can't!" she insisted.

"Why not! We need other opinions . . . other views!"

"But Jonathan," she pleaded, "if word gets out that our baby is the 'Child of Balance,' she'll never have any peace; I doubt she'll even be safe! I don't feel right telling anyone else about Nenia and Ryannon, either. Besides, it says right here that the riddle must be solved for or by her. She can't solve it if she hasn't even been born!" Gracielle was now pacing wildly in the small space available in front of the wall. "Oh . . . and how, exactly, do you think people will react to the news that Lor Mandela is dying? You know it'll cause world-wide panic! We *need* to keep this between us! The state of the world depends on it!"

Jonathan felt like his head was going to burst. Thoughts were racing rampant through his mind, piling haphazardly one on top of another. They all seemed to end in one horrific image though—Lor Mandela disintegrating into a fiery oblivion. He was overwhelmed and—for the first time in his somewhat sheltered and protected life—very frightened.

After a few uncomfortably silent seconds, he turned his attention back to the glowing crimson message on the wall.

"Her father's hatred die for love to grow?" he read. "What is that supposed to mean? Am I just supposed to forgive Ultara for killing my parents?"

Gracielle looked at him with a somewhat stunned expression on her face. "What? Do you really hate Ultara?" she asked. She knew that Jonathan was angry over his parent's deaths—and justifiably so—but she never imagined him capable of hatred.

"I don't know, Graci," he muttered. "I want her imprisoned."

Suddenly, his expression grew harsh and vengeful. "Actually, no," he seethed, "she deserves the same fate she dealt them. If my thinking that counts as hate . . . then I guess I do."

Gracielle gaped at him. They stood there in silence for several minutes.

It was Jonathan who finally spoke. "We need to write this down and work on it every available moment, Graci."

"But we have to be careful," she reiterated. "It's just us. No one else can know."

Jonathan only partially agreed. "Only until we get to a point where we need more help." Before Gracielle could object, he added, "Listen, Graci, I want to protect our daughter, and our people every bit as much as you do. But if we can't find a way to save Lor Mandela on our own, we won't be protecting anyone!" He started back toward the door. "I'm going to go get something to write this down on."

Jonathan left Gracielle standing in front of the Advantiere. She lowered herself onto the edge of a broken bench and read the part that the spirit had called 'The riddle.'

"Destruction from twins, and so it must end. They are the lock, yet they are not friends. The Child of Balance can only restore. Her father the key and she is the door. The riddle now told, the Advantiere presents, healing begins following future events." She breathed a heavy sigh as she stared at the glittering red enigmatic prophecy. "So, what does this all mean? And where are these twins supposed to come from now?"

CHAPTER IX
THE CHILD OF BALANCE

Months went by, but the meaning of the Advantiere and its riddle continued to be elusive. Jonathan had copied it down into a small, green, leather book and he and Gracielle pored over it whenever they could. Yet somehow, there always seemed to be pieces missing—more that they needed in order for anything to connect. Despite their efforts, Lor Mandela continued to deteriorate and decay. Many areas of the planet had become uninhabitable. Entire countries perished in tumultuous floods followed by bitter freezing, while others were destroyed by drought and intense heat. Savage winds ripped through cities, demolishing buildings, lifting large trees, and smothering anything that breathed in a thick blanket of suffocating dust.

Interestingly, however, the destruction seemed to be following a pattern. The areas that were hit first, and the hardest, were the ones with few or no inhabitants, followed by the regions on the far east side of Lor Mandela—those furthest away from Mandela City. It was as if the spirit of Lor Mandela was somehow controlling how it died—doing it in a way that would allow for life on the planet to be preserved as long as possible.

The deaths that had occurred were a result of those too stubborn to evacuate when it became necessary—or of the murders that were, sadly, becoming more prevalent as tension and fear escalated.

Notwithstanding all of the peril and uncertainty, however, today was a day of rejoicing. Gracielle had just given birth to a beautiful, healthy, baby girl named Audril.

"Are you warm enough, Ator?" Gracielle's companion servant, a young, red-haired, freckled girl, reached for a blanket.

"Hmm? Oh, yes. Thank you, Kahlie," Gracielle answered groggily. "I'm fine."

"The doctor said he'll be back in a while to give Audril a good checking over."

Kahlie smiled and looked at Audril, who was fast asleep. "Sure is amazing . . . isn't she?"

"Yes, she is," Gracielle agreed, "Kahlie?"

"Yes, Ator?"

"When the atoc gets back, I want you to go and get some sleep. You've been up all night with us."

"Oh, I don't mind," Kahlie smiled cheerfully. Besides, I have lessons to do." She twisted her face up into a scowl. "Tur Helene says that if I don't stop daydreaming and focus on language studies . . . ." she breathed heavily, "as if me misplacing a word on a test is gonna change how I scrub floors!"

All at once Kahlie gasped and her eyes widened. "I don't mean . . . I don't enjoy . . . it's not that I . . . I," she stammered.

Gracielle smiled. "It's okay, Kahlie. I'll speak to Tur Helene." She held out her hand and Kahlie took it. "A young woman at your age must have her beauty sleep. Studies can wait until tomorrow."

Kahlie giggled and nodded.

Just then, Jonathan peeked around the corner of the door. He smiled lovingly at Gracielle and walked across the room to her bed, pausing just long enough to tousle Kahlie's bright red curls as he passed.

"Hello, Milady," he greeted. "You've been taking good care of our new atoh, I hope?"

"Oh . . . oh yes sir," she answered nervously, "that's what I do best." Kahlie really liked both Ator Gracielle and Atoc Jonathan, but she was far more comfortable with Gracielle. Jonathan made her very uneasy.

She had only been at the palace for a few short weeks, and was told in the beginning that she had been brought to the palace to be a kitchen maid, not to fulfill the most sought after position a servant could acquire.

But one day, when she was cleaning in the main dining hall, her constant clumsiness finally paid off.

She had just finished wiping down what she counted to be forty-eight wooden chairs when Gracielle and her former Companion Servant, Dedri, happened into the room.

Kahlie almost fell over when she saw the ator, and bowed nervously before her.

Gracielle signaled for her to stand, smiled warmly and said, "Hello, young lady. I don't believe we've met. You're new here, aren't you?"

Kahlie nodded and sputtered, "Y . . . yes, ma'am." She had heard that Gracielle was very kind, but didn't expect her to treat such a young, lowly servant with so much respect and affability.

Gracielle continued, "I'm Gracielle and this is Dedri—my companion servant . . . and you are?"

"Kahlie, ma'am," she answered timidly.

"Well, welcome, Kahlie. It's a pleasure to meet you. Please don't let us bother you. We just have a few things to discuss."

Kahlie thought that Gracielle was the loveliest woman she'd ever seen. And that Dedri—with her squinty gray eyes, yellowish skin and very short, mousy brown hair—was one of the most frightening. She fantasized that Gracielle was an angel who'd been captured by the evil Matron of Doom, (Dedri), and that she, (Kahlie the Avenger), had been sent to save her with magical objects she'd produce from the Sorcerer's Cloth, (dust rag).

She tried to appear focused on polishing the long buffet table, but was really straining to hear what was being said by the beautiful Gracielle, who was speaking firmly to Dedri about something that had been neglected.

Ha! She knows who you are Matron. When she realizes who I am, you will meet your demise! Kahlie was so lost in her daydream, that she didn't notice that she had left one of the dining chairs slightly pulled out from the table. As she turned to walk to the other side of the buffet, her foot caught on a protruding leg and she tripped—stumbling across the room and smacking right into the companion servant—knocking both Dedri and herself to the ground.

"You clumsy brat!" Dedri shouted. She jumped up, yanked Kahlie to her feet, and slapped her hard across the face. "You could have hurt the ator!" She raised her hand again, but Gracielle grabbed it in mid-air.

"How dare you?" Gracielle seethed. "She is just a child and it . . . it was an accident!"

"She could have injured you or the baby," the servant argued.

"But she didn't!" Gracielle was livid. She was still clutching Dedri's arm and holding it high in the air. "Dedri, I have never seen such outrageous behavior in my life," she scolded as she dropped Dedri's arm and pointed toward the door. "You are dismissed! Pack up your things and leave this palace immediately!"

"But, Ator," Dedri pleaded, "who will care for you and your daughter?"

Gracielle moved in very close to Dedri and spoke right in her face. "Listen to me, Dedri. If you are unscrupulous enough to strike this young lady, what makes you think that I would allow you anywhere near my daughter?"

"But, your majesty, she's only a kitchen maid." Dedri was shaking and twitching. Kahlie couldn't tell if she was angry, or embarrassed, or just plain crazy.

Gracielle stepped back and placed her arm around Kahlie's shoulders. "No Dedri, she isn't. She is Kahlie—the companion servant of the ator of Lor Mandela." Kahlie gasped, and Gracielle added, "Now, would you like to bow to her before you leave, or shall I call the Guard and have you forcibly removed?"

Dedri glared in shock from Gracielle to Kahlie and then back to Gracielle again. "Forgive me. Good day, Milady," she sneered, as she bowed to Kahlie, and then turned and rushed from the room.

"Well," Gracielle chuckled as she watched Dedri angrily retreat, "I guess we'd better get you moved to your new chambers."

Kahlie stared at her gaping.

"And I probably should introduce you to the atoc."

And that's how it happened. It was like a dream come true for Kahlie, who had never dared to imagine herself in such a prestigious position, especially at such a young age; she had just turned fourteen.

Now, not only was she companion servant to Ator Gracielle, she would be helping with Audril as well. She walked over to where Audril was sleeping, kissed her own hand and touched it softly to Audril's rosy little cheek. She smiled at Gracielle and

Jonathan and said, "If you'll not be needing anything more . . . ."

Gracielle replied, "No, my dear. It's time for you to get that beauty sleep, remember?"

"Hmpf!" Jonathan chimed in grinning from ear to ear. "If this vision of loveliness gets any more beautiful, we'll have to assign her guards of her own, just to keep the young men away!"

Kahlie's freckles darkened as her face blushed to bright scarlet. "Th . . . thank you, Atoc," she giggled and headed off to her chambers.

"Now . . . ." Jonathan turned to Gracielle. "I know that *you* can't get any more beautiful . . . but you still need your sleep." He kissed her cheek and her eyes fluttered shut.

"Mmmm," she sighed, as she dozed peacefully.

Jonathan stood and walked to Audril's intricately carved, lace covered bassinet. "Hello, Angel," he whispered.

Her little eyes blinked open, as if she'd heard and understood him.

He leaned over and gently lifted her up, cradling her in his arms, and began to hum softly to her. She wriggled a bit, but then quickly fell back asleep.

Jonathan just held her; he watched her sleep for almost an hour, before finally laying her back down.

It was strange. Almost the moment that he set her in the bassinet, his emotions started to spin out of control. He was elated that she was finally here, but then worried about her future, and that wretched Advantiere. Then, he was happy that both she and Gracielle were healthy, and then suddenly angry—very angry! Angry that his parents weren't here; angry that Ultara had killed them; angry that Anika had started all of this chaos; angry that Lantalia hadn't been able to stop it, and even angry at Nenia, for disappearing and making him occasionally feel sorry for her mother.

It was at that point that he realized he *did* feel hatred for Ultara—very real, very strong hatred, and, fate of the world relying on it or not, he didn't know how to stop it. How could she have done this? His parents had respected her and treated her well; so did he and Gracielle. How could power have possibly been so important that she would descend to killing friends? The more he thought about it, the angrier he became, until the only thought racing through his mind was that Ultara had to die. He would never be able to forgive her and let go of his hatred unless justice was served.

And that's when it hit him. There was a way—a way to get into Trysta Palace to find Ultara. "Darian's . . . friends," he breathed.

Of course, he thought to himself. *Darian said he has Trysta spies! Why haven't I thought of this before?* He marched over to the door and looked out into the hall. A palace guard just happened to be strolling past.

"You there!" he commanded.

The guard froze in place.

"Send word to Darian of Brashnell. Inform him that I need to speak with him . . . this evening if possible."

The guard bowed. "Yes, Atoc," he replied.

Jonathan signaled for him to rise and added, "Let me know his answer as soon as you hear."

The guard nodded and sped quickly down the corridor.

"Jonathan? Is everything okay?" Gracielle's faint voice called out from behind him. She was still groggy, but had heard him talking to the guard. "What's Darian up to now?" she asked.

"Oh, it's nothing, Graci . . . nothing to worry about. Just go back to sleep."

"How's the baby?" she asked.

He didn't answer her at first. Instead he walked to Audril's bassinet, picked her up, and carried her over and laid her at Gracielle's side. "She's perfect, my love, and almost as beautiful as her mother." He smoothed Gracielle's silky raven hair back off of her cheeks as she drifted back to sleep.

A few seconds later, there was a soft knocking at the door. Jonathan didn't want to wake Gracielle by calling out, so he walked over and answered it. "Kahlie?"

He was surprised to see her back so soon. "Weren't you supposed to be getting some rest?" He pulled the door open wide, and signaled for Kahlie to come in.

"Um . . . y . . . yes, Atoc, but I couldn't sleep," she fluttered. "If it's all right, I'd rather be here, sir."

"Well, okay," he agreed, "but you'll need to sleep eventually, Milady."

Kahlie blushed again. It wasn't customary for the ator's companion servant to be referred to as 'Milady;' but ever since Gracielle told Jonathan about how Dedri had called 'Milady,' he had decided to do the same. "Oh, I . . . I promise I'll sleep while the ator and baby sleep tonight. I'm fine, really," she insisted.

"All right then," he replied, "I do have one or two little things I could to attend to."

"Uh . . . uh . . . of course, Atoc," she stammered, "Don't worry. I'll look after them now."

Jonathan stood and tousled her red curls again. "Well . . . that is what you do best," He replied. He bowed lowly to her and walked toward the door. "Thank you, Milady. I'll return shortly."

He had no sooner left the room when a familiar voice called out from behind him. "Atoc Jonathan! How fortunate!"

He turned and was surprised to see Darian himself coming down the hall toward him. "Oh, Darian," Jonathan began, "Hello . . . I didn't expect to see you so soon."

Darian bowed humbly and explained, "Yes, Sir. As it turns out, I've been in Mandela City all afternoon. With the northern evacuations, Brashnell has become quite . . . um, shall we say, cozy. I was hoping that the situation here was not as uncomfortable but," he chuckled, "I can see that you are facing the same dilemmas that we are."

Jonathan nodded in agreement. "I'm afraid so. Please, Darian, let's go someplace where we can talk."

"Of course, Atoc. Lead the way." Darian followed Jonathan out to the foyer and across it to a richly appointed lounge near the main palace doors.

Jonathan motioned for Darian to enter. "Can I get you anything, Darian?"

"Oh . . . thank you . . . no, sire." Darian waited for Jonathan to sit down before lowering onto a large leather bench across from him. "I understand congratulations are in order. I assume that the ator and new atoh are well?" he asked.

"Yes Darian, thank you." Jonathan hadn't planned what he would say to Darian, so he just got straight to the point. "Darian, you came and saw me and my father the night before he was murdered. Do you remember?"

The fires in Darian's dark eyes seemed to shrink slightly. "Yes, Atoc, I remember well."

Jonathan continued. "You warned us that Ultara was going to attack; I've never thanked you for that warning."

"There is no need, Sire," Darian assured, "I was only doing my duty. I'm just sorry that I couldn't have done more."

"Nonetheless, I owe you my thanks," Jonathan pressed, leaning forward in his chair. "I also wanted to apologize for my attitude toward you that night. As I recall, I was not very pleasant."

"Atoc," Darian stood and started wandering around the room. "I have many enemies on Lor Mandela. I've never worried about what others think or say about me. As such, I'm sure you've heard many rumors and stories about the Evil Darian. I would think you a fool to not be a little suspicious of me." He eyed Jonathan intently. "Now, what can I do for you, Atoc?"

Jonathan drew in a deep breath. "You mentioned that night that you had some Trysta friends. Is this still the case?"

Darian smiled. He strolled over to a row of shelves that lined one entire wall of the room and picked up a small jade statuette. He turned the figurine over and over in his hand, and then set it back down and redirected his attention to Jonathan. "I have a few," he smirked.

"What do you know of Ultara's whereabouts, Darian?" Jonathan quizzed.

Darian returned to the bench and lowered himself onto it. He leaned toward Jonathan and whispered, "She stays in the palace. She disappears for a couple of hours every once in a while, but the bulk of the time she is at the palace."

"Where does she go when she disappears?" Jonathan quizzed.

"I'm not certain," he replied casually.

Jonathan's expression became deathly serious. "Darian . . . how close can your people get to her?"

Darian shook his head. "My friends are very good listeners, Atoc, but you know how difficult it is to see the vritesse if you aren't on the council. They can only bring me what they hear. Believe me, Atoc, if I could have gotten someone close enough to her for long enough . . ."

He paused and looked at his hand for a second, then raised it to his mouth and bit at one of his fingernails before nonchalantly adding, "She would have been dead a long time ago."

Jonathan was suddenly questioning his plan. Darian had just admitted—without a hint of conscience—that he would murder Ultara if he had a chance. Was this the kind of man with whom the atoc of Lor Mandela should be conspiring? Although he deeply believed that Ultara should be sentenced to death, there were channels to be followed and now, in light of Darian's confession, this didn't feel right. "I don't suppose my plan will work then." He tried to bow out gracefully.

A sinister smile spread slowly across Darian's face. "No, I imagine not . . . but mine might."

"Yours? You have a plan, Darian?" Jonathan asked. "Why does that worry me?"

Darian laughed. "It's really quite simple, Atoc. You want Ultara to be brought to justice; I want the same."

"But you've already said that you can't get to her," Jonathan reminded. "Neither can I. She can't be brought to justice if no one can get their hands on her."

Darian smirked, "Perhaps not, Atoc, but I have a proposition for you."

"What do you mean?" Jonathan asked. He had no idea where this was heading, but he was sure that any proposition devised by Darian of Brashnell would be questionable at best.

"I have already told you that Ultara leaves the palace every once in a while," he explained.

"Yes, Darian," Jonathan acknowledged, "but what does that have to do with anything?"

"I propose this," Darian smirked, bristling with confidence. "I tell you where she is going, if you will allow me the privilege of being her executioner."

"What?" Jonathan blurted. "That's absurd! Besides, you just told me that you don't know where she goes!"

"No, Atoc," Darian corrected, "I said that I am not certain where she goes."

"Explain," Jonathan demanded.

"I've received information from one of my best informers, Atoc. She is someone who I generally deem quite reliable." Darian stood and started pacing again. "However, I make it a point to never absolutely accept what any of my spies tell me. They are spies, after all. Let's just say that I'm about ninety-eight percent sure."

"I just can't turn Ultara over to you, Darian," Jonathan began. "She will have to be tried and convicted before I can sign an order of execution."

"Of course, Atoc," Darian replied smugly, "I excel at being patient. I just want to be the one who takes care of her once and for all . . . when the time comes." He lowered back onto the bench and stared Jonathan in the eyes; his fiery pupils glistened savagely. "She killed your parents, Sire, and she is hiding in that palace like some coward . . . I am almost certain that she is responsible for what is happening to Lor Mandela, as well."

Jonathan became lost in his thoughts. Darian didn't know about the Advantiere, and that was just fine. There was no way that he was going to let him in on that secret. But Darian was right about the rest. Ultara had brutally attacked his parents, without provocation, and used her power and influence to hide herself away. She deserved to be brought to justice; she deserved to die. He felt the same unquenchable fury as earlier building inside him. He wanted her to answer for her crime; he wanted her to experience the horror to which she had subjected his parents.

After several minutes, he finally replied.

"Where does she go, Darian?" he breathed quietly. "If you want to be the one to kill her, I will arrange it."

Darian looked like a cat ready to pounce on its prey. He hunched over toward Jonathan—his face wild with anticipation. "Excellent, Atoc," he gushed. "You'll be very glad you've agreed. You see, when Ultara leaves Trysta Palace, she comes here."

"Here, as in Mandela City?"

"No, Sire. Here, as in Mandela Palace."

"What? Impossible!" Jonathan blurted.

"It's true, Sire. My source informs me that there is something she is trying to get her hands on here in the palace."

"How does your source know this?" Jonathan insisted.

"She was near the gate of that monstrosity of a wall when she spotted Ultara running toward it. Let's just say that it would have been unfortunate for this young lady if Ultara had seen her, so she quickly hid behind a bush or something."

Darian seemed embarrassed that one of his spies had done something so mundane.

"Ultara charged directly toward the gate, and just before she was about to crash into it, she shouted, 'Mandela Palace,' and disappeared." He leaned back on the bench and added, "Doesn't leave much to the imagination does it?"

"Why would she come here? If she gets caught, it's suicide." Jonathan asked, more to himself than Darian.

"Nonetheless," Darian answered, "I don't know what she's after, but I would be willing to bet that she is plotting another attack, Atoc. You had best be on your guard."

Horrifying thoughts raced through Jonathan's mind—thoughts of Ultara attacking Gracielle, or Audril.

If Ultara was coming to the palace, how would they know? She had confided in Gracielle that she had altering powers. She could make herself look like anyone!

This was a nightmare and Jonathan feared that his family was in grave danger. "If what you say is true, Darian, I have to go immediately and meet with my guards."

Darian nodded in agreement, "Yes, Atoc. You mustn't take any chances. I can rely on you to let me know when she's captured?" He looked at Jonathan earnestly.

"Of course, Darian. We have an agreement. Now, if you'll excuse me, I have work to do."

Darian stood and bowed. "Yes, certainly. Good evening, Atoc."

"Good evening, Darian."

Just outside the room in the hallway, there was a faint swishing and the flutter of black fabric. A dark, cloaked figure sped across the foyer to avoid being seen. Darian turned into the large entrance hall just as the intruder disappeared into a dim corridor across from him.

The cloaked figure was—of course—Ultara, and she'd heard everything.

CHAPTER X
GLARON AND GRACIELLE

"Unbelievable!" Ultara seethed as she stormed down the Executive Corridor at Trysta Palace.

A tall, lanky, brunette woman rushed up to her and bowed

Ultara didn't break her gait. "Get me Glaron! I'll be in the Throne Room!" she commanded forcefully.

"Yes, ma'am," the woman responded nervously and rushed away.

Ultara approached a tree-concealed doorway and threw her hand angrily in the air. The tree practically disintegrated as she stormed past. "Unbelievable!" she shouted again.

She entered the Throne Room, which was dim and dreary, in sharp contrast to the bright, ethereal areas in the rest of the palace. The damp, granite walls were lined with spiral torches that cast an eerie golden glow. The throne itself sat on a raised, silvery rock platform with odd cryptic characters etched in its jagged face. At the end of the platform, to the left and the right of the throne, two roughly hewn pillars reached skyward, tapering at the top into sleek, smooth points. The floor in front of the platform was inlaid with an ornate mosaic star formed by tiny moss green and white pebbles. It led to a stone bridge that spanned a wide stream with rapids slamming noisily against its rocky banks.

Dark twining branches, covered in sporadic clumps of glossy, green leaves twisted up out of the ground and formed a large tangled throne. The light cast by the torches flickered across it and created unnaturally shaped shadows on everything in the cold, misty room.

Ultara crossed the bridge, strode up to the throne and in one fluid motion, sank down onto the gnarled seat. She was fuming; her gold eyes shone like cat's eyes in the dimness. She sulked in her throne and waited for Glaron—her chief advisor. Within just a few seconds, an athletic man sporting a wavy, light brown ponytail appeared through the branches at the door. He strolled quickly over the bridge and approached Ultara, who was hunched over holding her hand over her forehead.

"Good Evening, Vritesse," he greeted as he lowered to one knee in the center of the mosaic star.

"Glaron," Ultara looked up and jumped right to the point. "I need you to do me a favor."

"Of course, Ultara." Glaron stood and leapt with relative ease up onto the platform. "What can I do for you?"

"I need you to go to Mandela Palace, and speak to Ator Gracielle."

Glaron's pale green eyes practically bulged out of his head. "You need me to what?"

"I need you to go talk to Gracielle," Ultara repeated insistently.

"But, why?" he complained. "Ultara, they'll slaughter me!"

She stood and walked over to one of the tall stone pillars and leaned against it. "Relax Glaron. Have you ever even been to Mandela Palace?" she asked.

"No," he replied quietly.

"Then you won't be recognized."

Glaron stared at Ultara, hoping to see some hint that she was joking. Unfortunately, no such hint existed. "I don't understand," he began, "isn't that where you've been sneaking off to . . . to work on the Advantiere? Why do you need me to go too?"

Ultara explained, "Darian's puppets have been at it again. One of them saw me transport to the palace." She walked to the edge of the platform and gracefully levitated to the ground below. "Darian, of course, ran as fast as he could to the atoc and made him a stellar deal."

"What kind of deal?" Glaron asked.

"He told Jonathan that I was making frequent visits to the palace, and in exchange for this information—when they catch me there—Darian gets my head."

"Really? That doesn't sound like something that Atoc Jonathan would agree to." Glaron walked to the edge of the platform and lowered to sitting with his feet dangling over the side.

"Oh, he agreed . . . didn't take him long either. He thinks I killed his parents, Glaron; he wants me dead." She cleared her throat and continued, "At any rate, I can't go back there now. It's too risky."

"Can't you just alter yourself?" Glaron asked, but quickly added, "Of course I'll go, but are you sure that this is the best option? I'm not the most eloquent man, you know."

"It's the only option right now, Glaron," she insisted. "I can only alter myself into female forms. Gracielle knows that it is impossible to alter gender. They'll be looking for a woman, and you are the only man I can trust."

"Gee, thanks," Glaron replied sarcastically, "so why do you want me to talk to the ator. Shouldn't I just go to the Advantiere room and copy down the Advantiere for you?"

"Need I remind you, Glaron that even I haven't been able to get into that room? Gracielle sealed it; she's the only one who can unseal it."

Glaron sighed heavily. "So, what exactly do you want me to say to her?"

"Well," Ultara answered, "we'll have to wait a few days. She just had a baby."

"Yeah, I suppose that would be the polite thing to do," Glaron quipped.

Ultara ignored him. "You should tell her that you have proof that I did not kill Cristoph and Jocelynne."

Glaron nearly choked. "I . . . I do?" he spluttered.

"No, of course not, but I need to see how she reacts. If she has any doubts at all, we can convince her," Ultara answered. "Hopefully, she has some doubts. It's clear that Jonathan doesn't."

"How do I get in? I mean, if they find out I'm a Trysta, they won't let me anywhere near the ator."

Ultara explained, "The Celebration of Light is in four weeks. Gracielle's dressmaker is scheduled to see her for a fitting ten days from now."

"You've been doing your homework," Glaron observed.

Ultara smirked at him. "Yes . . . I'll arrange for the dressmaker to be unavoidably detained, and you will go in his place."

"Only one minor problem, Vritesse. I'm not a dressmaker."

"No, Glaron," Ultara responded, "but in ten days you will learn how to be an apprentice dressmaker. That will be good enough."

"Okay," Glaron snipped, "so, I tell her that I'm the apprentice, and that you didn't kill Jonathan's parents; anything else?"

Ultara shook her head. "You know, Glaron, it's a good thing I understand your cynical sense of humor. You're probably the only Trysta who can get away with talking to me like that."

Glaron chuckled nervously. "Oh . . . sorry, Vritesse. I guess I got a little carried away."

Ultara raised a scolding eyebrow at him. "We'll fine tune the details and come up with a more specific plan over the next few days." She floated over to him and touched him on the arm. "The fate of Lor Mandela may very well rest on your able shoulders, my friend . . . if you succeed, you can talk to me as cynically as you like from now on!"

Over the next ten days, Glaron learned the fine art of dressmaking and he and Ultara concocted their plan. At last, the day arrived for him to go to Mandela Palace. The fitting was to take place right after breakfast, while the baby was down for her morning nap.

Glaron was admitted to the palace without incident and shown to a large white marble room with a phenomenal view of Mystad Lake and the surrounding hills. In each corner of the room stood a graceful, gilded statue of a brilliantly carved, winged angel. Although they were made of stone, Glaron could have sworn that they were in motion. In the middle of each wall, wispy ivory curtains billowed down alongside massive open windows—each etched in the center with images of the same four glorious angels. The room was two levels. Plush benches lined the upper level, each upholstered in a different color of rich velvet. Two long, stone steps led to the sunken lower level, which was carpeted with an enormous, elaborate tapestry woven in the same hues as the benches, and depicting scenes of Mandela City, Koria,

Brashnell, and all of the other territories of Lor Mandela.

Glaron waited for only a few moments before Gracielle entered the room with two of her handmaidens. She looked as stunning as ever.

Glaron had only ever seen her from a distance in council meetings, but he always found her quite lovely. She looked very well recovered from childbirth—no hint of a recent pregnancy at all.

She approached Glaron and held out her hand. "Good afternoon, um . . . ."

"Oh . . . it's Glaron, your Majesty." Glaron kissed her hand and bowed humbly.

"Ah, yes. Well, good morning, Glaron. You are here for my fitting?" The manner with which Gracielle carried herself was everything poised and elegant. She exuded absolute self-confidence and grace.

Glaron had to glance away momentarily to keep from gawking at her like some awkward adolescent.

She leaned in closely to him and whispered as if she knew he was up to something, "I was not aware that my dressmaker had changed."

Glaron cleared his throat nervously. "Uh, I'm the apprentice, Majesty. My master has fallen ill and asked me to come in his place. He will be overseeing my work, of course."

Gracielle turned toward her handmaidens who were standing across the room. "Helene, I think we'll be fine here." She spoke to the older of the two. "Will you please see that Kahlie is caught up on her studies?"

Helene bowed and left the room.

Gracielle then signaled to the other handmaiden to take a seat on one of the benches before turning her attention back to Glaron. "Now then, are you going to tell me who you *really* are, or do I have to figure out this mystery on my own?"

Glaron sighed; he realized that there was no point beating around the bush with this clearly intelligent woman. "My name really is Glaron, your Majesty," he whispered, then apprehensively added, "I . . . I'm a Trysta."

Gracielle's eyes widened at his confession.

He quickly interjected, "And I promise, I mean you no harm."

She eyed Glaron like she was looking straight through to his soul. "You know it's extremely dangerous for you to be here, don't you?"

Glaron glanced over at the handmaiden who was still sitting obediently in the corner. She did not appear to have heard any of their conversation.

"I was sent here by Ultara, with a message," he whispered, pretending to measure Gracielle's arm.

"*Ultara?*" she gasped, "but Cristoph and Jocelynne . . . . How can I . . . ."

Glaron interrupted, "She did not kill them, Ator." His eyes expressed the utmost sincerity.

She was silent for several seconds. Finally, after what appeared to be much deep thought, she looked straight into Glaron's eyes again and whispered, "I know."

"What! How?" he blurted loudly.

The handmaiden rose to her feet, but Gracielle held up her hand to signal that everything was all right.

"I know this will probably sound strange to you, but I've known she was innocent from the start."

"Unfortunately, your Majesty, nothing seems strange to me anymore!"

Gracielle chuckled. "Well, Glaron," she explained, "the problem is that the atoc won't believe she's innocent just because I think she is." Her eyes saddened. "He still feels excruciating pain at the loss of his parents. I've tried to talk to him about it, but I'm afraid it's no use."

"How can I help?" Glaron asked with obvious sincerity.

Gracielle smiled warmly. "What is your message, Glaron?" she asked.

"Ultara wants to help you solve the Advantiere, but she can't risk coming here to the palace anymore. She proposes that you and I work on it together."

"Does she have any idea what to do about the fact that there are no twins alive anymore?" She was careful not to mention Ryannon and Nenia. She didn't know if Ultara had shared her secret with Glaron.

Her question was answered by his reply. "No . . . and quite frankly, I'm not sure how to bring it up. I'm afraid she hasn't been able to let Nenia go. I think she still believes that her daughter's alive."

Gracielle nodded. Now that she was a mother, she couldn't imagine the horror of losing a child. She'd always assumed that it was a terrible thing for a mother to endure, but since giving birth to Audril, she'd come to understand even more.

"All right, Glaron. Go back to Ultara. Tell her that, for what it's worth, I believe her. I'll try to figure out how to clear her name, but I think it's gonna take some pretty substantial proof." She paused and asked, "Glaron, are you familiar with the Anaria?"

"Of course," he answered.

"Good. Meet me there three days from now, just after sundown. I'll bring a copy of the Advantiere for you to take back to Ultara." She patted Glaron on the arm. "We'll get this all straightened out. I'm sure we will."

Glaron smiled and cleared his throat, making sure that his voice projected far enough for the handmaiden to hear "Hmmm, hmm! I'll take these measurements back to my master, Majesty. He will see to your final fitting."

Gracielle's back was to her servant, so she allowed herself a quiet chuckle. "Um . . . thank you, sir. That will be all for today," she replied.

Glaron bowed and kissed Gracielle's hand again, and hurried back to Trysta Palace to share what he'd learned with Ultara.

Ultara was waiting for him in the Throne Room, pacing anxiously just inside the door. When Glaron came into the room, she stopped and breathed a deep sigh, relieved that he was back safely. "Well?" she asked impatiently.

Glaron took her by the arm, and together they started across the bridge toward the big platform. "It went very well, Vritesse . . . even better than well. The ator said that she's known that you were innocent all along!"

Ultara stopped in her tracks and gaped at him. "Really? Excellent!"

Glaron went on, "She's bringing me a copy of the Advantiere and she said that she will try to figure out how to clear you for the murders."

"This is wonderful news, Glaron. When are you meeting with her to get the copy?"

He told her where and when they planned to meet.

"Marvelous work," Ultara commended, "thank you."

Glaron smiled. "All in a day's work for a dressmaker's apprentice, ma'am." He bent over in a dramatic bow.

Ultara raised her eyebrows. "Are you finished?" she snapped.

"Sheesh," Glaron frowned, "you certainly change your moods quickly!"

Ultara shook her head; she turned him by the shoulders and faced him toward the door. "Good afternoon, Glaron."

He leaned backward and gave her a quick peck on the cheek. "Good afternoon, Vritesse," he answered and sauntered proudly out of the room.

Three days later, just before sunset, Glaron set off to meet with Gracielle. He crossed the big meadow adjoining Trysta Palace, but instead of climbing the hill that led to the caverns, he turned toward the north and meandered through the outskirts of Mandela City trying to keep a low profile. There was nothing about his appearance that was specifically Trysta—like glowing eyes or feet that don't entirely touch the ground—but he had conducted business in this area in the past, and knew that he might be recognized. He ducked behind buildings and walked down streets that were unlit to keep out of sight. In the distance, he could see the Anaria. He continued in the shadows until he reached the edge of the meadow in which it stood. The last rays of sunlight were disappearing behind the horizon. He had to hurry. He ran across the field and up to a massive tree that stood alone in the darkened meadow.

On one side of the tree was a big, cave-like hollow. Glaron approached it and whispered, "Hello . . . Ator?"

Gracielle appeared out of nowhere.

"Whoa!" Glaron shouted, and then lowered his voice to an anxious whisper. "You startled me!"

"Sorry," Gracielle smiled. "Come on."

They walked into the dark tree cave over a crunchy, leaf covered floor, and rounded a sharp turn. The further they walked into the tree, the brighter it became. Glaron was astounded that this much was hidden inside what simply seemed to be a big, old tree. Again, the trail curved and. . . .

"Wow!" he blurted, as they stepped into a large, elegant room furnished with lush chairs and settees upholstered in rich tones of green, gold, coral and purple. Beautiful dark wood shelves lined one wall and were covered with big, leather bound books. The other walls surrounding the circular room were covered in long, thick, globs of amber sap. A chandelier that looked like hundreds of dripping icicles hung at least twenty feet in the air over the center of the room; it illuminated the sap drips so that the walls appeared to be made of thick, bubbled glass.

"So this is the Ator's Anaria? No wonder all you ators are so fond of this place! I never understood why anyone would want to hang out in some big tree." Glaron was awe struck.

"Welcome, Sir Glaron," Gracielle smiled. She walked back over to the tunnel and peeked around the corner. "The cave should have sealed by now. Shall we get to work?"

"Sealed? You mean that cave's not always there?"

"No," she replied, "I opened it when I saw you coming."

"Ahhh, convenient," he sighed.

Gracielle sniggered and held out a small, brown, fabric covered notebook. "Here it is, Glaron," she breathed, "I'm sure I don't have to tell you how confidential this thing is."

Glaron nodded as he flipped slowly through the notebook. He felt like he was holding the most valuable item that had ever existed on Lor Mandela. Gracielle had written the Advantiere down over several pages, each one containing one line. "I'll protect it with my life, Ator," he assured.

"I wrote it out like this for a reason," she explained. "I left room on each page for our notes. When we get a line figured out, I would like you to tear it out and give it to Ultara for safekeeping."

"Sounds good," he agreed. "Where would you like to begin?"

She led him over to where two deep, violet chairs and a small, simple table stood. They sat down and initiated a process that—unbeknownst to them—would virtually consume their lives for the next four years—the process of solving Lantalia's Advantiere.

CHAPTER XI
A DAY OF BREAKTHROUGHS

Ator, Forgive me for sending this note. I hope that nothing is jeopardized by it. I've found something! Please don't risk sending a reply. Tonight at the usual time – URGENT.

Gracielle eagerly read the note from Glaron that had just been delivered. "Yes," she exclaimed aloud, "finally!" She folded it and tucked it into a small, porcelain box in her top bureau drawer. "Rynolts couldn't keep me away, my friend," she whispered. Over the last four years, she and Glaron had been secretly meeting in an effort to solve the Advantiere. They had dissected each of its lines into its most rudimentary parts, only to end up even more bewildered and frustrated. But now, Glaron was saying he'd found something!

This has got to be big! She thought to herself. *He wouldn't risk a surprise meeting, unless it was crucial.*

"Momma!" Gracielle's thoughts were suddenly interrupted by a spunky, rosy cheeked little girl with sparkling blue eyes and jet black bouncing curls who had bounded into the room. "When they will be here, Momma?" Audril brimmed with vivacity.

"Oh, dearest, your party isn't until this afternoon," she answered, mussing Audril's curly black hair. "Why don't you find Daddy and see if he's ready for breakfast yet?"

Audril put a round little fist to her mouth and giggled. She was looking past Gracielle, who knew that this was code for the morning ritual of "Daddy's sneaking up on you." She smiled and played along. "What are you giggling at, little girl?"

"Nuhfing," Audril sniggered through her small fist.

Jonathan poked Gracielle in her sides. "BUAH-HA!" he shouted.

"Aaaaaaa!" she shrieked, as she pretended to jump in her seat.

Audril moved her hand away from her mouth and laughed from her toes. "He gotcha, Momma! He gotcha!"

"Yes, he got me . . ." she smiled, "again." She smirked at Jonathan who leaned over and kissed her good morning.

"Daddy! Daddy!" Audril pulled on his pant leg. "You know what is today?"

Jonathan lifted her up and blew a raspberry on her pink cheek. "What is today?" he teased. "Is it the day I get a haircut?"

"Nooo," she smiled sheepishly.

"Oh! Well then it must be the day Momma gets new shoes! Yes . . . I'm sure! It's Momma New Shoe Day! Hooray!" He lifted her up above his head and repeated, "Hooray!"

"No, Daddy," Audril corrected, "iss my birfday!"

"Your birthday? That is exciting! I just love birthdays! So, let's see . . . you're two years old now, right?"

"Daddy, I'n four," she scolded.

Jonathan kissed her cheek and confessed, "I know you're four, my angel. Happy Birthday." He lowered her down to the floor; she jumped from his arms and bounced up and down excitedly next to him for a few seconds, then skipped over to a pile of picture books on the floor, and pulled out her favorite. She plopped down on the rug and started flipping through it, merrily humming to herself.

Jonathan chuckled. "So, what's on your agenda for today, my love?" he asked Gracielle.

"Just preparing for the event of the century," she grinned, "and you?"

"What else?" he answered. "Working on the Advantiere. I mean . . . have you seen Sybran Forest recently?"

Gracielle nodded.

"Half dead, I'm sure of it. It's getting too close for comfort, Graci. I'm afraid if we don't get some help . . . ."

"But, Jonathan," she pleaded, "can't we just wait a few more days?"

"Wait for what? Mandela City to explode? The world is coming to an end, Graci! It's time to get help!"

Gracielle glared scoldingly at him. She grabbed a small stick-like object from a nearby table and spoke into it. "Send for Kahlie," she instructed, and frowned at Jonathan again. "Will you be careful with that *'the world's coming to an end'* stuff in front of her?" she whispered, pointing the stick towards Audril.

He glanced over at their little girl who was lying on her stomach, kicking her legs back and forth while she read. "Oh . . . sorry," he apologized.

She shook her head and turned away. Her thoughts immediately turned to the condition of the planet. Jonathan was right. It was getting bad. But Glaron had found something, and if what he'd discovered was enough, they wouldn't have to tell anyone else about the Advantiere—and she wouldn't have to betray Ultara's secret again.

Just then, Kahlie tapped at the door and entered the room.

"Milady," Jonathan bowed dramatically, "welcome back. I hope you enjoyed the academy?" When he stood and actually looked at Kahlie, he almost fell over backward. This was not the gawky girl he'd expected to see. Instead, he found himself face to face with a beautiful and refined young woman. "Whoa! I . . . uh . . . I see you did! You . . . you look radiant, Milady!" He stared at her in awe. "Graci . . . what happened to that awkward little kid who used to be your Companion Servant?"

"Um . . . uh . . . Kahlie," Gracielle stammered, "you look gorgeous, positively gorgeous!"

Kahlie had just returned after a month away at a finishing academy. Gracielle had sent her there to learn about diplomacy and mediation, but she certainly didn't expect to see such a drastic physical transformation in her companion.

The girl she'd come to know had messy, curly red hair, and hardly ever wore more than a simple brown dress—which was frequently dirty—and light blue shoes with holes in the sides. But now, her hair was tamed into long, soft waves and she was wearing makeup! The celery green color of her suit brought out the vivid emerald in her eyes. Her nails were manicured; she was wearing shoes that matched her outfit; and she was adorned about the neck and wrists in elegant pearl and silver jewelry.

"Good Morning, Atoc . . . Ator," she greeted, lowering gracefully to her knee.

Gracielle beamed and choked back a giggle. "Oh, okay, Kahlie . . . that's enough of that! You know you don't have to be that formal with us!"

"Oh, I know," Kahlie grinned, "I just wanted to show you what I learned! Besides, the instructors at the academy would keel over if they ever found out I didn't bow to you! I mean . . . don't get me wrong. I'm thrilled, of course, that you sent me, Ator, but yeowch! Some of those instructors are just plain wacky and uptight!"

"Ahhhhh. There she is," Jonathan chuckled. He started toward her hair with his hand, but then thought the better of it. Kahlie caught the motion out of the corner of her eye, and felt the all too familiar burning in her cheeks that Jonathan seemed to be so talented at bringing on.

"Kahlieeeeee!" Audril had been so wrapped up in her book that she hadn't noticed Kahlie until now. She rushed over and jumped full-force onto Kahlie, who caught her and swung her around in a circle.

"My big four-year-old Buzzy Bug," she exclaimed. "Happy, happy birthday, Miss Audril!" She gave Audril a great big squeeze.

Audril ran her little hand through her smooth hair. "Kahlie?" she grimaced. "You look funny."

Jonathan, Gracielle and Kahlie all laughed.

"Yes I do," Kahlie agreed, and kissed Audril's round cheek.

Gracielle stifled her laughter. "Um . . . will you take our birthday girl to the dining room and get her some breakfast, Kahlie? The atoc and I have some important matters to discuss."

"Of course, ma'am," she nodded. "Come on, Buzzy Bug." She set Audril down, took her by the hand, and off they went.

"Did you see that?" Jonathan asked. "She's too young for all that fluff! They made her look twenty-five years old, at least!"

"Jonathan, stop!" Gracielle scolded. "She looks beautiful. She is eighteen now, you know."

A sudden bump of the ground and a distant rumbling reminded them why they needed to be talking about matters other than Kahlie's appearance.

Jonathan sighed and shook his head. "We can't wait anymore, Graci. We've waited too long already. We *really* need to get help."

She dropped down into her favorite big green chair and pondered the situation for a minute. If Glaron's discovery was enough to solve the Advantiere, what difference would it make if she agreed with Jonathan? Surely she could persuade him to wait until tomorrow to get the help he was seeking. "Okay," she sighed at last, "let's get help."

Jonathan's jaw dropped.

"Sweetheart," she explained, "I don't want their lives to be cut short because of my selfishness." She pointed at the door that Audril and Kahlie had just exited through. "But I'm scared. I don't know who we can trust with this."

"I'm sure we can trust Michelan and Statlen," he soothed. "They're our closest friends, and two of the smartest men I know."

Again, the floor jolted and the planet rumbled loudly.

"All right!" Gracielle yelled angrily skyward and let out an exasperated sigh. "Let me write down some notes . . . things we've already thought about, and ideas we've already tried. Maybe it'll be helpful. I'll do it after the party tonight."

"Thank you, Love." Jonathan leaned over and gave her a kiss. "I'm certain they'll respect our confidence, and be a great help to us."

"When will you talk to them?" she asked. "There won't be time today."

Jonathan thought for a minute and answered in exactly the way she hoped he would. "Yeah, you're right. It'll have to wait until Audril's party is out of the way."

"How about in the morning," she suggested. *After Glaron and I have it figured out*, she thought to herself.

A small piece of plaster from the ceiling dropped to the floor next to Jonathan, followed by a trail of white floating dust. "Yes, I think that's best," he answered, as he brushed at the fine powder that had just landed on his shoulder. "I'll send messages to them right away. Then, if you like," he volunteered, "I can come help you with the . . . um . . . extravaganza."

Gracielle smiled and thanked him.

He kissed her, and then went on his way.

A few minutes later, Kahlie and Audril returned from breakfast. "Momma," Audril announced, "we bringed you some muffins!"

"Oh, thank you, dearest." She took the fluffy, berry muffins that Audril was holding and set them down on a small table, and then slumped back into her chair and looked Kahlie over once more. "You really do look lovely, my dear."

Kahlie smiled warmly. "Thank you, Ator." She could tell that something was weighing heavily on Gracielle's mind. "Is everything all right, ma'am?"

"Oh, it's just the Advantiere again," Gracielle explained. She'd confided bits and pieces about the Advantiere to Kahlie over the years. Kahlie knew that a Trysta named Glaron was helping her—and that Jonathan didn't know about their meetings. She knew that Audril had a special part to play, and also that the strange happenings on Lor Mandela were directly related to the mysterious prophecy.

She scooted Audril over to an elegant, ivory doll house and opened it up for her. "Here, Buzzy. Why don't you play with your dolls?" Audril loved to pretend with the little doll family that lived in the house. She flopped down on to the floor, immediately picked up two of the little figures, and started a make-believe conversation between them.

Kahlie walked back over to Gracielle and asked, "Is there anything I can do?"

The ator didn't answer for some time; she just sat in the chair gazing blankly at Kahlie. All of a sudden, her face lit up and she started mumbling excitedly. "She . . . she was altered, and then disappeared! Of course . . . she would be . . . if Darian . . . ." She stopped and stared into space with a stunned expression on her face.

"What is it, ma'am?" Kahlie asked.

"Oh!" Gracielle blurted and jumped up from the chair, "It all makes sense! It . . . we . . . this means . . . we're not doomed, Kahlie! It can still be done!" She raced over and hugged Kahlie exuberantly. "Oh, thank you, Kahlie!" she exclaimed. "Thank you!"

Kahlie was confused, to say the least. "Thank you for what?" she inquired.

"Uh . . . well . . ." Gracielle bit on her lower lip. "I . . . I can't really say right now, but don't worry, Kahlie! Once I find out if my hunch is correct, you'll be the first to know." She started laughing. "Oh, I have to go get ready for the party," she bubbled.

"I'll be back at lunch." She hugged Kahlie again and dashed out of the room.

Kahlie shrugged her shoulders. "Okay, then," she chuckled. She shook her head and joined Audril at the doll house.

A few hours later, Gracielle and Jonathan returned to the room to escort Audril to her party. Audril was all dressed up in a tea length, white linen sun dress. Kahlie had stuck little yellow flowers in her hair, and even put some of her makeup on her—just because she was such a big girl now.

Audril was ecstatic when her parents arrived. "Iss time! Iss time!" she shouted. "Come on Kahlie!" She grabbed Kahlie's hand and pulled her toward the door. "Iss time for my party!"

"Okay . . . we're coming, Buzz," Kahlie giggled, and the four of them made their way to the Assembly Hall for the big event.

The party was a huge success. Hundreds of friends came to celebrate, bringing with them mountains of dolls, makeup sets, tea sets, drawing colors, building toys, books, purses, clothes—there was hardly a gift that Audril didn't receive. Games were played, food was served, songs were sung, and presents were unwrapped. In the end, there was a very tired, but very happy little atoh—and a colossal mess.

Kahlie took Audril back to her room to put her to bed.

Gracielle stayed to coordinate the clean up effort, while Jonathan went to see if there was word back from Michelan and Statlen.

Jonathan was almost to the main doors, when Statlen burst through them, disheveled and out of breath. "Forgive me, Atoc," he panted, "but there has been . . . a large land-slide . . . at the south end of Westrim. We believe that there are several fatalities, sir. Dr. Michelan is assisting there, and I'm afraid that I am needed as well."

"Yes . . . of course," Jonathan didn't waste a second; he was already speeding back across the foyer. "Wait here, Statlen. I'm coming with you," he commanded, "I just need to let Graci know." He raced back to the Assembly Hall and informed Gracielle who quickly instructed the servants to gather supplies and food for him and Statlen to take on the journey.

Within a few minutes, they were ready to leave. Gracielle escorted Jonathan out of the palace, and begged him to be careful.

"I'll send word once I have more details," he called back as they rushed away.

Gracielle stood on the front steps, watching them go and feeling very concerned. Why couldn't they figure this blasted thing out? People were dying now! It wasn't just random stories of tornadoes ripping through some evacuated country on the other side of the world anymore. The destruction was here—all around them. She looked up at the darkening sky and cried out to the spirit of Lor Mandela, "You know, just a little help would be nice! Like a hint or a clue or . . . ." She stopped short. "*Glaron!*" she gasped. The sun was setting and she realized that she should have been on her way to the Anaria by now! She looked down at the sparkly blue gown she was wearing and stomped her foot in frustration. Quickly, she ran back to her room. Kahlie was there waiting for her.

"I'm sorry, Kahlie," Gracielle yelled as she ran into the changing room. "I can't talk. I have to go! I'm supposed to be meeting Glaron . . . right now!"

"Yes, Ator, of course. But I . . . I heard about Westrim—that there was a slide and that people've been killed." One of Kahlie's closest friends, Dallin Doone, lived in Westrim.

Gracielle marveled at how quickly word had spread through the palace. She hurried back into the room—now wearing gray pants and an ivory shirt—reached for a rust colored jacket from a tall, narrow wardrobe and slipped it on. "Yes, Kahlie. Jonathan's on his way there now." She touched Kahlie on the shoulder and soothed, "I'm sure Dallin's fine, dear. It would take a lot more than a land slide to bring him down." She felt bad about leaving Kahlie when she was obviously distraught, but it was absolutely necessary. "I'll hurry back . . . I promise . . . just as soon as I can."

Kahlie nodded somberly, and Gracielle raced out of the room. She ran through the foyer and out the main doors. The sun had already fully set. "Hang on, Glaron! Please don't leave. I'm on my way." As soon as she was down the front steps and out into the courtyard she yelled, "The Anaria!" and vanished.

She popped up outside the big, old tree just as Glaron was turning to leave. "Ohhh," he yelped, "I wish you wouldn't do that!"

Without a word, she waved her hand in the air in a large "S" like pattern and the cave entrance rippled onto the surface of the peeling gray bark. As she did, there was a rumble and a crackling sound that emanated from the hills in the distance. The ground shook and vibrated, causing hundreds of dry, dead leaves to spill down from the Anaria's branches.

"Come on! Let's get inside," she insisted. They rushed into the cave and followed the path to the Anaria's main room. Gracielle waved her hand again to seal the entrance.

"I was beginning to wonder if you were coming," Glaron breathed. "I thought maybe my note had been intercepted, or that you'd gone to Westrim."

"Glaron, what did you figure out?" She asked in a way that reminded her of the anxiousness that Audril had exhibited all day. "It's been making me crazy!"

Glaron pulled the little brown book from his vest pocket and started leafing through it. "Well, you won't believe my luck, Ator. I was in the Transendar yesterday, when I came across an extremely old book. You've heard of the Derites, right?"

"Yeah, I think so," she answered. "They were a small civilization that existed in Koria thousands of years ago. They're the race that supposedly created the Caverns."

"Precisely," Glaron exclaimed, "this book was all about the Derite language. It's fascinating, really. They used a series of words, combined with gestures and magical tricks, to communicate."

"Really?" She'd never heard that.

"Anyway," he continued, "as I was flipping through the book, I came across this passage that was talking about their musical traditions." He read what he'd jotted down in their notebook. "It said, 'Solna Elahk Enta.'"

"Elahk?" Gracielle repeated anxiously.

"Exactly!" Glaron beamed. "It said that translated, this means *music creates love*." He paused for effect. "Elahk means create! I couldn't believe it, but then I started wondering if any thing else from the riddle was mentioned in this book, and are you ready?"

Gracielle nodded enthusiastically.

"I found that the letter E by itself means the same thing as our letter A. So, what we have here is 'Elahk E'—Create a."

"Create a?" Gracielle questioned. "Create a what?"

"Ber, of course," Glaron sniggered at his unparalleled wit.

Gracielle frowned at him.

"Hmm mmm, sorry," he apologized. "Actually, Ber in ancient Derite means *new*."

"Create a new . . . create a new . . . Lor Mandela?" Gracielle shrugged her shoulders. "I don't understand."

"Neither did I," Glaron admitted. "I was up half the night trying to figure it out. This morning, I took it to Ultara and asked her what she thought."

"And?"

"She didn't know at first either, but then she got that crazy look in her eyes . . . the one she always gets when she's about to kill somebody or something," he shuddered. "Kinda scared me."

"Glaron!" Gracielle snapped.

"Oh . . . well, she said that she believes this spell, Elahk E Ber, is what Anika did to start this whole process, look!"

He pointed at a page in the notebook. Gracielle followed along as he read, *'One comes swiftly in the morning*. Ultara said that the birth of Anika and Lantalia was sudden, and fast. Twenty minutes from start to finish. One birth . . . two infants born early one morning."

Gracielle stared at him wide-eyed. Was it all coming together? Were the pieces starting to fit?

Glaron continued. *"One unknowing moves in haste,"* he explained. "Anika didn't know that twin spirits couldn't be cloned. Impatience got the better of her."

"This is amazing!" Gracielle breathed.

"One beloved though mighty fallen has to refer to Satia. She was an amazing ruler. Beloved is a mild understatement! Or, it could've been your mother."

Gracielle nodded in agreement. Then she interjected, *"One is chosen to forget her place.* Of course . . . Anika's destiny must have been to forget her place and rebel against our ways."

Glaron smiled and nodded, "That's what Ultara thought, too! I checked it out . . . paid a visit to General Kort early this morning. He told me that Anika had learned how to clone souls from her great grandmother's journal . . . which Kort just happens to be in possession of now."

"And?"

"And, the spell used to clone is *Elahk E Ber.*"

Gracielle slapped her hand over her mouth to muffle a delighted squeal. She bounded forward and gave Glaron an enthusiastic hug. "That's half of the riddle Glaron! This is so great! So, what about the rest?"

"I . . . I don't know yet," he mumbled, "The strange thing is that the Derite translation of the letter A by itself is exactly the same as the E by itself. It's like we're supposed to create a new Lor Mandela . . . twice."

"Hmmm," Gracielle thought, "then why wouldn't it just say the exact same thing twice? Why the letter change?" She was deep in thought, when she remembered something. "Oh, Glaron," she exclaimed, "I almost forgot! I've made an incredible discovery of my own!" She hesitated, but then added, "It's something I need to tell Ultara in person, though."

"Wh . . . what?" he fumbled, "That's impossible! And dangerous! And impossible! Besides, why can't you just tell me? You know you can tell me anything, don't you?" He looked a little hurt.

"Oh, Glaron," Gracielle soothed, "I can tell you anything! But this is a personal matter—between me and Ultara. It wouldn't be right for me to talk to anyone else about it."

"Oh," he pouted, "well I guess I understand. But how in the world do you propose we pull *this* off? It's not like you can just come to Trysta Palace . . . and she certainly can't come visit you!"

Gracielle reached into her jacket pocket and pulled out a photograph. "Here." She handed a small photograph to Glaron. "This is Tur Helene. She's Kahlie and Audril's private tutor."

"Okay . . . so?"

"So, day after tomorrow, she will be away all day visiting her family. If Ultara can alter herself to look like this . . ." She pointed at the photo.

"Oh . . . I get it now," Glaron grimaced. "You want her to come to Mandela

114

Palace, day after tomorrow, disguised as this, erm, lovely lady?" He flicked at the picture with his index finger.

"Will you see to it, Glaron? Please! It really is very important!"

He half-smiled. "I guess I can try," he groaned, feeling put out that after he'd just handed her the biggest news in Lor Mandela's history she wouldn't tell him her big secret.

Suddenly, there was a loud boom and everything started shaking violently.

"Glaron! It's an earthquake! Quick, over here!" she yelled. She grabbed him by the arm and pulled him away from the back wall, just before every one of the bookshelves lining it toppled over like dominoes. He barely escaped the barrage of heavy books that spilled from one of the shelves.

The shaking intensified, sending furniture, lamps, statues, floral arrangements and the dumped books sliding and spinning indiscriminately across the agitating floor.

Glaron looked up nervously and saw the massive chandelier above swinging like a gigantic pendulum over their heads. If it came down, they were as good as dead.

He nudged Gracielle toward the tunnel; they tried to maneuver their way towards it, but the ground was shaking so fiercely—back and forth and up and down—that it was extremely difficult to make any headway. They inched their way to one side of the room, sputtering and coughing as a heavy cloud of dust filled the air. Gracielle grabbed one of the blobs of sap, and then another, and held on. She used the amber knobs to pull herself along the wall.

Glaron saw what she was doing and followed suit.

Slowly, they moved from blob to blob, using all the strength they could muster. After much effort, they reached the tunnel which was swaying and careening angrily.

"I don't think we should go in there!" Glaron yelled above the roar of the quake.

"I have to get back," she shouted, "Audril . . . and Kahlie!"

She took a step into the cave, keeping one of her hands against the wall, but as she tried to take another, the cave floor jolted wildly, knocking her to the ground.

"Gracielle!" Glaron yelled. He lowered to the ground and crawled over to make sure she was okay.

The floor of the tunnel gyrated and reeled even more ferociously than before.

Glaron reached Gracielle and helped her pull herself back up. "You can't!" he bellowed. "It's too dangerous!"

"I have to!" Gracielle choked on the thick dust. She cupped her hand over her mouth and in a muffled yell insisted, "I have to get back!"

She turned toward the tunnel again; Glaron grabbed her by the arm. He was not going to let her go, but all of a sudden there was a loud, low creak in the room behind them.

"THE CHANDELIER!" he cried out. The huge light was swaying ferociously and slipping out of the ceiling.

Glaron and Gracielle looked at each other, and then lunged into the cave as far as they could throw themselves. There was another moan from the bolts that held the massive fixture in the ceiling and then, crack! The bolts let go, and the chandelier plummeted to the ground disintegrating into millions of pieces in a deafening crash. Tiny shards of glass bulleted through the room sticking into the furniture, the sap bubbles, the walls, and into Glaron and Gracielle. They held onto each other inside the tunnel, scared, bloodied, and in pain.

Glaron held his hand over his left eye, which had been shredded to bits by the flying glass. It burned and scratched if he tried to open or close it.

"Aggghhhh!" he wailed miserably. He could hear the nauseating sound of the glass scraping against the bone in the socket. He panted heavily, trying to stay conscious.

Gracielle noticed that he was having difficulty, and wrapped her cut and bleeding arms around him. She started to pull him, best she could, down the tunnel. The ground, which refused to cease its brutal assault, continued rolling and jolting.

Glaron faded in and out of consciousness as Gracielle tugged him toward the entrance to the cave. With each tug, hundreds of stinging bits of glass dug deeper into her already torn up skin; tears streaked down her dust-covered cheeks. She had to get Glaron—who had now fainted and was dead weight—to safety. She lifted him under the arms and yanked him along, inch by inch, gasping in agony with each yank.

When at last she reached the end of the tunnel, she feebly waved one arm in the air, balancing Glaron's weight against her knee. Slowly, the cave opening shuddered onto the wall. She readjusted her arms around him and gave his limp body one more strong tug, pulling him through the opening, and out into the meadow. Finally, the rumbling stopped, and the ground bumped to a halt.

Gracielle toppled over backwards and Glaron landed right on top of her. "Aaooooh!" she moaned, as the glass stabbed in further under his weight. They were both covered in dust, glass crystals, tree sap and crimson blood. She carefully slid Glaron off of her and tried to revive him.

"Glaron," she coughed, "come on . . . wake up." She grabbed a handful of his sandy hair and tugged on it gently. She didn't dare touch his skin for fear of pushing more glass into him. She pulled his hair a second time. "Glaron . . . wake up! Please!" she begged.

Slowly, his good eye blinked and partially opened. "Awwwwwoooooow!" he groaned, dropping his hand back over the mangled one.

"Are . . . you okay?" she huffed weakly.

He coughed two or three times and panted, "Um . . . I . . . I . . . think so. It's . . . just . . . just my eye."

"We've got to get you some help," she insisted.

"I'll be all right," he gasped. He tried to stand but didn't have the strength. "I just need to . . . to rest for a minute. I'll . . . be . . . fine." It was a struggle for him to speak.

"No, Glaron," she wheezed, "you're not fine. We have to get you to a doctor. Here . . . ." She stood and reached out her hand to him. He took it and she yanked with all of her strength.

Glaron rose up in the air, almost to standing, but then started to slump back over.

Gracielle quickly bent under him, and he fell on to her back. She winced and gritted her teeth as his full weight smacked against her. She took a deep breath and started to run—not fast, but at least it was something.

Glaron bounced against her back, pushing more sharp glass into her skin. The pain was terrible, but she didn't stop. As soon as she gained enough speed, she looked skyward and yelled, "Trysta Palace!" and the two of them disappeared.

With a pop, they materialized just outside the imposing wall of Trysta Palace. Gracielle lowered Glaron to the ground. He was still conscious, but weak.

As Gracielle moved back from him his right eye suddenly grew large and he clutched frantically at his chest. His breathing became sporadic and labored. "Can't . . . breathe," he gasped. "Can't . . . breathe!"

Gracielle didn't know if he was choking on glass or injured internally or what the problem was. "Hang on!" she pleaded. She knew that it was dangerous for her to be here, but Glaron needed help, and he needed it now.

"Ator . . . noo!" he yelped, as he realized what she was doing.

Casting her own safety aside, she ran to the gate and started shouting. "Help! Help! Get a doctor! Someone help!"

Not more than a second later, an indiscernible smoky blur raced past her and a person in a black cloak suddenly appeared hovering over Glaron, attending to him. A soft golden glow radiated from under the cloak and floated down onto him. His breathing eased, and the scrapes and blood that had covered him started to gradually fade.

"Ultara?" she guessed.

Ultara didn't answer, but turned and faced Gracielle. Her eyes glowed vividly, making the rest of her face nearly invisible. Gracielle felt a calming warmth radiate through her. Ultara was using her healing power to cleanse the glass shards from her skin.

After a minute or two, Ultara's eyes dimmed and she rushed to Gracielle's side. "You have to get out of here!" she insisted. "Right now! You can't be seen!"

"Is he gonna be all right?" she begged.

"Yes. I will get him to the doctor. But you've got to go!"

"I know," Gracielle nodded, "I will, but I really need to speak with you! It's urgent!"

Ultara walked back over to check on Glaron. "Then speak to me!" she insisted, but before Gracielle could respond, a Trysta Guard burst through the gate.

"Vritesse!" he called out.

"Gracielle! Go!" she commanded in a whisper.

"Come to Mandela Palace in two days. Glaron knows how to get you in," Gracielle quickly instructed and then turned and sprinted away from the rapidly approaching guard. "Mandela Palace!" she shouted, and disappeared.

"Vritesse! What's happened? Are you all right?" the guard cried. "That looked like the ator."

"I'm fine, Branlor, but Glaron needs a doctor."

He tried again, "Was that the . . . ?"

Ultara cut him off abruptly. "Of course not, Branlor! Why would the ator come here?" She raised her eyebrows and looked at him as if to say, *you didn't see anything . . . understand?*

"Oh . . . uh . . . she wouldn't," he choked.

"That's right. Now quickly . . . let's get him inside." Ultara held her hand over Glaron and walked toward the gate. He rose a few inches off the ground and floated along next to her, sleeping peacefully.

She took him to a dimly lit room, which was cluttered with strange bottles of colored liquids, tattered books and odd looking instruments. A vat of putrid looking liquid bubbled in the center of the room; the light that oozed from it was yellow, then green, then lavender, then blue, and then yellow again. "Salera?" Ultara called out, "Get out here. I need your help."

"Eallo, Vreetessa." An exotic, yet frail looking woman, with green-gray toned skin, floating white hair, and sky blue eyes slid out of the shadows on the other side of the room. She drifted toward Glaron, took one look at him and in a very slow, dreamy, voice said, "Ahhh, he ees nealy daed." Her accent was thick and captivating. "Poonctured lung, a few ribz dat ees broken now, and 'e will need da new eye."

Ultara nodded. "Whatever it takes, Salera—I want him well taken care of."

"Oh yes, Vreetessa," she assured, "Salera fix heem rawt up."

The doctor went to work on Glaron as Ultara slid down into a chair across the room. She stared blankly at the vat of color changing lights—her thoughts centered on her encounter with Gracielle. She wondered why Gracielle wanted her to come to the palace. She wondered what she had to say—and why it was so urgent.

CHAPTER XII

MESSAGES

Gracielle hurried up the palace steps and quickly headed for her chambers. When she reached the door, rather than bursting in, she knocked softly. A couple of seconds later, Kahlie opened the door. Anticipating the reaction to her battered appearance, Gracielle slapped her hand over Kahlie's mouth to stifle the impending shriek.

"Shhhh," Gracielle insisted. Slowly she lowered her hand.

Kahlie's eyes were wide with concern. "Ator, wh . . . what happened?" she whispered.

"Is Audril sleeping?" Gracielle checked.

"Uh huh," Kahlie nodded, "she's on your bed."

Gracielle pushed the door open further, took Kahlie by the arm, and walked her back to the dressing area. Once they were behind the wall where they wouldn't be seen if Audril awakened, Gracielle asked, "Is she all right? Are you all right?"

"Yes," Kahlie assured, "she was a little scared, but after the quake ended, it didn't take long for her to fall back to sleep. What happened to you?"

"The chandelier came down in the Anaria," she explained. "It pretty much exploded when it hit the ground. Glaron was hurt badly, but Ultara was taking care of him when I left. She cleaned the glass out of my skin too. Trust me! I looked a lot worse before."

"What? Ultara was there?" Kahlie didn't know much about Ultara, but what she did know frightened her. Gracielle had told her that Ultara didn't kill Jonathan's parents, but so many other people thought she did.

"Actually, she wasn't at the Anaria," Gracielle confessed. "Glaron was in really bad shape. I couldn't leave him there, so I took him back to Trysta Palace for help."

"Trysta Palace! Oh, Ator . . . you could have been captured!" Kahlie exclaimed.

"Yes, but I wasn't." Gracielle casually slipped her ripped up jacket off and handed it to Kahlie. The shirt beneath was covered in big splotches of crimson blood.

Kahlie gasped. "You need a doctor, ma'am!"

Gracielle looked down at her tattered and torn appearance and admitted, "I guess that would be a good idea. I honestly don't know if I'm injured or not, Kahlie. I hurt all over."

"I'll go for a doctor immediately."

"You'll need to get Dr. Slade," Gracielle explained as she headed toward her dressing area to change out of the remainder of her shredded clothes. "Michelan's in Westrim with Jonathan."

Kahlie nodded and rushed quickly out of the room. After a few short minutes, she returned with a heavy-set, dark haired man with a thick, fuzzy mustache.

"Good Evening, Ator," The doctor greeted, lowering to his knee.

Gracielle had just come out of the dressing area, "Oh, hello, Dr. Slade. Please . . . ." She motioned for him to stand.

A look of concern spread across his face upon seeing Gracielle's cut up exterior. "My dear Ator, it would seem you've had quite a night."

Gracielle smiled. "I took a shower in glass, Doctor. Somebody told me it's good for your complexion. I think they lied."

The doctor smiled and indicated for her to sit down on the small burgundy bench that was against the wall behind her.

Kahlie excused herself, and went over to where Audril was sleeping. She picked her up and carried her to her own room.

Dr. Slade took a small, shiny, silver instrument from the black satchel he was carrying, pushed a button on the end of it, and it started to glow. As he lifted one of Gracielle's hands and waved the little glowing stick over it, the cuts on her skin turned a sickly shade of yellow, and started bubbling and sizzling. The process looked extremely painful, but Gracielle didn't seem to mind. As soon as the doctor moved the instrument away from the area, the sizzling stopped and the wounds melted away.

"This will take care of most of these scratches," he explained, "but a few marks will probably linger for a day or two."

Gracielle nodded. "As long as my family isn't afraid to look at me."

"Not likely," he smiled, as he continued working, clearing the cuts from one hand and arm and then starting on the other. "It looks as though you've had some Trysta help, huh?"

"Oh, um . . . ." Gracielle stammered, "well, of course. I am a Trysta, Doctor."

"I know," Dr. Slade continued, "I just didn't know that Trystas could use healing abilities on themselves."

"Well, not completely . . ." She wasn't about to explain any further. "That's why you're here, Doctor."

Just then, the door opened and Jonathan came through it. He was also dirty and a little scraped up. With him was a young man with a full, rugged beard and scraggly brown hair.

"Wh . . . what's going on here? Graci, are you alright?" he asked, surprised to find Dr. Slade busily removing cuts from her neck.

"I'm fine, Jonathan . . . just some scratches," she assured. "What's going on in Westrim?" She hadn't noticed the man who was there with Jonathan until just then. "Dallin," she exclaimed delightedly, "oh, Kahlie will be so relieved!"

"Hello Ator . . . uh . . . you look . . . well . . . um . . . ." Dallin stammered awkwardly. He knelt down without completing his sentence, and then rose clumsily back to his feet.

"What happened to you?" Jonathan tried again.

"Oh . . . well, after the party," she began, "I needed to unwind a bit. Kahlie had things under control here, so I went to the Anaria for some alone time." She hated lying to Jonathan, but knew he wouldn't understand. She'd never been able to convince him of Ultara's innocence, and he would certainly not approve of her meeting with Ultara's Chief Advisor. "There was a quake," she continued. "Did you feel it in Westrim?"

Both Jonathan and Dallin nodded.

"Well, you know the big chandelier in the Anaria? It fell as I was leaving to come back. The glass cut me up a bit, that's all." She didn't want to talk about this anymore; she wanted to know the status of their efforts. "Now, what about Westrim?" she pressed.

Jonathan looked at Dallin and pointed at two comfortable burgundy chairs; they walked over and dropped down into them. "It's bad, Graci," he began, "at least fifty people dead and hundreds missing. We've just come back to gather some more supplies and recruit more help."

Dr. Slade cleared his throat. "I will go wherever I am needed, Atoc," he volunteered.

"Thank you, Slade. I believe it would be best for you to stay here in Mandela City. We have eighteen emergency doctors in Westrim already; Dr. Michelan is coordinating things there. I would like for you to do the same here, if you would. We likely will need to bring back some of the injured."

"Of course, sir," Slade accepted.

"When will you be leaving again?" Gracielle asked.

"We'll round up volunteers tonight and then travel back first thing in the morning."

Dr. Slade healed the last of the cuts from Gracielle. She walked over to Jonathan and sat down on the arm of his chair. "What can I do?" she asked as she reached her arms around him and kissed his forehead.

"Just hold things down here," he answered. She ran her hand gently across several good-sized gashes on the side of his face. "Doctor, could you take care of these, please?" The doctor willingly obliged.

"So, uh . . . Kah . . . Kahlie is back from the academy?" Dallin asked nervously.

Gracielle smiled. She suspected that Dallin liked Kahlie as more than just a friend. "Yes," she answered, "she's putting Audril to bed. She should be back momentarily."

Dallin smiled. "Oh . . . um . . . good."

A moment later, a door at the back of the room clicked open. Dallin twisted around in his chair, and out of the corner of his eye, caught sight of Kahlie entering the room. He quickly rose to his feet and started toward her. After two or three steps though, he froze in his tracks; his eyes got big, and his jaw practically fell to his chest.

"Dallin!" Kahlie dashed across the room and embraced him warmly. "I was worried about you! When I heard about the slide, I . . . ."

Dallin cut her off. "*What* have they done to you?" he frowned.

"Uh . . . um . . . well . . . what do you mean? You don't like it?" she fumbled.

"It's okay I guess. You just look so . . . well . . . so girly." He reached up and lifted a lock of her hair in the air like it was a smelly sock.

"Hey!" She snapped, pulling her hair out of his hand. "I am a girl, you Slarp!" She slugged him in the shoulder and frowned back.

Dallin grimaced and rubbed his arm. "Yeah, I know Budge. I'm just not used to you looking like one."

"Well, I'm not used to you looking like one, either," she sassed.

Gracielle, Jonathan and the doctor sniggered from across the room.

Dallin just stood there and stared at her with a confused look on his scruffy face.

"I just decided it was time to look my age," she replied after several silent seconds. "And besides," she slapped his shoulder again; "I like it!" She spun around him indignantly and walked over to where Gracielle was sitting.

The doctor smiled at her as he finished mending Jonathan's injuries; he then excused himself to go prepare the other doctors in the area.

"We'd better get going too, Dallin," Jonathan observed. "We have a lot to get done tonight." He stood and looked at Kahlie. "Take care of the ator and atoh, Milady."

She bowed dramatically and replied with the standard response she used whenever Jonathan told her to take care of his girls, "That is what I do best, sir."

Jonathan looked at Dallin, who was staring, not at Kahlie, but at Gracielle. "Dallin?"

"Oh . . . uh . . . yes, sir." He snapped back into reality. "On my way."

"Goodbye, Dallin," Kahlie snipped, and turned rudely away from him.

He smiled playfully, rushed over and gave her a quick peck on the cheek. "Bye, Budge. By the way, you did very well. You look exactly your age."

She gave him a, "hmph," as he and Jonathan headed out the door.

"Well, this has been quite a day," Gracielle sighed.

"Yes, it has," Kahlie agreed. "I'm sorry you got hurt, Ator."

"It was worth it, Kahlie," she grinned. "Glaron and I actually made some headway on the Advantiere! Not just some headway, a lot of headway!"

"Really? Does this mean the disasters will be ending soon?" she asked.

"I hope so," Gracielle sighed. "We've solved about half of it. The rest should go quickly now. If we can . . . ." She gasped and stopped in the middle of her sentence. "Wait!" she breathed, "If the picture was damaged, how can Ultara . . . ?"

She turned and walked over to a small writing desk and started digging through one of the drawers. "Ah hah! I thought I had another one," she exclaimed as she took out a photograph, pulled a piece of stationery out of a tray on the top of the desk and started scribbling a note. "I need you to take this to the courier. Give it to Tabbit. She'll know what to do."

"Tabbit," Kahlie repeated, "yes, ma'am." She stood by the desk and waited for Gracielle to finish writing.

Gracielle folded the stationery in half, sealed it, and handed it to her. She also handed her the picture. It was Tur Helene—Kahlie and Audril's private teacher. Kahlie's face must have shown her confusion, because Gracielle quickly explained, "Don't worry! She's not in any kind of trouble."

"Will this be all, ma'am?" she asked.

"Yes, dear . . . just make sure you give it to Tabbit," she reiterated.

Kahlie nodded and hurried off to the courier office which was located in the below-ground levels of the palace. She made her way across the foyer into one of the many shimmery hallways and followed it nearly to its end. She walked through an arched passageway that led to a narrow spiral staircase, descended the stairs, and knocked on the door that was at the bottom of it.

A crooked, bony old man with a snarling voice peeked out around the door. "Oh, it's you! Why are you disturbing my sleep this time?" he asked gruffly.

"Good evening to you too, Snag," she snipped. "The ator needs this message delivered immediately."

"Hmpf," he growled, "the ator does, does she? Does the ator need me to do anything else? Break my legs? Eat poison? Wrestle a rynolt?" He swung the door open and held out his skeleton-like, gnarled hand.

"Um, actually, she would like Tabbit to take it, Snag."

"Ooooohhh! So Snag's not good enough for the noble ator, is that it?" He gestured for Kahlie to come in. "Too old, too slow?"

"No . . . just too bitter," she retorted.

Snag glowered at her most unpleasantly. "Shut the door, you little snippet! You'll let in a draft," he wheezed and staggered as he crossed the room. A large pile of papers lay on the floor in front of him; he kicked at it as he walked by. When he reached the back of the office he barked, "Tabbit! Get out here!"

Kahlie looked around the small, cluttered courier office. There were brown leather satchel bags and coin purses sloppily piled on the floor and stacks of papers strewn everywhere. However, despite the lack of organization and mess, Snag and his colleagues ran an impeccable, very reliable service.

Just a few seconds had passed when a demure fairy-like creature, dressed in a cropped blue top and a long, bright yellow skirt bounded around the corner. "Tabbit! Get out here!" She glowered, mimicking Snag almost perfectly, "yeses, mister Snags, sir?" Tabbit was no taller than a small child, and grinning ear to ear. Her big blue eyes were wild with anticipation. "Is it my turn?" she asked excitedly.

"Hello, Tabbit," Kahlie smiled. "How are you this evening?"

Snag huffed in disgust.

"How are you this evening?" she repeated, copying Kahlie's mannerisms almost perfectly. "I am fines, Miss Companions Servant, just fines," she bubbled.

"Good! The ator would like you to deliver these." She handed Tabbit the picture of Tur Helene and the note.

"The ator would like you to deliver these. Ooooo, the ator," she breathed softly. She bobbed her head up and down, causing her pure white wisps of long, wild hair to turn and twist strangely—almost as if they had a life of their own. "Ator want mees to takes important things. Yep!" She popped her arm up to a salute and pushed out her bulgy brown tummy. "Me know whats to do!"

"Lovely!" Snag sneered. "Then why don't you just do it and let me get some sleep!"

"Let me get some sleep!" she repeated. "Okie dokies, Mr. Snag, sir!" She bounced across the room, grabbed a satchel and a coin purse, waved enthusiastically at Kahlie and Snag, and then disappeared out the door.

Kahlie giggled at Tabbit's happy little departure, and at the drastic personality contrast between her and the skinny old man who was glaring at her irately. "Good grief, Snag!" she exclaimed. "You really should get some sleep! You look even more miserable than usual."

"Are you quite finished?" he scowled.

"Absolutely!" Having no desire to linger with this nasty grump any longer, she promptly backed out of the office and started up the stairs. She was about half way up when the door behind her slammed with a loud bang!

CHAPTER XIII
ULTARA'S ALTERING

Tabbit slipped out of the palace and across the courtyard. Her little figure was nearly undetectable in the crisp darkness. She hopped from place to place, nimbly maneuvering around buildings, trees, and rocks—anything that was in her path. She crossed through the city, and then into a rolling, rich meadow.

The trip from Mandela Palace to Trysta Palace would have taken most people several hours, but in just under two, she'd reached her destination. She stood shaking in the cold night air, in front of the towering wall at Trysta Palace, stuck her little head cautiously through the iron bars of the gate and looked side to side.

"No ones," she whispered, bringing her head back through the gate. She raised her arms out to her sides, closed her eyes, and pressed her entire body against the cold metal bars. "Brrrrrr," she shivered. Slowly, she melted into the gate, until all that could be seen were her large blue eyes blinking happily on two of the iron rods.

A Trysta guard strolled past, entirely missing her gazing eyeballs. Once the guard rounded a corner and was out of sight, she pushed herself forward and seemed to grow out of the other side of the gate. She was in!

She darted in a rapid zigzag across the courtyard. Whenever a guard came in to view, she would lift her arms and dissolve into whatever happened to be next to her—a statue, a plant, the wall. She skittered right past the main palace doors and darted along the sprawling, stony wall until she came to a dark, two-story window.

Again, she raised her skinny little arms; but this time, instead of melting herself into the building, she snapped her fingers, and a strong, focused wind—originating from her fingertips—blasted at the window, shaking the panes wildly.

The wind jiggled the window, making the latch on the inside shake back and forth until, at last, it popped open.

Tabbit moved her hands down a bit and aimed the strong currents of air at the window sill.

Slowly, the window rose. When it was fully lifted, she lowered her arms and the wind stopped. In one fluid motion, she leaped from the ground and right through the open window.

"Lady? Laaadyyy?" she called out in a tiny, squeaky voice.

Across the room was a closed door. Behind it, a light clicked on sending a glowing sliver of yellow spilling out from underneath. The door opened, and Ultara appeared in the doorway. "Tabbit," she began, "what are you doing here?"

Tabbit hopped over to her. "What are you doing here?" she repeated. "Message froms the ator, Lady." She gave Ultara the note and the photograph.

Ultara handed her a mesh bag containing a few shiny stones and a bunch of creepy, crawling bugs. "Oooooo! Very nices, Lady!" Tabbit poked at one of the bugs with a satisfied grin, and stuffed the whole mesh bag—bugs and all—into her coin purse. She nodded and made a strange little clicking noise with her tongue. "Good evenings, Lady!" she beamed, and then bounded across the room and back out the open window.

Ultara unfolded the note from Gracielle and read aloud:

"I thought the picture might have been destroyed, and thought having another would help. I hope my friend is recovering well. I await your visit."

Ultara studied the picture of Tur Helene. "And, why do I need this?" she asked aloud, knowing that Glaron would no doubt be the one with the answer. She stared at the picture again for a minute, shrugged her shoulders, and then returned to her chambers and went back to bed.

The following morning, she woke early and promptly went to check on Glaron.

Dr. Salera greeted her at the door.

Glaron was sitting on a low black chaise, wearing dark glasses and smiling broadly.

"'E ees good as new, Vritessa." In the daylight, Salera's eyes looked like crackled bits of ice—an eerie contrast against her strangely colored skin. "Ez eyes will be taken some tame to 'eel . . . two o' tree weeks, Salera tinks will be enov."

"Thank you, Salera." Ultara replied and glanced over at Glaron. "Come along, my friend. I think we should get you back to your place."

Glaron rose to his feet, and walked over to the waifish doctor. He put his arm around her dainty, clay-like shoulders, and said, "I owe you one, Doc."

Salera turned toward him and swirled her bony fingers through his wavy hair. "Mmmmm," she oozed seductively, "aye be collectin' laeta, deah Glayron."

Glaron cleared his throat and Ultara bit her lip trying not to laugh. "Um...all right then," he choked. "I'll be seeing you around." Ultara shot him a disgusted look and pulled him by the arm out of Salera's chambers.

"What?" he asked innocently.

She looked at him and shook her head. "Never mind, Lover Boy. We have more important things to discuss. Are you feeling up to breakfast in my chambers?"

"Hmmm," Glaron teased, "two offers in one morning. I think I should get hurt more often."

Ultara rolled her eyes. "Yep, you seem to be back to normal."

They arrived at Ultara's chambers, where a generous spread of food was already waiting. "Good thing I said yes," Glaron smiled, as he grabbed for a big piece of orange fruit.

Ultara walked over to a large console near her bed. "I received an interesting telegram last night." She picked up the picture and the note from

Gracielle. "Here. I'm sure these will make more sense to you than they do to me."

Glaron glanced at the picture and explained, "Oh, well this is the atoh's teacher. Gracielle must've figured my copy would have been damaged . . . ya know, by all the glass and stuff." He pulled the shredded remains of the original photo from his tattered vest. "Wow! She actually looks better like this," he quipped.

Ultara stood with her arms folded and her head cocked to one side. "You know, Glaron, I've met Tur Helene. She's a lovely woman. But I don't recall asking for a portrait of her for my throne room."

"Oh . . . um, sorry," he smirked. "Apparently, Gracielle has something very important that she can only talk to you about." There was the slightest hint of bitterness in his voice. "This Tur Helene person is supposed to be out of town tomorrow, visiting family. The ator would like you to alter yourself to look like her and come to Mandela Palace tomorrow morning . . . if it isn't too much trouble."

"She didn't give you any indication of what she wanted?" Ultara asked.

"Nope . . . none at all," he frowned, "just said it was personal . . . between the two of you."

"Tomorrow morning, huh? It's going to take me most of today to alter myself to this," Ultara observed as she studied the photo.

"Does it take longer to make yourself ugly?" Glaron sniggered.

Ultara glared at him. "How long do you have to wear those ridiculous glasses?" she asked, as she picked up a piece of bread and pulled it apart.

"Just for today," he answered. "Is that a problem? I mean . . . I can see just fine. They're just a little sensitive to the light, that's all."

"They? I thought you only injured one of your eyes."

"Yeah well, Dr. Salera said dat she was out o' da laet green eyes, zo she hed to use de derk green wohnz." He mimicked her beautifully. "I guess she replaced my right eye too, so they'd match."

"Drastic," Ultara criticized. "Anyway, I can really use your help today . . .

131

if you're up to it."

"I am ready for whatever you'd like to throw at me, Vritesse . . . unless, of course, it's a chandelier!"

They ate their breakfast quickly, and then went to work collecting the tools they would need for the altering. Mostly, it was just clothing and accessories to match Tur Helene's frumpy style; but they also gathered seven glow stones, a sizable piece of greelan bark, and several other minor ingredients for the altering spell. By late afternoon, they had acquired all they needed to begin the process.

First, Ultara placed the seven glow stones—which were similar in shape and size to a human skull—in a circular pattern on the floor. She laid Tur Helene's photo on the seventh stone, and one by one, they started to light up. The stone with the picture on top glowed a bright red as the others took on a soft, yellow luminescence. Ultara then took the greelan bark and broke it into bits; she used the broken pieces to fill the cracks and crevices around the rocks, thereby forming a solid radiant ring.

Glaron brought over a bowl which contained a gooey, tar-like mixture.

Ultara dipped her index finger into it and pulled some out.

It smelled awful! Glaron scrunched up his nose and turned his head. Ultara didn't seem to mind the smell though. She used the substance to paint a star-like symbol on the upper part of her chest, just below her left collar bone. She returned her finger to the goo, drew out some more and placed the same symbol on the right side; and then, one on her forehead.

She stepped inside the glowing stone ring and started to hum—low and strange.

Glaron stood back and watched as one of the glow stones turned purple and a thick ribbon of lavender light floated up from it, spiraling its way slowly around Ultara. Next, another stone turned orange, and an orange ribbon twisted up, then a green one . . . a blue one . . . a white one . . . and a silver one.

The red stone started to sputter and sizzle as, all at once, a heavy shower of red sparks flew up from it, engulfing Ultara in a fountain of light. One by one, the twining ribbons dissolved into the crimson spray, turning it finally to a dark burgundy fire.

Ultara stood, still humming, in a column of maroon flames.

Glaron could feel the heat radiating from the fire; the intensity of the light stabbed painfully at his sensitive eyes. He had the urge to look away, but he was not going to miss this! He was probably one of only a handful of Trystas who had ever watched an altering.

Suddenly, the symbols on Ultara's chest and face began to glow bright white, and the crimson flames from the fire started pouring into them. The symbols consumed the flames until nothing remained but the stones, the bark, and Ultara. Everything had returned to how it was before.

Much to Glaron's dismay, Ultara did not appear to be changed in any way. "It didn't work," he moaned.

"Of course it worked," she corrected. "The actual change will take several hours."

"Then, how do you know it worked?" Glaron asked.

"I just know, Glaron," she insisted. "Now, if you'll clean this all up for me, I have to go to sleep."

"Huh? Why?"

"Well," Ultara explained, "if you must know . . . the process hurts." She twisted her head from side to side like she was already trying to relieve some tension in her neck. "The pain is unbearable if you're awake."

"Really?" he asked compassionately. "I'm sorry. I didn't know."

"Oh, it's all right, Glaron," she assured. "I'll be fine. I have done this before, remember?"

"Is there anything I can do for you?" he asked.

Ultara started rubbing her arm. She was already feeling a lot of pain. "Just clean this up and meet me back here first thing tomorrow morning."

CHAPTER XIV

THE MEETING

"**G**reat . . . big . . . son of a slarp!" Glaron exclaimed as he entered into the Throne Room and beheld the "altered" Ultara. "You look just like her!" he gasped.

"Well, that is the general idea." Ultara sounded like herself, but didn't look it. Her normally flowing auburn locks were now a tight, silver, up-swept bun and her tall, svelte physique was slouchy and short. Squinty brown eyes—which were all but hidden by thick, orange-rimmed glasses—blinked where large, sultry gold ones had been before, and she'd aged by at least twenty-five years.

"Does it still hurt?" Glaron asked as he circled around her, surveying the transformation from every available angle.

"No," she replied, "altering only really hurts while the most dramatic changes are happening. I used the left over greelan bark to make some tea before bed. I actually slept quite well."

"Ahh . . . yes . . . well . . . that's good," he muttered inattentively, as he scrutinized her left ear at a rather close range.

Ultara jerked away and frowned at him. "Do you mind?" she snapped.

"Sorry! It's just kind of . . . well . . . weird."

Ultara sighed in exasperation. "Just make sure you have everything together when I get back! I would like to look like this for as short a time as possible."

Glaron smiled. "I will. Have fun with your, uh, girl talk!" he sniggered.

Ultara adjusted her simple floral dress, picked up a small peach colored hat and matching handbag and shuffled across the bridge.

Glaron tried to restrain himself, but he just couldn't hold it in. Seeing Ultara as a frumpy, little old lady holding a handbag was too much. He sputtered, and then erupted into wild hysterical laughter.

Ultara rolled her eyes and continued on her way. Once outside the palace, she made a quick check to ensure that no one would see her, started running toward the gate, and shouted, "Mandela Palace!" She vanished with a pop, reappearing behind a large green topiary in the palace's main courtyard. Again she straightened her clothes, took a deep breath, and made her way to the front doors.

"Good Morning, Tur Helene," greeted one of the gardeners, who was busily pruning the hedges.

She nodded politely and continued on.

"Hello, Helene." Another worker rushed up and opened the doors for her.

"Thank you," she mumbled in her best Tur Helene accent. She entered the foyer and looked around. "Couldn't make this easy, and just meet me here, could you, Gracielle?" she whispered.

Just then, a handsome, young guard entered the foyer and rushed up to her. "You must be Tur Helene?" he began.

"Yes, I am," she answered.

"Excellent, ma'am. The ator would like for you to come to the Advantage . . . Adventer . . . Advisitor."

"Advantiere?" she blurted.

"Oh . . . yes . . . that's the one! The Advantiere Room," he said.

The young guard was incredibly good looking—with his dark olive skin, straight, dark brown hair, muscular build, chiseled facial features, and big green eyes—but he was obviously not the brightest man. "You, uh, know where that is, don't you?"

She smiled devilishly at him and replied, "Oh, I think so, but I would love for you to escort me there." She ran her fingers in a walking pattern up his bicep. *Might as well have some fun*, she thought.

"Uh . . . um . . . actually," he stammered nervously, "I . . . I . . . I'm pretty new here. I don't think anyone's shown me where that room is yet."

"Mmmm," she cooed as she leaned against him. "You *are* pretty something, that's for sure. How do you feel about . . . older women?" She put her face very close to his.

"Ma'am?" he squeaked uncomfortably. "I . . . uh . . . I should be getting back to work now."

"Pity," she pouted. "I guess I'll just go meet the ator then, my big, strong, guard." She blew him a playful kiss. "See you around."

He opened his mouth to speak, but nothing came out. He just stood, staring wide-eyed at this little old lady who was throwing herself at him. After a few seconds, he turned around and practically sprinted across the foyer and into one of the hallways.

"That was entertaining!" Ultara sniggered. She fussed with her dress again, and then proceeded to the Advantiere room.

Once she was out of sight, the guard snuck back into the foyer. His encounter with the very forward Tur Helene had him so flustered, that he'd forgotten he was supposed to be leaving the palace in the first place. He rushed to the doors immediately—for fear of being seen by her again—checking over his shoulder as he went. While looking backwards, he failed to notice that someone was on their way in.

He spun around and . . . *thwack*! He and the stranger hit hard and both tumbled to the ground.

"Oh! Pardon me, sir," he yelped, jumping to his feet, and thinking that this was possibly the worst beginning of a day he'd ever experienced. He reached out his hand to help up the man he'd just flattened.

The dark haired gentleman grabbed his hand and pulled himself to standing again. "Don't worry, young man. No harm done." He brushed himself off and introduced himself to the shaken young guard. "Darian of Brashnell."

"Oh, I'm Captain Morringe, sir."

"Delighted, Captain." They shook hands and Darian asked, "Is the atoc back from Westrim, sir?"

"Not yet," Morringe answered, "he's expected back this afternoon."

"Ahhh," Darian nodded.

"The ator is in the Advantiere room, though. It's in that direction." Morringe offered and pointed to the hallway that Ultara had gone down.

Darian smiled, "Thank you, Captain Morringe. You've been most helpful."

The young guard nodded and scrambled down the steps.

"Well," Darian thought aloud, "The ator without her entrusted. It's not often I get an opportunity like that." He strutted across the foyer and added, "Time to turn on the charm."

By the time he got to the Advantiere Room, Gracielle and Ultara were already locked in a heated discussion. Darian heard their shouting voices as he approached and stopped cold in his tracks outside the closed door. "Ultara?" he gasped, recognizing her voice immediately. "How interesting." He leaned against the frame of the door and listened.

"I can't believe you told him! You swore that you'd keep it a secret!"

"I know! But you were nowhere to be found! I needed help! He's my entrusted! It's not like I told a total stranger!" Gracielle's plan to come clean with Ultara was not going as planned. "You can trust him, Ultara. He's a good man."

"Trust him! He wants me dead!" Ultara shrieked.

"Of course he doesn't!"

"Yes, he does! How can I trust him? He's never had evidence that I killed his parents, but just because I happened to be here the day they were killed . . . ."

"The paper the curse was on was pretty incriminating!" Gracielle retorted.

"This is unbelievable! Don't you realize that your entrusted and Darian have been in cahoots for years . . . they have this great plan to bring me to justice?"

"What *are* you talking about?"

"I overheard Jonathan and Darian talking one night."

"Oh you did, did you?" Darian breathed.

Ultara continued. "They made a deal. Darian feeds Jonathan information on me, and in exchange—if they happen to catch me—my beloved former entrusted gets to be my executioner."

"Impossible," Gracielle argued, "Jonathan would never agree to that."

"I *heard* him agree to that!" Ultara insisted. "That's why I started sending

Glaron here! This is just fantastic! He's probably told Darian about the twins!"

"Told me what? What twins?" Darian was contemplating bursting into the room in an attempt to catch Ultara, but it was risky. She was very powerful, and her chances of escaping when he was the only one there to apprehend her were fairly good. Besides, the conversation thus far was quite illuminating. He carefully cracked the door open so he could better hear.

"Ultara, I'm sorry! Honestly, I didn't know . . . and I needed his help." Gracielle's voice was sincere and calmer now. "Listen, I will ask Jonathan what, if anything, has been said to Darian. I was adamant in the beginning that he was not to breathe a word of this to Darian."

Go ahead, Ator . . . why don't you just tell me what this is all about? Darian thought to himself.

Ultara seemed a little calmer now, too. She took a deep breath and reasoned, "Well, Darian may have an advantage over us, I suppose. But he can't get his hands on Audril, and without Audril, he is powerless."

"Without Audril?" Darian breathed.

Just then, two people turned into the far end of the hallway.

Darian quickly turned to leave, but as he did, he kicked over a small box that someone had left outside the room. Several metal brackets spilled from the box and slid noisily across the stone floor. He spun around and dashed away just as quickly as he could.

"What was that?" Gracielle gasped, and rushed over to the door. She peered into the hallway, just missing the last billowing corner of Darian's cloak as it disappeared around the corner. She looked down, saw the scattered brackets, and then turned and looked the other way. Much to her horror, she saw Jonathan walking down the corridor, and with him Tur Helene.

"Oh, no!" she gasped and rushed back to Ultara. "You have to hide . . . now!" She grabbed Ultara by the arm and moved her toward the other side of the room.

"What? Why? What are you doing?"

Gracielle forcefully pulled her along. "Jonathan's coming . . . and Tur Helene!"

Ultara was now moving all by herself, but then suddenly stopped. "Wait,

Gracielle," she chuckled, "this is ridiculous! I'm the vritesse! I can transport, you know."

Gracielle didn't find as much comfort in this as Ultara. "Then do it! Now!" she insisted.

"But . . . you had something you were supposed to tell me! You haven't even . . . ." Ultara didn't have time to finish her thought. The sound of Jonathan's voice came from right outside the door.

"Yes, thank you, Helene. We'll see you tomorrow, then."

"There's not time!" Gracielle whispered frantically. "Just send Glaron . . . the Anaria . . . tomorrow night . . . usual time! I'll just have to tell him instead!"

Ultara was moving toward the back of the room to put as much distance between the atoc and herself as possible. "But wait! I thought the Anaria was destroyed!"

"Don't worry! We can still get in . . . He's coming! Go on!" Gracielle's eyes grew wide as Jonathan started pushing the door open.

Ultara ran toward the back wall of the room "Koria!" she shouted, and disappeared in a blue flash.

"Jonathan!" Gracielle shrieked excitedly in an effort to drown out Ultara's shout. "You're home!" She rushed over to him and threw her arms around his neck.

"Are you okay, Graci? Who was that?" Jonathan asked suspiciously.

Gracielle's heart stopped. "Who?" she asked innocently, trying to buy time to formulate a good excuse. She was not about to tell him that she'd been meeting with Ultara; but if he had seen someone disappear, he would know that it was a Trysta heiress.

"Who?" he blurted. "Darian, that's who! What was he doing here?"

"Darian?" Gracielle was clearly confused. "Darian was here?"

"Yeah! I saw him coming out of this room, Graci. He seemed in an awfully big hurry, too." Jonathan's voice sounded like he'd just caught her with another man. Indeed, Gracielle thought that he must be thinking exactly that.

"What? No, Jonathan! I didn't see . . . ." Gracielle stopped mid-sentence.

"Darian?" she breathed anxiously. "He must've been who kicked over the box in the hall . . . and then he rushed away. Why would he rush away, unless he'd been . . . ?" She looked Jonathan in the eyes and whispered, ". . . eavesdropping."

A look of panic swept across her face. "Please tell me that you've never told Darian about this." She pointed at the Advantiere, which even after almost five years, still glowed brightly on the wall.

"Graci, what is going on?"

"Please, Jonathan," she begged, "you haven't told him about the twins have you . . . or about Audril?"

"Of course I haven't," he answered, "but, if you didn't want him knowing about the Advantiere, this probably wasn't the best room to meet him in." His voice was accusatory again.

"I wasn't meeting him," she insisted. "I think he may have been spying on me!"

"Spying on you? Why would Darian be spying on you?"

At that moment, Gracielle came very close to revealing everything; how she'd been meeting with Glaron all this time on Ultara's orders, and how she'd just seen Ultara in person. She was about to begin her story when a horrifying thought entered her mind. It was what Ultara said before they heard the noise in the hall. *"Without Audril . . . he is powerless."*

"Oh no," she shrieked, "Jonathan, he's after Audril!" She ran past him and out of the room.

"What?" Jonathan turned and chased after her. She was waving her arm towards Audril's bedroom door by the time he caught up. "What is going on?" he panted, trying to catch his breath.

The bedroom door flew open. Kahlie and Audril, who had been reading a story together, both jumped in surprise.

"Momma!" Audril beamed as Gracielle scooped her up and hugged her tightly.

Kahlie looked at Gracielle and then at Jonathan. "Is everything alright, Atoc?" she asked.

"Yes, Kahlie. It's fine." His response assured her that everything was *not* fine. He never called her by her real name, unless he was upset. "May I have a word with you, Ator?" He grimaced at Gracielle and pointed toward the door that led to their chambers.

She set Audril down and nodded like a child who was being punished. Jonathan moved toward the door and Gracielle followed, but before she left, she leaned back to Kahlie and said, "Don't answer the door for anyone! I mean it, no one! I'll explain when I get back."

Kahlie nodded obediently.

The second Gracielle stepped into their room and shut the door, Jonathan began. "Will you please tell me what is going on?" His voice was eerily calm—but that didn't last very long. "I have been dealing with chaos . . . and mud . . . and pain . . . and DEATH FOR MORE THAN FORTY-EIGHT HOURS, GRACIELLE, AND I AM NOT IN THE MOOD FOR GUESSING GAMES!" His voice was now a roar.

Gracielle's instinctive reaction was to yell back—he had no idea what she'd been through either—but she realized that there were more important things to worry about at present. Audril was in very real danger, and she knew it. "I think that Darian overheard me talking about the Advantiere."

"Talking? To who?" Jonathan was still fuming, but at least he wasn't yelling anymore.

"Um . . . uh . . . to myself," she stammered. "I was thinking out loud—reading the Advantiere. I said that Darian might have an advantage over us because he has Ryannon, but I also said something like 'at least he doesn't have Audril, and that makes him powerless.'"

"You said that?" Jonathan didn't seem quite convinced. "And what makes you so sure that he heard you?"

"Right after I said it," she explained, "there was a crash in the hallway. Not only that, but I am *sure* I closed the door when I went into that room—I never leave the door to the Advantiere room open. Anyway, I heard the crash in the hall, and when I went to go see what it was, the door was cracked open."

Jonathan thought for a moment. "I suppose that would explain why he was rushing away."

"Exactly," she sighed. "We need to assign more guards to Audril right away!" Gracielle was clearly worried.

Jonathan nodded. "I'll see to it," He replied, his tone far more comforting now. "You know I've never trusted Darian. I don't think he'd be stupid enough to try anything, though. If he finds out much more, however, it might be too much of a temptation for him." He looked into his entrusted's frightened eyes. "Don't worry, Graci. I'll assign our best guards. Darian won't be allowed within a mile of our little girl!" He stood to leave, but stopped on his way out and kissed Gracielle's cheek. "I'm sorry I yelled."

Meanwhile, back at Trysta Palace, Ultara had undergone the altering process again—to restore her appearance to normal. She told Glaron about the fiasco of a meeting, and how he would have to be the one that Gracielle confided in after all. They were sitting together, wrapping up a few loose ends before she headed back to bed, when suddenly, she stopped talking and jumped to her feet. "Glaron," she gasped, "do you know how the Grasping Curse was delivered to Cristoph and Jocelynne?"

"Uh . . . no," he answered, "no one does. The people who received it are . . . well, they're dead."

"But Gracielle said something this morning! She said that the paper the curse was on was incriminating."

"Yeah . . . so?" Glaron didn't see where this was going.

"What would make a piece of paper incriminating, Glaron?" she asked.

"I dunno. I guess if it was your personal stationery, or had your fingerprints all over it, or if it had your seal on it, or . . . ."

"Exactly!" she interrupted. "It would be pretty conclusive that I was the murderer if my seal was on the paper! Why didn't I realize it before?"

"Realize what?"

"Glaron, do you remember that general who we were going to have executed for treason about two years ago? Oh . . . what was his name? It started with an O, I think?"

"General Omer?" Glaron recalled.

"Yes! Omer . . . Blansten discovered that he'd been spying for Brashnell . . . taking Trysta intelligence directly to Darian."

Glaron interjected, "Yeah, a lot of people were disappointed when he escaped. He wasn't what you'd call a popular fella."

"The morning that Cristoph and Jocelynne were murdered, I was at Mandela Palace checking on Gracielle," Ultara explained.

"I remember."

"It was also the morning Nenia disappeared. Jonathan was acting strange. I thought he and Gracielle were fighting or something. I figured I'd give them a moment alone, so I went to the dining room to get some food."

"And?" Glaron still didn't know what the point was, but it was clear that Ultara had one.

"I was returning to their chambers when I was given the note about Nenia. Guess who delivered it to me?"

Glaron shook his head.

"It was Omer! He handed me a note . . . said it was urgent . . . so I opened it right then and there. It was just a blank piece of paper. He acted like it was an accident." She looked at Glaron, then continued, "He took the blank paper back, handed me the note about Nenia, and then ran off. My fingerprints would have been all over that paper. If he acted quickly, he would have had time to apply the grasping curse and my seal to the paper."

"But, I thought that heiress seals had to be pressed on by the actual . . . um . . . heiress," Glaron questioned.

"That's what most people think, but in reality, it's the fingerprint that creates the seal, not pressure applied by a specific person. Darian knows this. He and I discussed it."

"So you think that Darian sent his spy to kill Cristoph and Jocelynne and frame you for doing it?"

"Exactly."

Glaron furrowed his brow pensively. "But, how did he even know you were going to be there that morning?"

"I don't know." She thought for a minute. "Wait," she blurted, "Omer knew. My calling was supposed to be that day. I'd briefed all of the generals on my mother's death the night before. I gave them all assignments to help with the transition and told them that I would be going to Mandela Palace in the morning and that when I returned I'd be expecting a status report from each of them."

"Whoa," Glaron sighed, "but surely Darian couldn't foresee a rynolt attack, unless . . . ."

Ultara sank down into a chair at her side. "Unless a rynolt didn't attack my daughter . . . but he did! Oh, no," she breathed, "he's doing it, Glaron! He's just waiting for the perfect opportunity. He's going to . . . he knew if he divided us . . . ."

"What Ultara? What's he doing?" Glaron asked anxiously.

"He's going to attack Mandela City."

"What?" Glaron exclaimed, "What makes you think he would do that? It would be crazy for him to go against Mandela! Jonathan has a massive army."

"So does he," she replied. "Listen, Glaron, I know Darian. As soon as he sees an opportune moment, he *will* attack. We're just fortunate it hasn't happened already."

"But what makes you think so?" he tried again.

"When Darian and I were together, we came up with a plan. We were going to join forces after I became vritesse and attack Mandela City. It would give us control over all of Lor Mandela."

"And if you never became vritesse?" Glaron questioned.

"We had a plan for that as well. Listen, I'm not proud of this, Glaron. It actually all started out as a joke . . . a 'what if' kind of scenario. But then we both got wrapped up in it. I don't think Darian's ever let go of the possibility. If he murdered Cristoph and Jocelynne and pinned me for it, his intention clearly was to divide the Mandelans and the Trystas. And why else would he do that, except to divide and conquer?"

"But then why hasn't he done anything yet?" Glaron asked. "Cristoph and Jocelynne were killed almost five years ago."

Fourteen

"I don't know. He must be waiting for something . . . but what?" She dropped her head into her hands. "Unless," she looked back up at Glaron, her golden eyes as big as he had ever seen them. "What if Jonathan did tell him about the Advantiere? What if he knows that it has to be solved by or for Audril, and what if he knows about the twins?" Her eyes grew wide. "If he knew about the twins, he'd know that he needs Nenia . . . alive."

"What are you saying, Ultara?"

"Maybe the reason he hasn't attacked yet is because he hasn't been able to get his hands on Audril. And maybe he didn't actually kill Nenia, but just took her so that he'd have both of the twins."

Glaron felt a little overwhelmed. If Ultara was right, then Darian was plotting something that would lead the people of Lor Mandela to a world wide war.

"Hold on," he sighed, "that still doesn't explain what he's waiting for. I mean, if I were someone like Darian and knew that I just needed one particular person to control the world, I'd do everything in my power to get that person. As far as I know, there's never been an attempt to abduct the atoh. I'm sure her mother would have told me if there had been."

Ultara looked away and muttered, "Surely he understands that the planet is dying. Would he risk losing everything just so he can wait for the right moment?" She turned back to Glaron and shook her head. "I don't know, Glaron. But Darian has always boasted about his patience. Maybe he's just waiting for us to solve the Advantiere for him . . . or something like that. You're right, though. He would do everything he could to get her." She ran her hand through her hair and let out an exasperated sigh. "No, he's got to be holding out for a reason . . . but what?"

Glaron shrugged his shoulders. "It could be anything! At any rate, I have to warn Gracielle about Darian."

"Yes. Tomorrow night when you meet her, and make sure you tell her about Omer, too."

CHAPTER XV
DARIAN'S WAIT COMES TO AN END

It was about four o'clock the following morning when it started, and there was not a resident of Lor Mandela who did not hear it. At first, it was deep and quiet—coming from somewhere far, far away. But as the day progressed, the sound grew…and grew…and grew. By midday, the entire planet was immersed in a loud, mournful, haunting moan that seemed to be coming from the very center of the world. Every person—and in fact, every living thing on Lor Mandela—was set on edge. The sound was unrelenting…unceasing…unnerving. Ultara knew what it meant, as did Gracielle. They knew that the planet didn't have much time left to live. It was groaning in pain as it struggled to maintain the last anemic fragments of its remaining life.

The day developed only to cold and dreary. The sky was dull and colorless with an icy, sickly, green fog hanging just over the dark horizon.

In Brashnell, Darian sat with his back to an enormous, heavily carved, wooden desk, staring out the window at the bleak scene. "Audril . . ." he mumbled to himself, "without Audril I am . . . powerless? Why? Why would a small child be so important to me?" He lowered his face into his hands. "Without Audril . . . ." he moaned.

A sudden rustling outside drew his attention. He stood and walked to the large glass door across the room.

"Audril . . . ." he breathed again shaking his head.

He opened the door and stepped out into a large courtyard surrounded by tall, columnar trees. He shivered, and pulled the dark green jacket he wore tightly around him. "Well, where are you, you wretched animal?"

The trees directly in front of him started to shake and sway.

"Come on!" he demanded.

The trees rustled again throwing hundreds of tiny leaves twisting through the misty air; at the bottom of the trees, the massive leg of an animal suddenly appeared.

The leg was charcoal grey, thick and strong like a huge plow horse, and easily five feet high. Jutting out from the shimmering black hoof were three, long, curved claws that clicked noisily on the gravel ground. The trees shook violently once more, and through them burst the rest of the enormous animal, thrashing its head and prancing nervously.

"Syltar! Relax!" Darian commanded.

The animal approached and lowered his dragon-like head.

Darian reached out and patted him firmly on the neck. "Calm yourself, my pet."

The planet moaned again and Syltar reared up onto his muscular hind legs. The huge, black wings that normally rested at his side like a vampire's cloak, unfolded and slashed at the air.

"All right, then . . . here!" Darian reached behind a green hedge near the door and lifted out a small cage. A little creature zipped around in the cage, screeching wildly.

Syltar reared up again, and roared with excitement.

Darian pulled the small, furry animal from the cage and threw it forcefully skyward.

Syltar watched with his foggy, icy, grey eyes as his prey flew high above him. Once it began to descend, he unfolded his enormous jagged wings, bounded upward and hung in the air just a few inches from the ground. He snatched the little animal in his front teeth, and shook it ferociously back and forth. Then he tossed it back up, and caught it again. Once more, he shook it and hurled it upward; only this time, as it came down, he opened his strong jaws wide, and swallowed the now limp animal in one noisy gulp.

Darian smiled. "Very good. Now, Syltar, will you please calm down and let me think?"

Again a loud groan lifted from the depths of the planet.

Syltar fidgeted a bit in the air but seemed to calm fairly quickly; he lowered to the ground with a thud.

"Frolnisk blood," Darian oozed, "works every time."

Syltar's eyes fluttered shut and loud blasts of air snorted out of his nostrils. He staggered a bit, and then collapsed into a large dark heap.

"Oh, that's a good boy," Darian smirked, and then turned and retreated into the warmth of the indoors. "Cursed animal," he hissed under his breath as he walked back inside.

His thoughts instantly returned to what he'd overheard Ultara say the morning before. He went to the desk, picked up a long black stick and spoke into the end of it. "Omer, get in here!" he insisted.

A young, serious looking Trysta man entered the room almost immediately. "Yes, sir?" Omer brushed a stray strand of straight black hair away from his narrow green eyes. "How may I be of service, Milord?"

Darian couldn't help but smile smugly at the respect and loyalty being shown him. "Omer, who is Glaron?" he asked.

"Glaron?" Omer smirked. "You mean Ultara's little pet? He is her chief advisor . . . the eldest son of Malynda."

"I want him followed. Ultara has been sending him to meet with the ator, and I want to know why," Darian insisted.

"Of course, Milord, I shall see to it myself." Omer was only too delighted to be involved in any plot against Ultara.

"Good." Darian paced back and forth for a minute and then quizzed, "He and Ultara . . . they're close then?" The fires in his eyes blazed intensely.

Omer sensed the jealousy in Darian's voice. He smiled slyly and played along, "Lovers . . . or so I've heard."

Darian's jaw set and a thick vein in his forehead became more prominent. "I see," he fumed. "In that case, Omer, learn what you can and when you have all that you think we can use, feel free to kill him." He turned away from Omer, struggling to control his rage. "That is all, General."

"Yes, sir! It will be my pleasure." Omer bowed and backed out of the room.

He immediately set off for his home to gather a few necessities; a traveling cloak to keep him warm and somewhat hidden, some food in case he was away for an extended period, and his weapon of choice, a vystoran sleeve—a simple silver tube loaded with small blood red disks called vystorans, which were virtually harmless, until they were shot from the sleeve. With a forceful impact, a vystoran would rupture, oozing a runny, slime green substance. The substance would slowly and painfully freeze the internal organs of the victim who had been shot, starting with the heart—regardless of where on the body they'd been hit. Omer checked the vystoran supply in the sleeve, packed it away into a simple black duffel bag, and left quickly for Koria in search of Glaron.

The spirit of the planet continued to groan in agony. The green fog had become denser, as the temperature of the air plummeted. It was early evening now, and the combination of the dreadful moaning and the icy air was keeping almost everyone indoors. Hardly a soul was out, creating the perfect scenario for Omer, who had not been seen by anyone on his way to Koria.

He arrived at the gate of the palace just before sundown. He was hidden behind a large rock, formulating a strategy to get in, when—much to his delight—the gate swung open, and Glaron himself crept out around it.

Glaron glanced nervously around as the iron gate clanked shut. The planet wailed loudly again. "I'm on my way! Hold on," he whispered into the air.

Omer fumbled through his duffel bag and pulled out the vystoran sleeve. He waited until Glaron was several yards away from him, and then began his pursuit. He followed at a safe distance, through the outskirts of Mandela City, jumping behind trees and buildings periodically to stay out of sight. He stopped in back of an old abandoned farm that sat at the end of the city and watched Glaron start across the field toward the Anaria.

Suddenly, a horrific screech; more earsplitting and disturbing than any other sound that had been heard that day, bulleted from the core of the planet. Blasts of wind shot straight upward from the ground, obliterating the fog and ripping apart trees, roofs of buildings, fences—anything not securely anchored.

Omer hurled himself away from the old building he was hiding behind to keep from being hit by a barrage of flying bricks.

The screech lasted for several seconds, twisting pathetically through the evening air, and then, with an eerie abruptness, it stopped. There was nothing but complete and total silence. There was no moaning; no rustling grasses; no wind; no sounds of moving animals; absolute, dark, cold silence.

Glaron breathed heavily, waiting, hoping that the thick quiet would be disturbed by some sound—any sound—but nothing. "Oh, no," he breathed and took off at a full run toward the Anaria.

Omer quickly followed.

Gracielle met Glaron at the Anaria's entrance. She grabbed him by the shirt and yanked him inside. "Watch out," she warned, "there's still a lot of glass." They hurried down the glass-covered tunnel. "Hurry! There's not much time." The sound of the crunching glass shards beneath their feet was strangely amplified by the overwhelming silence of the planet.

"Gracielle, what's going on?" Glaron asked frantically. "Why is it so quiet?"

She spun toward him. "Do you have the book with you? We need to get this thing figured out, *now!*"

"Here," Glaron glanced around at the shredded remains of the once elegant room. He handed the small brown book to Gracielle, who grabbed it and started anxiously leafing through it.

Meanwhile, Omer inched his way down the tunnel towards them. He knew that he would be heard if he stepped on any glass. He took off one of his gloves, bent down and carefully swept a section of the floor clear with it before taking each step. He didn't have to strain at all to hear every single thing that Glaron and Gracielle were saying.

"Gracielle, I have to tell you something! It's Darian. Ultara thinks he is after Audril."

"Me too," she replied, "I think he heard us talking yesterday."

"She thinks Jonathan told him the . . . wait! What?" Glaron blurted, "You think he . . . yesterday?"

"Wait," Gracielle questioned, "what are you talking about?"

Just then, the ground jolted violently, knocking them both to their knees.

The jolt threw Omer as well, tossing him into a pile of sharp glass fragments. "Ahhhuhhh!" he wailed pitifully, as he pulled himself up from the ground. His voice reverberated against the wooden cave walls.

"What was that?" Glaron whispered, as he helped Gracielle back to her feet.

Gracielle slapped her hand over his mouth. "Jonathan," she mouthed and pulled Glaron towards the back of the room.

Horrific thoughts of what the atoc would do upon finding him—a Trysta man—there alone with Gracielle raced through his mind. "Not good . . . not good!" he muttered under his breath.

They maneuvered around piles of tattered books and broken glass to the back wall; Gracielle waved one of her hands across the wall and a sprawling maze of tangled tree-root tunnels instantly appeared where the wall had been. The floor cracked behind them and they spun around to see Omer staggering into the room.

"Even worse! Even worse!" Glaron yelled as Omer aimed the vystoran sleeve directly at him. Gracielle flicked her wrist, and the floor beneath Omer bumped hard, throwing him off balance. A vystoran zipped from the sleeve and raced across the room; it smacked against the wall above her head. Glaron grabbed her by the arm and pulled her backward into one of the tunnels. They dashed down the tunnel and Omer pursued.

"Glaron, here! Take my hand! It's easy to get lost in here," Gracielle instructed as they ran further into the maze. She yanked him around one sharp turn...then another. . .then another, and then stopped and motioned for him to keep quiet. They could hear Omer's heavy footsteps directly on the other side of the wall. His pace slowed as he tried to figure out which of the many paths they had taken.

He took a few slow steps, and as he did, Glaron saw his shadow heading in their direction.

Gracielle lifted her arm across Glaron's chest, and gently coaxed him back against the wall of roots behind them. She pushed him further back until he was smashed uncomfortably against the jutting roots.

Omer turned the corner, peered down the tunnel and looked almost directly at them, but the tangled shadows of the roots camouflaged them completely, hiding them from his view. He squinted down the corridor, and then retreated slowly back around the wall.

Gracielle waited a few seconds and then pressed her hand against the other side of the tunnel. It dissolved away and another long, dark corridor appeared. "Go straight," she whispered, "don't take any turns. It goes to Koria."

"But, what about you? Where are you gonna go?" he mouthed.

"I'll be all right. The palace is this way." She pointed toward another tangled passage. "I'll figure out where we can meet again tomorrow."

"Where are you, Ator?" Omer's sinister voice taunted from what sounded like just a few feet away.

"Get out of here!" Gracielle insisted quietly, "Go!"

Glaron watched as Gracielle took off toward the palace, and then reluctantly sped off in the direction she had indicated.

In the meantime, Omer was feeling a little nervous about being able to navigate his way back out of the labyrinth. He decided that it would be unwise to continue pursuing Glaron and Gracielle any further.

He started back out of the maze, but suddenly noticed an object lying on the ground a few feet in front of him. As he got closer, he could see that it was a small, brown notebook. He picked it up and flipped through the pages.

There were bizarre lines written neatly on each page, surrounded by notes, scribbled in a different hand. He started on the first page and read aloud, *"Destruction from Twins, and so it must end."* The other notes on this page were, *"Lor Mandela's spirit dying—caused by Anika."* and *"Ryannon and Nenia?"* He didn't know what it meant, but he knew who Anika was, and that Ryannon was Darian's son, and Nenia was Ultara's dead daughter. "I wonder," he began, "if this nonsense would be worth anything to *His Majesty*." He rolled his eyes at the mention of Darian then tucked the little notebook in his cloak and started back to Brashnell. The strange silence still hung eerily in the night air as he made his way back.

It was very late when Omer finally reached Darian's mansion. He would have waited until morning to report, but he knew that if, by chance, Darian found some value in this little notebook, the consequences of him not sharing his discovery immediately would be far worse than the consequences of waking Darian from his sleep. Luckily though, Darian had not yet retired. Omer found him in the same place he'd left him earlier that day—standing in front of the large desk in the mansion's study.

"Back so soon, Omer. I assume he's dead," Darian raised his eyebrows and added, "or that you have at least, brought me something relevant."

Omer reached for the book. "I assure you, Milord, Glaron will be eliminated. Today just wasn't the day. I hope, however, that this will be helpful."

Darian didn't look at all pleased. He ripped the notebook out of Omer's hands and started studying its pages. As he read, his eyes grew wide and the fires that danced in them surged and flared. "Anika? Anika caused this?" he hissed. "And Audril's the only one who can fix it." His mind was racing. "No wonder Ultara said . . . ."

He lowered the book and looked at Omer who was relieved that his findings seemed to be well-received. "General, how many battalions are fully battle-ready?"

"Three hundred and twelve, sir," he smiled proudly. Roughly two hundred thousand soldiers."

An evil smile spread slowly across Darian's thin lips. "And what is the size of the Mandelan Army?"

"We've confirmed nearly the same amount . . . two hundred thousand," he answered.

"Yes," Darian paced the floor and reasoned aloud, "but thanks to my son, our weapons are far superior."

"Ryannon's technical advances in weaponry are, indeed, unparalleled, sir," Omer agreed.

"General," Darian's eyes burned excitedly, "ready Syltar for me and gather the Commanders for an emergency briefing!" He smiled and added, "Prepare your troops, Omer. Tomorrow we ride for Mandela City."

CHAPTER XVI
THE JOURNAL OF KAHLIE

My name is Kahlie. I am a servant in the Palace of Borloc, in the city of Mandela, first city of the beautiful world of Lor Mandela. I have been the companion servant of Ator Gracielle Borloc since I was fourteen years old. Shortly after I arrived at the palace, the ator gave birth to her beloved daughter, Audril. My duty has been to care for them both.

I am writing this now because something very strange has happened. I don't know what exactly, but I'm sure that I was the only witness—at least the only witness who lived through it.

This morning, Ator Gracielle and I were walking near Mystad Lake, attempting to discuss plans for the upcoming Celebration of Light. The ator said something about how she hoped that Lor Mandela would make it to the Celebration, which I thought was an unusual comment. Sure, there were some weird things happening, but it seemed like she was afraid the entire world was going to fall apart. When I asked her what she meant, she just smiled, and said that she was being overly dramatic. But, I could tell she was really worried. It showed on her face.

She started talking about the Celebration again—about the flowers she wanted for the paths—but then she stopped short and stared at Tur Helene, (mine and Audril's private teacher) and Audril. They were down by Mystad Lake, studying small drifter bugs that played on the grasses near the water. She stood motionless for several moments and stared at her daughter as if there were nothing else in the world. I glanced from her to Audril and back to her again. I studied her expression, wondering what was behind her unusually serious mood and this sudden break in our conversation.

After what seemed like several minutes, she grabbed my hand. Her gaze was still fixed on her little girl.

"Kahlie," she said, with an expression of utmost concern on her face, "promise me something?"

"Anything you wish, Ator," I replied.

"Have you ever met Darian of Brashnell?" she asked me, strengthening her grip slightly when she said his name.

I told her I hadn't, but I'd heard of him.

She said, "I fear that Darian is not to be trusted. We've tried to keep an alliance with him, but he is dangerous— more so now than ever before."

I nodded and listened as she went on.

"He's after Audril. He overheard me telling someone that Audril is the key to stopping all of this chaos, and now he wants her so he can gain control over everything!"

I didn't understand. I was trying to figure out a polite way to ask her what she was talking about, when she looked me right in the eyes and said, "DO NOT let anything happen to Audril, Kahlie."

"Of course, Ator," I answered, "I would guard her with my own life if necessary."

She acted as if she hadn't heard me at all. "You have no idea just how important she is; Lor Mandela will die without her. You have to . . . ." She stopped in the middle of her sentence and stared in shock at the hills behind the lake. And that's when I heard the noise.

It started as a low hum that steadily grew to a thunderous roar. On the horizon, in every direction, a thin line of black started to appear. It was then that I realized what was happening. The army of Brashnell was flowing over the foothills, spilling into Mandela like a gigantic swarm of bees.

Terror gripped every part of me as countless thousands of Warriors and beasts—all adorned in glistening black—moved closer and closer.

Gracielle's words, "DO NOT let anything happen to Audril," echoed over again and again in my head.

I felt like my soul and body had somehow separated, as I picked Audril up with one hand, grabbed Gracielle by the arm with the other, and pulled her with me toward the palace.

Gracielle was yelling back at Tur Helene to get to the plaza and rally the troops.

I could tell that she was only hearing part of what the ator was yelling at her, but she understood enough to run toward town.

As the great army grew nearer, the thunder was punctuated by the distinct sounds of hoof beats and clanging armor.

Gracielle spun around and waved her arm. A huge crack opened up in the ground in front of us, separating us, at least momentarily, from the oncoming horde. I looked back to the town, and saw hundreds of our own soldiers running at full-speed toward the palace.

I grabbed Gracielle's arm again, and pulled her across the courtyard. I had the feeling that had I not been there, she would have stayed and tried to take on Darian's Army all by herself.

The moment we reached the stone steps, she began to scream out for Atoc Jonathan. We ran through the large double doors, into the grand marble foyer. The atoc was nowhere to be seen.

Gracielle pulled me toward a hallway that led to the kitchens and the servant's quarters. I was still holding Audril, who was crying and obviously very frightened. Gracielle was frantically trying to find the atoc. She kept shouting his name, but there was no reply.

As we moved down the long hall, I saw a man at the other end of it, running toward us. He was in full battle armor and a cloak with a hood so we couldn't tell who he was— or at least, I couldn't.

Gracielle let go of me and flew down the hallway as though she had wings on her feet. "Jonathan!" she shouted.

When she reached him, the atoc embraced her quickly and motioned back toward the kitchens. He quickly pushed the three of us behind a large cupboard and told us to stay put.

At that moment, I realized that the battle had not only reached the palace, it was in full-force all around us. Outside of our kitchen, soldiers were killing each other with swords, vystorans, spike darts and axes. Others— servants and soldiers alike—were being slaughtered as they tried to escape.

"Kahlie," Gracielle's whisper startled me. "Inside that closet behind us there is a door. It's in the floor, under the shelves that line the back wall. It leads to tunnels that run under ground. The tunnel on the left will take you to the Anaria. Get Audril and GO! Jonathan and I will be right behind you!"

"But, Ator," I protested, "YOU and your family must get to safety! You're the last Borlocs! I can create a diversion so that you and Audril won't be seen, and so the atoc can break free as well. I would never forgive myself if I left and anything happened to one of you!"

I'd no sooner finished speaking when at least a dozen Black Warriors burst in from a door at the back of the kitchen.

"KAHLIE, GO NOW!" Gracielle was pushing me toward the closet.

Although the atoc was extremely outnumbered, he was battling ferociously. He was taking down Brashnell warriors as quickly as they were coming at him.

More Black Warriors ran in through another back door directly behind us.

We were no longer hidden. In addition, all of our escape routes—including the one in the closet—were cut off.

Gracielle's eyes glowed bright blue and three of the Brashnell soldiers fell screaming to the ground.

Atoc Jonathan picked up a knife from one of the tables, and flung it at one of the Black Warriors near us, hitting him squarely in the back of the neck. He fell to the ground, and at that moment I knew what I needed to do.

I lunged toward the fallen warrior and grabbed his sword. I don't recall ever handling a sword in my past, but I wielded it as if I'd been dueling all of my life. Nothing had ever come so naturally to me.

One by one, I defeated the Black Warriors.

As I turned to face another attacker, I realized that one of them had made their way to where Gracielle and Audril were.

Gracielle was trying to shove Audril into the closet, as still another of Darian's soldiers was charging toward them. Gracielle turned to face them when another one appeared behind her.

I ran for him as fast as I could, but it was too late. He raised his sword in the air, and thrust it forcefully into Gracielle's back, and she fell, lifeless, to the ground.

Jonathan screamed and charged at the smiling warrior as I stood motionless; too shocked to do anything.

The Brashnellan soldier looked at Jonathan and then at Audril, who'd run crying into a corner.

A look of panic swept over the atoc's face as he realized that his daughter had become the new target of this evil warrior.

Both the atoc and the Brashnellan Warrior ran toward Audril. I charged toward her also, but I was twice as far away from her as the two men were.

Atoc Jonathan reached her first, sliding on his knees and grabbing her around the shoulders. He turned and put her behind him, but as he did, the Warrior raised his sword high in the air and lunged toward him.

I watched in horror as the enemy's sword thrust downward toward Jonathan's skull.

All of a sudden, there was a loud dull THUD and time seemed to stand still. I saw every detail of what was going on around me. Audril was back in front of the atoc, and had her head buried in his chest; there were two more warriors near the door to the hall who stood watching as the atoc was about to be slain; and Gracielle lay on the floor, her lifeless eyes staring into the heavens.

At that moment, Audril turned around and looked right at me. She nodded and raised her small arm into the air; my arm flew into the air with hers. I didn't have any control over it—she was controlling me! She opened her mouth to speak, but as she did, the words yelled out of my mouth instead. "ELAHK E BER LOR MANDELA!"

I had no idea what I'd just said, what it meant or where it had come from. But, as soon as the words left my lips, there was a startling CRACK and a flash of blue light . . . and everything was gone! The atoc was gone . . . Audril was gone . . . The warriors were all gone. All that remained was my dear Gracielle's body . . . and me.

I stood alone in a quiet kitchen, in a quiet palace. I let the sword slip out of my hands; the only sound that echoed through the halls was its clanging against the brick floor.

That is all I know. I am frightened, and I am alone. I know I must leave the palace, but I fear what I will find. I've written this because I don't know what will happen to me once I do leave.

If you are reading this, YOU MUST TRY TO FIND OUT WHAT HAPPENED TO AUDRIL! PLEASE! Her mother said that Lor Mandela will die without her. We need to find her—no matter what—please . . . find Audril!

Part Two

And So
It
Must End

CHAPTER XVII

THE SWIM

It was a phrase Maggie Baker had heard a million times. Her father, Nathan seemed especially skilled at repeating it. "Be careful what you wish for, Smaggs. You just might get it."

Despite his warning, Maggie went right on wishing. She longed for something—anything that would exalt her from the mundane, non-eventful, duller-than-dirt existence she had come to despise. Somewhere deep inside her, she felt that she was destined for so much more than the commonplace and her dad's repetitious recital of the tired old adage only made her crave excitement all the more. Maggie didn't realize, however, that her dad's over-used cliché was about to become a surprisingly accurate premonition. "Be careful what you wish for, Smaggs. You just might get it."

It all began at quarter past four in the afternoon on a sweltering Friday in August. Maggie's Godfather, Dr. Paul Brockman, who had been staying with them for the last week, was packing to return home to Connecticut when he received a phone call from an officer of the Glenhill, Iowa Police Department.

Now, he found himself standing in the kitchen of the Bakers' old Victorian farm house in the midst of a situation which, despite his years of training as a physician, was nonetheless quite awkward.

Before him stood a soaking wet Maggie clothed in nothing, save a faded blue bath towel (hence the awkwardness.) Her arms were folded, and there was a hint of indignation on her slightly freckled face.

"What on Earth were you thinking, Maggs?" scolded the doctor, trying not to look in the wrong place or appear too unnerved by Maggie's near-nakedness. "I thought you had more common sense than to do something this crazy?"

Maggie tucked a sopping black curl behind her ear and plopped dramatically onto a pumpkin-colored, vinyl dining chair. "Oh, please! C'mon, Doc. I don't see what the big deal is. It's a hundred and three out, and that pit of a house out by the pond has been vacant for almost two years; nobody would've even seen us if it hadn't been for Lorrine. Besides, what else is there to do in Glenhill? Seriously . . . life here is absolutely, nauseatingly boring! If I didn't at least try to mix it up, I'd keel over from a lack of stimulation!"

"Ahhhh, so I see we're still on the 'my life is so boring' kick." The doctor breathed a heavy sigh. "Ya know, Boo, sometimes boring can be good."

"Uh, yeah, right," snipped Maggie, "well, my life is way too boring. I mean, how much more blah could it be? I live in Dullsville, U.S.A.; I go to Ho Hum High; my dad is a freakin' accountant, for heaven's sake! Face it, Doc; I am the Mistress of Mediocre!"

Dr. Brockman choked on a laugh. "Mistress of Mediocre, huh?" He rolled his emerald eyes and shook his head. "Now I see why they voted you Vice President of the Drama Club."

"Ha, ha," Maggie grimaced, "ya know, none of this would have happened if Miss Perfectly Perfect Lorrine would've just come with us. She's supposed to be our friend, but the first time we try to do anything even remotely adventurous, she runs home and tattles. So *not* cool!"

"Oh, come on, now. Don't go blaming this all on Lorrine," he rebuked. "It isn't her fault you made a poor decision, Boo. She was just looking out for . . . ."

"WHAT! You're kidding me, right?" Maggie blurted, jumping up from the chair—her fair face reddening with rage. "Why don't you get it? We were just trying to have a little fun!"

She moved around the table until she was uncomfortably close to Dr. Brockman. "I am *so sick* of this dinky little town, and my pathetic excuse of a life!"

The doctor took a step backward but Maggie quickly compensated by stepping forward again. "Nothing *ever* happens here!" she continued bellowing. "You . . . you got to travel all over the world when you were my age! But if I want any excitement, I have to make it myself! And then you just say . . . you can stand there and act . . . how could you? I thought you cared!"

She stomped hard on the floor, causing the tucked-in corner of her bath towel to un-tuck and slip downward. Frantically, she grabbed at the loosening wrap, but to no avail. The edge of the towel slid through her fingers and dropped to the floor.

Dr. Brockman slapped his hands over his eyes and turned away.

Maggie shrieked and snatched up the towel. A flood of crimson washed across her face, as she rushed from the kitchen, both mortified and infuriated.

After a few seconds, Dr. Brockman cautiously peeked out through his fingers to see if the coast was clear, and then lowered onto one of the garage sale chairs and ran his hand through his sandy blonde hair. "How does this happen?" he sighed. "How do I get myself roped into these things?"

Just then, the sound of a sickly car engine sputtered outside the storm door, making a loud *clunk* as it came to a stop. The sound was followed by the unpleasant screech of the driver's door swinging open, and the equally unpleasant screech of it swinging back shut.

A frantic-looking, floppy-haired man in his early forties raced up to the door. In his hands he carried a disheveled pile of papers and an old black brief case that looked to have mustard stains splattered across it. He made a spastic effort to push the door latch with his elbow, but when that failed, he angrily kicked the door open with his foot.

"Where is she?" he asked, dropping three or four papers onto the black and white tile floor as he tripped across the threshold. "Where is my daughter, the felon?"

"Now, just relax, Nathan," answered Dr. Brockman. "She's upstairs getting dried off and dressed." He took the papers and briefcase from his friend, and motioned for him to sit down.

Nathan smoothed the front of his orange plaid shirt and ignored Doc's invitation to sit. Instead, he anxiously circled the kitchen table. "This is the last straw, Paul. Her with her 'boring this' and 'dinky that'! There are plenty of fun things to do in Glenhill, ya know? Things that don't involve trespassing and nudity—but nooo! Let's just frolic around like . . . like . . . like naked nudists!"

"Oh c'mon, Nate," the doctor replied. "Don't be too hard on her. She's pretty embarrassed. Besides, she's already had an earful from me."

"Well," Nathan sneered and glared at the ceiling, "that means she still has another ear to be filled."

"Wh . . . what?" gulped Dr. Brockman, choking on a chuckle. "Did you hear what you just said?" Nathan stared blankly at him for a moment and sniggered; then they both erupted into full-fledged laughter.

Maggie, who was now clothed in faded blue jeans and a dark plum t-shirt, sat on the edge of her bed upstairs listening to the raucous guffawing that permeated the floor and walls of the old house. "Unbelievable," she breathed, "what a couple of dorks." She stood and walked over to the open window and looked out past the gnarled maple tree that grew near the house. "And they say I have mood swings!"

Just then, a whisper—louder than was needed—hissed out from behind the maple's massive trunk. "Maggs . . . pssst! Maggs!"

"Bridge?" Maggie answered. "Shhh!"

A tall, willowy blonde with gleaming brown eyes and a mouth full of braces peered out around the tree. "Get down here. I have something to tell you," she whispered, once again more than a little too loudly.

"Bridgette! Honestly. You whisper louder than most people talk!"

Maggie could still hear her dad and Dr. Brockman talking and snickering downstairs. She glanced over her shoulder to make sure her door was shut, and then climbed out onto a large branch that hugged the house just below her window.

Skillfully, she scooted across the length of the branch and alongside the rickety old tree house that her non-mechanically inclined father built for her when she was seven. The only structurally sound part of the crooked little house was a chain ladder he had purchased ready-made. Maggie scaled down the ladder and, skipping the bottom rung, dropped to the ground in front of Bridgette.

"Hiya!" Bridgette beamed and gave her a hug and a playful peck on the cheek. "So, how long you in for?"

"Don't know yet," answered Maggie. "He's in the kitchen talking to Doc about his criminal daughter and laughing it up over her naked nudity."

Bridgette's eyes lit up. "Doc's still here?" she asked. "Oh, that's good. He always takes your side."

Maggie frowned. "The only reason it's good that Doc's still here is because you think he's cute. And besides, I'll have you know, it sounded like he was taking Lorrine's side—not mine."

"Ewww! I do *not* think Doc is cute!" Bridgette retorted. "He's ancient! Maybe he's cute for my mom, or my grandma, but not . . . oh, wait! Lorrine! That's why I came over. Lorrine wasn't the one who snitched!"

"Huh?" Maggie asked, "Whatta you mean? Who else could it have been?"

Bridgette explained. "Well, I heard that *totally hot* cop—the one who helped you out of the pond . . ." Maggie blushed violently, ". . . tell my mom that a realtor from Cedar Rapids brought a couple of investor guys from Georgia to look at the house. They're the ones who saw us. Apparently one of the suits saw more than he bargained for and called the cops."

Maggie blushed violently, again.

"So we can't be mad at Lor . . . ."

Before Bridgette was able to finish, Nathan's voice rang out from around the back of the house. "Margaret Amanda Baker, come down here! Now!"

Maggie reacted quickly and began a rapid ascent of the chain ladder. "See ya at school Monday, Bridge," she called back quietly.

Doc poked his head around the corner of the house and whispered, "Hurry up! I'll try to stall."

Bridgette giggled and batted her lashes.

"Ancient, huh?" groaned Maggie, who was already working her way across the big branch.

The doctor paid no attention to either of the girls, but instead turned and rushed back into the house.

Bridgette grinned in his direction as he darted out of sight. "Bye," she mumbled, waving an airy hand toward Maggie while staring dreamily at where the doctor had been.

Maggie nimbly slipped through the window and ran to her dresser. She grabbed her MP3 player from the top drawer, crammed the earphones into her ears, and dove for her bed—landing not two seconds before her dad stormed into the room.

"Dad?" she sat up and looked at him in faux-surprise while she tugged the earphone from one ear. "Did you knock?"

"No," he replied, "I was calling for you to come downstairs."

She motioned toward the earphone that was dangling at her chest and shrugged. "Sorry, couldn't hear ya."

"Well, can you hear me now?" he barked, placing both fists angrily onto his hips.

"Yes, Daddy," she replied, "but are you sure you want to talk about this now? You seem upset." The words had no sooner left her lips when she realized she probably shouldn't have said them.

Nathan's eyes bulged in their sockets and the possibility of steam hissing from his ears seemed to increase by the second, but then suddenly, and much to Maggie's surprise, he appeared to calm down.

"No," he began in a subdued tone, "I'm not upset. I'm confused." He started pacing back and forth in front of Maggie. "I'm confused because I seem to remember a certain young lady dragging me into The Edge Boutique in Glenhill Galleria to show me this *adorable* little swimsuit that she absolutely had to have. I also remember telling this young lady that there was no way on this green Earth that I was gonna spend sixty-four dollars on a swimsuit. But," he continued, "this particular young lady looked at me with big, blue, puppy dog eyes, and pouted and whined until finally, I gave in."

He stopped pacing and looked at Maggie who was doing her best to appear guilty.

"Evidently . . . since you prefer to swim without a suit . . . THIS WAS MONEY ILL-SPENT!" His tone was no longer calm and subdued.

"Dad, I . . . ."

"No, Maggie! I really don't wanna hear it! The way I see it, you owe me sixty-four dollars plus tax, and you will earn this by spending the next four Saturday afternoons cleaning Mr. Pratt's office for him."

"Dad, you're being ridiculous!" she protested. "I'm supposed to go to Omaha with Bridgette next weekend, and my birthday's the Saturday after that! Why can't you just ground me like a normal parent?"

Nathan smirked triumphantly. "Because I know what gets to you, Smaggs, and grounding usually aint it! Besides, I'm not a normal parent."

"Oh, you can say that again," she groaned as she slumped down onto her bed.

Nathan sat down next to her. "Ya know, Smaggs. What you did could've been dangerous. What if some sicko woulda seen you—or what if the boys from school get wind of this? You'll never live it down."

"Boys from school?" Maggie smirked. "The opinions of twelve nerds, twenty-five dumb jocks, and six druggies don't really matter, Dad. Besides, I've known them all since we were little. None of them would dare harass me . . . not with the dirt I could dish out."

Nathan just looked at her and shook his head. "Just promise me you won't do anything like this again," he pleaded. "I'm not a huge fan of being called home early from work by the Glenhill PD."

"Fine," Maggie moaned.

He held out a hand and helped her to her feet. "Alright then. C'mon. I've gotta get Doc to the airport."

Downstairs, Doctor Brockman was sprawled out on the big, brown, living room sofa watching TV, but sat up and clicked off the television when he saw them coming. Three tan hound's-tooth bags sat on the floor near his feet. "We all good now?" he asked smiling.

"Yeah, we're good." Maggie looked at her dad and nodded. "I just came down for a Doc Brock hug to tide me over 'til next time. You *are* coming back for my birthday, aren't you?"

"Of course, Boodle! I wouldn't miss it," he replied as he wrapped his arms around her and lifted her off the ground. "Oh, hey, that reminds me. What would Madame like for big number one-seven?"

"Well," she answered coyly, "maybe a diamond, or a hot little sports car, or a private jet. Ya know . . . teenager stuff."

"Hmm," Dr. Brockman played along. "I was thinking just a small gift this year. Like a yacht or a Caribbean island or something."

"Oh, I understand, money's a little tight," she giggled. "Well, I s'pose that'll have to do."

She leaned forward, and pretended to kiss him on the cheek, but instead whispered, "Thanks for calming down the accountant."

Dr. Brockman gave her another quick squeeze. As he and Nathan picked up the suitcases and headed for the front door, he called back, "Anything for the Mistress of Mediocre."

Maggie smiled and followed them as far as the porch, waving as they drove away toward the Des Moines International Airport. A twinge of disappointment floated through her, as it usually did whenever Doc left. She viewed his visits as a much-needed break from the endless monotony that was her life.

True, he wasn't some rich, famous tycoon from an exotic locale, but he had managed to gain some notoriety in his profession, and was from the most populous city in Connecticut, which gave their dear family friend an air of glamour in Maggie's eyes.

She sighed and slouched back into the house, anticipating the inevitable return to what she called "small town stale-ity"—and stale it was.

The following week was even more boring than usual. Bridgette had been grounded for the escapade at the pond, so beyond going to school, Maggie barely left the house.

By the time Saturday finally rolled around, she was actually looking forward to her cleaning punishment at Mr. Pratt's office.

The job probably should have only taken about two hours, but Maggie dragged it out to three. It was early afternoon when she arrived home, and had just begun sifting through a pile of mail in the kitchen, when Nathan's cell phone buzzed on the counter.

"Yikes," she complained, picking it up and checking the caller ID, "when will he learn that he can take this thing with him?

"Daaaa-aaaad!" she yelled out into the backyard where Nathan was mowing the lawn. "Doc's on the phone!"

Nathan hollered back over the roar of the mower, "Okay, honey, I'll be there in just a sec."

She flipped the phone open and answered it cheerfully. "Hey, Doc. What's new?"

His reply was short and uncharacteristically serious. "Boo, I need to talk to your dad. It's important."

"Er, yeah . . . okay," she answered, "he'll be here in just a . . . oh wait, here he is."

Nathan came through the old storm door. He was covered in grass clippings and patches of dirt, and his straight black hair was matted to the sides of his head with sweat. He smiled exhaustedly at Maggie and reached out for the phone.

She handed it to him with a perplexed look on her face, shrugged her shoulders and then ducked out into the living room.

"Paul, muh-man!" greeted Nathan as he brushed a bead of sweat from his brow with the back of his hand. "Whaz up?"

"Nathan? Are you okay? I mean . . . how are the two of you doing?" Doc asked. His voice was strangely intense and urgent. "Are you all right? Is Maggie all right?"

"Yeahhh," Nathan answered slowly, "shouldn't we be?"

"You're sure there's nothing wrong?"

"Um, Paul, what's going on?" Nathan quizzed. There was something disturbing about the way his friend was interrogating him. "We're just fine. Why are you acting so . . . er, bothered?"

Doc's voice softened a bit. "Good . . . good," he sighed, "I'm glad to hear it. I know this sounds nuts, but I just had a feeling that something was wrong."

"You had a feeling? Yeah, that does sound nuts."

"I know," he continued. "I thought so too. But I just couldn't shake it—that feeling. I had to call, just to be sure."

"Well, thanks for your concern, but everyone's perfectly fine here." Nathan smiled at Maggie as she came back into the kitchen to get a glass of water. She poured one for herself and one for him and sat down at the table to see if she could glean any information regarding Doc's unusual mood.

"So, did you just call to see if we're . . . ?"

Bang! Suddenly, a loud crash echoed through the house. Maggie froze mid-drink; her azure eyes widened.

"What was that?" Nathan asked as he rose to his feet and started toward the living room door.

Maggie followed.

"What was what?" Dr. Brockman's voice cried out from the phone.

"Nothing. Something just fell upstairs," Nathan reassured.

Boom! This time, a deep, heavy thud rattled through the floor above their heads.

"Okay . . . something just fell upstairs, again."

"Nathan!" Doc shrieked into the phone, "Get out of the house! Call the police! Where's Maggie?"

"Paul," Nathan snapped, "calm down! I'm sure it's nothing. Maggie's right here. She's fine."

"Nathan, listen to me! Take Maggie and get out of the house! Don't go up there! I mean it. Get out! I'm hanging up right now so you can call the police!"

With that, there was a click and the phone went silent.

CHAPTER XVIII

INTRUDERS

Nathan paused halfway up the stairs and stared at the cell phone in his hand. *What if Paul's right?* He thought to himself. *What if we're in some sort of danger? Maybe I should . . . wait a second! This is absurd!* He shook his head and continued climbing the staircase.

Thud-dump! Another loud noise sounded from down the hall. Maggie quickly ran up behind him. She put her hands on his shoulders, squeezing a little harder than was comfortable.

"Hey Smaggs, did you leave your window open? I bet a squirrel's gotten in again. The branches have grown kinda close to . . ."

He stopped suddenly.

"Dad, wha . . ."

"Shhhh!" Nathan blurted, thrusting his hand up in front of her face. His eyes were wide with panic—and Maggie was about to discover why.

"Hey, look! I found it." An unfamiliar man's voice sounded from somewhere down the hall.

Maggie's heart pounded in her chest and a sense of horror washed over her. Frantically, she started jabbing her dad repeatedly in the shoulder.

"Hah! I knew it," another man replied.

Nathan breathed heavily, but didn't move—despite Maggie's desperate poking, he stood frozen in place, listening.

"I knew it was them; this proves it." The stranger's voice was low and gruff.

The second man, who sounded younger than the first, asked, "Is that

Tab . . .?"

"Shhh! Yes!" the gruff man answered. "We'll have to show this to Ultara. There won't be any question, now."

Nathan looked questioningly at Maggie. She stopped poking him and shook her head wildly back and forth.

All at once, the husky voice became louder and clearer as Maggie's door began to creak open. "He and his daughter . . . where are they now?"

The other man responded, "They're downstairs."

"Perfect," the gruff man answered, "let's go."

Nathan jumped. "Go on," he whispered insistently. He turned and pushed Maggie. "Go . . . go . . . go!" he continued urging as they sprinted down the stairs and out the front door. Once outside, he pulled Maggie across the driveway and behind a privet hedge, flipped open his phone, and dialed 911.

"Hello? Yes. There's someone in my house!" He glanced around the hedge to make sure they hadn't been followed. "Yessss!" He kept his voice low. "They're still in there! No . . . no, we're outside. My daughter and I got out of there. We're in the bushes!"

Maggie curled up with her back pressed against the hedge. She was shaking and praying out loud—this was not *at all* what she had in mind when she had wished for a less boring life.

"Yes ma'am, it's 2163 East Cedar." He stayed on the line with the 911 operator until a Glenhill Police car squealed around the corner and screeched into the drive.

A tall, muscular officer stepped out and walked toward him. "Mr. Baker?"

"Yeah, that's me," Nathan answered, bolting out from behind the bushes and stumbling awkwardly across the driveway. "Sir, there are men in my house. At least two of 'em, upstairs! I thought maybe it was squirrels, but my daughter and I . . ." He pointed to Maggie whose dark curls were barely visible over the hedge, "We heard voices. So, ya know, it couldn'ta been squirrels."

Another short, muscular officer stepped from the squad car and joined them. "Okay, Mr. Baker, just relax. We'll check this out." He put his hand up in

Nathan's face. "You'd better wait here, sir." Both officers drew their guns and entered the house.

Neither Nathan nor Maggie had any intention of following the gun-toting police officers back inside. They were both sufficiently spooked, and perfectly content to wait outside, as they had been instructed to do.

After more than twenty-five minutes, the shorter officer stepped out onto the front porch, and rubbed his shaved head. "Uh . . . Mr. Baker? It appears that there was an intruder in your house."

Maggie, who had finally come out from her hiding place behind the privets, looked at him as though that was one of the stupidest things she'd ever heard. "Yeah, duh," she snipped, "my dad told you that when you got here! We heard 'em talking, remember!"

Nathan looked at her and scowled. "So, you didn't catch 'em then?"

"No, sir, but we checked the whole house. It's all clear now." The officer glanced sideways at Maggie and a sly smile spread across his face. "Oh, hello, young lady! I didn't recognize you with your clothes on."

Maggie's mouth dropped open. In the chaos, she had failed to notice that this was the *totally hot* cop who had helped her out of the pond.

He chuckled at her obvious embarrassment, and then cleared his throat. "Hm-hmm. Would you come with me please, folks?"

They followed him back into the house and directly upstairs.

"Whoever it was . . . well, it looks like they only went into one room." He stopped outside of Maggie's bedroom door and pushed it open.

"Oh, *no way!*" Maggie exclaimed. "Look at my room!"

Nathan slapped both hands onto his cheeks and slowly slid them down his face. "Whoa," he moaned.

The room was completely destroyed. Papers were strewn all over the floor. The bedding was pulled off the bed. Maggie's clothes were pulled out of the dresser drawers, and the drawers themselves were flung everywhere and in pieces. Many of her belongings lay smashed in shattered little piles of rubble.

"Sir," the taller officer pulled out a little blue notebook. "It looks as though the intruders were looking for something. Do you have any idea what that might have been?"

"No, I . . . uh . . . I don't." Nathan answered, trying his best to appear calm, but the horrifying fact that someone had rummaged through his daughter's room left him feeling quite uneasy.

"Wait a second," Maggie blurted, "they said they had to show someone something, remember?" She struggled to recall what she had heard. "One of them said 'we have to show this to' um . . . oh . . . what was it? Utalar? Ultrala? No . . . it was Ultara!"

"That's right . . . Ultara," Nathan nodded. "They were talking about a 'tab' too."

The taller officer diligently scribbled down their comments. "Ultara . . . tab, eh? Either of those things familiar to you?"

They both shook their heads.

"Is there anything else you can remember?" the hot cop asked.

"I . . . I don't know," Nathan replied. "We didn't hear much. It all happened pretty fast."

The officer handed Nathan a business card with the name **Sgt. Bradley S. Jacobsen** printed on it. "This is my direct number. If you think of anything else or have any questions, you can reach me here." He pointed to a phone number at the bottom of the card.

"Thank you, Sergeant." Nathan shook his hand.

While her dad finished up with the police, Maggie walked around her room inspecting what had been done. It was overwhelming. Her things had been touched by someone she didn't know. They had gone through all of her stuff. They were looking for something she supposedly had, and felt they had the right to just come in and take it. It left her feeling violated, scared, and angry. They said they had found something—but what? What was missing?

She continued wandering through the debris, but then stopped suddenly. "Oh no," she gasped. She dashed to the other side of the room and ran her hands frantically across the top of her dresser. "Oh no, oh no, oh nooooo!" She started digging through clothes and papers, tossing things violently through the air. "Where is she? *Where is she?*"

"Who?" Nathan asked. "What are you looking for?"

Maggie was breathing heavily, mumbling to herself furiously. "My hiding seeker, Dad! She's not here! They took Hidey! She's gone!"

"What?" he asked with a surprised chuckle. "Why on Earth would anyone take that?"

Sergeant Jacobsen turned an inquisitive eye on Maggie. "Excuse me, young lady. Your hiding what?"

Maggie, who had no intention of making eye contact with Sergeant Jacobsen, returned to flinging clothes around and ignored him entirely.

"Oh," Nathan jumped in, "it's nothing Sergeant . . . just a little statue thing she's had for years."

"Did it have any significant monetary value, sir?"

Nathan frowned at him. "Uh, nooo. It was just a . . . a toy, given to her by . . . ." He stopped short. There was no way this could be a coincidence. Dr. Brockman had warned him that they were in danger just seconds before the intrusion, and Dr. Brockman had given Maggie the hiding seeker.

"By?" Officer Jacobsen pressed.

"Oh, uh . . . ."

Nathan didn't think he'd better say anything about it just yet. He didn't want this to get any more complicated. After all, Paul Brockman was his best friend. There had to be a simple explanation—one that didn't require the intervention of the law. "I'm sorry," he apologized. "It was given to her by a very good family friend.

The officer raised an eyebrow. "Hmmm, well all right then, if there's nothing more, we'll just . . . ."

Nathan cut him off. "Nope, don't think so."

The officer eyed him suspiciously. "You'll, uh, call me then if you happen to think of anything else?"

Oh, absolutely!" Nathan replied. He patted the policeman condescendingly on the shoulder. "Thanks for your help, Sergeant! C'mon, I'll show you out."

Maggie stopped digging and watched her dad. He was acting strange all of a sudden—strange even for him. She followed him and the two officers downstairs and looked on as her father noticeably rushed them out the door.

"Thanks again, Sergeant J.!" He waved from the front porch smiling widely. "You guys be safe out there!"

As soon as the police car was out of sight, Nathan's face dropped. "Okay, Paul, time to explain," he seethed, pulling his phone out of his pocket and whipping it open.

"Dad?" Maggie stepped out onto the porch with him. "What're you doing? You don't honestly think Doc had anything to do with this, do you?"

Nathan ignored her completely.

"Paul, it's Nathan," he barked.

Maggie had never heard her dad use such a curt tone with Doc.

"Oh, Nathan! Oh, thank goodness. You're all right."

"I am most certainly *not* all right, Paul!"

"Dad? What are you . . . ?"Maggie pleaded.

"Shhhh!" he snapped.

"Nathan, what's going on?" the doctor asked. "What's happened?"

"My house was broken into, Paul; but I guess you know that."

Maggie gasped loudly. She tried to grab the phone away from Nathan, but he turned so she couldn't reach it. "Dad! Stop it!" she insisted.

He covered the phone with his hand. "Maggie, I will handle this," he scolded, glaring at her sternly.

"But . . . ."

He angrily raised his eyebrows as he put the phone back to his ear. "Well?"

"Nathan, listen," Doc began, "it's not what you think. I had nothing to do with your house being broken into."

"But you knew it was going to happen," he accused.

"No, I didn't know for sure."

"What do you mean?"

Eighteen

Doc was quiet for a second and then asked, "Is Maggie okay? This probably really freaked her out."

"What? Yeah, she's fine," Nathan snipped, annoyed that Doctor Brockman seemed to be purposely withholding information. "As fine as someone can be when their room's been ransacked and their most prized possession's been stolen."

"What?" Doc exclaimed. "What's been stolen?"

"That silly little figurine you gave her."

Doctor Brockman was silent for several seconds. "Oh, no," he finally breathed, sounding like someone had just died. "Nathan, please tell me you're not serious."

CHAPTER XIX

DOC RETURNS

D r. Brockman's flight arrived at 10:45 a.m. Nathan couldn't get off work, so Maggie skipped school and made the two hour drive to the airport. It was 10:57 when she got to the baggage claim, where they'd agreed to meet. Doc was there waiting.

"Boodle!" he exclaimed, when he spotted her rushing toward the luggage carousel. He sped over, picked her up and swung her around in a circle. "How is it that you're even more gorgeous than you were last time?"

"You always ask me that, Doc," she grinned, and kissed him on the cheek.

"Well, stop getting more gorgeous then," he scolded, as he grabbed his suitcase from the carousel with a jerk.

They walked arm and arm to the parking garage, climbed into Nathan and Maggie's old silver sedan, and embarked on the long drive back to Glenhill.

Their conversation started in the standard way—Doc asking if she had gotten a boyfriend in the last two weeks and when her dad was going to stop living like a monk and find a nice lady; Maggie telling him that there would never be any prospects for her in Glenhill, and to forget her dad. He was never going to find a nice lady. He wasn't even looking! It was a conversation that took place at least once every time they were together. It would always end with Doc saying, "I just care about you guys. I want you to be happy."—A phrase that Maggie would mockingly mouth along with him as he said it.

They'd just finished their little dating chat when Maggie asked, "How weird is it that both of our houses got broken into?"

Doc became noticeably uneasy. "It's really weird, Boo. You okay though?"

Maggie shrugged her shoulders. "I dunno. I thought I was, but I still had to sleep in Dad's room last night."

"Yeah," he answered, "I haven't been sleeping lately myself. I've been really worried about you guys. I wish I could have gotten back here sooner, but I was needed at the hospital."

"So, I've been wondering. How did you know that they were coming to our house after yours?" Maggie tried. "Dad wouldn't tell me. He said it would freak me out."

Dr. Brockman shook his head. "Then what makes you think I'm going to tell you?"

Maggie smiled and batted her eyelashes. "Because you know I'm a big girl and that I can handle it . . . and because someone promised that he wouldn't ever keep secrets from me."

"Oh there it is . . . just go ahead and throw that one up in my face again," he shook his head and grudgingly relented. "Fine. Here's what happened.

"I'd just gotten off work and ran home to change before going to the gym. When I got to the house, the front door was open. At first I thought maybe the housekeeper had forgotten to shut it, but then I heard voices. There were at least two men . . . talking. They were saying '*it wasn't here*' and '*it has to be with the others*.' I had no idea what they were talking about."

Maggie listened intently as he continued.

"One of them said '*He gave it to the girl, the one with black hair and blue eyes*', and then he asked the other guy if they should '*go to Iowa and get it*'. That's all I heard before I realized they were coming toward the door. I ran to my car, and headed straight for the police station; I called you guys on my way there."

Now, he seemed to be talking to himself. "They must have . . . It's the only way they could've gotten there so fast."

"But why would a couple of creeps break into houses in two different states to steal a little statue of a strange fairy-looking thing? It just doesn't make any sense."

"I know, Boo. I can't figure it out either," Doc replied.

"And why did they have to take my hiding-seeker? I was completely bummed out. I loved her." She tilted her head gently onto Doc's shoulder.

He smiled and told her to watch the road.

"Remember that dopey story you told me when you gave her to me," she sniggered, "about how you met her in your enchanted garden?"

Doc shook his head, "I almost had you. You totally believed that she was good luck!"

"Never!" Maggie insisted, "I just *acted* like I believed you. You wouldn't give her to me unless I said I believed."

"Well," he began, "what if I told you that it was all the truth. That I really do have an enchanted garden, and that I was walking through it one day and bumped right into her, and that she hit me over the head with a big blue rose and told me to get out of her house?" He grinned ear to ear.

"I'd say I need to hook you up with Bridgette's mom," Maggie smirked. Bridgette was the daughter of quite a famous psychologist who had authored a series of best-selling, self-help books.

Dr. Brockman glared at her with his deep green eyes. "Very funny, Boodle. I swear no imagination whatsoever! Okay, so I got her at the flea market," he admitted, "but that's kind of like an enchanted garden."

Maggie giggled. "I'll miss my little Hidey though. She's always been there for me."

"I'll see if I can find you another one," Doc soothed, "maybe for your birthday tomorrow, ya know . . . to go along with your island."

It was early afternoon when they arrived back at the house and they were greeted by a huge—bordering on obnoxious—hand-drawn banner framed by red and gold balloons sprawling from one end of the white wooden front porch to the other. The very colorful "HAPPY 17TH BIRTHDAY, SMAGGS!" message simply screamed Bridgette.

"Oh my gosh," Maggie groaned. "What is she doing?"

Doc chuckled. "Looks like we're having a party."

Just then, Bridgette and three other girls burst out onto the porch. Bridgette waved gregariously and bounded over to the car. "We couldn't wait 'til tomorrow," she squealed, "ditched World History and Anatomy!"

"Anatomy's important," Dr. Brockman scolded playfully as he pulled his duffle bag from the back seat. "How are you ever going to take over my practice if you flunk out, Bridge?"

"Uhhh . . . ." she breathed, gazing longingly at the man who had just made her weak simply by speaking to her.

Doc smiled and decided to give her an even bigger thrill. As he walked past, he leaned over and kissed her on the cheek. "Just teasing," he whispered, and continued into the house.

Bridgette's face was as red as the balloons on the banner. She tried to talk, but all that came out was a pathetic, mousy squeak.

Maggie shook her head and grabbed a hold of Bridgette's arm. "Come on, Bubbles. The party's waiting," she urged, and then added, "Man, I'd hate to see how you'd act if you *did* think he was cute."

The weekend was a whirlwind of fun, compared to most weekends in Glenhill. After the party, Nathan treated everyone to a barbeque in their back yard and, in honor of her birthday; he even let Maggie out of her office cleaning duties for the next day. She and Doc spent most of Saturday birthday shopping at the Glenhill Galleria, where he spoiled her mercilessly, and then on Sunday, she and Bridgette hung out and watched movies after attending church services in a neighboring town.

It was nearly ten o'clock Sunday night when Nathan left to take Dr. Brockman to the airport. Maggie changed into her pajamas and watched a little television in her room before finally dozing off to sleep.

CHAPTER XX

THE VRITESSE

Ultara sat emotionless on her tangled throne. Two of her warriors, Torschel and Linetal, entered the room with their arms locked around a man who was struggling violently to escape their grasp. They dragged him across the rough rocks that formed the bridge and pushed him forcefully onto the floor.

"Ahhh, yes . . . Linden Torak isn't it?" she began. "I've been told, Master Torak, that you were present at the battle." She cut right to the chase. Ultara was in no mood to mess around.

Linden looked up at her—his face bruised and bleeding. He snarled angrily, but did not answer.

"Don't be foolish, Torak." She looked directly at his battered face, and a soft golden glow surged from her eyes. "Ahhhh, so Darian has taught you how to block a mind penetration . . . very good."

She rose from the throne and paced back and forth on the platform in front of Linden. Her black gown billowed like thick smoke all around her. The long, fiery locks that spilled over her shoulders and her bright golden eyes were a stark contrast to the cold, shadowy room. Her confidence, and the exaggerated calm in her voice, only added to her sublimely intimidating presence. "Did your dear Darian also teach you that a successful mind block requires every tiny ounce of strength in your body?"

Linden remained silent and sneering.

The glow in Ultara's eyes began to intensify, pulsating and surging brighter and brighter until the room was completely flooded in golden light.

As the glow in her eyes intensified, Linden began to wince and cringe. After just a few seconds of fighting with all of his strength, he was overcome. "Aaaaaaarraahh!"

he cried out in agony, his body contorting and twitching uncontrollably.

Ultara's eyes continued to surge brighter and brighter as she spoke. "What you are feeling right now, Master Torak, is an energy jolt equivalent to a bolt of lightning." She spoke loudly in order to rise above his screams, but maintained the eerie calmness in her tone, "Several have felt it; few have survived."

The glow in her eyes faded away. She stepped down from the platform and walked over to where Linden slumped, reached down, and with unbelievable strength, yanked him to his feet. He groaned miserably, as she looked him squarely in the eye and stated matter-of-factly, "Let me explain. You won't have the strength to keep this up for long. Mind blocks don't work on the vritesse. I will be able to read your thoughts. Why suffer more than necessary?"

Linden glowered at her angrily. He turned his head slightly to the side and made a sound like he was going to spit.

Ultara threw him forcefully to the floor. He landed in a hard thud and screamed out in pain. "If you do not tell me what you know, Torak, you *will* die." The light in her eyes intensified again as she sent another brutal jolt.

Linden was strong-willed and physically strong as well, but the strongest of men would not live through more than two or three of Ultara's powerful shock waves.

Finally, Linden succumbed and broke his silence. "All right! I was there," he coughed weakly. He doubted that cooperation would spare his life, but he hoped for a moment to rest between assaults.

Ultara raised her eyebrows. "Now, that's better," she oozed, "but you know, Torak, I am aware that you were there. What can you tell me that I am *not* aware of?"

"I don't know how they got away," he gasped. "We had the palace surrounded!" He fought for breath as he spoke, as it had been knocked out of him by Ultara's crushing attack.

Just then, Commander Branlor burst into the room and quickly ran to where she stood. "Vritesse," he knelt down humbly before her.

As he lifted his eyes, he noticed the crumpled heap of a man lying on the ground a few feet away from him. A sickening fear flooded through his core as he realized that he'd just interrupted one of Ultara's poignant interrogations. "Please forgive my bold intrusion, Ma'am, but I have news."

"Rise, Branlor, what is it?" Ultara kept her eyes focused on Linden and paced slowly back and forth.

"We've found them!"

Ultara stopped in her tracks and turned her gaze from Linden to Branlor. "You know where they are?" She looked like a cat that had been turned loose on an unsuspecting bird.

Linden, too, seemed very interested in the news.

Ultara noticed his sudden interest out of the corner of her eye. Once more, her eyes lit up brilliant gold; she sent a powerful, fatal burst of energy coursing through Linden's body. He shrieked and convulsed wildly, and then, let out his final, painful breath.

Linden Torak lay rigid—eyes wide open—and dead right in the center of the mosaic star.

Branlor stood gaping—stunned by Ultara's apparent indifference to the fact that she'd just ended a man's life so easily.

"We can't risk anything, Branlor," she explained. "He was a spy, and your information about the Borlocs most definitely would not have remained between us. Besides, his thoughts revealed nothing useful."

She looked down at his stiffened form and motioned to Linetal and Torschel, "Take him away, and the next time I ask you to bring me information," her eyes lit up just a little as both Linetal and Torschel winced fearfully, "make sure you bring me someone who actually has some!"

They bowed, and dragged Linden's body across the bridge and out of the room.

"Now, Branlor, where are they?"

"They were found on Drolana," he responded, still a little shaken, but not wanting to show it.

"What? So your theory was right. It was Glaron?"

"It appears so, Vritesse. If Glaron was able to get his receptors onto the atoc and atoh he could have channeled enough energy through his own body to transport them with his Traveler powers."

Ultara nodded and dropped down slowly into her throne; her eyes saddened. "So, he sacrificed himself to get them out."

Branlor nodded. "Verolite went to Drolana himself and confirmed it. He saw the atoh swimming in a pond and recognized her by her hair and eyes. He and Linetal followed her." He held out a small figurine and handed it to Ultara. "She had this."

Ultara gazed down at the little statue in her hand. "A Squanki?"

"Yes, Milady."

"Shadow Squanki don't exist outside of Lor Mandela, that I'm aware," she muttered. She sat thoughtfully for a moment, and then stood and commanded, "Branlor, I want you to oversee this personally. Go to Drolana. You'll need to take at least a thousand Travelers with you. It will take five receptors on each of the Borlocs to bring them back."

"Five?" Branlor was shocked by her request. "How can we place that many without being detected?"

"It will be difficult, but not impossible. Yes, Branlor, five on each. Any less will be unstable." She stopped and stared at him threateningly, "I can't trust this to someone with doubts, Commander."

Branlor gulped. "Whose receptors should we place, Ma'am?"

"Mine of course! They must be brought back to me. I'm counting on you, Commander. I'm sure you understand how important this is. Do not let me down."

"Yes, Vritesse." Branlor bowed nervously.

The dark wisps of Ultara's gown flowed around him as she turned and strode up the slope to the platform. She lowered herself gracefully onto her throne again. "At last . . . ." she breathed.

Branlor bowed once more and quickly set out to recruit one thousand Trysta Travelers.

It didn't take long before he had a large group assembled in the main conference room.

"Verolite has informed me that the atoc and his daughter are alive, and on Drolana," he enlightened. "We have a great challenge before us. We must place five of Ultara's receptors on each of the Borlocs."

The room erupted with the shocked whispers of a thousand men and women. Nothing like this had ever been attempted.

"Silence!" Branlor boomed over the din. He was far more intimidating when he was not addressing Ultara.

He continued, "Most of you will be used to create a diversion with your lights. Torschel, Blansten, Verolite, Linetal, and I will carry the receptors, as we are able to penetrate solid surfaces. This will not be easy to accomplish, as I am aware, but the atoc and atoh must be brought back to Ultara."

Many of the assembled Trystas still looked at him in disbelief. It was one thing to place one receptor without being discovered, but placing five on two different individuals would be an unbelievable, close to impossible, feat.

"Are there any objections?" Branlor thundered with authority. The murmuring and whispering stopped abruptly. The Trystas were all keenly aware that Branlor was now second in command to Ultara. This gave him a tremendous amount of power. Not a soul in the room wanted to risk having him report them to Ultara for insubordination; a fate like that of Linden Torak would be theirs if he did.

"I suggest you get over your concerns quickly. We leave in one hour!" Branlor turned and walked authoritatively from the conference room.

Again the air filled with mumbling and complaining. "This is a death sentence!" one man shouted. "How is such a difficult task to be accomplished?"

"It will be a death sentence . . ." a female general spoke up and everyone in the room quieted. It was extremely rare for a high-ranking female official such as this to speak ill of an order set forth by the vritesse, "if we do not obey!"

One hour later, one thousand Trysta Travelers took to the air. Small lights flickered and a faint buzzing emanated through the dusky sky of the Sybran Forest. They climbed higher and higher until their lights disappeared and the buzzing ceased. The large group of Travelers bulleted through the vaporous border of Lor Mandela and headed towards the almost insurmountable challenge that awaited them on Drolana.

CHAPTER XXI
MONDAY MORNING IN GLENHILL, IOWA

The alarm clock clicked from 6:04 to 6:05 a.m., and let out a sadistic buzz which jolted Maggie from a deep, comfortable sleep. With great effort and a disgusted moan, she reached out and smacked the top of the clock, hitting the snooze button for the first of three routine extra ten minutes. The room was quiet and almost completely dark; a faint cool breeze played with the sheer curtains that hung on the open window. In Maggie's estimation, these were the ideal sleeping conditions—a fact that only added to the cruelty of it being morning already.

Bzzzzz. Smack!

Wrapped in her favorite blanket and surrounded by a mountain of pillows, she wandered back and forth between awake and asleep—one moment aware of her surroundings, the next, slipping effortlessly into the beginnings of nonsensical dreams.

Bzzzzz. Smack!

She pulled herself upright and sat, still half asleep, on the edge of the bed. Her eyelids dropped, and her head bobbled around as she nodded back off; a sudden falling sensation brought her instantly back to life with a jolt. Her eyes popped open, but then, once again, blinked slowly shut.

She had just started to doze back off, when she realized that she had seen something in between blinks.

"What in the . . . ?" she mumbled as she forced herself to wake up. She rubbed the sleep from her eyes and squinted toward the other side of the room.

There, outside her second story window, two bright white lights—no bigger than a dime—darted around behind the fluttering curtains. They zipped to the right, stopped, and held still for a second, and then spiraled down together to the left. They made a faint but peculiar noise as they jumped from place to place, like a cross between static on a television and chirping crickets.

Maggie had been a little skittish since the break-in, but at this moment, curiosity was stronger than fear, so she stood and started toward the window. As she walked, the floorboards of the old house creaked ominously beneath her feet, causing her confidence in the situation to rapidly decline. By the time she was half way across the room, she was forcing herself to stay calm.

"C'mon, Maggs! Don't be such a wimp!" she scolded under her breath. "It's probably just lightning bugs!"

She reached the window and lifted her hand to pull back the curtain for a better look. All at once, two more little lights zipped up and joined the first. Maggie jumped and her breath caught in her chest. Her heart began to race as an uneasy feeling stirred—the feeling that she was being watched. She inched her way backwards.

"It's okay," she breathed. "They're just bugs."

The four tiny illuminations whizzed around in formation for a second or two, and then the lights started to multiply. Out of nowhere and everywhere all at once, hundreds and hundreds of bright, piercing, white orbs whirled and buzzed outside her open window, creating a riotous screech. Maggie slapped her hands over her ears as the volume of the bizarre noise grew…and grew…and grew. Blinding flashes, like bolts of lightning, burst in through the window and ricocheted around the room, creating a turbulent strobe effect. They crashed into the walls and the floor, making the whole room convulse violently.

Maggie's fear grew to sheer terror! She turned and tried to run, but as she did, the floor bumped hard, knocking her to her knees with a painful smack. She screamed, but her voice was drowned out by the horrendous buzzing of the chaotic little lights.

Horrified, she curled up into a ball on the floor—hands clasped tightly over her ears, eyes squeezed shut—and begged, "Oh please . . . oh please . . . oh please! Someone help me!"

Just then, her bedroom door swung open. Within a split second, the multitude of lights vanished; the quaking stopped, and the dreadful noise came to an abrupt halt. All was as it had been before.

"Smaggs?" The familiar voice of her dad caught Maggie off guard, but she was, nonetheless, very relieved to hear it.

Nathan expected to find her still in bed, not in the fetal position on the floor. "Whatayadoin'?" he half-chuckled. "Have you lost something? Are you okay?"

Maggie sat up shakily—tears streaming down her cheeks—and turned toward her dad who was standing in the doorway. She tried to speak, but was completely unnerved. A shaky "Wh-aat was that?" was all she could manage.

"Um, Princess, you all right?" Nathan asked again. He walked over to help her back to her feet. "What was what?" he asked, puzzled by his daughter's peculiar behavior.

Maggie couldn't believe that her dad was messing around with her like this when she was obviously traumatized.

"Dad, come on," she pleaded as she took his hand and pulled herself to her feet. "Why are you playing with me? That was totally freaky!"

"Smaggs . . . look at me. Are you sick?" Her dad put his hand on her forehead to see if she had a fever.

Maggie stared at him in disbelief. His face was concerned and serious, and she realized that he really didn't have any idea what she was talking about. But how on Earth could he have not seen the lights, or felt the ground shaking, or heard that awful noise?

She felt faint and leaned into him to keep from falling down again.

"Whoa! Hey, c'mon, Sweetie! Come sit down." Nathan walked her over to her bed and sat next to her. She was so shocked that she couldn't speak at all. As strange and frightening as the lights had been, her dad being oblivious to them put her into a stupor.

"Maggie," Nathan spoke softly, "what is it, honey?"

"You . . . you didn't hear that?" she tried.

"Hear what, sweetheart?"

"Did we, um . . . maybe have a tornado or something?"

Nathan chuckled, but then realized that she was being completely serious. "Smaggs, I think maybe you mighta just had a bad dream, or somethin'."

"B . . . but I . . . there," she stuttered, "It . . . I mean, it was *really, really real*, Dad!"

"Oh . . . well, sometimes dreams feel that way, Sweetie," he replied. "Maybe you just had a doozer!" He wiped a stray tear from her cheek.

Maggie stared at him. She knew she hadn't been dreaming, but her dad had obviously experienced nothing. After a few silent moments, she whispered a resigned, "Okay."

Nathan sat with her for a while to make sure she was all right but after about fifteen minutes, he stood and kissed her on the forehead. "You feelin' better now, 'cause we'd best get goin', or we'll be late."

Maggie nodded and her dad backed out into the hall. She glanced around her once again normal room and got up and walked to her dresser; she ran her hand over the top of it and sighed. She really wanted her hiding seeker right now.

As she stood staring at the top of the dresser, Maggie's thoughts drifted back to the odd little lights and her own personal tornado.

The harder she tried not to think about it, the more the images flooded through her, until finally she found herself reliving the whole crazy incident all over again. It wasn't like she was just thinking about it, either. It was as if it were happening again.

She saw and felt every detail.

First, she watched as two little lights started bouncing around outside the dark window. She felt herself stand and walk, but she was not moving. She heard the floorboards creak and then watched two additional lights join the first, followed by thousands of them zipping around with ear-splitting volume. She felt the ground shake and her knees smack against the hard floor, even though she remained on her feet. Then, just as before, it stopped suddenly when, in her mind, she saw the door open.

She'd no sooner come out of this trance, when the whole thing started again. A nauseating fear swelled in the pit of her stomach, paralyzing her movement, and with it, her ability to think about anything else other than the pictures flashing vividly before her eyes.

This episode ended and she managed to make her way across the hall to the bathroom.

Once more, she found herself watching the scene again…and again…and again. She was caught up in what she now knew was *no* dream for about the tenth time, when Nathan called from downstairs.

"Smaggs! We have to leave in fifteen minutes! If you're gonna eat breakfast, you'd better get down here and do it!"

"Oh . . . breakfast . . . yeah . . . ." Her dazed response was hardly audible.

Suddenly, she snapped back into reality. "What? Oh, no!" she shouted, jumping as she realized that she hadn't even started to get ready for school yet.

She took a couple of quick steps toward her room, but was instantly tugged back by a strange, inexplicable force. Her insides lurched and a sickening, paralyzing fear washed over her.

Again, she saw the lights, heard the noise, felt the ground shake, and felt the burning pain of her knees slamming against the floor. She was cold, but sweating profusely. Her head was spinning, and she was sure that this time she was actually going to pass out.

"C'mon! Stop it!" she scolded herself. "I . . . have . . . to . . . get . . . ready!"

Every word was a struggle to get out.

She took several deep breaths and with great effort, haphazardly lifted her long black hair up into a curly, messy ponytail.

Again, the lights danced before her in her window.

"No!" she insisted, taking three or four more deep breaths and spastically flinging herself into her bedroom.

Once more, she felt herself slipping back into a daze, a nauseating fear twisting and churning inside her stomach.

"Clo . . . clo . . . clothes!" She huffed, grabbing a bright yellow t-shirt from the laundry basket.

The fight to stay alert was now very much a battle between her mind and her body. Her movements were jerky and wild, as she bounced back and forth between subconscious thought and conscious will. It took every ounce of energy she could muster just to get dressed.

Finally, after several minutes of exasperating effort, she managed to finish dressing, but not before knocking her alarm clock off the nightstand and kicking over her butterfly shaped CD rack, sending CDs crashing and sliding in a plastic *screeeeech* across the wood floor.

She staggered out of her room and climbed down the stairs.

"Where've you been, Smaggs? We gotta leave in two minutes! What in the world have you been doing up there? Aren't you gonna eat anything?" Nathan quizzed without taking a breath, as he ran around trying to gather up papers he needed to take to the Pratt and Miller Accounting Firm where he'd been working for the last thirteen years.

He didn't wait for Maggie to answer. He grabbed his car keys off of a hook in the kitchen, and ran out the front door yelling back at her, "C'mon Smaggs! If I'm late again, Mr. Pratt will have my . . . . " He jumped into the car and shut the door before finishing his sentence.

Maggie slowly picked up her purse and book bag and followed her dad out to the car. She was still very queasy, and drained of all her energy. Walking was almost more than she could manage at the moment because her legs were wobbly and heavy. She clutched the rusty car door handle, and fell into the front seat of their old silver sedan.

The car door had been dented a couple of months ago when Nathan ran into a pole in the grocery store parking lot. Ever since, it had to be slammed hard to get it shut all the way.

When Maggie attempted to close the door it made a swishing sound against the rubber strip on the door frame and bounced back open; she didn't have the strength to get the stupid door closed.

Nathan glanced over at her with a puzzled expression. "What's up with you?" he asked, tilting his head to one side. "Still weirded out by your dream?"

Maggie just stared blankly at him.

"Yoo-hoo? Ya in there?"

"I'm . . . I'm kinda tired, dad. I don't know what's goin' on," she answered in a dazed mumble.

Nathan shrugged his shoulders, shook his head, and got out of the car. He sprinted around to Maggie's side and kicked the door with the bottom of his shoe. It slammed shut with a *bang* which made Maggie nearly jump out of her seat, and then he ran back around to his side of the car, jumped in, shoved it into gear and backed quickly out of the driveway.

The dented car door, in addition to being quite ugly, had the tendency to rattle loudly when the car was driven over 40 miles per hour.

This morning, the clattering was even more unnerving to Maggie than usual. She covered her ears with her hands and closed her eyes.

That's when she noticed it. She wasn't fighting to control her mind anymore; she was actually feeling much better.

She sat still for a minute just to make sure. "It's gone," she blurted, not realizing she had said it out loud.

"Wh . . . what's gone?" Nathan quizzed.

"Um . . . uh . . ." she stammered, trying to think of something intelligent and believable to say to her dad. "Oh! The billboard of the guy with the . . . uh . . . striped suit." She glanced out the window to hide the disgusted face she was making over her lame answer.

"Oookaaay," Nathan looked at her like she was perfectly insane.

Despite her idiotic comment and her dad's thinking she was losing it, she was incredibly relieved that she was back in control of herself again. She took a deep breath and sighed loudly.

Misreading Maggie's sigh as left over tension from her troubling dream—or the alarming disappointment that her favorite billboard was missing—Nathan tried to joke around with her. "Hey homey, ya wanna boogie down to the super groovy mall later and catch a flick?"

Maggie rolled her eyes and couldn't help but smirk. No matter how hard he tried—and he seemed obsessed with trying—her dad just didn't get how to be cool.

He took great pains to be cool, though. He was constantly checking out what the guys at Maggie's school were wearing, how they were styling their hair, and what the latest cool "lingo" was. The problem lied chiefly in his interpretation. It was always just a little—no, a lot—off.

If the guys were wearing baggy jeans, he'd wear baggy jeans that were too short or way too long. If the "in" style was to grow a goatee, his would be complemented by a big, furry black mustache.

His latest attempt was his hair. He'd grown it out to about eight inches all over, but instead of letting his straight dark hair hang naturally—which Maggie thought would look really good—he would slick the sides back and let the top flop all over the place.

Maggie knew that if he ever let go of his eternal quest for cool, he would be quite handsome, but she'd given up on that a while ago.

"No, Dad," she answered. "I think I'm okay now. It's just . . . well . . . it's been a really weird morning!" She frowned slightly and added, "Hey, have you noticed that you always ask me out when you're trying to cheer me up?"

"Oh, what! Am I not good enough for you?" Nathan teasingly protested, "Wha-ell, I never!" he sniffled as though he was truly hurt by his daughter's rejection.

She rolled her eyes. "Okay, Dad. Give it a rest!"

He chuckled and mussed the top of her hair. "And you say your life is boring."

Maggie just shook her head and looked away. As she stared out the window at the passing fields, she thought about what had happened to her that morning and tried to make some sense of it. This was more bizarre than anything she had ever experienced, or even heard of.

What were those lights? How could her dad not have seen or heard anything? Why did she keep seeing them over and over again? And—Heaven forbid—what if it ever happened again?

What Maggie was unaware of was that this morning's strange event was only the beginning—this unexplainable experience would definitely not be her last.

CHAPTER XXII
THE MATH NAZI AND THE NEW KID

Nathan dropped Maggie off in front of the school at 8:15—about ten minutes later than usual. She was feeling better—now that she wasn't fighting the demons in her head—but was still not entirely back to her normal energetic self. Nonetheless, she was able to get up the "oomph" to lean across the car, kiss her dad on the cheek and, in one swift move force the dented door open and lift herself up and out on to the sidewalk. She knew that she would be late if she didn't hustle.

"Bye, Smaggs!" her dad yelled after her as she dashed up the school steps and disappeared behind the large brown doors.

"Margaret Amanda Baker! Where have you been?" Bridgette was waiting just inside the school. "I've been worried sick!"

Bridgette's braces gleamed under the fluorescent lights as she giggled at her own humor. Her big brown eyes twinkled and her pretty face glowed. It was amazing how she could find happiness in every situation. Everyone in the school seemed to be drawn to her, not only because of her beauty, but also because of her optimistic outlook.

Together, she and Maggie were quite the photogenic pair, Bridge at five foot ten, deep brown eyes and shimmering, straight blonde hair, and Maggie—who looked tall, even though she was three inches shorter than Bridgette—with shocking, electric blue eyes and long black curls.

"Bridgey . . . you wouldn't believe it if I told you." Maggie dropped her book bag right in the middle of the hall and started digging around in it frantically.

"Look at you, Maggs! You're a mess!" Bridgette observed, still grinning widely and playfully tousling Maggie's curly ponytail. "What *are* you looking for?"

"I need my math book, Bridge . . . ah ha! There you are!" Maggie pulled a large red book out of the bag, picked it up with a jerk, and started running down the hall toward her class.

"Okay, Miss Marge," Bridgette yelled after her down the now-deserted corridor, "but ya owe me an explanation later!"

"At lunch, Bubbles! Mr. Lee will be uglier than usual if I'm late again!"

"Ewwww! Not possible!" Bridgette whispered to herself as Maggie swung the door to her classroom open and vanished. She made it to her desk with no more than ten seconds to spare.

At the front of the room, Mr. Wilbur H. Lee sat hunched over, flipping through several papers that were piled messily on his desk. Everyone in the school un-lovingly referred to him as the "Math Nazi." He was a frightening looking man, nearly bald on the top of his head, but with a mangy brown beard, and a tiny, Hitler-like mustache that earned him his title. He was average height, but horribly skinny and frail looking. His clothes never matched and usually looked like they had never been washed. In addition to his unfortunate looks, he was, without a doubt, the strictest, nastiest, most unfair teacher in the entire school.

He adorned his desk with cute little snippets like '**Children should be seen—not heard!**' and '**Stop talking to me like I care!**' and—Maggie's personal favorite—'**If at first you don't succeed, that's what I expected.**' He'd arranged these niceties in such a way that if any of his fellow educators happened into the room, he could hide them quickly by simply shuffling some of the hundreds of papers that were always present on the desk.

Generally, Maggie somewhat enjoyed school, but this year, she found herself dreading first period every day. It seemed that no matter how hard she tried she could not please this terribly cruel and tragically ugly man.

"Open your books to chapter eighteen and read the review." Mr. Lee's gravelly monotone voice made Maggie, and everyone else in the class, cringe. For some reason, he always sounded like he had rocks in his mouth and when he spoke his nose would scrunch, his eyes would blink abnormally, and his beard would twitch spastically, which made it look like he was chewing on something foul.

"Miss Baker!" he shrieked, glaring at Maggie with his blinky little eyes. "Book open!" Maggie had only paused long enough to shudder at his creepiness, but Mr. Lee had very little patience for hesitation once he had given an order. Normally, everyone in the class jumped the second he spoke, but Maggie's energy was still a little depleted and apparently she'd been kind of slow. She plopped her book open, flipped a few pages, and started reading.

Michelle, the freckle-faced, red haired girl who sat next to her glanced over, rolled her eyes, smiled pleasantly and shook her head. Michelle was constantly getting picked on by the Math Nazi, too.

As the class read quietly, the door creaked open and in sauntered a boy about Maggie's age. Glenhill is a very small community. Everyone knows everyone, but Maggie had never seen this guy before.

He was tall and lanky with shoulder length wavy blonde hair and a dark tan. His clothes were—to say the least—a little odd. He had on a vivid orange and green, short sleeve, Hawaiian print shirt, which he wore over the top of a navy blue long sleeve t-shirt. His khaki shorts looked at least four sizes too big and hung down to the middle of his tanned calves. He had on short black socks and bright red high-top basketball sneakers. More than one of the students in the class chuckled quietly at the sight of him, but that didn't seem to bother him in the slightest.

"Well?" Mr. Lee frowned and tapped the ends of his long, bony fingers together, waiting for some explanation as to why this person had just interrupted his class.

"Name's Holden, dude! Holden Guarlo." Holden virtually skipped over to Mr. Lee's desk and enthusiastically shook his hand.

"Do *not* touch me!" Mr. Lee hissed as he ripped his hand out of Holden's and quickly jumped to his feet, grabbing a bottle of hand sanitizer from under some papers and squeezing a generous blob into his hand.

"Whoa! Someone needs to relax!" Holden chuckled, pointing at Mr. Lee with his thumb and talking to the other students as though he were on stage. Several of them gasped at Holden's audacity — or blissful stupidity.

"What do you want?" Veins in the Math Nazi's forehead bulged and his face turned purple with rage; beads of perspiration formed on the top of his bald head.

"Dude, you are totally, like, gonna blow a fuse if you don't chill out!" Holden—who had a solid four inches and at least thirty pounds on Mr. Lee—practically picked up the livid teacher by the shoulders and sat him down at his desk.

At this point, the room sounded like a tire with a leak. Everyone was trying as hard as they could not to explode into laughter.

Holden patted Mr. Lee on his sweaty head, wiped his hand on the front of his shirt, and said, "That's okay, man. Someone obviously forgot to take his meds this mornin'. I'll just find my own seat."

He strolled toward a row of empty desks and looked across the room, right at Maggie. "Hey, Blue Eyes!" he shouted with an enthusiastic wave. "You look different than you did down at the pond. Oh . . . dude! It's 'cause you're dressed!"

As though on cue, everyone turned their attention to a completely horrified Maggie who slid down in her chair and blushed through about six different shades of red.

Holden winked as if he and Maggie had known each other for years and plunked down at an empty desk at the other side of the room.

Again, as if they were cued to do it, every student slowly turned their attention from Maggie to Mr. Lee who was now shaking uncontrollably, breathing sporadically, and clutching the sides of his desk. His tiny sunken eyes bulged widely in the sockets. Slowly, and without saying another word, he stood and walked toward the door. He practically ripped the handle off of it as he flung it open and staggered out into the hall.

Cynthia Dix, the straight "A" braniac in the class quietly speculated, "Oh my gosh! He's having a coronary!"

Other students added their comments, and the buzz of twenty-two murmuring teenagers filled the usually silent classroom.

Maggie glanced over at Holden. He was leaning toward a group of girls who were whispering to each other, grinning widely and listening intently as if he were trying to overhear some juicy bit of gossip. He sat back up, but then leaned toward another group in exactly the same way.

After several minutes, the door flew open and Mr. Lee finally strode back into the room and glared angrily at Holden. All conversation came to an abrupt halt. He was still quite scarlet in the face, but his breathing seemed to be more normal. After a long pause, he sneered, "We are reading the Chapter eighteen review, Mr. Guarlo."

For a few seconds, Holden just stared at Mr. Lee's twitching face in awe. Then, he shrugged his shoulders, looked down at his still closed text book, and quipped, "Cool Mr. L . . . but where I come from that's like third grade stuff."

Several students gasped aloud at Holden's unbelievable nerve.

"Oh, really," Mr. Lee sneered, weaving his way through a maze of desks until he was standing directly in front of Holden. "Why don't you just prove that, Mr. Guarlo?" He slapped Holden's desk, but was far too wimpy for the slap to make much of an impact. "I want a ten page essay on rational expressions, including examples and information sources on my desk by the end of the day this Friday."

Mr. Lee's entire body seemed to be shaking in an effort to keep from strangling his new student. "I want it typed and single spaced," he hissed as he tried to come up with anything else he could add on to make the assignment more difficult. "If you fail this assignment, Mr. Guarlo, you will fail my class!"

The Math Nazi smiled triumphantly, confident that there was not enough information in the world to produce a ten page report on this particular subject. He tapped a bony finger on Holden's book, and in his usual garbled voice said,

"You'd better get started." He turned and walked back up to the front of the room and sat back smugly in his desk chair.

Holden's face still bore a ridiculous grin, as he reached in the tattered brown book bag at his feet and pulled out a yellow paper folder. From where Maggie sat, she could see that written on the front of it, in beautiful black calligraphy, were the words;

"Rational Expressions Defined"

A Report by Holden Guarlo

Positively stunned, she watched as Holden sauntered up to Mr. Lee's desk and casually placed the yellow folder on it in front of a ghostly pale, sweaty, wide-eyed and shaking Math Nazi.

"Thank you," he hissed and threw the folder onto the heap of papers. "Just go sit down and leave me *alone!*"

Holden chuckled. "Duuude, two words . . . day . . . spa."

This time, almost everyone in the room laughed out loud.

"Silence!" The Math Nazi's voice was much higher-pitched than normal. "Read!"

The class fell silent.

Holden looked over at Maggie once more, shrugged and whispered, "Sheesh."

She lowered her head, glanced around nervously out of the corner of her eye, and pretended to be reading. She didn't move again until the bell rang.

CHAPTER XXIII
VOICES IN THE FOG

During the break between first period and second, the halls of the high school came alive. The seven minutes in between classes were always pretty loud, but as students hurried down the musty halls and toward their next classes, all conversation seemed to be centered on this new, crazily dressed, and overly confident Holden Guarlo. (Glenhill is a very small community after all—news travels quickly.) Even Maggie was excitedly telling Bridgette and Lorrine, about Holden's psychological assault on Mr. Lee.

"It was so bizarre," she shouted over the din. "I mean, he had a report on Rational Expressions already written in his book bag! How many people do that?"

Lorrine pushed her plastic rimmed glasses up on her nose, shrugged her shoulders, and looked at a group of kids that were walking past.

It appeared that there was one very annoying side effect to Holden's arrival at Glenhill High. Everyone assumed that Maggie knew him somehow; and now they were all eyeing her suspiciously.

"Why is everyone staring at you, Margaret?" Lorrine inquired.

Maggie glanced around at the herds of students making their way through the school. They were whispering amongst themselves and looking at her like she'd grown another head.

"Well," she explained, "he sort of singled me out in class."

"What do you mean?" Bridgette asked.

"Um . . . he acted like . . . well, he said that he saw us that day at the pond," she explained.

Suddenly an odd sinking sensation welled up in the pit of her stomach. She felt queasy and dizzy, just like she had at home earlier. "Uh . . . I . . . uh . . . ."

"Hey, are you all right?" Lorrine asked. "You're looking rather pallid!"

Maggie leaned up against her locker for support and shot Lorrine a desperate, pleading look. Both Bridgette and Lorrine stared at her with concern.

"What's wrong?" Bridgette asked. Her normal smile disappeared as she watched Maggie's color change from pure white to a sickly purple.

She couldn't answer. She felt strange. It was almost like she had been lassoed around the middle and was being tugged backward. Only, it felt like the lasso was attached to the inside of her body—like someone was trying to pull her insides out through her back.

"Lorrie," Bridgette's voice seemed distant. "I think we'd better get her to the nurse's office. She looks like she's gonna pass out!"

Suddenly, Maggie heard a faint "whooshing" sound coming from somewhere behind her. The sound faded in and out, but grew increasingly louder with each whoosh.

"All right, but can you take her?" Lorrine answered, "I can't be late for my next class."

"What? Well neither can I!" Bridgette protested.

They started arguing back and forth, both blurting out a list of reasons why the other should go.

"Fine," Lorrine finally exclaimed, "I will do it!" She glanced over to see how Maggie was hanging in, but then frowned and asked, "Hey, where did she go?"

Both of Maggie's friends looked straight at her with confused and bewildered expressions on their faces.

Bridgette shrugged her shoulders and suggested, "Maybe she ran to the bathroom. She did kinda look like she was gonna puke!"

"Hey! Hello!" Maggie snapped. "I'm right here!" She felt like she was about to be pulled backwards through her locker. "Hellooo!"

Bridgette and Lorrine, who seemed oblivious to the fact that she was standing right in front of them, turned and started to walk away.

"Hey! You guys! Where are you going?" she called out desperately. Just then the whooshing sound stopped and the yanking and tugging on her insides ceased so suddenly, that she almost fell over backward.

She glanced down at her feet and realized that she was no longer standing on the grimy grey linoleum that covered the floors of the school. She was instead in a large open field; thick, tall grasses of deep brown and rust swayed gently around her.

Hanging in the air, just above the grass, was a bizarre, pale green fog. The fog filled the sky as high as Maggie could see.

"Oh, no," she panicked. "Am I . . ." Her blue eyes widened, "*dead?*" She whispered the word "dead" as she felt her stomach and sides. Everything seemed to be intact. "Okay, girl," she said, taking a deep breath to calm herself down. "Get a grip! Think! If I'm dead, Bridge and Lorrine would have seen me being, well, dead. They're acting like I'm invisi . . . ."

She stopped short, absolutely refusing to say something so absurd. "So, what's going on?" she questioned aloud.

She turned back toward Bridgette and Lorrine and saw them talking as they walked further and further away from her. "Bridge! Lorrine! You guys," she cried out, but they just kept walking. They could not hear her calling.

She was somehow in two places at once. She could see the halls of the school and the few students who were now hustling to make it to class on time, but behind her—where a row of lockers should be—was the large, foggy field. She looked toward the big double doors of the school, only to find that they had become part of the field. In the distance, dark, undefined shapes moved behind the murkiness.

As she watched the shapes twist slowly through the fog, she heard a faint sound—a woman's voice—coming from where the shapes were. Maggie closed her eyes and listened, trying to make out what the woman was saying.

"Grass? Grass?" The woman's voice was distant and quiet, but it sounded like she was saying "grass."

"Grass?" Maggie had hoped for something a little more enlightening. She was perfectly aware that she was standing in a field of grass!

She squinted, in an effort to make out what was moving in the haze, but all she could see were the shadows.

As she leaned closer to the blurred forms, the "whoosh" that she had heard before, started whooshing again. It grew until it had amplified to a loud roar. As the roar reached a riotous crescendo, there was a blinding flash of blue light, and Maggie was back, standing in front of a row of purple and gold lockers.

She looked at the floor, which was once again dirty, gray vinyl, and at the double doors which were where they were supposed to be.

She stood alone in the high school hall, trying to figure out what had just happened.

"What in the world is going on with me?" she questioned out loud. She searched her thoughts for some logical explanation for how the morning had unfolded, but nothing came readily to mind. In the few short hours since she had gotten out of bed, there had been nothing but chaos.

After lingering for a few more stunned seconds, she decided that she had better get to her next class. She didn't want to walk into class late—that was always awkward—but she couldn't think of anything else to do instead.

"I got sick . . . I was in the bathroom throwing up . . . I must've eaten something . . . ." She tried to think up a good excuse to give her teacher for her tardiness. "Well, at least it's Ms. Devereaux, and not Mr. Lee." She shuddered at the mere mention of him.

After a few minutes, she reached the back auditorium door leading to the stage where her advanced drama class met. This was Maggie's favorite class due largely to Ms. Devereaux, the eccentric, but always cheerful drama teacher. Ms. Devereaux's quirky charm was a welcome ray of sunshine after dealing with Mr. "Math Nazi" Lee.

"Oh, Maggie dear," Ms. Devereaux smiled sweetly as she came in.

She half-heartedly smiled back as she stopped to take in today's version of her wonderfully unique teacher.

One could never be sure what to expect when they entered into the presence of Angelique Devereaux. Today, she wore a bright pink, ankle-length taffeta skirt that was held out widely at the bottom by layers and layers of lime green netting. Her top was a flowing, white peasant blouse with small, pink polka dots on the large, billowing sleeves. Her long, thick, silvery hair was tied up in a green scarf with crinkly fringe on the ends, and her eyes were framed by large, hot pink glasses. Due to the brightest pink lipstick imaginable, her lips seemed to be leaping off her face.

She walked over to Maggie and took her warmly by the hand. "I was worried about you, love. You do look pale! Brigeet said that you were not feeling well." Ms. Devereaux's voice was soft and soothing, with the slightest hint of a French accent. "Will you be here tomorrow, do you think?"

"Um," Maggie frowned, "I'm here now."

She realized as she spoke that something wasn't right. As she looked past her teacher to the students busily rehearsing skits, she noticed that these were not her usual classmates.

"Oh, fantastic!" she moaned. She couldn't believe that yet another bizarre twist had been thrown into her day. She looked at the back wall of the auditorium where large Roman numerals formed a gigantic clock.

"You've got to be kidding!" she moaned.

The clock read 11:35—nearly two hours after her friends had left her standing in the misty field at her locker.

Maggie stood staring at the auditorium clock without moving for several seconds. It wasn't hard for Ms. Devereaux to see that she was upset. Tears welled up in her eyes and spilled down her cheeks; her breath was choppy and her chin quivered uncontrollably.

The kind and caring teacher touched her on the shoulder in an effort to console her, but it was too late for that. Maggie was convinced that she was on a fast train to Looneyville, and no amount of consolation could stop it.

"Uh . . . I've . . . gotta go!" she mumbled shakily. She couldn't think clearly anymore. She had to get out—right now!

She took three steps backward and turned away from the eyes of the other students who had stopped acting to look at her. As she ran across the stage and back towards the hall, her eyes became so clouded with tears that she didn't see the large stage curtain right in front of her.

"Oh! Uh . . . Maggie!" Ms. Devereaux tried to warn her, but it was too late! She smacked into the heavy purple velvet curtain so hard that it knocked her feet out from under her; she landed flat on her back on the floor with a loud thud.

Several gasps and a few sniggers filled the room behind her.

She heard Ms. Devereaux repeating, "Oh, my dear . . . oh, my dear!" as she rushed over to see if she was hurt.

Maggie gasped, trying to regain the breath that had been knocked out of her by the hard wooden stage floor. She knew that she couldn't bear to face anyone after the way she had just humiliated herself. She sprang to her feet and ran clumsily across the stage, down the steps to the door, and out into the hall.

The tears now literally jumped from her eyes and onto her wet cheeks. She leaned against a locker, and sliding slowly down it to the floor, curled up into a sobbing, hysterical ball. "Wh-at . . . is . . . is happening to me-he . . . he?" she blubbered. She looked up at the ceiling and yelled, "What else could *possibly* happen?"

"Hey, Blue Eyes!"

She couldn't believe it! There, standing a couple of feet away was none other than Holden Guarlo, sporting a big, goofy grin. Without saying another word he sidled up next to her, and slid down right beside her on the floor.

She couldn't speak. She was somewhere between shocked and furious. She clenched her fists and seriously thought about slugging Holden as hard as she could, but as she turned to face him, something caught her off guard.

Up close, Holden had the most incredible eyes. They were not just green, but fluorescent emerald. She stared at his incredible eyes for several seconds, completely mesmerized.

"Hellooooo," Holden waved his hand in front of her face. "I know I'm B-

E-A-Utiful, but you are totally making me blush by staring!" He frowned just a little.

Maggie snapped back into reality and sighed disgustedly. "What are *you* doing here?"

Holden's nerdy smile was back. "Rough day?" he asked, ignoring her question entirely.

"I don't want to talk about it."

Again, Holden ignored her and continued, "Ya know, it's crazy, Blue . . . things happen you can't explain . . . you think you're losin' your marbles . . . and then someone comes along who understands, and it all seems to be okay." He spoke like he was some sort of great philosopher.

Maggie's jaw dropped open. He seemed to understand a little too well— with the exception of someone coming along and making things okay.

"What are you talking about?" she asked, almost afraid of what the answer would be. "Are you some sort of freakish mind reader or something?"

"Nah," Holden chuckled.

"Okay, then." She wanted some answers. "How is it that you knew I had blue eyes from across the room," she stood up and started to yell, "and you just *happened* to have a ten page report on rational expressions with you . . . and you knew about the pond! How can you sit here and tell me exactly what I am feeling, when I haven't told you a thing? Who are you?"

Fortunately, they were in the hall where the only classroom was the stage used by the drama classes. Everyone was used to overly exuberant conversations emanating from this area of the school. Otherwise, Maggie's shouting would have drawn a great deal of attention.

Holden, too, jumped to his feet; he grabbed Maggie by the shoulders. She tried to pull away, but he had a very firm grip. He looked at her with condescension, shook her three or four times, and then let go.

Maggie couldn't believe he'd just done that! She gaped at him for a second or two, and then suddenly, the whole incident seemed absolutely hilarious. She tried to hold back, but she couldn't help laughing out loud.

Holden quickly joined in, and within a few seconds, they were both rolling hysterically.

"I am *definitely* losing it," she finally said, as she struggled to gain her composure again. She wiped her eyes, and took a deep breath.

"Losing what?" Holden questioned.

Maggie just stared.

"No, seriously," she began, "how did you happen to have a ten page report on rational expressions in your book bag?"

"I didn't," Holden answered, "it was thirteen pages."

"But . . . ."

"Kinda cool that I had to do that same report at my last school," he interrupted, "and, also kinda cool that I never clean out my bag. Ya never know when somethin' you didn't throw away might come in handy."

Maggie just stared again. Her stare was suddenly interrupted by the bell ringing, signaling that lunchtime had arrived.

"Um . . . I'd better go find Bridgette and Lorrine," she excused. "They'll be wondering what happened to me. Of course, they're gonna think I've gone mental!"

"You're not gonna tell 'em, are ya?" Holden practically screamed.

Maggie jumped. "Tell them what?"

"Um, uh . . . about um . . . the report thing," he stammered.

"Nooo," she answered slowly, eyeing him suspiciously. "Not if you don't want me to."

"Right on, Blue! It'll be like our little secret . . . cool! See ya later!" He bounded off toward the lunchroom, grinning ear to ear.

"Weirdo . . . ." Maggie sighed, and went to go find her friends.

CHAPTER XXIV

ONLY ONE

Ultara retreated—as she often did—to the Caverns, to await the Travelers' return. She leaned against a long, silvery rock and gazed out over the edge of a bottomless cliff. At present, her thoughts were consumed by the news; after more than a year, the missing Nobles—Atoc Jonathan and the Atoh Audril—had been found.

She came to the Caverns to think and to strategize. She knew it would not be easy for Branlor and his company of Travelers to get the Borlocs back from the other world; she was well aware that any less than five receptors would cause instability in the energy force that pulled them back.

Five, she thought to herself, *impossible!*

Just then, Commander Branlor appeared at the bottom of the path. He was out of breath and his eyes were bloodshot; his usually well-groomed, wavy, brown hair looked like it'd been sucked up in a tornado.

Ultara floated down the path towards him. Although she was intimidating, Branlor had always felt that she was the most unbelievably beautiful woman he'd ever laid eyes on.

He watched fixedly as she moved toward him—her auburn hair drifting and swaying. Her voluptuous form was enhanced by the tight-fitting, slate blue suit she wore, and silhouetted exotically by a billowing black cloak. On several occasions, Branlor had lost himself while staring into her brilliant gold eyes, and now, as she swept down the path, he couldn't help imagining that she was coming toward him to lean her incredible body against his and kiss him passionately.

"Well? Is it done?" Ultara questioned coolly, snapping him out of his fantasy. She had noticed his disheveled appearance, but kept her expression stone-cold. She never allowed herself to exhibit too much emotion.

Branlor was winded—but not for the same reason as when he'd arrived. "Milady," he lowered his eyes out of fear that she would read his thoughts. "I believe we found the atoh, but we were only able to get one receptor onto her."

"You believe?" She stared Branlor down. "What is that supposed to mean?"

"Verolite assures me that this was the right girl," he explained, "and she did have the Borloc characteristics."

"But?"

"But, it's just that this girl looked older than the atoh."

"Older, Branlor? How much older?" She paced around him like a lioness preparing to pounce.

"W . . . well, I really didn't get a good look at her," he sputtered. "We had to move quickly." He was afraid to admit that the girl they had placed a receptor on looked to be at least ten years older than the atoh. "She did have black hair and blue eyes," he rationalized, "that much I did see."

"Then it has to be her . . . but only one receptor, Commander?" Ultara tsked in disapproval, "you were sent to place five . . . on them both. This will make things very difficult. She could be pulled anywhere on Lor Mandela."

Branlor was noticeably worried. "Y . . . yes, Ma'am. Someone came into the room. We had to leave."

There was a long, uneasy silence as Ultara paced. When at last she spoke, her voice was smooth as silk. "Of course, it was probably the atoc, which would have made your mission more successful," she paused sadistically and watched Branlor squirm, "but I suppose you were wise to leave. We can't risk being discovered."

Branlor—though disappointed that she hadn't fallen into his arms—was very relieved that Ultara wasn't sending bolts of lightning through him.

"It was *my* receptor, correct?" she asked, already formulating a new strategy to work with the present situation.

"Yes," he answered, "of course."

She stared straight into his eyes as she had done so many times before. Branlor instantly felt weak. "Give me the other four receptors, Branlor; I will place them on the atoh myself when she arrives."

"Yes, Ma'am." He pulled his gaze away from her captivating eyes and handed her a small leather pouch.

"Inform everyone to keep an eye out, Commander. She could show up anywhere. And send for Lortu. We'll need the Dwellers' help."

He nodded and lowered reverently to his knee. She dismissed him with a wave and he rose and rushed down the path that led out of the Caverns.

A slow, delighted smile spread across Ultara's face. At least the Travelers had been able to place one of her receptors. When Audril was tugged back to Lor Mandela, the little atoh would likely—even if the pull was only slightly stable—be brought directly to her. Placing the other four receptors on a child would be easy. And once Audril was on Lor Mandela permanently, the atoc would come without a fight; he wouldn't want to be separated from his precious little girl.

"Thank you, Branlor," she breathed to herself and smiled mischievously. "If you keep this up . . . and perhaps fix your hair . . . you may eventually get that kiss."

She gazed out over the steep jagged cliffs. "You've done well, Commander . . . not perfectly, but well."

CHAPTER XXV
THE SPIES' REPORT

On Lor Mandela, Ultara wasn't the only one interested in the whereabouts of the Borlocs. Darian also spent a great majority of his time trying to discover what had happened to Atoc Jonathan and his daughter during the battle at Mandela City.

"My loyal followers," he addressed a large congregation of his troops one hot summer morning. "We must be wary. I have been informed that Jonathan and his little girl have gone into hiding. As I speak, the Mandelans are refortifying their army, preparing to attack us." The fact was, though, none of his spies had issued such news. They were as unaware of the atoc and atoh's location as he was.

"They are the enemy!" he continued. His voice echoed through the large courtyard below the balcony on which he stood. "Only when they are discovered, can we ensure the safety of our families, and homes, and indeed all things that we hold dear!" An explosion of cheers filled the streets.

Darian smiled and waved to the onlookers and then walked back inside. Instantly, his smile turned into a scowl. "Where are they?" he fumed, "it's been a year. They couldn't have just disappeared!"

"My Lord," Omer suddenly appeared out of thin air and knelt in front of a startled Darian.

"What is it, Omer?" Darian glared at him. "You had better have a good excuse for popping in like this!"

Omer cleared his throat nervously. He knew he'd irritated Darian, but the news he brought was too important to worry about following standard protocol.

"Last evening, Grayden and I were on our way back from hunting in the Sybran. We were on our way back toward your estate . . . ."

"Palace!" Darian insisted.

"Oh . . . yes. Your palace," Omer corrected quickly.

Shortly after the disappearance of Jonathan and Audril, Darian had named himself atoc, and insisted that all of the Brashnellans refer to him as such.

"Anyway, as we were walking we noticed hundreds of Trysta World Travelers flying overhead."

"Trystas?" Darian's interest was piqued. "Did you follow them?"

"Yes, My Lord. We followed them to Drolana," he answered, exhibiting a little more confidence than he had shown thus far in their conversation.

Since Trysta Travelers are nearly invisible to anyone but a Trysta, Darian relied very heavily on Grayden and Omer and his other Trysta spies to keep him up to speed on any Traveler activity.

"What were they doing there?" Darian questioned.

Grayden, a rugged, dark-skinned, muscular man suddenly materialized next to Omer. "They were attempting to place receptors on a girl who they seem to think is Atoh Audril," he answered smugly.

Darian was too engrossed by the news to be put off by Grayden's intrusive entrance. He glanced briefly at him, and then back to Omer for his input.

Omer stammered, "Y . . . yes, they think they've found both of them."

"They think . . . they think?" he quizzed impatiently. "What do you mean they think? How would Jonathan and his daughter have gotten to Drolana?"

Grayden stepped up and stared Darian in the eyes. He showed no sign of intimidation whatsoever. "They didn't! Ultara is insane! The girl that the Trystas claim to be the atoh is at least seventeen or eighteen years old."

"What? That's impossible," Darian exclaimed. "They *must* be insane!"

Omer shrugged his shoulders, "Atoc, the girl did have black hair and blue eyes."

"Those fools!" Darian threw his hands in the air and began pacing. "It isn't unheard of to have black hair and blue eyes on Drolana!"

All of a sudden he stopped and became pensive and a mischievous smile oozed across his handsome face. "Were they successful at placing receptors, Grayden?" he asked. The fires in his eyes flickered wildly.

"Only partially," Grayden decided to play with him a bit. He was the only one in the Brashnellan Empire who was not scared of Darian. They were approximately the same size and build, but he had *real* magical powers. Darian could only perform his magic out of spell books.

Darian responded with a "don't you dare" expression.

"Actually," Grayden continued, "they were only able to get a single receptor onto her. As I'm sure you know, Atoc, it would take five or six to have enough stability to pull her back to the right person . . . and to keep her here long enough to get more receptors on her. We'll just have to keep our eyes out for this girl. She could show up anywhere!"

"Yes, my *confident* friend," Darian glared at Grayden, "I am aware of this."

Omer, who did not want to get involved in their intense banter, had kept quiet, but suddenly cleared his throat to interrupt. "They placed one, Atoc," he explained, "and I was also able to place one."

Both Darian and Grayden looked at Omer in complete astonishment. Darian was clearly impressed. "You, Omer? You placed one of your receptors on her?"

Omer smiled. "No, Majesty. The receptor I placed belongs to someone else."

Darian normally would have been upset by his indirectness, but Omer so rarely impressed him, that he decided to allow him to enjoy his moment.

"Well then, Omer. Whose receptor was it?"

Omer saw a hint of tension rising in Darian's face, and knew he'd better get to the point. "When I spotted the Travelers, Milord, I decided to join them and see if I could find out what they were up to. I had to be careful not to be recognized, of course. I approached a Traveler I hadn't seen before and asked if they needed any help. He said that they already had the Travelers they needed, but told me that they were off on some fool mission to put five receptors on the atoh and the atoc, who had been found on Drolana. He didn't seem too thrilled about the mission and was all too eager to fill me in.

"I came back here, grabbed the receptors that I thought would do us the most good, told Grayden to come with me, and re-joined the Trystas. The receptors I took were your son's . . . Ryannon's."

"Ryannon's?" Darian repeated excitedly; the fires in his dark eyes glistened. "Oh, General, that's delightful. Does he know?"

"Yes, Sire, I've just told him that he may have an unexpected visitor."

"This is excellent! You've seen my son. Women find him quite . . . um . . . irresistible. He'll have no trouble getting this young lady to fall for him. Then . . . ." He started pacing again, and no longer addressed his generals directly. He plotted out loud, to himself. "Yes . . . then . . . even though she is not the atoh . . . we'll convince the Mandelans that their beloved Audril has been brought back to us! We'll make up some story about a time warp between here and Drolana. It shouldn't be difficult to convince these idiots. Then no one else will be looking for the real Child of Balance, the one I need to become . . . ."

He turned on his heels, and without finishing his previous thought, barked, "Grayden, Omer! Let it be known that the reward has just tripled for anyone who brings me this *Atoh Audril* alive! Go!"

Omer bowed and Grayden nodded, and then they headed off to make the announcement.

"Excellent . . . excellent . . . Ryannon's!" Darian chuckled, "it seems that having a Trysta for a son is finally working to my advantage." His thin, evil smirk seemed even more malicious than usual. "I think I need to go have a little chat with my son."

CHAPTER XXVI
TWO HEADS ARE SCARIER THAN ONE

Maggie walked slowly toward the cafeteria, trying to figure out how to explain her sudden "disappearance" to Bridgette and Lorrine. She had run through several different scenarios in her head—including the truth—but decided she had better just stick with the "I got sick" excuse.

"Oh! Maggieeee!" Bridgette ran toward her, grinning, wide-eyed, and pulling Lorrine along by the arm.

"Hey, Bridge. Hey, Lorrie."

Out of the corner of her eye, she saw an arm slowly reach out from behind Bridgette and steadily wrap itself around her waist. All at once, blonde curls sprung up from behind Bridgette's head, followed by the inane grin that had become all too familiar.

"Oh, and erm . . . hey, Holden?" she stammered.

Bridgette glanced over her shoulder at Holden and giggled sheepishly at Maggie's stunned reaction to him. "Hey, Maggs. Holden's been telling us all about your awful morning! Are you okay, sweetie?" Bridgette questioned.

Maggie gazed from Bridgette—who was staring at her blankly and grinning ear to ear—to Lorrine, who was rolling her eyes, and then, to the wacky new kid, Holden whose mouth was twisted up in a playful little knot.

She raised her eyebrows at him and whispered an annoyed, "What?"

"Man," Holden looked away from her, and directed his focus on Bridgette. "Ya know, Pretty Dude, I hate pukin'. Nothing worse! 'Cept maybe a Neptune Cocktail after a particularly gnarly wipeout. It's like *whoa!*" He stumbled dramatically. "Fierce! But then ya usually puke anyway," he chuckled, and Bridgette

218

giggled again.

Maggie grimaced and caught Lorrine doing the same.

Lorrine shrugged her shoulders and glared at Bridgette. "Ugh! Come along, Margaret. Let's go get something to drink. I suddenly feel an acute case of nausea coming on!"

"Yeah, um okay . . . sure," she answered slowly. She glanced, perplexed, at her best friend and her strange new buddy as Lorrine guided her away. "What's up with that?" she asked.

Lorrine stopped walking and spun to face her. "Positively unfathomable! What absolute imbeciles! They've known each other barely ten minutes, and it's 'hee hee hee,' 'ho ho ho' 'giggle giggle giggle'. Entirely embarrassing . . . that is what it is!"

Maggie was well aware that the whole "giddy girly" thing was extremely annoying to Lorrine. She was what most teenagers weren't—serious, refined, and totally into school. She dressed like a sophisticated business woman most of the time—suits, briefcases and all—and wore studious glasses despite her perfect vision. Her shoulder-length, mousy hair was always twisted into a conservative ponytail at the nape of her neck. She was also quite fond of using large words like 'unfathomable' and insisted upon calling people by their given names—no nicknames or abbreviations.

"What happened? I mean, I *just* saw him in the hall right before the bell rang. How'd they get to know each other so fast?"

"Oh, well . . . he just walked up and started talking to her. At first she remained appropriately aloof, but by the time he got to, 'Whoa, Pretty Dude, your eyes are like a shiny new penny, sprayed with that glittery spray stuff,' she was blushing and giggling like a lunatic!"

Maggie nearly choked. "He said that? Really?"

"I am afraid so."

"Wow. That is one of the stupidest lines I've ever heard! I can't believe she fell for it."

"Hook, line, and sinker, my friend."

Maggie and Lorrine bought a couple of sodas from a vending machine, and then—disgusted or not—sat and watched Bridgette and Holden schmooze and giggle at each other from across the cafeteria.

"She is not even aware that we are gone, is she?" Lorrine shook her head and sighed disapprovingly.

"Uh, nope, I don't think so." Maggie responded, her gaze still fixed on her best friend and this suddenly omnipresent surfer dude.

"Well, I've had quite enough," Lorrine sighed. "Come along, Margaret. We should go to Biology early, and organize the lab stations for Mr. Berg."

Maggie thought to herself, *I have the weirdest friends*, but she went along to Biology with Lorrine anyway.

Luckily, and much to Maggie's relief, the rest of the school day was pretty uneventful.

Bridgette wanted to tell her all about Holden after school, but Maggie had already put up with a little more of Holden Guarlo than she'd wanted to in one day. It was bad enough that he had embarrassed her in Math class, shook her like a toddler in the drama hall, and had become an instant obsession for her best friend; but as it turned out, he was in two more of her classes as well.

"I missed English this morning, Bridge," she tried, "I should go back and pick up my work, or I'll get behind. I'll call ya later and you can tell me all about him."

"Oh, all right," Bridgette sighed, "but he's sooo sweet and he really listens to me and . . . oh, my gosh! Did you see his eyes?"

"Bridge . . . really, I need to go! I'll call you tonight! I promise!"

Bridgette reluctantly nodded and gave Maggie a fake peck on the cheek.

Maggie smiled and shook her head, and then went back inside the school. She wasn't really that worried about getting behind in English, but decided to see if her teacher had any make up work anyway.

She called her dad and asked him if he would pick her up after he got off work.

It was around four o'clock when Maggie walked out the big double brown doors and sought out a good spot on the deserted school lawn to wait for Nathan.

She was never so relieved that a day was almost over—bizarre, strange, unusual, wacky, off-the-wall—no words seemed to even come close to describing it.

She decided on waiting in the shade of the school marquee, and had just dropped her bag on the lawn when she heard something—a sound surging in and out directly behind her.

She froze. Her heart began to pound. Her breath seized inside her with a gasp. It was back—the strange "whooshing" sound! It was happening again!

"Oh no!" she shouted. Instinctively, she dashed back toward the stone steps, not even pausing to pick up her bag.

As her foot hit the third step from the top, an "internal lasso", just like the one before, grabbed her abruptly. With a loud *whoosh* and a pop, she was again standing, dazed and alarmed, in an unfamiliar place.

This time the picture in front of her was much clearer than it had been before—clearer and more frightening. She was in a large meadow, but it wasn't like earlier. It was night this time—dark and eerily quiet.

The still, black canopy above was shredded by literally millions of jagged stars which, by virtue of their numbers, should have been far more illuminating than they were.

Across the field was the scariest looking forest she had ever seen.

All of the trees appeared to be nearly dead and leafless. Their twisted, gnarled, charcoal branches jutted out at odd angles creating a chaotic maze of tangled limbs.

A dense murkiness hung close to the ground, tightly encircling the distorted tree trunks. The muck looked as though it was trying to strangle away any life that the trees might have had left in them.

Behind the forest, a small, crooked mountain protruded up from out of nowhere. It was steep and harsh with a sharp, angry form. The shadows that were cast by the sadistic stars overhead played on its crevices and outcroppings, sending demonic faces rippling across its surface.

The scene was straight out of a horror movie, and as Maggie took it all in, a chilling wave of fear rippled through her body.

She attempted to remain calm, but what she saw next ripped the calmness right out of her and threw it to the low, howling wind.

There was a faint rustling in the mangled trees, and then a loud crash as an enormous two-headed creature burst out and thundered onto the meadow.

"Okay, okay," Maggie's eyes widened with terror. "Don't panic! Two headed . . . *two headed . . . not real!*"

The creature turned back toward the dark forest and let out a deafening shriek. Slowly, it paced back and forth in front of the twisted trees.

In the piercing starlight, Maggie could see the massive, frightening animal quite clearly. It was unlike anything she'd ever seen or heard of—a huge, mythical-looking beast with a thick, muscular body, resembling an enormous horse, but at least twice a horse's size. It was black and scaly with powerful, long, prancing legs, and a sleek, full, spiked tail. At the top of each swaying reptilian neck was an oblong, hooded head, similar to a king cobra's.

It turned, giving Maggie a full view of one of the heads. It had creepy, glowing, silver slits for eyes, an enormous mouth and gleaming, long, sharp, dripping fangs that gnashed wildly at the hazy air.

The thing hadn't seen her yet, and she most definitely did not want it to see her—ever! She was next to a large outcropping of rocks, behind which she swiftly ducked. She glanced around the edge of the rocks and watched in horror as a small, furry animal darted out from behind a shrub at the edge of the forest. It twittered about for a bit, but then noticed the monster and froze in its tracks.

The beast sniffed the air, reared up on its hind legs, and one of its snake-like heads swayed backward. Suddenly, as fast as a bolt of lightning, it plunged toward the little animal and snatched it with its twisted fangs.

It threw the furry creature—which was shrieking and thrashing—high into the air and as the tiny animal fell, the beast's jaws snapped on it ferociously, and the shrieking silenced.

Maggie panted, trying not to panic. She was still attempting to convince herself that none of this was really happening.

Cold beads of sweat formed on her forehead and upper lip. She wanted to cry. She wanted to go home. "Someone," she pleaded quietly, "please . . . please help me!"

Suddenly, a cloaked man burst out from the trees, yelling wildly, and running full-force at the beast. Maggie jumped and slapped her hand over her mouth to stifle her scream.

The animal lunged at the man and one of the powerful jaws snapped loudly, narrowly missing his leg.

Maggie gasped and tried to get herself further behind the rocks, but she failed to see a large tree root that was sticking up out of the ground next to her. As she pulled herself back, she lost her balance and fell over the root, landing with a thud on the wet meadow—right out in the open.

At once, the beast froze. It turned its heads away from the cloaked man and stared across the field. Both heads lowered and sniffed the ground, and then four evil, silver eyes locked their gaze directly on Maggie.

Maggie's heart pounded so hard, it felt like it was going to burst through her chest. She couldn't catch her breath. She felt like every muscle was being stabbed by hot, sharp needles. Multiple thoughts twisted frantically around in her head, tangling together and piling one on top of another. "Oh, no," she whimpered, *"I'm dead!"*

The creature let out another deafening screech. It took two or three slow, deliberate steps toward Maggie, and then broke out into a full, thunderous run across the field.

Every inch of her felt heavy. She tried, but couldn't move. It was as though her mind and her body had disconnected. She just lay on the warm, dank grass, watching as the monster came closer and closer.

"Get up! Run! Run! What's wrong with you? Ruunnnn!" The cloaked man chased quickly behind the animal, yelling loudly and waving his hands frantically. "Are you crazy? Run!" He raised a gloved arm out in front of himself and shot what looked like long, golden spikes at the rapidly-moving creature.

Several of the spikes glanced off the monster's back, which slowed it down a little, giving Maggie time to finally snap out of her horrified trance. Quickly, she sprang to her feet and started running—hoping to put as much space between her and the animal as possible.

But the situation was only getting worse. She didn't know where she was, so she didn't know where to go.

The rocks wouldn't hide her anymore and it looked as though were the only shelter at all on this side of the field. Additionally, the beast was heading right toward them. The only other cover in sight was the spooky forest across the field, but running toward impending doom didn't seem like a good option either.

The beast was approaching rapidly.

The man kept up his attempts to slow it down with the spikes, but they didn't seem to be having an effect any longer.

Maggie heard the monster behind her, and within just a few short seconds, its hot breath was blasting down on the back of her neck.

Instantly, she stopped running and dropped to the ground, curling into a ball. The creature was caught so off guard, that it flew right over her—one of its back legs barely missing her head. She jumped back to her feet. The beast stopped and swung around in front of her and a dripping, fanged mouth bulleted towards her.

Maggie jumped to one side, narrowly escaping its bite as the other head screeched and bolted toward her in the same way as the first. She lunged just as it snapped dangerously close to her right shoulder.

Both heads were now weaving and swaying above her.

She turned to face the beast and realized that it had her right where it wanted. The heads were poised on either side of her—in perfect striking position.

She froze—too panic-stricken to think of anything else to do—and waited for her untimely death.

"What are you doing?" The cloaked man yelled from the middle of the field. "Moooooovve!"

But she couldn't. She just stared at the massive, glimmering heads weaving and swaying high above her, and waited. The creature hissed and then roared loudly again; its stale, hot breath exploded across her face and blasted through her hair. Her eyes shifted from one head to the other, but, the rest of her stayed frozen in place.

"Oh please . . . I'm dead! This is it! Come on body! Please . . . MOVE!" Blinding tears welled in her eyes. "Please . . . ." she whimpered out loud.

Both of the monster's heads reared back—their slit-like eyes glinting in the harsh starlight. Maggie watched as they began their deadly descent, straight towards her.

Time seemed to slow.

"Move!" The man's voice echoed somewhere in the distance.

The only thing Maggie could hear clearly was her own pounding heart.

The beast's heads weaved downward—their silver, pupil-less eyes wide as their razor-sharp fangs came closer and closer. One of the heads was now only inches away from her—and its jaws were spreading wide.

Finally, and without a second to spare, instinct took over. She bent to the side, almost folding completely in half, and then twisted around so fast that her legs left the ground and pushed her skyward into a perfectly graceful aerial. She flipped in the air, dropped, and rolled across the ground.

One of the monster's heads grazed across her back as she rolled, cutting a long gash in her shirt.

Time zipped back to normal as an ear-splitting, earth-shaking thud sounded behind her, followed by a deafening shriek. She looked back, expecting to see the thing coming toward her again, but it wasn't. It was pounding its enormous hooves wildly on the ground, and bellowing.

It staggered a bit, back and forth, shrieked again, and then dropped hard— sending up a thick cloud of dust—landing right next to where Maggie had stopped rolling.

Quickly, she scrambled backwards to get away from the gigantic scaly animal before its next strike, but oddly, it didn't appear to be moving. It just laid still and quiet in the damp grass.

She scooted back a few more feet, and as she did, what had happened became clear.

Her flip had caused the monster to miss her and instead bite one of its own heads clean off. The creature was dead—its severed head thrashing and flopping uncontrollably across the ground.

"That was unbelievable! Amazing! Unbelievable!" the man yelled as he ran toward her, his black cloak billowing largely behind him. "Are you all right?" He held out a gloved arm and helped her to her feet. "I've never seen anyone escape a rynolt like that! *Amazing!*" he repeated.

What she saw next almost knocked her back to the ground. She lifted her head and found herself face to face with arguably the most beautiful man she'd ever set eyes on.

"Whoa," she breathed, and stumbled clumsily.

He was an absolute Adonis—at least six-foot-four, muscular and strong. Dark, wavy hair hung down and rested on his broad shoulders, framing his square, chiseled jaw. As if all of this wasn't enough, his eyes were completely intoxicating. Maggie couldn't tell for sure what color they were—only that they were dark—but little flecks of bright red sparkled and flashed across them in the starlight.

As the stranger looked at Maggie, a breathtaking, knee-shaking, glistening white smile grew across his handsome face. He bowed and then lowered down on one knee.

"Your Highness. Please forgive me. I didn't realize . . . What an honor this is for me!"

"Wha?" Maggie was more than a little stunned.

"You are all right, aren't you? How may I be of service, Highness?" He stayed on his knee, but looked up into Maggie's eyes—awaiting her command.

She was panting heavily, and not just because of the ordeal she had just been through with the freaky two-headed thing. "Wha . . . I mean . . . um . . . who are you?" she stammered, feeling stupid that she couldn't think of anything to say.

He stood up and looked deep into her eyes.

Her cheeks burned and her heart pounded.

"Oh, yes. I'm sorry, I am . . . ."

But before the handsome stranger could finish, there was a sudden whoosh, a flash of blue light, and a loud *crack!* Maggie was instantly—and quite unwillingly—yanked back to the stone steps of Glenhill High School.

CHAPTER XXVII
THE TABLE TALK

"Wait!" Maggie bellowed angrily. "No! No! *Nooooo!*" She dropped down onto the darkened school steps and buried her head in her hands. "You gotta be kidding me! This is so totally unfair!" she cried.

Just then, she heard the clunking and clattering of her dad's old sedan, followed by Nathan's frantic, shrieking voice. "Maggie! There you are! Finally! Good grief! Where have you been?

She looked up to see her dad sprinting toward her with a wild and terrified look on his face. He reached the steps so quickly that she wasn't sure how he'd done it. He grabbed a hold of her and hugged and kissed the top of her head repeatedly.

"Da-ad!" She wriggled out of his clutches. "What are you doing? What's wrong with you?"

"What do you mean, what am I doing," he yelled loudly. "I've been looking for you for over *three* hours!"

"What?" She knew she shouldn't be surprised, but she was nonetheless.

"Three hours," he repeated. "Where've you been?" He eyed her disheveled and tattered appearance and added, "And what the devil have you been doing?"

"Dad, I . . ." She brushed a clump of mud from her ripped T-shirt and fussed with her damp, half-fallen-out ponytail. She couldn't tell him. He'd never believe it. "I . . . I was . . . um, with some friends. I'm sorry. I musta lost track of time!"

"You lost . . . I can't belie . . . *what?*" Nathan's face was red with rage. "You told me to pick you up here! I came to pick you up, and you were *nowhere!* Now I find you looking like you've been beaten and all you can say is 'I lost track of time'?" He ran his hand through his floppy hair. "How in the world did you end up looking like this anyway?" He asked, motioning toward her dirty, wet clothing.

Maggie glanced down at her mud-covered jeans. "I . . . uh . . . well . . . we were . . . um. We were just . . . you know, wrestling around on the lawn," she stammered.

"Wrestling?" Nathan grimaced. "And who exactly is this we you were wrestling with?" His tone was interrogatory. "You and a girl friend . . . or you and a *boy* friend?"

"Oh, yikes! Come on, Dad!" Maggie protested, "Girls, dad! Really! I . . . I was with Lorrine and Bridgette."

Nathan's furious expression softened a little. "Lorrine and Bridgette?" he repeated. "Hmm, Lorrine and . . . uh, Bridgette?" Suddenly, he looked very angry again. "Then how do you explain the fact that BRIDGETTE HAS BEEN WITH ME SINCE 4:30? SHE'S BEEN HELPING ME SEARCH FOR YOU!"

Maggie sighed disgustedly. She'd been caught, but instead of feeling the slightest bit apologetic, she was mad. She had been through so much in one day, including almost being killed by some freakish animal, and then, just when something nice happened, it was yanked away before it could even get started! Now, to be caught lying to her dad, only because he would never believe the truth? It all seemed to be so below-the-belt, and it made her mad!

"Fine, Dad," she snapped, "whatever! Why don't you just punish me and get it over with!"

Nathan glared at her. He didn't want to let on that he was incredibly relieved that she was okay. "Oh, I'm gonna punish you all right." He pointed emphatically at the car. "March, young lady! We'll discuss this when we get home!"

"Fine!" She stomped across the lawn, snatched up her book bag from where she had left it laying, and headed for the still-idling sedan. She practically ripped the car door off as she opened it, and then plopped down into the seat and yanked the door back shut with a slam.

The ride home was very tense. Neither of them made a sound. He just drove, and she just stared out the window, fuming.

It's not my fault! She consoled her nagging conscience; *I didn't choose to disappear for three hours! And what am I supposed to do? Worry him even more with all this crazy junk?*

She glanced sideways at her dad. He looked miserable. In fact, it looked like he was trying not to cry. Maggie's mood slightly shifted from anger and a sense of injustice, to a tiny twinge of concern for what her dad had been through. It occurred to her that he must have been pretty scared when he couldn't find her. Then, to discover her battered and beaten—after three hours, no less—only to be lied to? It was no wonder that he was upset.

Nathan turned the corner onto their street and pulled into their long, flat driveway.

"Dad?" Maggie tried.

Nathan didn't answer. He slid from the car and slumped up the small walkway that led to the front porch.

"Dad, c'mon! Really. I'm sorry," she called after him.

Nathan climbed the rickety old porch steps, head bowed and shoulders sagging, and pulled open the white wooden door.

Why don't you just tell him? Her conscience urged. *Tell him everything— about the little lights, and disappearing at your locker, and the attack of the two-headed snake-horse.*

She followed him into the house.

Two-headed snake horse? Yeah, he's gonna believe that!

Nathan switched on the living room light and tossed the car keys half-heartedly onto the small hall table just inside the door. He glanced back at Maggie with sad puppy-dog eyes, and then dragged himself towards the kitchen.

"Dad, please wait. I need to talk to you. Table talk?" she suggested.

Over the years, whenever they needed to discuss something serious, Nathan would make his special peppermint hot cocoa with miniature marshmallows, and they would sit at the kitchen table and talk. Somehow the whole ceremony of it, combined with the cocoa, provided comfort, no matter how uncomfortable the subject. They now referred to these father-daughter chats as "table talks."

"I think that's a relatively good idea," Nathan agreed, although this was one table talk he was dreading. He was convinced that Maggie had been out rolling around with some hormone-crazed teenage guy, and that she was "madly in love" and soon to be engaged to the next future pig wrestler of America. "Why don't ya go change out of those wet clothes, and I'll put on the water."

Maggie nodded and headed upstairs.

Nathan went to the kitchen and pulled out a dented red teapot. "I'm not ready for this," he mumbled to himself as he filled the pot from the tap and placed it on their old gas stove. "Only last week she was starting Kindergarten," he muttered as he waited for the battered kettle's melancholy whistle.

A few minutes later, Maggie came into the kitchen and sat down at one of the mismatched chairs around their garage-sale, metal dining table. Her black curls were smoothed back into a tame ponytail, and she had changed into her comfy pink and white polka-dotted flannel pajamas, puffy white bath robe, and fuzzy pink slippers.

Nathan brought the cocoa cups to the table and sat down across from her. He poured the steaming water into the small white cups, stirred the contents of each a few times, and then plopped a small handful of marshmallows in.

Maggie breathed in a deep whiff of the heavenly peppermint-chocolate aroma as she reached for her cup and slid it toward her.

Nathan took a slow, slurping sip, and began with, "Well?"

"Okay, first," she started, "I didn't mean to lie to you. It's just . . . I didn't think you'd understand."

"Oh man, I knew it!" Nathan blurted. "Listen Smaggs, I know you think you're old enough to know about these things, but you're still young! You don't wanna make decisions now that you'll eventually regret! You have to think about the future. You can't just dive into things without standing back and thinking about the future! And pig wrestling isn't all it's cracked up to be."

"What? Da-ad! What on Earth are you talking about," she frowned. "You don't have any idea what I was going to say! Wait! Pig wrestling?"

"Oh . . . um, sorry," Nathan stammered, "I just . . . well, I was thinking that maybe . . . ."

"Yeah, I know what you were thinking. Yikes! I was not out with a guy, Dad . . . and give me a little credit! I'm not gonna marry a pig wrestler!" She grimaced and shook her head. "Honestly."

Nathan took a sip of cocoa and smiled sheepishly. "Yeah, I guess I got a little carried away."

Maggie picked up her cup and giggled. "A little."

"So, what's on your mind, Smaggs?"

She drew in a big breath and started. "Remember that dream I had this morning? Well, it wasn't a dream." She told him about the incident in detail, and about what had happened at her locker. "I felt like something was pulling me, and then I was in this field. I wasn't at my locker anymore."

She paused to check her dad's reaction.

He was staring at her blankly.

"Dad, I know this sounds . . . ."

Suddenly, she stopped short. Her eyes widened and she held her breath. It was back! The low, pulsating, *whoosh. . .whoosh. . .whoosh.*

It surged in and out behind her, growing louder with each whoosh.

Her pulse raced; she grabbed the sides of the kitchen table and closed her eyes. Oddly though, the sound only whooshed three times and then stopped; nothing happened.

"What was that?" Nathan walked over and looked out the screen door, searching for the source of the strange sound. "I wonder what those blasted Harrisons are up to this time."

"You heard that?"

"Yeah . . . shouldn't I have?"

Maggie felt frantic as she realized that, at any moment, she could be pulled away again. "Dad! Listen! I keep hearing that whoosh, and then I end up somewhere else! It's happened to me twice already," she yelled. "I go somewhere . . . somewhere I've never been before. That's what happened at my locker, and that's what happened after school! Don't you see? That's why you couldn't find me! I was somewhere else!"

Nathan frowned. "Smaggs! Calm down! You're kinda freakin' out here."

"No, Dad! I'm not freaking out . . . I mean, yeah . . . I sorta am, but it's because I keep leaving! I can't control it! There's a whoosh and then a lasso and then 'pop' and I'm outta here!"

She barely finished her sentence when it started again.

Whoosh. . .whoosh. . .whoooooooosh!

"Oh, no . . . *Daaaaad!*"

Nathan grimaced and looked around the room. "What is that?" he asked again, "it's kinda annoying!"

Maggie's eyes were wide with fear. The familiar tugging was back. Nathan glanced over at his panic-stricken daughter, who was panting heavily and clutching the table so hard that her knuckles were white.

"What's the matter with you, Ma . . . .?"Suddenly, there was a deafening crack and a bright blue flash, and Maggie was gone!

Nathan shrieked hysterically and started spinning around in spastic little circles. "Maggieeee!" he screamed, "Maggieeeee! Margaret Amanda Baker! I am not amused!"

He dropped to his knees and looked under the table. Then he started frantically opening cupboards, the pantry, and the refrigerator. "*Maggieeeee!*"

He ran to the back door and out into the dark yard. He looked around the corner of the house behind the big maple tree—and then up in the big maple tree. His eyes were bulging, and his black hair was flopping wildly as he jumped up and down, looking over the fence.

"Maggie! This isn't funny! Where are you," he shouted desperately.

His back fence neighbor, Mr. Harrison, stood at his flaming barbecue, holding a long spatula, and staring at him like he was crazy.

"Margaret," he squealed again as he ran back inside and started madly searching the house.

But Maggie was not there. She had, once again, been taken to an unfamiliar place.

CHAPTER XXVIII
KAHLIE AND RYANNON

Maggie stood in a strange meadow that she didn't recognize, and although it had been late evening in Glenhill, it was broad daylight here.

At first she thought that this was the same place she had been earlier. There were certain similarities. It was a vast field, with a forest in the distance, backed by a tall, narrow mountain, but there was nothing scary about this place. It was warm, peaceful, and gloriously beautiful. The lush green field was blanketed in soft waving grass, punctuated by tiny frills of yellow and purple blossoms.

Breaking up the rolling ocean of green were tall outcroppings of twisting brown rock, jutting up boldly at sharp angles from the ground. Tiny bits of crystal in the rock glistened in a myriad of sparkling, jewel-toned colors as the sun danced across the unusual formations.

The sunlight itself was also unusual. It glowed brightly, but seemed to be filtered and softened somehow. Its soothing warmth flooded over Maggie, dissolving into her, and made her feel both sleepy and energized at the same time.

In the distance was a forest, bordered by a grove of stately swaying trees. Their long leafy branches hung to the ground and flowed softly in the gentle gusts of cool air that wafted through them.

The sky above the forest was brilliant blue—bluer than any ocean Maggie had ever seen in pictures. A steep, majestic mountain rose high behind the trees and into the azure sky. It was covered in a blanket of luxurious velvet green, except for the contrasting white snow caps that topped its highest peaks.

"Wow!" Maggie breathed as she took in the view, "this place is awesome!"

She fiddled with her hair and smoothed her clothes just in case she should meet up with a handsome stranger again. She was wishing that she had a mirror and her makeup bag, when a horrible realization struck.

"Oh, perfect," she moaned as she looked down at herself. "I'm still in my pajamas! This is just great!" She pulled her bathrobe around her tightly and cinched the tie, as if that would help somehow.

She glimpsed across the field and realized that she was not the only person presently occupying it. "Just great!" she repeated.

Near the grove of trees across the field, and apparently unaware that Maggie was there, a woman sat, quietly reading on one of the smaller rock formations.

Maggie's first reaction was to scope out cover, but the woman didn't appear to be much of a threat. *Hmmm, she thought, she looks pretty harmless . . . only one head and all. Maybe she can help me.* Maggie started across the field.

The woman was completely engrossed in her book and unaware that anyone else was near. In fact, the entire time it took for Maggie to cross the large field, the woman didn't budge or look up.

"Ahem," Maggie timidly cleared her throat when she was a few feet away.

The sudden break in the silence startled the lady so, that she nearly fell off her rock. "I'm trying to read here!" she snipped, and shot an agitated look in Maggie's direction, but then slid quickly off of the formation and—much to Maggie's surprise—dropped to her knees. "Forgive me, Majesty." The woman was shaking like a leaf and obviously quite unnerved by Maggie's appearance.

"I uh . . . I . . . ." Maggie stammered.

The woman looked up, but not directly at Maggie's eyes. "How? I mean . . . I . . . I thought you were dead!" Tiny tears dropped from the woman's eyes and slid down her face as she spoke.

"Wait a sec, what?" Maggie blurted in response to the morbid comment, "what do you mean? We . . . we don't even know each other, do we?"

The woman timidly looked at Maggie's face but did not rise. "Oh, you're not . . . but I thought . . . forgive me."

Maggie could hardly imagine what needed to be forgiven. "Please, you really don't need to stay down there." She felt awkward about the recent rash of people bowing down to her.

"Oh yes, Majesty . . . of course." She wiped the tears off of her cheeks and rose to her feet.

This was the first look Maggie really got of her. Up close, she was younger than Maggie had first thought, perhaps about twenty years old or so, with long, curly auburn hair and slightly freckled skin. Her features were graceful and very refined. She was sprite-like in her overall appearance, which intrigued Maggie greatly.

"I'm sorry," Maggie apologized, "I didn't mean to upset you. It's just . . . well, you're the second person to kneel down and call me Majesty. I don't think that I'm who you think I am."

The woman stared at her blankly. Obviously, Maggie's comment didn't compute.

"Okay," Maggie gave it another try. "My name is Maggie Baker." She smiled and dipped in a small curtsy. "From Glenhill, Iowa."

The woman continued to stare, but nodded affirmatively as Maggie spoke.

"I'm just, um . . . you know. I'm not royalty, or anything. I'm just an ordinary teenager." She tilted her head as if to say, do you get what I'm saying to you?

"Oh, I see, Your Highness." Clearly there was a gap in the communication somewhere. "I can't believe it," she burst out suddenly, "a Borloc . . . still alive . . . Maggiebaker Borloc . . . Where is the house of Glenowa, or was it Glenohiowa?"

"Uh . . . I . . ." Maggie let out an exasperated sigh. "Maybe we should start over. Please, call me Maggie."

"As you wish, Maggie."

"And you are?"

"My name is Kahlie. I am . . . I mean, I was the Ator's Companion

Servant."

Maggie had no idea what she was talking about, but at least she had a name to work with.

"Kahlie," she went for broke, "who is it, exactly, that you think I am?"

"You are Maggie, correct?" Kahlie smiled.

"Yes," Maggie smiled back "but, why did you call me Your Majesty and Highness?"

"Because . . . well, at first I thought you were the ator . . . I mean . . . because you are a Borloc, of course."

"What's a Borloc?"

Kahlie's mouth gaped open. She was speechless for several seconds. "Well," she finally began, "wait! How can you not know what a Borloc is? You are one!"

Maggie grimaced. "Kahlie, I really have no idea what you're talking about."

"A Borloc! You know? Guardians and rulers of Lor Mandela," she yelped, gesturing excitedly with her hands.

"Rulers? Yikes! Hold on a second! I already told you! I'm just an ordinary teenager from Iowa. What on Earth makes you think that I am one of these . . . these Borlocs?"

Kahlie took a couple of deep breaths and calmly continued. "You have black hair."

Maggie grimaced again.

"And blue eyes?" Kahlie waited for Maggie to respond. Maggie waited for Kahlie to say something that made sense.

"You really don't know what I'm talking about, do you?"

"No, Kahlie. I don't. What do my eyes and the color of my hair have to do with anything?"

Kahlie's smile returned. It was warm and compassionate now. "I'm sorry, Maggie. It's just that, well . . . only Borlocs have black hair and blue eyes."

Maggie chuckled, "You're kidding, right? I can think of about half a dozen or so people in my school alone with black hair and blue eyes."

"Really?" Kahlie was awestruck. "How is that possible? Where did you say you're from again?"

"I'm from a small town in Iowa."

"I'm not familiar with Iowa. Is it near Koria?"

"Um, I don't think so."

Maggie decided to lay it all out in the open. She hoped that her experiences might seem normal and have a logical explanation in this place.

"Kahlie," she started, "there've been some really bizarre things happening to me."

"Well, yes, just the fact that you don't know you're a Borloc seems a bit odd."

Maggie frowned. *Borloc, schmorloc!* She thought to herself. *Jeez lady! Give it a rest!* She proceeded to tell Kahlie about all of the weird things that had happened that day.

She longed for answers, but judging from the puzzled look on Kahlie's face, she wasn't going to get them.

"So, you have no idea why you're here?" Kahlie asked.

"Oh," Maggie moaned, "so, I guess you don't get it either. I kinda hoped you'd understand all of this better than I do."

Kahlie shrugged her shoulders. "I'm sorry," she tried. She could see that Maggie was disappointed and desperately wanted to help. "You know what, though? I'm sure the answers are here somewhere. We'll just have to keep our eyes open."

"Yeah," Maggie sighed. "So . . . where on Earth am I?"

"Earth?" Kahlie inquired innocently. "What's an Earth?"

Maggie just stared at her. Slowly—and quite frightened of what the answer would be—she asked, "Wh . . . what is your planet called?"

"Planet?"

"World?" she tried again.

"Yeah, I know what a planet is," Kahlie answered. "Are you telling me that you're not from Lor Mandela?"

"Lor Man Whatta?"

"This world . . . Lor Mandela," Kahlie explained. "Maggie! This is extraordinary!"

"I don't understand. I'm not on Earth," she mumbled in horror. "This is not extraordinary, Kahlie! This is terrible! I don't want to be on Lor Whatever! I want to go home! Now!"

"Okay, just calm down. We'll figure this out," Kahlie soothed as she took Maggie by the hand. "We should go to the Transendar. Yeah, of course! Come on! If there's any information on the things that have been happening to you, we'll be able to find it there."

She grabbed the book she'd been reading and—with Maggie in tow—started for the trees. Maggie had no idea what Transendar was, but she didn't ask. At the moment, she was just trying not to cry. Her only consolation was that Kahlie seemed to want to help, and perhaps because Kahlie was close to her own age, she felt comfortable with her. She gulped back her tears and followed Kahlie toward the forest without resistance.

Up close, the trees at the edge of the forest were more gigantic than Maggie had initially thought—more gigantic and more beautiful. Although they were imposing, there was a hypnotic, airy quality to them. The branches swished and swayed rhythmically back and forth; the silvery leaves sparkled in the filtered sunlight.

As they approached, the branches stopped swaying and slowly parted; they rose in the air like a thick, green stage curtain.

Maggie gasped, but Kahlie smiled reassuringly so she continued to follow. As soon as they passed underneath, the branches dropped and began undulating side to side again, as though nothing had changed.

Each tree they came to did the same. It would stop swishing as they drew near, and lift its branches politely so they could pass through. Then the branches would drop back down and return to their metrical swaying.

When Maggie looked back, all she could see behind them was a wall of wispy, swinging, green branches.

They moved on, past the mysterious trees, and down a narrow path. Lacy, exotic-looking orange, yellow and chartreuse green bushes and more odd rock formations lined the sides of the path. The bushes shook and rustled as small furry animals, unlike any Maggie had seen before, darted and scurried around and in and out of them. Pure white bird-type creatures floated overhead. They were so bright white that it was difficult for Maggie to look at them against the vivid blue backdrop of the sky without squinting. As they walked deeper into the forest, the path took a sudden sharp turn and opened into another spacious field.

"Wait! Kahlie!" Maggie burst out suddenly, "I've been here before!" She looked up at the pale green fog that hung in the air above their heads. "This is the field I came to this morning—when I was at school!"

"What?" Kahlie looked shocked. "No . . . there's no way."

"No way, what?"

"I think I saw you here! I thought you were Gracielle. You look just like her!"

"Grass!" Maggie exclaimed. "Ohhhh, you were calling me Grass . . . or, I guess, Grac . . . ielle? Who's Gracielle?"

Suddenly, there was a loud, abrupt *whoosh* and a crackling flash of blue light, and Maggie landed with abrupt bump that knocked her to the ground. She heard a commotion of some sort behind her and then felt an arm wrap around her and someone lift her to her feet.

"Hey! What's the big idea? Let go of . . . ." She stopped short when she spun around and realized that it was the handsome, mysterious guy from the creepy field.

He smiled and looked Maggie directly in the eyes. She attempted to smile back, but found herself quite paralyzed by his hypnotic stare. He lowered to his knee, all the while maintaining eye contact and a playful smile.

"Good afternoon, Your Highness." He finally broke his gaze as he reverently bowed his head. "I was hoping we'd meet again. How are you? Recovered from the rynolt attack last evening?"

"Um, uh-huh. I . . . uh just . . ." Maggie stammered. "Please . . . um . . . stand?" For someone who usually was at no loss for words, whenever she was in this man's presence, she found herself with absolutely no idea what to say.

The young man rose to his feet and eyed Maggie's ensemble.

She gasped and dropped her head into her hands in disgust. "Oh, my gosh! I don't normally . . . I mean . . . I was getting ready for bed and . . . ." She sighed and tried to straighten her slightly twisted polka-dotted pajamas.

The stranger chuckled and placed his hand on her shoulder. "Don't worry, Highness. You look lovely."

Maggie felt herself blush violently. "Yeah, right," she mumbled, looking down at her feet.

The stranger gently lifted her chin and smiled again. "Yes . . . you do," he insisted.

"Wh . . . who are you?" Maggie pleaded, not knowing what else to say.

"My name is Ryannon," he stepped back a bit in case he was making Maggie uncomfortable. He bowed slightly and added, "and if you'll excuse me, Highness, who are you?"

"I'm Maggie . . . Maggie Baker. Do you think I am a Borloc too?"

Ryannon nodded, "Well, of course, aren't you?"

Finally! Someone who listened. "No! I'm just a normal girl."

Ryannon's amazing smile returned, "I wouldn't say just normal."

Maggie gulped. Was it possible that this absolutely perfect man was flirting with her?

Ryannon motioned toward a large rock formation indicating that they should sit down. She fussed with her pajamas again and moved towards the rock.

"Have you figured it out yet?" Ryannon asked, politely waiting for Maggie to sit before taking a seat himself.

"Figured what out?" she asked.

"Why you're here?" Maggie must have looked faint, because Ryannon reached out like he was preparing to catch her.

"Whatta you mean," she started. "You know what's going on with me?"

"Ahhhh," Ryannon answered, "so you haven't figured it out." He flicked a small pebble off the rock next to him. "I owe you an apology. Well actually, my parents owe you an apology, though I doubt you'll get it. This is all their fault." He grimaced and then added, "Of course, I thought you'd at least be a Borloc. What were they thinking?"

"Your parents?" Maggie quizzed.

"And their respective bands of lackeys," Ryannon looked slightly disgusted.

"What? What do you mean?"

Ryannon explained, "For some reason, my mother thinks you are the atoh, so she sent her army to put receptors on you. A couple of my father's spies saw them going and honed in. They took my receptors."

Maggie sensed, as Ryannon spoke, that he wasn't a huge fan of either of his parents.

"See, my mother and my father loathe each other. They're always at each other's throats! Anyway, the Trystas supposedly placed one of her receptors on you, and my father's little puppets placed one of mine."

Maggie stared at him blankly.

He chuckled and guessed, "You have no idea what I'm talking about, do you?"

"No . . . no idea at all," she whispered. "What's a receptor? And why do your . . . *Wait!* THEY PUT SOMETHING ON ME?" She wasn't whispering anymore. In fact, she was speaking very loudly and feeling rather mortified that a strange army of alien spies had put some sort of object on her without her knowing about it. She searched her arms frantically for any sign of a foreign object.

"It's okay, Maggie," he assured, "they're not dangerous. They were invented to bring Travelers back to Lor Mandela in difficult situations."

His explanation did little to calm Maggie, who felt violated. "It's not okay, Ryannon! I feel like I was just abducted by aliens!" She bolted up off the rock, and paced wildly, flinging her arms in the air and yelling. "I was! I was! That's what this is, isn't it! And you . . . you probably don't even look like that! You probably just made yourself gorgeous so I'd feel all relaxed and like you!"

Ryannon jumped up and followed after her. He caught up to her and grabbed her from behind by the shoulders. She spun around and his arms wrapped completely around her. Suddenly, she was very silent.

Ryannon held her close, looked at her with his black and red sparkling eyes, and whispered, "Everything will be fine. I will make sure. Just leave it to me."

Then, he did something completely unexpected. He blushed! "Wait! You think I'm gorgeous?" He stumbled back and stared down at his feet.

There was a long awkward silence before he spoke again. "Listen, Maggie. My mother thinks you are the Child of Balance . . . the one and only person who can restore Lor Mandela. "

"Restore it? It's a planet. What's there to restore?" She slipped back down on the rock formation.

"You're kidding, right," he mused, pointing toward the creepy, dead forest behind him.

Maggie realized that this was exactly where she had met Ryannon before, when she had almost been eaten by the two-headed thing. Just the thought of it sent a chill shivering down her spine. "So, this place didn't always look like this?"

"No," Ryannon explained, "about six years ago, my grandmother did some kind of messed up spell and corrupted Lor Mandela. Apparently, only the Child of Balance can fix it." He came over and sat down next to her. "For some reason, Ultara—my mother and ruler of the Trystas—thinks you are her."

"That's ridiculous," Maggie insisted. "I'm not!"

"I know," Ryannon assured, "but she's going to be looking for you."

"Looking for me? Why?" Maggie asked uncomfortably.

"I'm not sure," Ryannon sighed. "I've never really met her. My father took me from her at birth so that I wasn't put to death."

"WHAT," she blurted. "What kind of a place is this? People who think they can abduct other people and mothers who kill their own children? Get me out of here!"

Ryannon placed his hand reassuringly on her shoulder. "Listen, Maggie . . . you need to know . . . Ultara isn't the only one you have to worry about!"

A sick emptiness twisted through Maggie's insides. She didn't know what Ryannon was going to say next, but it obviously wasn't going to be good news.

"My father, Darian, has always wanted to take over Lor Mandela. He is going to use you as a distraction while he tracks down the real Child of Balance. After he finds her, you'll only be in the way."

"WHAT," Maggie yelped, jumping up from the rock again. "You're kidding me! Get me out of here, Ryannon! You've got to get me out of here! Your mother and your father are both insane! They can't just use people like this!"

Ryannon jumped up too and tried to console her by putting his hands back on her shoulders. This time, Maggie ducked away from him. She didn't want to be consoled; she wanted to go home! She marched quickly across the field, away from Ryannon.

"Maggie! I will help you however I can! I promise," he called after her, "but you have to make sure they don't get receptors onto your father!"

Maggie froze in place and then slowly turned to face him. "My dad," she questioned. "What are you talking about?"

Ryannon answered as he walked toward her, "I can protect you, Maggie. My father has ordered his people not to harm you, so I just have to keep you away from him. But your father . . ." he took a deep breath.

"What? What about him, Ryannon?" she barked.

He sighed and continued, "Almost half a million soldiers have been ordered to kill *him* on sight."

CHAPTER XXIX
FRIENDS DON'T LIE

Nathan sat at the kitchen table in a daze, cell phone in hand, numbly dialing every one of Maggie's friends he could think of.

"Hello . . . Charlotte? This is Nathan Baker. Have you seen Maggie? Okay . . . thanks."

He pushed another set of buttons.

"Hello . . . Lorrine? This is Nathan Baker. Have you seen Maggie? Okay . . . thanks."

Still staring blankly ahead, he pushed yet another set of buttons.

"Hello . . . Emily? This is . . . ."

Just then, there was a loud crack, followed by a brilliant blue flash, and quite suddenly Maggie appeared—from out of nowhere—across the table from him.

Startled, he sprang to his feet and stumbled backwards into the refrigerator, dropping his phone to the floor.

"Hello . . . Hellooo . . . Mr. Baker? Are you there?" A muffled voice emanated from the upside down phone.

Maggie hesitated just long enough to get her bearings, then walked over, picked up the phone and hung up on Emily without saying a word. Her dad was frozen in place, and looking at her like he'd just seen a ghost.

"Dad?" She waved her hand in front of Nathan's eyes. "Dad, it's me . . . I'm back. Are you all right?"

Nathan's hair was sticking up all over the place and his eyes were practically bulging out of the sockets. He very calmly began, "You were right there and you just . . . you just . . . ."

"I know," she interrupted softly.

"YOUNG LADY," he bellowed, "I absolutely forbid you to disappear ever again! I am a nice father . . . very few rules . . . but this?" He collapsed back onto one of their mismatched dining chairs, and ran his hand through his messy hair. "I just don't . . . I can't . . . I . . . What am I supposed to . . . disappearing? Three and a half hours. Three and a half!" He buried his face in his hands, and continued ranting nonsensically, his voice muffled, and his hair flipping back and forth as he shook his head.

Maggie sat down on a chair next to him and touched him gingerly on the shoulder. "Dad, I tried to tell you. It's that whooshing noise."

Nathan raised his head and stared blankly at her.

"Dad, please," she begged. "Something weird is happening to me."

He responded as though he hadn't heard a word. "I can't believe you would do this to me Maggie. It's just not funny."

"WHAT," she roared. "What do you mean?" She couldn't believe that *he* was acting like the victim. "I did not do this on purpose, dad! This isn't some sort of joke!" She slapped the top of the table angrily. "What do you think? That I've taken up magic just to freak you out?"

"Okay, fine," he retorted, his voice escalating to match hers. "Well then, where have you been? People just don't disappear, Maggie! They just don't!"

"If you must know," she blurted, jumping to her feet, "I've been to Lor Mandela, Dad! It's another planet! Do you hear me? I keep going to this other place! Another world . . . Lor Mandela!" She was tired, and scared, and quite sick of trying to explain. She was so angry that if she stayed any longer, she knew she was either going to say something very mean, or burst into tears. "I'm going to bed," she shrieked with a stomp, and stormed out of the kitchen and up the stairs.

Nathan jumped up from his chair, practically knocking it over. "Hold it just a second," he shouted as Maggie sprinted across the living room. "This isn't over young lady! Get back here!" Maggie didn't hesitate in the slightest. She ran up the stairs, skipping every other step and sped down the hall to her room; she slammed the door shut with a violent *bang* that shook the walls and made Nathan flinch.

He took a deep breath and started up the stairs. Despite his efforts to remain calm, he could feel anger and frustration building like a bomb inside him, just waiting to explode. By the time he reached the bedroom door and grabbed the knob, his blood was boiling. He was just about to rip the door clean off its hinges, when he heard Maggie sobbing on the other side of it.

Slowly, he backed away. He hated to hear her cry. As he stood there, staring at the crystal doorknob, listening to his daughter's sobs, his anger began to subside. Still, for the life of him, he couldn't understand what she was up to and why she was making up these wild stories; but at least for now, he decided that it would probably be in the best interest of them both to wait until morning to pursue the matter any further.

Maggie threw herself onto her bed, blubbering uncontrollably. It had not been her intention to get into a fight with her dad. She'd just wanted him to believe her, but that wasn't the only reason she was upset. It was Ryannon's last comment that left her completely terrified. His father—and an entire army—were looking for her dad, just waiting to kill him; that they were safely on Earth at the moment did little to calm her. Ryannon's parents had been able to get *her* to Lor Mandela. It was only a matter of time before they would be able to get her father there too. And then what? She couldn't bear the thought of losing him. He was more than just her dad, he was her entire world—the only family she knew. She lay there, sobbing and panic stricken, for nearly two hours before exhaustion finally took over and pulled her down into a heavy, dreamless sleep.

At 6:05, the alarm blasted. She bolted upright and hit the switch to "off" rather than pushing the snooze button. She rubbed her eyes—which were burning and puffy from crying—dressed quickly and hurried toward Nathan's bedroom. Part of her didn't want to face him after the previous night's argument, but she needed to check on him and make sure he was safe. She cracked his door open just a little, and peered in. A twinge of terror swept through her at the sight of his bed, which appeared to have not been slept in. She opened the door further, and stuck her head around it to see if his bathroom light was on. It was dark. Quickly, she turned on her heels and darted down the hall. "Dad," she called out nervously.

"Dad!" She was half-way down the stairs when she crashed into him hard, nearly knocking both of them down.

Nathan grabbed her around the shoulders. "Whoa, where ya goin', Speedy?"

She threw her arms around him and squeezed.

"Good Morning?" he questioned, wondering to what he owed this outpouring of affection. "You're up early."

Maggie finally let go. "Dad," she began, "I'm sorry. I didn't . . . ."

"Shh . . . it's okay, Smaggs," Nathan soothed, "I mean, we wouldn't be a normal dad-slash-teenage daughter if we didn't have a tiff now and then, would we? I think we were both jus' tired and cranky, that's all. What say we try to have a better day today, eh? We can talk about all this magic and other world stuff later, okay?"

Maggie grimaced at him. An, "I believe you," or "I should have listened" would have been nice—especially after she had disappeared and reappeared in front of him—but at least he wasn't yelling, or rehashing the whole episode, which he did have the tendency to do from time to time, so she decided, that at least for now, she would take what she could get and concentrate her energies on keeping her dad away from Lor Mandela. "Okay, I'll try," she finally agreed.

The two of them readied for their day, and headed off in the usual manner— Nathan driving her to school, dropping her off just outside the big brown double doors, and then speeding off toward the Old Downtown district of Glenhill in his rusty sedan with the noisy, dented door.

Maggie watched from the school steps as he drove away and muttered a quiet, "keep him safe," into the air. She turned and started up the steps but didn't get far before something she saw stopped her cold in her tracks. It was Bridgette and Holden who were locked in a smoldering, passionate, "oblivious to the world around them" make out session, just outside the school doors.

"Hey! What are you trying to do," she shouted racing toward them. "Get expelled?" She grabbed Bridgette by the shoulders and yanked. "Yikes you two!"

Of course, it wasn't her concern over her best friend being reprimanded by school authorities that motivated her to act; it was complete shock and disbelief that Bridgette seemed to be flinging herself at this stranger-than-strange, well, stranger.

"What are *you* doing?" Bridgette snapped, spinning around and facing Maggie all out of breath and flushed. "Maggie! What's wrong with you?"

Holden chuckled. "Hey Blue! Welcome to beautiful Glenhill High."

Maggie shot him a look of disdain.

Holden smiled his dorky smile, flipped his long blonde locks, and quipped, "Oh, ho, I get it!" He continued in a hushed tone. "You ladies need to C-O-municate."

"As a matter of fact, we do!" Maggie seethed through clenched teeth.

Bridgette scoffed, and glared at her.

"Okay! Laters, Pretty Dude! Laters, Blue." He gave Bridgette a peck on the cheek, walked over to Maggie and tousled her curls and then quickly bounded away before Maggie was able to get a good shot at him with her clenched fist.

"What are you doing, Maggie?" Bridgette repeated—her brown eyes devoid of their usual sparkle.

"What do you mean," she retorted. "You've only known him a day and you're all over him!"

Bridgette gasped. "Well, excuse me, Miss Morality Police! Haven't you ever heard of love at first sight?"

"But Bridge, you hardly know him! And you haven't even talked to me . . . your best friend about . . . ."

Bridgette cut her off mid-sentence. "Hold it right there, Maggie! I've *tried* to talk to you! But you were either too busy or off who-knows-where doing who-knows what and worrying your poor dad and me to death! So don't even lecture me about talking to you!" She spun around, turning her back on Maggie. "I . . . I've got to get to class," she sniffled.

Maggie rolled her eyes. Bridge could never get mad at someone without bursting into tears. "Yikes, Bridge, wait," she sighed realizing that she might have overstepped her bounds just a bit. "I guess you're right. I haven't been around. I'm sorry."

Bridgette slowly turned to face her. "Can't you just be happy for me," she whined.

Maggie put her hand on Bridgette's arm. "Of course I'm happy for you. If you're happy, I'm happy," she soothed.

Bridgette locked her arm around Maggie's and smiled. The sparkle was back. "C'mon. We'll talk more at lunch!" She led Maggie into the school and down the hall toward Mr. Lee's classroom. "Gosh, it feels like we haven't seen each other for days," she gushed.

They reached the door and Maggie started through it.

Bridgette peeked in around her and blew a kiss to Holden, who was at the back of the room, leaning back in his seat with his hands clasped behind his head.

He winked and blew one back.

"See ya, Maggs," Bridgette beamed. "Oh, I can't wait to hear what you were up to yesterday! You really had your dad goin' crazy!" She flipped her silky hair with her hand and slipped back into a crowd of students who were hurrying down the hallway.

"Yeah, great!" Maggie moaned, "more lies."

"Lies, Miss Baker?" The familiar gravelly growl of Mr. Lee's voice scraped through the air behind her. "Who are we planning on lying to now?"

Maggie didn't want to look at him; he really freaked her out, but slowly she turned and faced her snarling teacher. "What? Um . . . oh, no one, Mr. Lee." She shivered at the mere sight of him. "It's well, uh . . . me. I'm the one who is being lied to." She tried to maintain eye contact so she would seem believable, but it was difficult. Mr. Lee's stare was creepy and intimidating, to say the least.

"Well, let's just hope you're not planning on lying to me." As usual, his scrawny mustache twitched as he spoke. "Oh believe me. I can, and will, make things very uncomfortable if I even have the slightest inkling that you are being deceitful, Miss Baker."

Maggie just nodded.

Mr. Lee sniggered and turned to go to his desk, but as he did he smacked right into Holden, who was standing directly behind him. Maggie had no idea how he got there without her seeing him, but she was relieved that Mr. Lee would have a new target on which to vent his frustrations. What happened next, however, was not at all what she expected.

Holden's face became chillingly serious. He stared Mr. Lee boldly in the eye, and in a quiet voice only audible to the three of them, and so daunting that it didn't even sound like his own, he gave Mr. Lee a dose of his own medicine.

"Mr. Lee," he began, "you will *never* use that tone with her again!" He didn't break his intense stare. "I *fully* expect you to treat her with the esteem and dignity that she deserves or I will have you removed from this school permanently."

Maggie was dumbfounded. Mr. Lee actually appeared to be trembling in fear.

Holden continued, "Do you understand me, Wilbur?" The Math Nazi slowly bobbed his sweaty head up and down. Holden raised his eyebrows condescendingly. "Good! Now take your seat."

Without a word, Mr. Lee obediently shuffled over to his desk and sat down, as if in a trance. Holden glanced at Maggie and then returned to the back of the class where he resumed his casual position—leaning back with his hands clasped behind his head.

It was several seconds before Mr. Lee moved again. Finally, he blinked once or twice, looked up at Maggie and said, "Miss Baker, would you please take your seat so we can begin?" There was nothing spiteful or vindictive at all in his tone. Maggie glanced over at Holden who was grinning widely as she walked slowly to her desk.

Math class had never been more pleasant. Although Mr. Lee was far from sappy sweet, he'd actually behaved decently. He hadn't growled, grimaced or glared at anyone. And, when Cynthia Dix asked him to repeat the page number of the assignment, he praised her for having the courage to ask. At the end of the period, he announced that the students were free to take extra time to finish their assignment—something he'd never done before—and informed them that it would be due the next morning.

The bell sounded and the buzz of comments began. Some students guessed that he'd gotten in trouble with the administration. Others assumed that he'd gone to the doctor after his "near-heart attack" the day before, and been told that death was imminent if he didn't relax. Whatever the reason, they were all sure that the change was temporary, and that the Math Nazi would surely return with a vengeance.

Maggie waited near the door as everyone exited. As Holden passed her she grabbed a hold of his sleeve and yanked him into the hall. "Okay," she insisted, "you and I need to talk!"

Holden shrugged his shoulders and replied, "Sure, Blue Eyes."

She pulled him down the hall and out a door that led to the football field; she continued down the steps between the bleachers and out onto the field.

A group of four or five kids who obviously had no plans to attend any of their classes huddled across the field from them, and briefly acknowledged the intrusion.

Maggie got straight to the point. "Okay. Who are you," she insisted—finally letting go of Holden's sleeve.

He straightened his shirt and casually replied, "I'm exactly who I say I am, you?"

Maggie stomped her foot. "You know what I mean, Holden! Stop playing around and tell me what's going on!"

He strolled over to one of the benches alongside the field and sat down. "Listen, Blue," he began, "it's no big. I've had some trainin', that's all. Ya know . . . taught how to handle bullies? Doesn't matter if they're kids or adults, I know how to deal with 'em."

He stood up and gave Maggie an awkward squeeze around the shoulders with one arm. "Ya know, Blue, I accept that I'm D-I-F-ferent. Most people just gimme my space, which is cool, but you and Pretty Du . . . uh, Bridgette . . . you've been like totally great."

A twinge of guilt twisted in Maggie's gut. She hadn't been "totally great" at all. She'd yelled at him, stopped him from kissing Bridgette, dragged him through the school like a mother punishing a five-year-old, and practically accused him of being—well—something strange.

"Holden," she sighed at length, "I haven't been that cool. I've actually been kinda mean."

"Hey! It's all good, Blue," he assured, "you're just stressed. I get it . . . been a couple of whacked out days. Nothin' like the boring stuff you're used to."

"Yeah . . . well . . . ." She looked at him suspiciously again. He knew somehow. She could see it in his emerald eyes. There was something hiding there. She took a deep breath and went for broke. "Holden, have you ever heard of Lor Mandela?"

He didn't answer right away; he seemed confused by the question. "Huh," he finally muttered, tilting his head to one side. "I dunno, seems kinda familiar. Are they a band?"

Maggie frowned. "Uh huh . . . um, never mind."

Just then a bell sounded from within the school.

"Dang it!" She grabbed Holden by the sleeve again and started pulling. "Come on! We're gonna be late!"

They dashed up the steps and back into the school. Maggie pointed down the hall that ran to the right. "Drama," she shouted.

"Chem," Holden replied, pointing straight ahead.

"See ya!" She turned and sprinted off toward the auditorium, and barely made it as the final late bell sounded.

"Ahhh, Jolie, Maggie," Ms. Devereaux greeted as she burst through the purple curtain completely out of breath. "You look much better today."

Maggie gasped a bit, and then replied, "Thanks. I . . . I am." She quickly joined the other students who were sitting in a circle on the stage floor.

Ms. Devereaux—who today was wearing grey and black horizontal striped tights under black shorts that were rolled to just above her knee; a long grey jacket, a white T-shirt, a charcoal beret, and black ankle-high boots—strolled slowly and dramatically toward the circle.

"Today, loves, we will pair off and practeese for our production of 'Meet Me in St. Louis'. . . Gabby?" She touched a lovely auburn haired girl on the head,

"You with Michelle." She pointed toward a skinny boy with glasses. "Michael, you with Robert." She smiled and nodded at Bridgette. "Brigeet, you and Maggie." She clapped her hands twice and instructed, "Everyone else, peek a partner."

Two by two, the students paired off and found a corner or secluded spot to run lines. Maggie and Bridgette went to the very back of the auditorium in a corner lit only by the green rays of the exit sign overhead.

"We're not really going to practice this again, are we?" Bridgette sighed, "I can recite these lines in my sleep."

Maggie smiled. "Oh really, Ms. Ballard?" She turned her nose up and dramatically continued. "Well, that's only because you're an Eastern snob!" The two of them giggled quietly.

Bridgette pretended to look at the script in her hand. "So, we're okay . . . aren't we?"

"Yeah, we're okay," Maggie smiled. "That boyfriend of yours is really . . . ummmm . . . interesting."

Bridgette, who spied Ms. Devereaux glancing in their direction, made a bold gesture with her arm. "I know the two of you didn't get off to a good start, but . . . ."

Maggie stopped her. "No, really, we're totally cool now. We talked for a minute after Math. That's why I was almost late."

"Why, Lon . . . you're down for the first dance!" Bridgette grabbed Maggie's arm as Ms. Devereaux ambled past. They heard a quiet, "lovely," as she continued on.

"So, where were you yesterday? After school?" Bridgette whispered.

Maggie knew this question would come up, but had neglected to think of what her answer should be. "Uh well, I . . . I thought . . . I thought I heard your voice out by the baseball diamonds," she smiled nervously. "Turns out, it wasn't you, of course . . . but I sat down out there to wait for my dad. I musta fallen asleep."

Bridgette squinted her eyes. Something wasn't right, and Maggie could see it.

She'd been caught. She braced herself and waited for the blow.

Bridgette said nothing. She didn't have to. After a few seconds of silence, Maggie looked down at her shoes and mumbled, "You checked there, didn't you?"

Bridgette nodded. Big tears were welling up in her brown eyes again.

Maggie reached for her arm but Bridgette yanked it away. "Bridge, come on. I'm sorry," she whined. "Yesterday was so weird! I'll tell you the truth . . . the real deal . . . but I promise; you'll never believe it."

Bridgette just stared. Maggie pulled her gently by the arm to one of the auditorium seats and motioned for her to sit down.

"Okay," she breathed, "this is what really happened." She started with the bizarre light incident at her bedroom window. She explained in detail what had really gone down the day before at her locker. Then, she told Bridgette all about Lor Mandela, Kahlie, and the rynolt—and of course, Ryannon.

When she finished, she tried to read Bridgette's reaction, but there was nothing to read—no emotion, hint of an odd expression, or anything.

After several moments, Bridgette muttered, "Wow," and stood and walked away.

Maggie quickly followed. "Bridge? Bridgey?"

But Bridgette completely ignored her.

She rushed after her best friend but had to be quiet, so as not to disturb the other students who were rehearsing.

Just then, the bell rang and everyone stampeded back toward the stage. Several students pushed in front of Maggie, preventing her from catching up to Bridgette—who was grabbing her purse and making a beeline for the stage door.

Maggie quickly gathered her things and resumed the chase. Down the corridor outside of the auditorium, she watched Bridgette nimbly weave her way in and out through a sea of people. She tried to keep up but it wasn't working. After just a few seconds, Bridgette disappeared around the corner at the end of the hall.

Maggie stopped and sighed. Suddenly, a knowing look came into her eyes. "She's got geometry now," she whispered to herself, "and Brian's an Office Aide."

She smiled mischievously, turned around, and headed off in the opposite direction. She reached the school's Main Office, and waited outside the door. About two minutes later, a tall, beefy guy in a letterman's jacket came toward her. "Bri Guy!" she shouted and waved cheerfully.

Brian almost dropped the football he was carrying. "Um . . . Maggie," he sniggered and tried to act cool, "Whu . . . whuzzup?"

"I need a little favor, Bri."

Brian looked like he had just been handed the Heisman. "Um, yeah . . . sure . . . anything!"

"Can you get Bridgette out of Martin's class? I need to talk to her *really* bad!"

Brian looked around from side to side. "We're not supposed to . . . ." he breathed.

Maggie interrupted. "I know," she pouted playfully, "It's just *really* important."

Brian looked at her big, blue, doe-eyes and blushed. "Okay," he sighed, "I'll try." He smiled widely, displaying the gaping hole where his upper left central incisor had been prior to last year's championship football game.

Maggie bit her lip to keep from giggling. "Thanks, Bri. I owe you one! I'll be waiting over there," She pointed toward a stairwell across from them. "Down by the dance studio."

Brian nodded and headed into the office.

A few minutes later, Maggie heard Bridgette's voice. "Brian, I swear, if you don't tell me what's going on I . . . *baby*," she squealed. "You did this? Just so you could see me?"

Maggie climbed up a couple of stairs and peered out. Bridgette was across the hall from her, hugging, none other than Holden Guarlo. "Great! This guy's everywhere," she whispered.

Brian just stood there with a blank, bewildered stare—Holden did too.

Bridgette took his hand and started leading him toward the very stairwell in which Maggie was hiding. Quickly, she jumped back down to the bottom, and darted into the girl's locker room which was, thankfully, abandoned at the moment. Through the door, she could hear Bridgette's voice.

"She's totally ticking me off! You wouldn't believe the story she told me!"

Maggie knew who the topic of this conversation was.

"What'd she tell ya?" Holden asked.

Bridgette's paraphrased version hit all the pertinent points and Maggie realized how totally far-fetched the whole story sounded. Hearing it from someone else simply confirmed that no one in their right mind would *ever* believe it.

Apparently, Holden was not in his right mind. "So, what's the pro-blemo? Are ya mad 'cause you didn't get to go with her, or what?"

Bridgette's reply was louder than it probably should've been. "The pro-blemo is that she lied to me! She's my best friend and she lied to me! Best friends don't lie to each other!"

Holden's voice was calm and almost too quiet to hear through the thick wooden door. Maggie leaned in closer to it. "I don't think she was lyin', Pretty Dude, and it sounds like you didn't give her too much of a chance."

Maggie could only imagine Bridgette's face at the moment.

"But Holden, there's no way," Bridgette whined.

"Blue doesn't seem like she'd risk losin' you by lyin', Babe. Besides, what if she's like totally tellin' the truth? If you had all that crazy biz goin' down, down, down, wouldn't you want your best bud to believe ya?"

Holden had once again stunned Maggie. He was her ally, and despite what happened next, she knew that it would be better to face Bridgette with him there than it would be to do it alone.

Slowly, she opened the door. Bridgette was facing her, and Holden, having had his back to the door, turned to face her as well. There was silence for a moment—but then a *whoosh* and a crack—and Maggie disappeared...right in front of them.

CHAPTER XXX
LORTU OF THE SHADOWS

In a dim, misty cave with a roaring river running through the center, Maggie materialized with a pop. This was, once again, a new and unknown place. Just to her left, a tall, pointy, stone pillar seemed like the logical thing to dodge behind—just in case she turned out to be in unfriendly territory again. She glanced around the pillar toward the river. Neither Ryannon nor Kahlie were anywhere in sight; but she did spy what looked to be a chair of some sort, made out of twisting, mangled tree branches, perched on a platform, facing out into the cave. Suddenly, the branches of the chair moved. Maggie pulled back behind the pillar, but only far enough to hide herself a little better. She watched from her sheltered location, as a cloaked figure stood up from the chair and walked to the edge of the platform.

"It's useless for you to hide from me, Lortu." A woman's voice—deep, rich and silky—floated out from under the cloak. "I can sense Shadow Dwellers, surely, you know that."

The woman lowered the cloak's hood down to her shoulders, revealing wild, fiery orange hair. As she turned to pace across the length of the platform, Maggie caught a momentary glimpse of her face. It was beautiful, and yet eerie somehow, almost too beautiful, too perfect. The look of complete arrogance and power in her metallic golden eyes sent shivers flooding down Maggie's spine. Maggie guessed that this woman must have heard her arrive, and was, at the moment, mistaking her for a Shadow Dweller—whatever that was. It didn't take long before she found out *exactly* what it was.

On the other side of the river, the room's walls were alive with dancing reflections of the water and flickering glints of light from the torches that lined them. Suddenly, something about the shadows became abnormal. A section toward the center of the wall started to take shape and form. Quickly, and quite seamlessly, a human-like creature emerged from the shadows. It was a thin, yet muscular man wearing only a tattered animal skin which wrapped around his waist and hung nearly to his knees. His shoulder length hair twisted and weaved out of the shadows, gradually brightening from a gloomy bluish black to pure white. It floated around as if it had a mind of its own. Even in the dim light, and from easily thirty feet away, Maggie could see that this mysterious creature's eyes were either white, or a very pale, icy blue. As the last bit of him separated from the shadowy wall, he leaned over so that his knuckles were almost on the ground and then broke into a phenomenally fast gallop across the bridge. He stopped abruptly in front of the platform, nodded—not bowed—to the woman, and spoke in a deep thick accent.

"Iee do not hide frahm you, deah Ooltara. Iee moust only be carfohl." His words rolled from his lips very slowly, as if he was trying to lull a restless child to sleep.

"Ultara?" Maggie mouthed. She'd heard that name before. *Ultara.* She tried to remember. *Where have I heard that name?* Suddenly, it clicked. "Ultara!" she gasped—almost loud enough to be heard. The men who'd broken into her house had mentioned Ultara, and so had Ryannon. Ultara was Ryannon's mother!

"What ees it dat Iee may do for you, Vritessa?"

Ultara studied the Shadow Dweller and then replied, "I need to ask a favor of you, Lortu . . . of you and your followers. I guarantee that it will profit you."

Lortu's interest was piqued. "Iee am leesteneeng."

Ultara returned to her tree throne, and explained, "My generals have found the missing atoc and atoh."

Lortu's eyes widened, "Found dem?

"Yes," she answered.

"I tot dey would be daed bye now." Lortu casually pulled a bug, or a leaf, or some other small object from his hair, and threw it over his shoulder into the water behind him.

"Well, they are not. They were transported off of Lor Mandela at the time of the battle. That's why no one has found them . . . they aren't here."

"Transported? Dat would 'ave been deeficult. How did dey get transported," he questioned. "An' how do you plan to bring dem back to de Lor Mandela?"

"How they got there is not important," Ultara replied. "The problem I'm facing now is that I sent my travelers to put receptors on them . . . to bring them back . . . but they were only able to get one . . . onto the girl."

Maggie's stomach lurched at the mere reminder that these odd and frightening creatures had put something on her, and had done so completely unbeknownst to her.

"Ahhhhh, so you be needing us to find 'er and breeng 'er to you. Dat ees what you want?" A haughty smile grew on Lortu's face. "De Trystas ees not clever enov?"

In less time than it would've taken for Maggie to blink, Ultara was out of her chair, to the front of the platform, and holding a long, shiny, black spear-type object at Lortu's throat. Lortu looked stunned, and very frightened.

"You forget to whom you owe your life, Shadow Dweller," Ultara seethed. "My troops happen to be occupied with other things at the moment, and since your clan seems to have infiltrated Mandela City and the Sybran, you can easily keep an eye out."

Lortu took a small step backward and cautiously pushed the spear away from his neck. "Hahmble apologees, Vritessa.'Ow may we serve?"

She lowered the spear. "I want you to find Atoh Audril. Notify me as soon as she is found. Bring her to the Caverns. I don't want anyone here to see her."

"And what of de atoc?"

"Once the atoc is made aware of the situation . . . once he knows that I have his beloved little Audril, I'm sure he will come back to us willingly."

Lortu smiled and nodded in understanding, "Ov course. Der ees just one more ting, den."

"Ahhh, yes," Ultara answered, "your compensation." She leaned down and put her face close to his. "Bring me Audril, Lortu, and your life debt will be paid."

Lortu's pale eyes grew even wider than they were before. Maggie imagined that this would be the exact look on someone's face after they found out they'd won the lottery.

"Dat makes you de best offer den." Lortu nodded slowly, and without saying another word, bowed and backed his way across the bridge. Then—just as he had appeared— he disappeared into the shadows.

Ultara looked down at the spear still clutched in her hand and flung it across the room. Just as it was about to smack into the wall, it exploded with a bang and disintegrated into a cloud of black smoke. She was staring out across the span of the river, when she heard a strange sound.

Whoosh, whoooooshhhhh.

She whipped around and looked in the direction of the sound. Her eyes glowed bright gold, illuminating the entire platform.

Maggie gasped and pushed herself around tightly against the pillar. *Come on,* she pleaded silently, *get me out of here!*

The whooshing continued as the glow from Ultara's eyes became brighter and brighter.

"Tug, dang it! Where's the tug?" she whispered frantically.

The golden light intensified as Ultara drew nearer.

Maggie decided that her only hope was going to be to make a run for it, so she took a deep breath and readied herself for a chase. She hunched down and was about to sprint away, when Ultara rounded the corner and bumped right into her.

Ultara jumped back; her eyes instantly dimmed. The look on her face was one of shock and disbelief.

Maggie couldn't move; she remained frozen in her crouched position, staring at Ultara, who was standing motionless, staring back at her. She was so terrified, that when the tugging in her stomach actually began, she mistook it for the sickening sensation that would naturally accompany the panic that was currently paralyzing her. In an instant, a blast of blue light flashed above her head, followed by a loud, startling *crack*, and she was out of there.

Unfortunately, where she landed next was not much better. She popped into the middle of a large, stone room—with tall windows along one wall—occupied by two men, both of whom were, luckily, facing away from her.

The man furthest from her was yelling loudly at the other.

". . . CRUCIAL INFORMATION TO BE DISCOVERED ON LOR MANDELA IN MORE THAN A YEAR AND ULTARA FINDS OUT BEFORE I DO?" He started to turn to face the other man, but as he did, a hand slapped over Maggie's mouth; another grabbed her by the waist.

She was promptly yanked out of the room and behind the door. She managed to turn her head to find that it was Ryannon pulling her backwards. He cautiously let go of her waist, put his finger to his lips, and whispered, "Shhh." He moved his other hand slowly from her mouth and pointed back towards the room. "My father," he breathed.

Maggie nodded as he motioned for her to move in closer and together they listened from the hallway to the heated conversation brewing just beyond the door.

"I tried to get the information to you first, Milord, but the vritesse has been having all of us watched. She trusts no one, not even her own generals!"

"Well, obviously that is wise." Darian's voice was now calm and deliberate. "Tell me, General Linetal, where is Atoh Audril right now?"

"I . . . uh . . . I am not sure, sir."

"No, of course you aren't. That would be because only two receptors were placed, not five." He paused for a moment, and then asked, "And where is her father?"

Again the answer came, "I . . . I don't know."

"And, that, my friend is simply because I made the mistake of counting on you in the first place. But I will let you in on a little secret, General Linetal. I have a plan to fix all of this."

"How may I be of assistance, sire?"

Darian calmly oozed, "No need, no need. You see, General, it turns out that I still have spies I *can* count on. They are on their way to Drolana right now to find Atoc Jonathan and to bring him back to me, and I guarantee you *they* will not fail me as you have."

"Wh . . . what's that? What are you doing?" The voice of General Linetal took on a discernible tone of panic.

Ryannon slowly leaned around the door to get a better look and Maggie leaned with him. From her vantage point, she observed an older silver-haired man—who she assumed to be the general—on his knees looking pleadingly at Ryannon's father, a man with long, straight, dark, hair, strong chiseled features, and flickering eyes. He was holding a thin silver tube and aiming it toward the general's head. Ryannon noticed it too and quickly grabbed Maggie by the arm and started pulling her away.

"Oh, not good . . . ." he whispered. "We've got to get out of here!"

Maggie didn't question him. She could tell that something bad was about to happen to Linetal, and had no desire to stay and watch. She and Ryannon sped down a wide corridor, away from the room. Suddenly, the shrill, agonizing screams of a man echoed through the corridor, and Maggie stopped in her tracks. Ryannon rushed back to her; he quickly wrapped his arms around her and pulled her head into his chest to try to muffle the horrible shrieks. She could still hear them though, and knew with a nauseating certainty that General Linetal was being killed. The cries of the poor man became more and more anguished, and then stopped, leaving behind a sickening silence.

Maggie felt dizzy. The room around her began to spin and twist. Ryannon sensed that she was in trouble and shifted his arms upward, holding her firmly by the shoulders. She looked up into his glinting eyes and tried to breathe, but it was useless. All at once, she felt her knees buckle and everything went black.

At length, she blinked her eyes back open. Ryannon was kneeling over her, gently patting her on the cheek. They were outdoors on a small half-dead lawn, completely surrounded by tall brown hedges.

"Maggie . . . Maggie, are you all right?" he asked, looking rather concerned.

"Uh . . . I . . . I think so." Maggie mumbled. She moved to sit up, and Ryannon put his arm behind her to help. "Is . . . is he dead? The general, I mean."

Ryannon looked down at the ground and nodded. He lifted himself to his feet, and with his back to her muttered, "I'm sorry, Maggie. This is all my fault."

"Your fault," she questioned. "How could this possibly be your fault, Ryannon? You didn't kill that man. Your father did!"

He turned and looked at her with guilt and sadness in his eyes. "My father is a monster . . . a monster that I have helped create." He looked around at the wilted hedges that encircled them and explained, "When I was very young, I used to come out here and pretend to be a mighty hunter. I was armed with my pointy stick and some rocks I found lying on the ground." He smiled in remembrance.

Maggie pictured an adorable little boy with dark hair dodging stealthily from bush to bush, in search of unsuspecting prey.

"It didn't take long for me to realize that my weapons were completely inadequate. The other night, when you were fighting off that rynolt, did you see the darts I was shooting?"

"Yes," she answered, "I mean . . . not up close or anything." She timidly added, "I was a little busy."

Ryannon chuckled and sat back down next to her. "Yeah, I guess you were. Anyway, they're called spike darts. They were the first weapon I ever invented when I was about four years old."

"Four?" Maggie gasped.

"Uh huh. My father was so impressed, that he immediately recruited an elite group of tutors for me . . . masters in the fields of engineering, weaponry and warfare. Great start for a four year old child, huh?" He seemed to be lost in his thoughts for a moment. "I've been referred to as the 'Brashnellan Minister of Defense' since I was ten. I've developed hundreds of weapons . . . weapons that I was convinced were made for the purpose of defending Brashnell, not for senseless murders. That thing my father used on Linetal . . . it's called a vystoran . . . one of my most deadly and horrific inventions." He looked down in shame.

"But you didn't use it," she tried to soothe, "your father did."

Ryannon glanced up and their eyes met. Maggie felt as though she was being pulled into his beautiful eyes by a magnetic force. They didn't say a word as they moved closer and closer to each other. Ryannon lifted his hand and placed it gently on her cheek. Their lips were about to touch when Ryannon stopped, pulled back, and sprung to his feet. "Wait," he exclaimed, "your father! When did you see him last?"

Maggie shook her head, flustered by the abrupt change of mood.

"Didn't you hear him?" Ryannon blurted. "He said that his spies were on their way to Drolana to get Atoc Jonathan. If the Trystas thought you were Atoh Audril, then they think your father is . . . ."

"DROLANA IS EARTH?" Maggie screeched, also jumping to her feet.

Ryannon nodded. "You've got to get to your dad before they do! Here." He reached into his jacket pocket and pulled out a thin, black metal box. He opened it and took out a tiny, square, wafer-like object and handed it to Maggie.

"What is it," she asked.

"This is an inhibitor. The only way they can get him here is the same way they got you. An inhibitor will render the receptors useless." He added, "I went to work on them just as soon as you left me the last time. They haven't been tested, but they're all we've got. It's imperative that the inhibitor be placed first, though . . . before any receptors are. I haven't been able to come up with one that will reverse a prior placement."

"W . . . wait! What do I do with it?" Maggie was becoming more and more frightened by the second. What if they were already too late? What if Darian's spies had already found her dad? What if they'd already . . . ?

Ryannon could see that she was beginning to panic. "Maggie, it's easy! All you have to do is get him to ingest it."

"What," she blurted, "he has to swallow it? How am I supposed to get him to do that?"

"Just drop it in a drink. It dissolves in water."

"But, what if they already . . . ."

Ryannon put a comforting hand on her shoulder. "Listen to me. You can't lose hope. When *you* travel between Dro . . . um . . . I mean Earth and Lor

Mandela, it's instant, right?"

Maggie nodded.

"It takes the Travelers hours to get there."

This did little to calm her. "But . . . but the last time I saw my dad was this morning when he dropped me off at school."

"Okay, and where did he go from there?"

"To work. Why?"

"Is this work in a public place?"

"I . . . I guess," she explained. "There are maybe 20 people or so in his office."

Ryannon smiled. "See now, even the spies among the Travelers are leery of being seen on another world. They won't risk it unless he's alone, *and* unless it appears that he will be alone long enough for them to do what they need to do."

Maggie felt a little better but was still teetering on the verge of tears. "Ryannon," she breathed, "you said they were ordered to kill him on sight. What if they don't bring him back? What if they just kill him there?" Her voice was weak and shaky.

Ryannon looked into her eyes. "They won't," he assured. "Didn't you hear what my father said? He said that his spies were on their way to Drolana to *bring* Atoc Jonathan back to him. You saw what he did to Linetal. My father makes it very clear to his generals that if they don't follow his instructions to the letter, they won't live to make the mistake again. They're bringing him back here, Maggie, and I promise, if they happen to get to him before you do, I'll do everything in my power to keep him safe."

Maggie nodded slowly and blotted a stray tear with her index finger. "Th . . . thanks, Ryannon."

He smiled, and ran his hand gently down the side of her cheek. "You're welcome," he whispered softly. All at once, his face became serious and his breathing heavier, as he slid his hand back from her cheek and through her raven curls.

Maggie's breath deepened, matching the intensity and rhythm of his. His hand moved through her hair, slowly down her back and wrapped around her waist as he locked her in an intense smoldering stare and leaned towards her.

"Kiss me," he begged in a breathless whisper.

Maggie's breath caught in her chest. She moved closer and closed her eyes as she felt his lips softly brush against hers. Time stood still, and everything except the two of them disappeared from the world. She didn't hear the whoosh, or see the flash this time. As Ryannon unwrapped his strong arms from around her and stepped away, she opened her eyes, and was stunned to find that she was standing near the door of the girls' locker room—right where she'd vanished from earlier.

It took her a moment to get oriented; she was in complete emotional overload. Suddenly, she noticed the time on the clock above the door—4:24. Her dad would be leaving his office and heading for home any minute now. "The inhibitor," she gasped, opening her fist to verify that the little wafer was still there before sprinting out of the locker room and up the steps.

School had been out for over an hour, so the halls were deserted. She burst through the brown double doors and down the front steps.

"Maggie!" Bridgette and Holden raced toward her from the parking lot, but she strategically jumped to one side and kept running—right past them. "Maggie . . . wait," Bridgette yelped. "Where are you going?"

"I have to get to my dad! There's no time to explain!" She sprinted across the grassy lawn, through the parking lot, and out toward the highway that ran in front of the school. She would have kept on running—right across it—had she not heard Bridgette yell, "You live seven miles from here, ya goon! Are ya gonna run the whole way, or would you like a ride?"

Maggie spun around, confused. Bridgette didn't have a car. Her mom picked her up every day. She glanced questioningly at Bridgette and then noticed Holden, who was smiling and dangling a set of keys in his hand. "Let's go, Blue!"

CHAPTER XXXI
THE RACE FOR NATHAN

Maggie rushed back across the parking lot toward Holden and Bridgette.

"Over here," Bridgette directed, pointing to one of the only three cars still parked in the lot.

Maggie stopped and her jaw dropped. Bridgette was pointing at an amazingly gorgeous, black convertible sports car. "Whoooa! That's yours?" she gasped, eyeing Holden in disbelief.

Holden shrugged his shoulders and pushed a button on a black key fob that dangled near the top of his conglomeration of keys. There was a quick triple chirp, and the headlights of his one-of-a-kind custom two-seater blinked from left to right and then right to left. Bridgette ran around to the passenger side, pulled open the door and motioned to Maggie to join her; they quickly piled into the seat together.

Holden didn't bother with his door. He jumped over the side of the car and landed squarely in the seat. "Buckle up, groovy dudes," he yelled as he shifted gears and screeched out of the parking lot.

Bridgette gave Maggie a playful hug. "Welcome back," she yelled to be heard over the roar of the car. "So, where'd ya go this time?" She winked at Maggie as she struggled to fasten a seat belt over them both.

Maggie sighed. It was such a relief to have someone on Earth who finally believed her. "It's a long story, Bridgey! Right now I have to get to my dad! Darian . . . this completely horrible man . . . has spies coming after him, right now! They can't find him! They just can't!!"

Holden and Bridgette both looked over at Maggie as though she'd said something too impossible to believe.

"*Duuuudes!*" Holden hollered, stomping down on the gas pedal. "We gotta jam! Which exit?"

"Mansfield!" Bridgette and Maggie replied in unison.

He flew down the freeway at easily ninety miles per hour, masterfully weaving in and out of the few cars on that stretch of highway. As they approached the Mansfield exit, he wrenched the steering wheel to the side, sending them screeching and skidding across two lanes. Maggie grabbed at the dashboard and Bridgette shrieked. Holden just grinned, and nonchalantly maneuvered the car like a pro, skillfully avoiding a slow-moving Freightliner that was coasting along in the right lane. "Where to?" he yelled as they soared down the ramp.

The stunned girls just pointed. A few minutes later—following continued navigational pointing—they pulled up in front of Maggie's house and squealed to a stop. Holden again dismounted his ride by leaping over the door. He ran to the passenger side and let Bridgette and Maggie out, and together, they all ran across the front lawn, jumped on to the porch, and exploded through the front door.

"Dad?" Maggie called out, "Dad!"

She ran into the kitchen, followed by Holden and Bridgette. There, they found Nathan, sitting at the dining table with a sober look on his face. He didn't seem at all surprised that three frantic, winded teenagers had just burst into the room.

"Da . . . dad?" Maggie huffed.

He looked up and slowly answered, "Hey, Smaggs. Ya know that thing that happened to you? With the lights in your room?"

"Dad, what? What is it," she snapped impatiently.

"I just had the weirdest thing happen."

Maggie's heart and stomach dropped into her toes. "Uh, Dad? Wh . . . what're you talking about?"

Nathan turned his head toward the back patio door and with a confused frown, explained, "I was hungry and decided to make myself a ham sandwich. These weird little lights . . . they started flying around outside the back door." He pointed, indicating exactly where the phenomena had taken place. "At first, there were only a few of 'em. But then, a bunch more showed up. You all musta scared 'em though, 'cause when you guys came in they flew off."

Maggie looked at Holden and then at Bridgette. They both appeared as concerned as she felt.

"Oh, okay . . . um dude," Holden asked apprehensively, "did the walls shake?" He glanced nervously at Maggie and added, "uh, ya know . . . like hers did?"

"Whattya mean, duuuuude?" Nathan quipped. Maggie couldn't believe that in the midst of all this, he was still trying to be cool. "Whattya mean, did they shake? What in devil's name is going on?"

Holden didn't answer. He was distracted by Maggie, who'd gone over to the cupboards, pulled out a glass, and was standing at the sink filling the glass with tap water. She didn't even try to hide the inhibitor as she dropped it in and swirled it around. "Dad, you've got to drink this . . . now!"

"What? No. I just downed a soda. I'm not really thirsty, Smaggs."

"This has nothing to do with being thirsty, Dad," she insisted. "Please, just drink it."

"Yeah dude, please," Holden chimed in, "it's kinda a life or death . . . thing!"

Nathan's eyes grew wide.

"Er, at least I think it is. I mean . . . ya know . . . kinda?"

Nathan glanced from Holden to Maggie, who was still holding the glass of water out in front of him, staring at him pleadingly.

"Okay, fine! I'll drink it."

She handed him the glass, and then glared at Holden. He knew something—something about Lor Mandela and all of the stuff that was going on; that much was obvious. He understood way too much.

"So, Holden," she tried, "why does it matter . . . I mean, if the walls shook or not?"

The look on Holden's face confirmed that he was hiding something. "It means that they came through 'em," he resigned.

Nathan, Maggie and Bridgette all turned and stared at him, gaping.

"How on Earth do you know that?" Bridgette mumbled. "What's going on?"

Holden ignored her and tried again. "Did they shake, Mr. B? The walls?"

Nathan grimaced. "Uh, no. I don't think so."

His answer sent a flood of relief coursing through Maggie, but it only lasted for a moment.

Whooosh...whoooooosh!

This time, the sound came so loudly that no one within a quarter mile could've missed it.

"No! No! Not now!" Maggie shouted in panic—clapping her hands over her ears in an effort to shut out the deafening noise.

Nathan panicked too. "Maggie, wait!" He jumped up from his chair and grabbed her by the arm. "Leave her alone! You can't have her," he yelled frantically toward the ceiling.

"What is that?" Bridgette shrieked.

The whooshing became so thunderous that the entire house was shaking.

"Dude! Get away! Don't touch her!" Holden bellowed at Nathan, "BLUE! DON'T LET HIM TOUCH YOU!"

Maggie yanked backwards, freeing herself from her father, who immediately reached out to grab her again. "No! Dad, don't!" She jerked back and ran around the kitchen table to put more space between them.

Regardless of what Holden or Maggie was saying Nathan was not going to let his daughter be abducted again—not without one heck of a fight! He started around the table after her, arms outstretched.

Maggie grabbed a hold of a chair and slid it between them, then turned and sprinted toward the back door, reaching out for the handle. As if it had been choreographed, both Nathan and Holden simultaneously dove through the air towards her. They were mid-lunge, when a brilliant flash of blue light sent a powerful shockwave rippling through the room, momentarily blinding everyone.

Bridgette let out an earsplitting scream.

Holden smacked right into Maggie, knocking her forcefully to the ground.

Maggie blinked and squinted, straining to focus in on where she'd been taken, but her eyes weren't adjusting to the light very quickly. Through the twinkling flashes in front of her eyes, she saw a hand move toward her to help her up. She grabbed the hand and tried to make out who it belonged to.

"Holden?" she muttered. Now she understood why he'd yelled for her dad not to touch her. Apparently, whoever was in contact with her when she was taken would be taken as well.

"Where are we?"

As Holden's face became clearer, an even more confused look spread across it. "Uh, we're um . . . we're still in your kitchen, Blue."

Maggie jumped up and frantically scanned the room. Her stomach bottomed out. She stared wide-eyed from Holden to Bridgette, back to Holden and then back to Bridgette. "Where is he? Where is he?" she cried as—much to her horror—she realized that this time, it was her dad who was gone.

CHAPTER XXXII
NATHAN'S DISCOVERY

"**A**aaaaaaaaaaaaa!" Nathan had thrown himself across the kitchen with such momentum, that when he materialized, he was still hurling—arms and legs flailing—through the air. He bulleted right through the top of a large shrub, hit the muddy ground with both feet, flipped forward, landed with a thud on his back, and then rolled sideways down a small hill. "Goo . . . hoo . . . hood . . . night!" He exclaimed when he finally came to a stop.

Taking a deep breath to restore the air that had been knocked out of him, he pulled himself to his feet, and brushed at the sticky, dark mud that was now covering his blue jeans. "Maggie," he called out. "Smaggs? Where the devil are you?" He scanned the area around him, and realized that he'd not just simply tossed himself out into the backyard. "And, uh . . . wh . . . where the devil am I?"

He stared off in a daze for several seconds. "How on Earth," he mumbled. Suddenly his eyes widened and a knowing smile spread across his face. "Wait a second," he exclaimed, "maybe if I jump again . . . ."

He closed his eyes tightly, and flung himself into the air, hoping to undo what had just been done. Unfortunately, all he succeeded in "undoing" was his vertical orientation. He hit the ground and tumbled down another grassy hill. When he came to a stop, he was face-down, and even more covered in mud and grass stains. He pulled himself up to sitting, and looked blankly out at the dew-covered meadows and lush green foothills that stretched before him as far as he could see.

"This is definitely not Glenhill," he muttered, as a somewhat frightening realization took hold of his senses. He'd left Earth—he didn't know how or why—and he had no idea how to get back again.

"Sma . . . aggs," he called out shakily, but there was no reply. Maggie was nowhere to be seen. In fact, there was no one at all to be seen. He was alone. He got back up to his feet, and took a deep breath. Again, he browsed the scenery around him.

Despite being less than thrilled with this present unfamiliar locale, he had to admit the view was quite beautiful. The bottom rays of the sun were just beginning to descend behind the emerald hills, and the sky was slowly changing from soft pink to brilliant orange.

"Come on, Smaggs, where're ya at?" He started back up the hill, ascending the gentle slopes with little effort. As he reached the top and looked down the other side, his legs became wobbly and he very nearly collapsed.

Before him sprawled a massive, unbelievably beautiful, glowing city, the likes of which he'd never, ever seen. Its shimmering buildings and flowery gardens glistened in the soft light of the setting sun. The city was surrounded on two sides—the one where he stood and the one to his right—by lush, deep green, rolling hills. To his left huge trees reached skyward.

The hills were dotted with quaint structures that reminded him of French Chateaus, but with one very distinct difference. They weren't made of brick, or stone, or wood, like the houses he was used to. They seemed to be constructed of a thick, pearly, almost liquid-looking substance, colored in shades of white, tan, silver, and a pale, grayish-blue. Several people were out and about near the houses, visiting, working in the yards, reading, tending to animals and performing a myriad of other tasks. Children happily played together in large groups on the hillsides. *Hmmm,* he thought to himself, *they don't look like aliens.*

At the base of the hills, a wide, winding river separated the quaint villages from hundreds and hundreds of much taller and larger edifices—each made of the same pearly material as the smaller houses, but in varying shades of grey—surrounded by their own lavish, perfectly manicured gardens. The mass of tall, stately buildings stretched for miles toward a hazy mountain in the far-off distance that was glowing golden from the reflection of the sunset on its face. The whole scene looked like an ethereal, living, moving, watercolor painting.

"Tabbit, look! There he is!" Suddenly, a woman's voice sounded from somewhere below, breaking Nathan away from the mesmerizing view.

A red-haired young woman and a wild-looking child with crazy white hair were running up the hill toward him. His first instinct was to turn and run away, and he was about to do just that, when he heard the woman again.

"Mr. Baker! Wait! We're here to help!"

He stopped and turned to face them. "Help," he quizzed, "Who are . . . ?" Upon seeing the young woman up close, he was instantly rendered speechless. She was stunning—with her big green eyes, flowing auburn hair and pale, slightly freckled skin—and arguably the most beautiful woman he'd ever laid eyes on. "Um, hi," he fumbled. "Do . . . do I know you?"

The young lady squinted at him for a few seconds. "Uh . . . no. I'm afraid not." Her tone implied a hint of disappointment. "Your daughter, Maggie . . . she told me about you, that's all." She looked cautiously around and then grabbed him by the arm. "Now, come on. We have to get you out of here."

"Hold it just a doggone minute," he protested. "Who are you, and exactly where are you taking me?"

Just then, he felt a soft tugging on the leg of his jeans. He looked down at the little wild-haired girl, and stumbled backwards in shock. "You . . . you're . . . wha . . . wait . . . no . . . there's no way . . . how . . . ?" He ran his hand across his forehead. "You're that thing Paul gave Maggie! The one that was stolen! O . . . only, you're *alive!*" he whispered.

Tabbit looked up at him with a crazy grin on her face. "You . . . you're . . . wha . . . wait . . . no . . . there's no way . . . how . . . ? You're that thing Paul gave Maggie! The one that was stolen! O . . . only, you're *alive,*" she mimicked. "I is not a thing, sir. Tabbit's the name, sir. Yeses . . . very much alive, sir!" She rolled up and down on her little brown, bare toes, beaming happily.

"Uh, pleased to meet you?" he replied, eyeing Tabbit like she was nuts.

The woman cleared her throat. "Um, we really should be going," she insisted. "We can make small talk after we get to the palace." She started down the hill, tugging Nathan along by the arm.

"Palace? What palace?" Nathan gasped. "Listen, uh . . . ?"

"Kahlie."

"Okay, good . . . Kahlie. I'm not goin' anywhere until you tell me what in the devil's goin' on!" He yanked his arm out of her hand and stopped walking.

Kahlie froze in her tracks and glared at him, annoyed.

"Fine, Mr. Baker," she snapped. "Here is what's going on! I am trying to save your life, and you are making it very difficult. *That* is what is going on, all right? Now let's go!" She started off down the hill with Tabbit and Nathan in pursuit.

"Save my life? Sheesh! First Maggie and that California beach bum . . . now you? Why in blazes does everyone seem to think my life's in danger?" Nathan panted as he rushed up behind Kahlie.

"Because it is," she answered matter-of-factly.

Nathan glanced down at Tabbit who was bouncing along beside him, grinning up at him, and nodding. "Because it is. Yesses, big danger . . . Darian very bads!"

He shook his head and continued to follow Kahlie, who was moving at a fairly fast clip. He increased his stride to a sort of jog-walk to keep up.

After a few seconds, they reached the bottom of the hill, and started toward the river. Directly in front of them, a large, flat rock spanned from one bank to the other, creating a solid natural bridge.

As they approached the bridge, a small, lime green, disc-shaped object with two long crystals jutting from its top came soaring past, barely missing Kahlie and falling to the ground very close to the river's edge.

"Obeeo!" Tabbit squealed delightedly, dashing over to where the object had landed.

"Tabbit," Kahlie scolded, "what are you doing?"

She stopped in her tracks, and looked at Kahlie as though she was mournfully ashamed of herself.

Just then, three teenage kids—two boys and a girl—raced out from behind one of the little chateau houses, yelling loudly and laughing. "Obeeo! Obeeo!" they roared as they pursued the crystalline disc. They ran toward it, barely noticing that others were present.

All at once, the girl froze in place. It didn't take long for the boys to realize she wasn't with them and they stopped running as well. The girl was standing completely still, eyes wide, and gaping at Nathan. One of the boys gasped, and rushed back to her side. He grabbed her hand and yanked it downward. At once, all three of the teenagers dropped to their knees and bowed.

Kahlie cringed. "Oh, um, all right. Thank you," she groaned, grabbing Nathan by the arm and pulling him toward the bridge. "You have honored the house of Borloc. Please, go in peace. Return to your activities." She shook her head in frustration and told Tabbit to give them back their obeeo.

"What the blazes?" Nathan muttered, watching as the three stunned kids rose back to their feet, their eyes fixed on him. Even when Tabbit handed the obeeo back to the taller of the boys, he didn't as much as blink.

Kahlie was agitated. "How could you, Tabbit? We weren't to be seen, remember?" She motioned for Nathan to cross the bridge in front of her.

"How could you, Tabbit? We weren't to be seen, remember?" Tabbit echoed sadly. "Me is sorry, Miss Companions Servant. Mees loves Obeeo!" She hopped up onto the rock and sauntered slowly across.

Kahlie sighed.

"Come on," Nathan gasped, "they're just kids. You don't think they're tryin' to knock me off do you?"

"If word gets out that you're here, it's only a matter of time. Darian *will* find out," she explained. "He has spies all over Lor Mandela."

Nathan glanced backwards at the three teens whispering amongst themselves, still staring. "Weird . . . ." he muttered as he reached the edge of the rock bridge and stepped out onto it.

Kahlie finally slowed the pace a bit, and made eye contact with him. He knew that he should be concerned that some madman was after him, but he couldn't help thinking just how beautiful she was.

"Listen," she explained, "I'm sorry that I've been a little demanding, really, but you have to understand. This is serious. On this world . . . Lor Mandela . . . only members of the ruling family Borloc have black hair and blue eyes. Darian thinks you are Atoc Jonathan Borloc, our High Ruler. He thinks Maggie is the Child of Balance. He is planning to use her to gain power and he has already commanded his soldiers to kill you on sight."

Nathan gulped. Up until now this whole experience had seemed surreal—like a dream. But suddenly it was sinking in. He was on Lor Mandela—not Earth. An army of assassins was after him—or after the person they thought he was—and this Darian character was trying to get to Maggie, too.

"Yeah, okay, Kahlie. I understand. I'll do whatever ya say, and I appreciate you watchin' out for me, but please," he hesitated, "do not let anything happen to Maggie."

"I won't," she assured. She smiled and patted him gently on the hand—a gesture that caused a most unexpected reaction. A surge of pulsating heat flooded through his body and he felt himself blush from head to toe.

He cleared his throat, and responded in a very deep, manly tone, "Uh, yeah. Thank . . . mm hmm . . . thank you, Kahlie." He glanced away, hoping the faint daylight that remained was not enough to illuminate his reddened face.

Tabbit giggled.

The trio made their way up from the banks of the river and onto a wide street that wove its way through the tall, pearly buildings. It was now dark out, but the streets were well-lit by small, pale, yellow lights that hung in the trees and larger bushes of the gardens. "What is this place called?" Nathan inquired.

"This is Mandela City," Kahlie smiled with pride. "Is it like your first city?"

He shook his head, "I don't think there's anything like this on Earth. Least not anything I've ever seen." He looked down at the street which appeared to be made of large slabs of polished stone, pieced together in a giant glistening mosaic, and then glanced at Tabbit who was swatting at what appeared to be something similar to a lightning bug. The little bug darted just out of reach, but then became distracted by a large ruffled flower that hung from a nearby shrub. As it stopped to investigate, Tabbit slapped her little hands around it and popped it into her mouth.

"Ughhh," Nathan moaned as he watched a small little lump—obviously the still-alive bug—writhe and wriggle down Tabbit's throat. A few seconds later, and much to his disgust and amazement, the lump reappeared on her big, bulgy tummy. The bug was bumping and banging against the inside of her belly, still trying to escape. This went on for several seconds, concluding with Tabbit jumping up and down a couple of times and belching loudly.

Kahlie noticed his repulsed expression and sniggered.

"What? Is that normal here," he asked. "Do you eat like that, too?"

"No, of course not," Kahlie laughed. "Tabbit's a Shadow Squanki. Everything is like a game to them. You should've seen your face!" she giggled, poking him playfully in the shoulder.

"Well, ha ha ha," he retorted. "I'm sorry! That was just . . . ." Suddenly, he stopped and his jaw dropped open. "Whooooa! Is that the . . .?"

"Mandela Palace," Kahlie smiled.

They stood at the outskirts of the city, on the edge of a large grassy meadow. The sprawling field was devoid of anything vertical except a large, oddly shaped tree that twisted up just a few feet away from them. Across the meadow, at the base of the mountain, stood Mandela Palace—an amazing structure, easily the size of the entire town of Glenhill. It looked like someone had taken the best ideas of the world's most brilliant architects and combined them into one absolutely stunning work of art. It was a spectacular luminescent white constructed of the same pearly material as the other buildings and embellished with dark, elaborate roofs, intricate window frames, Gothic gable decorations and extensive verandas and balconies. It stood glowing and majestic nestled in a serene, mountainous valley, bordering a sparkling, crystal lake. All Nathan could manage to do was shake his head back and forth.

"You like it?" Kahlie's asked; her question barely registered.

"Like it? I'm . . . uh," he stammered. "It's well . . . just look at that thing!"

"Good," Kahlie smiled. "I'm sure it'll be a comfortable home for you while we get this mess straightened out."

"Home?" Nathan muttered as they started across the large expanse of grass.

"Home?" Tabbit repeated, and skittered off toward the palace singing, "You is the atoc . . . You is the atoc!"

"Tabbit!" Kahlie snapped, "That's enough! I already told you. Mr. Baker is not the atoc!"

Nathan chuckled, "That's okay . . . and I'd really prefer it if ya called me Nathan. Mr. Baker sounds so old."

"Oh, I'm sorry . . . uh, Nathan."

Tabbit was now almost half way across the meadow—ignoring Kahlie completely—and still bantering on. "Oh, I'm sorry . . . uh, Nathan. Nathan is the atoc, Nathan is the atoc!"

"She's um, somethin' else, huh?" Nathan laughed, "Ya know what's weird?"

"Uh . . . yeah," Kahlie teased, "you?"

"Oh, ha, ha!" Nathan smirked, and lunged toward her like he was going to grab her.

Kahlie giggled, and took off running.

"Hey! You get back here, Missy," Nathan insisted.

Kahlie shook her head "no" as she sprinted away. She was pretty fast, but Nathan was faster, and within a minute or two he caught up to her and grabbed her around the waist, lifting her off the ground. "Ahhhh," she squealed, still laughing like a little girl. "Put me down!"

Nathan smiled victoriously and let go. "You are no match for the atox," he shouted.

Kahlie sniggered. "The atoc," she corrected.

"Whatever." Nathan bent over and took a couple of deep breaths. "Whew, I haven't had a good run like that for a while."

Kahlie wasn't at all winded. "Yeah, well that didn't stop you from catching me, did it?"

He stood up straight and puffed out his chest. In a deep, formal voice, he proclaimed, "You are a very formidable racing opponent, M'lady!"

All of a sudden, Kahlie wasn't smiling. She looked mortified. "That . . . that is what I do best," she whispered.

Nathan looked into her serious eyes, and all of a sudden, a flood of memories raced through his mind—flashes of another time—another place. No, not another place, *this place!* Suddenly he was recalling copious amounts of information—his mother, his father, his friends, his home, the palace, Mandela City, Mystad Lake, Koria, the Mandelan army, the Trystas, Shadow Squanki, Shadow Dwellers—he knew it all! He'd been here before, too. They were in the East Mystad—the field just outside the palace. The field that led to the. . . . "The Anaria!" he gasped. He turned toward the massive tree and then glanced back at Kahlie.

"Kahlie! Oh, Kahlie! I'm back! I'm back!" He grabbed her and lifted her into the air. "Whoohoo! *I'm back!*" He lowered her to the ground and kissed her cheek, and then, the full gravity of the situation kicked in. Both he and Kahlie just stood there, stunned—panting and gaping at each other in disbelief.

It was Kahlie who spoke first. "But how? You don't look . . . I mean there's a little similarity, I guess, but . . . ."

He was now staring at his shoes and looking quite overwhelmed. "Graci," he muttered sadly.

Kahlie put her hand on his shoulder.

Just then, the quietness of the field was blasted away by a loud *whoosh, whoosh, whoosh!*

"What's that?" Kahlie yelled between surges.

"Kahlie! Hang on! Don't let go!" He thrust his hand out toward her and she obediently grabbed a hold. He pulled her to him and wrapped his arms around her shoulders as the sky filled with a brilliant blue light, followed by a deafening crack, and they disappeared.

They landed with a splash into something warm and wet.

"Whoa! Hold on! Don't move! I'm on my way." A male voice boomed through the light.

Even if Kahlie had wanted to move, Nathan was holding her so tightly that she couldn't. Despite this, however, she tried to look around to see where they'd been taken.

"Oh no," she gasped, "Eternity Pools . . . yeah . . . don't move."

"I know," Nathan breathed. "Don't panic. We'll figure this out."

They had been transported to an area just outside of Koria known as the Eternity Pools. The Pools appeared to be nothing more than a group of several ponds of water, but in reality, contained something far more treacherous—Deroxis—a strange, carnivorous plant. When an animal or—in this case—a person happened to land in one of the Pools, the Deroxis took on the appearance and feel of a warm, soothing spring. But, the moment the plant's prey attempted to get out, the Deroxis' leaf-like appendages would spread and wrap themselves tightly around it, smothering it before pulling it down deep below ground and slowly devouring it. The pools were called the Eternity Pools because the myth among the Trysta people was that the process of being consumed would take all of eternity.

Just a few feet away, a young man jumped from spot to spot, skillfully avoiding the deadly Pools. "Hang on, almost there!" he assured as he teetered on a small rock, and then leapt from it. Within a moment, he reached the side of the pool, knelt down and removed a coiled rope from the side of his belt. He quickly tied a few knots and flung the rope out around them. "Don't move a muscle!" he reiterated as he reached out and tucked part of the lasso into Nathan's hand. "Okay, now very slowly . . . take a hold of the rope."

Nathan carefully rolled his fingers into a fist. His heart pounded as, much to his horror, the water-like substance around him started to ripple.

"Alright, on my order, tense up." The stranger watched as the tip of a leaf formed near Kahlie's back.

"What? Tense up? We tense up and we're dead!" she retorted.

"You're going to have to trust me!" He stood and pulled the rope taut. "Ready . . ." he began, "*Now!*"

Kahlie and Nathan tightened their muscles. Masses of large, black-green leaves shot upward, momentarily creating a small space around them. The young man flipped the rope, spiraling it around and around Kahlie and Nathan. "Grab it!" he yelled. Nathan clenched his fist. The man had managed to twist the rope into something resembling a noose.

The treacherous leaves spun toward them, and the man leaned back and pulled as hard as he could on the rope. It was obvious that he was strong, but the rope itself seemed to be doing the work now. In an instant, Kahlie and Nathan were pulled from the Pool, just as the lethal Deroxis crashed inward. They landed forcefully on the ground, and rolled to a stop just before sliding into another deadly Pool.

"Whoa!" The young man gave a small tug on the rope and it virtually disintegrated. Nathan brushed the remaining bits of it off, and helped Kahlie to her feet.

She leaned in closely to him and whispered. "Don't say a word. We can't trust anyone, remember?"

Nathan gestured with an inconspicuous nod toward the young man. "Ryannon . . . Darian's son," he whispered back.

Kahlie's eyes grew wide; she turned and faced Ryannon. "Thank you for your help, sir. We are in your debt."

"Ah, you must be Maggie's father," Ryannon smiled. "I'm Ryannon."

"Ryannon, of course. Yes, as a matter of fact, I am Maggie's father. I'm Nathan . . . Nathan Baker. This is my friend, Kahlie."

Ryannon smiled and nodded. "I wish we were meeting under different circumstances, sir. I don't know how much you know."

"I know that your father has sentenced me to death," he retorted coolly.

Ryannon sighed. "I'm so sorry. My father is deranged, but I have a plan. I can help you."

"Really?" Kahlie interjected. "Why should we trust you to help? How do we know that you aren't up to something yourself?"

"I did just save you, didn't I?"

"Kahlie," Nathan assured, "maybe we should listen. I mean, given the circumstances I don't think we have much of a choice."

Kahlie looked at him like he was crazy.

"First," Ryannon began, "you'll need this." He pulled something from his coat pocket.

"What is it?" Nathan asked.

"Well, since you're here, I can only assume that the inhibitor I gave Maggie didn't work. This new one should do the trick. He placed a small object on the back of Nathan's hand which instantly dissolved into his skin. "There, now. Once you go back home, you'll stay."

Kahlie gasped. "WHAT! What are you thinking? You can't just put things on people without their permission! Do you have any idea what you've done?"

Ryannon looked at her like a cat that had just caught a mouse.

"Kahlie, it's okay," Nathan glared at her, wide-eyed. "Calm down. It'll be okay."

"We really should get out of here," Ryannon suggested, "I think it would be best if we got you out of plain sight."

Nathan nodded in agreement. "Lead the way, Ryannon. I have absolutely no idea where I'm going!"

As they cautiously made their way out of the Eternity Pools, Nathan allowed Ryannon to get a little ahead of him and Kahlie, and then grabbed her hand. She looked at him in surprise. With his head, he motioned toward the hand on which Ryannon had placed the object before.

"That was a receptor," he whispered.

CHAPTER XXXIII
TO CATCH A SQUANKI

Maggie was frantic. She looked at Bridgette pleadingly, grabbed her by the shoulders and yelled, "We're too late! They've got him!" Bridgette was simply trying to process what had happened.

Holden dropped into one of the kitchen chairs and buried his face in his hands. He seemed to be as upset as Maggie; but at this particular moment, she could feel no sympathy toward him. She stomped over to where he was sitting and slugged him in the shoulder.

"Ow!" he yelped.

"This is all your fault," she shrieked. "You did this when you bumped him out of the way!"

"WHAT?" Holden's face turned red with rage. "Thirteen years!" he bellowed. His voice sounded much older suddenly. "I've been trying to get back . . . been stuck on this lousy planet, with nothing more to do than follow you around and keep your butt out of trouble!" He stood from the chair and paced the floor. "I wasn't even part of your ridiculous . . . I was just trying to help your . . . *ugh!* I get a chance . . . one stupid chance in thirteen years, and now . . . it's all *my* fault? This is what I get for trying to help! Every time! Every time . . . something like this happens!"

Maggie and Bridgette stared at him, mouths gaping and eyes wide.

"I think, Holden that you have a bit of explaining to do." Maggie insisted calmly, yet deliberately.

Holden glanced from Maggie to Bridgette—who looked like she was in shock—and then back to Maggie. "Listen," he sighed, "I can explain later, and I promise I will. It's just right now, there's not time. We have to figure out how to get to Lor Mandela or your dad's in real serious . . . ."

"What do you mean, get back to Lor Mandela?" Maggie snapped. "You just said you've had one chance in thirteen years, and I can't exactly control when I have the pleasure of visiting!"

"I know!" Holden barked back, "but we've got to figure it out! We don't have a choice!"

Maggie was about to retort, when Bridgette touched her gently on the forearm.

"Holden," she began quietly, "what do you suggest we do?"

His reply was not what either of the girls anticipated. "We need a Shadow Squanki."

"A what?" Bridgette and Maggie quizzed in unison.

"A Squanki," he repeated. "They create portals between worlds. I've been trying to catch one in particular here for years, but she's been kinda elusive." The girls' faces must have shown their confusion, because he was quick to elaborate. "Oh, Squanki are these little creatures that live on Lor Mandela. They come here from time to time to get crickets. Maybe if all three of us keep an eye out, we can track one down."

"Crickets?" Maggie frowned. "You're saying that you want us to find a little creature that comes from another planet because we have crickets here? Is that supposed to make any sense?"

"No. It's not," he answered abruptly, "but as I see it, we have only two ways to find your dad. One, we find a Squanki and have it lead us to a portal, or two, you get transported back and I make dang good and sure that I go with you. So, for right now, we need to round up as many crickets as possible, and you need to stay very close to me so that if you start to go 'whoosh, whoosh' again, I can grab on and enjoy the ride!"

"But where are we going to get crickets?" Bridgette asked blankly. She felt like she was in some sort of weird, illogical dream and that at any moment her mom was going to come in and wake her for breakfast.

Holden smiled at her. "Well, usually I just look under rocks, or around wood piles and stuff. C'mon, we'll have to find a bunch if we want to attract a Squanki." He moved with determination toward the back door.

"Or," Maggie interjected, "we could just go to the pet store."

Holden stopped in his tracks and turned around. "The pet store?" he chuckled. "Just how many people do you know that have a pet cricket?"

Bridgette and Maggie gawked at each other in utter surprise.

"Haven't you ever heard of a lizard?" Maggie scoffed. "Crickets are pet food, not pet . . . pets! They probably have hundreds of them at Pet Land in the mall."

"Hundreds?" Holden gasped. "You're kidding me."

Maggie just shook her head.

Holden grimaced and threw his hands in the air. "Let's go then," he groaned as he stepped out through the storm door. Maggie and Bridgette shrugged their shoulders and followed after him.

They jumped back into his car and he put it in gear and ran his hand through his hair. "You mean to tell me all this time, I could've just gone to the pet store? I coulda found at least a dozen Squanki by now!" He pulled out onto the road with a squeal, and took off toward the Glenhill Galleria.

The drive from the Baker house to the mall usually took about fifteen minutes, but they got there in ten. During the whirlwind car ride, Maggie pressed Holden for information, but he refused. It was obvious that he was from Lor Mandela, and that he'd been trying to get back, but why had he been following her around for the last thirteen years? Why did she need someone keeping her "butt" out of trouble? Who was he really? Every question she asked, he answered with, "The less you know right now, the safer we'll both be," or, "I can't tell you. You just have to trust me!"

The mall was unusually busy for a Tuesday, but they managed to find a parking space in fairly close proximity to Pet Land—The Midwest's Greatest Pet Super Store. This was no little mall pet shop. It was almost as large as the other three anchor department stores in the Glenhill Galleria.

Once inside, Maggie flagged down a tall, skinny, freckle-faced employee, identified as "Brody" by his nametag.

"Excuse me? Brody? Hi."

Brody became uneasy, presumably because an attractive girl was speaking to him.

"I need to get some crickets."

"Um . . . okay," he squeaked, "uh . . . how many do you need?"

Holden piped in. "Uh, how many do you have?"

Brody smiled, thinking this was some kind of joke.

"A bunch," he answered. "We just got 'em in like twenty minutes ago."

"We'll take everything you've got, bro. How much for all of 'em?" Holden's surfer accent was back.

Brody's freckle-covered face flushed to a bright magenta; he shifted back and forth on his feet, giggling. "Uh . . . I'm gonna get my manager to help you," he wheezed, and sprinted away.

"Great," Maggie groaned, "that's not suspicious at all!"

"Whatta ya mean?" Holden asked. "You said people buy 'em for their lizards."

"Yeah! Maybe fifty or so! Not a billion at a time!"

"Well . . . my lizard is a healthy eater," Holden quipped, causing Bridgette to giggle.

Maggie rolled her eyes at him.

Just then, a tall, middle-aged, bald man in a bright blue dress shirt and black tie approached. His gold nametag read, "Mr. Butler – Store Manager."

"Hello," he greeted enthusiastically. "I understand you folks need some crickets. What kind of pet are you feeding?"

"Dude," Surfer Holden began, "I've got, like, fourteen lizards—big ones, ya know—and they're, like, totally starving."

"Really," Mr. Butler replied—a hint of disdain in his tone. "That's quite a collection. What kinds of lizards are they?"

"Hey, Bro. They're, like, all different ones, ya know, but they all totally need food. I ran out of crickets last night, and if they don't eat soon, they're gonna get, like, totally cranky!"

Bridgette smiled and Maggie sighed disgustedly.

He continued, "Dude, I seriously need to buy, like, all of your crickets, bro!"

The feigned smile that had been on Mr. Butler's face was now gone. He leaned over to Holden and whispered, "Listen, mister. I don't know what you're up to, but if this is some sort of sick teenage prank, I'll have the cops down here faster than you can blink!"

Just then, Maggie caught something out of the corner of her eye.

"No way," she breathed.

"No way, what?" Bridgette asked.

"Bridge, I think I know what a Shadow Squanki is! Follow me!" She grabbed Bridgette's arm and pulled her down an aisle a few feet away from where they'd been standing. They could still hear Holden insisting to Mr. Butler that he didn't know anything about the recent rash of cricket disappearances in the store.

"What are we looking for?" Bridgette questioned.

"A kid that looks like my hiding-seeker," she replied, peering around the end of the aisle. "I swear I just saw her!"

Bridgette, who was still convinced she was dreaming, nodded and played along. They were heading toward the back of the store when it started.

Whoosh...whoosh....

"Holllldennnn!" Bridgette cried. She and Maggie turned and sprinted back toward where they'd left him. "Holden! Come quick!" she shrieked as they turned the corner and he and Mr. Butler came back into view.

"What's that?" Mr. Butler asked as the whooshing grew louder.

"Oh, no!" Holden shouted, and almost knocked Mr. Butler over as he dashed toward Maggie.

Suddenly, the store illuminated in a flash of blue light. There was a loud *crack*, and right in front of Mr. Butler and a store full of shoppers and Pet Land employees, Maggie disappeared into thin air.

"Where'd she go?" Mr. Butler yelped. "Wh... what are you three up to?"

Holden slowly turned to face him. He opened his mouth to speak, but nothing came out. He glanced around the store, and then back at Mr. Butler.

All at once, he erupted into a deafening primal scream. "Aaaaaaaaaahhhhhhhhhh!"

Everyone in the place stopped what they were doing, and stared at this madman who was bellowing in the middle of the pet store. His stunning outburst went on for a solid ten seconds before Mr. Butler grabbed him by the arm and escorted him—still screaming—toward the front of the store.

"You too, Blondie," he yelled back at Bridgette. "Both of you . . . out!"

Three uniformed mall security guards hurried through the front doors. Two of them got on either side of Holden, and took him from Mr. Butler's grasp. The other walked over to Bridgette and grabbed her by the arm.

"Do you mind?" she snapped, as she yanked her arm away. "I'm perfectly capable of walking myself out!"

One of the guards clutching Holden—a very muscular, rather dull looking character—grunted as they reached the mall doors, "Uh, we see you in here again, the cops will 'rest you!" He gave Holden a shove out and glared back at Bridgette, who quickly joined him outside.

Holden waited for the mall cops to walk away, and then started shouting.

"WHAT WERE YOU TWO DOING? SHE WAS SUPPOSED TO STAY CLOSE TO ME!"

Bridgette's big brown eyes filled with tears.

"You . . . you were arguing with that manager guy and Maggie thought she saw her hiding-seeker . . . well probably not her hiding-seeker . . . but another one, in Pet Land. We were just trying to find her for you," she whimpered as the tears literally jumped from her eyes.

All at once Holden felt like a clod. "Hey, whoa! It's okay. It's not your fault, Pretty Dude," he soothed. "Wait! She saw one?"

Bridgette nodded and sniffled, "Yeah, in the store. Was that a . . . ."

Holden didn't wait for her to finish. "Bridge, we need to get back into that store!"

"Yeah, okay," she replied sarcastically, wiping the wetness from her cheeks, "And how're we gonna do that? Didn't you hear Quasi? 'The cops will 'rest you!'" she mimicked.

"We're just gonna have to come up with something," he explained as he paced back and forth in front of the big, glass, mall doors.

His thoughts were suddenly interrupted by the wild screeching of car tires. A Channel 4 news van raced through the parking lot and squealed to a stop just a few feet away. Four news people toting microphones, cameras and lights piled out of the van and rushed right past them into the mall.

"What's this all about," Bridgette wondered aloud. "They're not here because of us, are they?"

Holden shrugged his shoulders. "I kinda doubt it, but hey! I think I know how we can find out." He smiled and pointed at the news van. The sliding side door was wide open, and inside, a single technician watched the unfolding story on a small monitor. "C'mon!"

They ran over to the van, and Holden reverted instantly into his surfer routine.

"Dude, like what's goin' down?"

The technician was all too happy to fill them in. "Pet Land was just robbed at gun point. But a customer stopped the guy."

Bridgette gasped. "We were just in there!"

They watched the monitor as the field reporter—a very dignified blonde woman—began her report. "I'm standing outside of the Glenhill Galleria Pet Land, where an attempted robbery has just been thwarted by a brave customer. Officers are on the scene. Our sources have confirmed that moments ago, a man armed with a high-powered rifle entered the store, and demanded that the manager give him all of the money from the cash registers and the store safe. Apparently, however, a shopper in the store was able to catch the gunman off-guard, and disarm him. Police have the robber in custody and should be escorting him out momentarily. Michael, it looks as though someone is coming out of the store now."

"Hey! That's Brody!" Bridgette exclaimed. They watched as the reporter rushed over to him.

"Excuse me, young man. Can you tell us what happened in there?"

"Aw, man," Holden started. "He looks like he's gonna pass out!"

Brody wiped at his sweaty forehead with the back of his hand. "I dunno. I've never seen anything like that before. It was all wild and bouncy and it went totally psycho on that guy when it saw the gun!" He gazed pleadingly at the reporter, "What was that thing?"

"Thing?" The reporter asked. "Wasn't it a customer that stopped the robbery?"

"Uht-uh," Brody sighed, "it was this fat little bug-eyed . . . um . . . thing! It was psycho . . . totally psycho!"

Bridgette and Holden glanced knowingly at each other. They turned their attention back to the monitor, and did so right at the most opportune time. "Bridgette! There it is!" Holden yelped.

"What? Did you see her?"

"No! Look!" Holden pushed past the technician and pointed at the screen. There, just below the Pet Land display window, a mere sliver of steel blue light ran perfectly down the edge of a wood molding strip. Neither Bridgette nor the technician would have even seen it if Holden hadn't pointed it out. Suddenly, the area around the blue light rippled strangely, and then—visible for only a split second—a wild, white-haired, bulgy-eyed, bubble-bellied, little creature materialized out of the shadows. The little figure promptly jumped toward the light—which flashed vividly—and disappeared.

Bridgette gasped, and the bewildered tech just stared at the screen.

Holden took her by the arm and quickly led her away from the van and back toward the mall doors. "That was her! That's her portal. We've gotta get in there now!" Holden peered in through the glass doors. "Come on!" He pushed one of the doors open. "Just keep an eye out for security."

Bridgette grabbed him by the arm and followed closely behind. They were only a few steps inside when they heard a man shouting. "There they are! They are the ones that created a diversion for the robber!" One of the guards who had escorted them out was running toward them and pointing. He was followed closely by two Glenhill police officers. Bridgette shrieked and she and Holden spun around and sped back out the doors.

"Over here!" he yelled, pointing toward a large hedge that skirted the north side of the mall parking lot. "I know where we can hide!"

They dashed toward the hedge. Holden ran to a spot where there was a small break in the bushes, grabbed Bridgette and practically pushed her through. He lunged and tumbled through himself, barely pulling his feet in, as the officers burst out of the mall.

Holden jumped up, and pointed to a spot where the leaves of the hedge were thin. He and Bridgette peeked through the spot, watching in horror as the news technician rushed from his van to meet the police officers.

Bridgette's heart sank into her stomach. "I can't believe he's gonna rat us out," she whispered.

"Guys!" The tech waved toward the parking lot. "They took off," he panted. "Dark blue sedan was waiting for 'em. No plates! They went south, toward the Interstate!"

"Duuuude!" Holden chuckled as he watched one of the police officers radio in the tip. The technician looked in the direction of the hedge and winked.

"Yesss!" Bridgette sighed, and gave Holden a hug and a peck on the cheek. "That was *so* cool!"

"Yeah, great," he agreed, "'cept we still have one teeny problem." He ran his hand through his wavy blonde hair. "How do we get to that portal?"

CHAPTER XXXIV
DALLIN DOONE

D allin Doone was not what one would call "overly social." He lived alone on a small farm in Westrim, a quaint, yet politically strategic township, situated just over the hills from Mandela City. Since his parents' untimely deaths when he was just fourteen, he had worked the farm primarily by himself. Occasionally, he would hire one or two hands to help, but only when imperative. He preferred solitude—not having to worry about social graces or being accepted—or more accurately, not having to worry about getting close to someone, only to have them taken away, as his parents had been.

There were only two people he had ever allowed himself to get close to, Atoc Jonathan and Kahlie.

A young Aton Jonathan approached him one summer day, during a period of political unrest between Brashnell and Koria. Dallin's farm was situated in such a way that it was almost completely hidden between two hills. It would have made an advantageous hideout for the Trystas, had Darian moved to attack. Fortunately, however, the battle between the Trystas and the Brashnellans never took place. But Jonathan took pity on Dallin, and returned to visit him often—usually on the premise that he was there on military business, which was really never the case. Over the years they had become very close, and Dallin was always eager to help his friend whenever his help was required.

Shortly after Kahlie came to the palace, Jonathan decided that he should introduce her to Dallin. He was impressed by their similar personalities and interests, and felt that they would get along well; he was right. Almost immediately, they clicked—acting like brother and sister—teasing one another, laughing and sometimes fighting, but never for long. Perhaps one of the biggest similarities and bonds between them though, was that they were each hopelessly, passionately—and unfortunately—victims of forbidden love. Dallin, in a moment of gloominess, admitted to Kahlie that he was head-over-heels for his true friend's entrusted, Ator Gracielle. This, in turn, inspired Kahlie to reveal that she was, in fact, head-over-heels for his true friend, Atoc Jonathan.

Gracielle's death—coupled with the disappearance of Jonathan—was almost intolerable for Dallin. It very nearly destroyed him. Immediately following the battle, he withdrew from society—even more than before—and limited his contact with others to only the entirely necessary. Even Kahlie hadn't seen him in close to a year. The first time she tried to visit, he slammed the door in her face and told her to go away, and that if he was going to lose her too, it was going to be on his terms. He continued working the farm; but now, whenever anyone approached, he would swiftly head for the house and disappear into it.

It was a particularly hot afternoon, and feeling tired and melancholy, Dallin returned early from his daily chores. He sat in a dim, well-ordered room, eating a meager meal and reminiscing about a time when he had been at the palace, helping with some renovations.

He remembered how, on that day, he'd left his tools out in the courtyard, and had come from one room into the next on his way to retrieve them. He wasn't paying attention and as he turned a corner, he accidentally bumped into Gracielle.

He closed his eyes and recalled how she'd looked that morning; her stunning blue eyes vividly glowing in contrast to the silvery satin shirt she wore; her silky, straight black hair, and her mesmerizing soft coral lips. He remembered the sweet scent of her perfume and the soft tone of her voice as she apologized for her clumsiness. He also recalled the guilt that flooded over him for thinking about her the way he did.

But at this particular moment, there was no guilt. He dreamt of a different situation, one in which Kahlie was Jonathan's entrusted, and Gracielle was merely a servant in the palace. He rose to his feet and imagined that instead of muttering and stuttering, as he'd actually done on that day, he wrapped his arm around her waist to catch her from losing her balance; and she, overwhelmed by the moment and their instant closeness, pressed against him, and touched her lips to his.

He stood in the shadowy room, eyes closed, lips slightly puckered and lost in his thoughts, when suddenly there was a brilliant flash of light, and a young woman—who resembled Gracielle in more ways than one—materialized in front of him right where Gracielle had been in his fantasy—her mouth awkwardly against his.

"What the . . . ?" he yelped, stumbling backward over the stool he'd been sitting on earlier, sending it and several other things crashing and banging to the floor, before landing hard on his backside.

Maggie, who was startled herself, didn't know whether to scream, faint, cry, help this poor guy up off the floor, or what. She stood frozen in place, staring straight ahead, like a statue.

Dallin scrambled back to his feet and grabbed a long pointy stick-type object from the shelf next to him. "Okay! Who are you, and how did you do that?" he demanded.

Maggie opened her mouth, but no words came out—only a tiny squeak.

"Well?" Dallin insisted.

She couldn't answer; she was dazed and disoriented. After a few dumbfounded moments, she snapped back into reality, suddenly aware that precious time was wasting. In her head, she commanded herself to get it together.

"I . . . I'm sorry to intrude," she began. "I don't *know* how I did that . . . something about Trystas and receptors . . . but I have to find my father right now. It's an emergency! So, if you'll excuse me." She turned and looked around in an attempt to find the door.

Now, it was Dallin who was in a daze. Other than the tight curls that cascaded over her shoulders, this girl was the spitting image of Gracielle! And, not only did she look like her—a lot—but she sounded like her, carried herself the same confident way, and seemed to have the same mannerisms.

"Who are you?" he asked again; only this time it was as though he would cease to exist if he didn't find out.

His pleading manner made Maggie uncomfortable. After all, here she was in a stranger's house—someone with whom she'd unwillingly found herself in a lip-lock—and he was acting really weird.

"Uh," She started backing slowly around a corner into another room. "I'm sorry! I, uh, gotta go." She bolted for the door at the other side of the room, and flung it open. She was not two steps outside, when she realized that she had no idea where she was, or where she needed to go next. There was nothing but fields and hills around her—nothing at all that she'd seen before. She stopped in her tracks and sighed deeply, knowing that she was going to have to ask the strange man inside for directions. She turned around and was startled as he came barreling out through the door.

"Wait," he panted, "let me help you."

She nervously looked down at her toes and conceded. "All right, I guess, since I have no clue where I am."

Dallin smiled and tilted his head toward the hill next to his house. "You're in Westrim. I'm Dallin . . . Dallin Doone, and you are?"

"Oh, I'm Maggie Baker." For the first time since materializing, she stopped to notice Dallin's face. He was younger than she originally thought—possibly in his early twenties—but his countenance was care-worn and rugged. His brown, curly hair was messy and a little on the long side, and his chin was covered in scraggly, untrimmed whiskers. Despite this apparent lack of personal grooming, however, his eyes were bright, and his smile was quite nice.

"I really *am* sorry that I popped in like that," Maggie blushed. "I've been doing that a lot lately."

"No worries," Dallin assured. "So, you need to find your dad? Any ideas?"

"No," she admitted. "I'm pretty sure he's here on Lor Mandela, but I don't know where. He's in really huge trouble, though. Do you know who Darian is?"

"Whoa!" Dallin replied, thoroughly taken aback by her question. "What do you want with that slarp?"

"How 'bout his head on a stick," Maggie sneered. "He thinks my dad is your missing atoc guy. He's ordered his army to kill him on sight. If anything's happened to him, I'll . . . ."

"What? Why would he think your dad is the atoc?" Dallin's insides knotted at the thought of what Darian might do to anyone he believed to be Jonathan.

Maggie lifted up a curly lock of her hair, "Black hair . . . blue eyes," she explained. "I'm just hoping Kahlie found him and is keeping him . . . ."

"Kahlie?" Dallin interrupted. Suddenly his expression turned bitter. "I should've known!" He turned away and headed for the house. "Find your dad yourself!" he called back angrily as he stormed inside and slammed the door.

Maggie was shocked by his outburst—and livid! How dare he? She walked right over to the door, and ripped it open. "What was that about?" she yelled into the darkness. "Dallin! Dallin! Get back out here!"

"No!" his voice called back. "You and Kahlie have had your fun, now leave me alone!"

Maggie made her way into the house. "Where are the blasted lights in here?" she seethed as she fumbled through the room. "What are you talking about? *Owww!*" She smacked her shin on the edge of a small table and almost fell over. There was a faint click followed by light—dim at first, but gradually brightening, to softly illuminate the whole room.

Dallin stood next to the wall across from her. "How did you do it? Are you a Trysta?" he asked calmly, yet Maggie could sense that he was still pretty angry.

"No, I'm not," she answered. "I'm from Earth, or . . . or Drolana?"

"Did she think that because you look like . . . .?" He continued as though Maggie's comments hadn't registered. "Is this some sort of sick plot to get me to come back to the palace?"

"Listen, Dallin," Maggie retorted, "I don't know what you're talking about. Kahlie doesn't even know I'm here right now. But I really, *really* need your help!"

Dallin studied Maggie's face. She was *so* beautiful. He wanted to help, but his pride and his fear were too strong. "I'm sorry," he muttered sadly. He turned around and without another word, retreated down a hallway into the dark.

Maggie felt an overwhelming surge—panic, anger, and frustration. Her chin quivered and tears welled in her eyes.

"*Fine!*" she screamed toward the hall. "I'll figure it out myself! Thanks for *nothing!*" She turned on her heels and raced out of the house. She looked around, wiped her eyes with the back of her hand, and started across the field in front of her. "Jerk," she hissed, "who needs ya?"

She was just reaching the edge of the field, when, much to her relief, she saw a familiar sight in the distance—the big swaying trees that lined the forest with the tall narrow mountain behind them. "Yes!" she sighed. It was starting to get darker, so the sight of anything recognizable was a comfort. Maybe—she anticipated eagerly—Kahlie would be close to where they had met before. Maybe her dad would be there too. She took off running, hoping with everything in her that her hunches would prove correct.

By the time she'd crossed the meadows and fields she was out of breath and the last glints of sunlight had given way to a starry night. "Kahlie?" she panted, "Dad?" There was no answer. The only sound was a faint buzzing, presumably the noises made by bugs. "Great," she huffed, "so, now what?" She looked at the softly swaying branches of the trees, and then back at the large meadow behind her. *You're nuts to go into a forest at night*, the logical part of her mind cautioned. "Maybe, I'll just take a peek," she justified. She reached out toward one of the trees, and the curtain of branches parted and swung upward. Cautiously, she leaned in and squinted. As she lifted her foot to take a step, she felt someone grab her around the waist from behind. She screamed and struggled to get away.

"Stop it! What do you think you are doing?" Dallin's familiar voice boomed. "Are you tryin' to get yourself killed?"

Maggie didn't stop struggling, and Dallin didn't let go. "You stop," she insisted. "Put me down!"

"You got it," Dallin snipped, and pulled his arm back let go.

Maggie almost fell over frontward. "What are you doing here? Are you stalking me?" She turned around and gave him a shove on his shoulders.

"Don't flatter yourself!" Dallin retorted. "I had a feeling you'd try something stupid! Goin' into the Sybran at night? You were walking right into the Shadow Bogs! What were you thinkin'?"

"I am trying to find my dad! Do you think some lame forest is gonna stop me? My dad's life is at stake," she retorted. She was unbelievably grateful that Dallin had come, but there was absolutely no way she was going to show it.

"Then let us try using our brains, shall we? You can't help your dad if you're dead!" Dallin snipped back. He was unbelievably grateful that Maggie was all right, but there was absolutely no way *he* was going to show it.

"Fine!" Maggie flipped her hair indignantly. "What did you have in mind?"

"We need a Shadow Dweller." He dropped a backpack from his shoulder to the ground. "I just hope I brought enough."

"Enough what?" Maggie watched as he unfastened the loop at the top of the bag. "Wait," she exclaimed. "A Shadow Dweller? One of those freaky, white-haired things? Like that, um . . . Lortu?"

"Lortu?" Dallin chuckled nervously. "Yeah, just like that Lortu. He would be a good one to have helping us."

"Why do we need one of them?"

Dallin explained, "Shadow Dwellers know things. They see everything. They probably know where your father is right now."

"Really," Maggie exclaimed excitedly, "well, let's find one then! Where do they live?"

"It's not that easy." He flipped open the top flap of the pack, revealing what appeared to be softball-sized diamonds.

"Whoa. What are those for?" Maggie leaned down to get a better look.

Dallin flipped the bag shut again and explained, "Payment. Dwellers only help if it profits them. They are only loyal to . . . ."

"The best offer," Maggie interrupted, remembering that Lortu had told Ultara that she was his best offer—when she offered to absolve his life debt if he brought her Audril.

"Exactly," Dallin continued, pulling the backpack up to his shoulder. "Dwellers live in an area of the Sybran known as the Shadow Bogs, just beyond those trees there. They use these things to hypnotize their victims."

"What? Their victims?" Maggie's stomach lurched.

"Yeah. These are grazixs. You look at one long enough, you'll walk right into a rynolt's mouth if you're told to. The Dwellers love 'em. They like to tease their prey before they kill." He signaled toward a rock outcropping and headed toward it. Maggie stayed right on his heels. She was feeling more than a little uncomfortable now after hearing about Shadow Dwellers.

"Ya ever been in a place so dark that you can feel the weight of the darkness?" he asked quietly. "That's the Bogs. There's no light at all. Ya can't see anything but black . . . cold, heavy, black. Dwellers and Squanki are the only things that can see in there. You *do not* want to go into the Bogs at night! Squanki are harmless, but Dwellers will catch you, hypnotize you into doing whatever they feel like, and then kill you without even thinkin' about it."

"Oh come on, you've gotta be kidding me!" Maggie gulped, "Isn't there anyone else who can help?"

"Relax! We're safe as long as we have these grazixs," Dallin assured. "Just keep your eyes on the shadows." He set the pack on the rocks and slid down to the ground. He patted the soft grass next to him, signaling for Maggie to take a seat. Reluctantly, she sat down next to him and together they waited.

After several quiet moments, Maggie decided to try to alleviate the awkward silence.

"So, do you mind if I ask you a personal question?"

Dallin looked at her suspiciously. "Okay. What?"

"Well, I was just wondering why you hate Kahlie so much."

He glanced down at the ground. "Hate Kahlie?" he repeated. "I don't hate her. She's actually my only friend."

Maggie was surprised. "What? Then why did you get so upset when I mentioned her name earlier?"

Dallin sat quietly for a moment. Maggie thought perhaps she'd overstepped her bounds, but then he explained, "When I was a kid, my parents both got sick and died."

"Oh, I'm sorry," Maggie muttered.

"Yeah, well, at the time, it was horrible, but I eventually learned how to be okay on my own." He continued, "Then, 'bout a year ago, I lost someone else who I cared very much about, actually, someone who looks an awful lot like you."

"So, what does that have to do with Kahlie?" Maggie pressed. She understood that he had to be talking about Gracielle.

"I guess I lost it. I didn't want to get close to anyone ever again. I pushed Kahlie away. She was like my sister, but I was afraid if I went on being her friend, something bad would happen to her too!" He became agitated as he continued. "Everyone I've ever cared about has been taken from me! My parents, Atoc Jonathan, everyone!"

It intrigued Maggie that he wouldn't mention Gracielle's name; he was obviously in love with her.

"When you said that you knew Kahlie, I just assumed that she sent you to get me to come back to the palace."

"Because I look like Gracielle?" Maggie tried.

Dallin's eyes grew wide. "Oh, so you know about Gracielle," he sighed.

"Uh, not really. Just that I look like her. If you don't mind me asking, what happened to her?" she quickly added, "You don't have to tell me if you don't want to."

Dallin glanced down at the ground. "She was killed at the battle," he mumbled.

"I'm so sorry," Maggie tried to comfort. "That must've been so hard for you."

Dallin just nodded in response.

"Listen Dallin, Kahlie didn't send me . . . nobody did. She doesn't even know I'm here right now." She paused, and then asked, "Do I really look that much like her?"

Dallin looked deeply into her blue eyes, and studied her face. A strange knot twisted and turned in the pit of her stomach as he leaned a little closer. "Yeah," he breathed quietly, "you look just like her."

Maggie quickly glanced away and locked her gaze on the swinging branches of the trees. Suddenly, she spotted something moving. "Uh, Dallin," she started nervously, "I think we have company."

The silhouettes of the trees were waving and rippling oddly. One at a time, Shadow Dwellers began to materialize out of the shadows cast by the massive trees. Within seconds, roughly thirty of them were standing at the edge of the forest. In the center of the group was a familiar being.

"Lortu," Maggie gasped.

Dallin looked at her and whispered, "Stay close."

"Wat ees dis?" Lortu oozed in his deep rhythmic voice. "Whay do you deesturb the Shadow Dwellerz?

Maggie looked around at the group of strange, unearthly creatures. Their wild hair waved and floated around their heads. They all had light, glowing eyes and their grayish skin was scantily covered by battered animal skins. The scene was like something straight out of a fantasy movie.

Dallin bowed. "We bring an offering and ask for your help, wise Lortu."

"De girl?" Lortu looked directly at Maggie like she was a trophy to be won. "Ees dis da famed Maggie Baker?"

Maggie gasped.

"Yes," Dallin replied, "she is looking for her father."

Lortu started laughing wildly, followed by the rest of the Shadow Dwellers. "Aye am shooa she ees!" he rolled. He waved his scrawny arm skyward and in a blinding instant, the Shadow Dwellers surrounded Dallin and Maggie. They swooped around them, disappearing and reappearing as they moved in and out of the shadows. Where there had been perhaps thirty Shadow Dwellers before, now there were hundreds—circling rapidly, in a creepy, riotous frenzied blur.

"Dallin!" Maggie cried out, only to come face to face with a wide-eyed, cackling Lortu. He tilted his head back and forth, laughing, and held up Dallin's back pack in front of her. "We ees not needing heem anymore!"

"Hang on!" Dallin called back. She couldn't see him at all through the chaotic horde.

She made a grabbing motion toward the bag, but both it and Lortu vanished; she caught a glimpse of him again as he tossed the bag to another Dweller. Suddenly, she felt something wrap around her legs, followed by the unmistakable realization that she was being hoisted into the air. "*Dallin!*" she screamed wildly. She waved her fists frantically, hoping to make contact with whatever had a hold of her—and make contact she did. With a thud, her fist bashed into the bare back of the Shadow Dweller holding her over its shoulder. From the maniacal laugh that followed, she realized that it was Lortu. He hefted her a little further on, like she weighed nothing at all, lowered his other shoulder so that his arm was nearly touching the ground, and then, followed by the entire multitude, took off in a breakneck gallop toward the trees.

"Maggie!" Dallin yelled as he watched them carry her off. He started running as fast as he could after them. "Maggiiiieeee!"

She could see him chasing and watched in horror as a small group of Dwellers stopped to restrain him. He kicked and flailed his arms trying to break through them to get to her. The last clear vision she had was Dallin hitting one of them right in the face and then everything became pitch…black…dark.

They had entered the Bogs. The darkness was just as Dallin had described—so overwhelming, so heavy and thick, that Maggie found herself gasping for breath. Her heart pounded so hard that it felt like it was trying to beat its way out of her chest.

As they moved further into the heavy gloom, she heard a silky smooth female voice. "Lortu, whay ees we not taken heir to Ooltara?" They were moving extremely fast, yet the voice didn't falter in the slightest.

"De Trystas ees not maye best offer," Lortu replied, also with an eerily steady tone. "Aye 'ave bettair plans for 'er!"

Lortu's answer produced horrific thoughts of being hypnotized, tortured, molested, and brutally murdered. She felt like she was being held under water— thick, suffocating, black water. Her lungs burned as she sputtered and panted, groping for air. Finally, sheer terror, exacerbated by hyperventilation, consumed her, and the darkness of the Bogs was replaced by the darkness of total unconsciousness.

CHAPTER XXXV
YOAH FATE

Dallin fought vigorously to break free from the Shadow Dwellers. It was only after several minutes of hitting and kicking that he realized, aside from one of them holding him by the arm, they were not fighting back. Three other Dwellers were simply standing off to the side of the meadow, watching him pummel their companion. This caught him so off guard that he stopped for a moment and just stared, bewildered at them.

"Eef yoah ah feenished," one of the observers began, "we ah tryeeng to 'elp de Borlocs, and you ah deelayeeng us."

"Help the Borlocs," Dallin replied cynically, "by abducting an innocent bystander?"

The Dweller that had been holding on to him stepped back and studied his face. He circled slowly around him and explained, "Shee ees de atoha, Dallin Doone. Shee ees joust not knowin' eet yet."

Dallin grimaced. Could it be? Could this Dweller be right? Shadow Dwellers always seemed to know more than anyone else and were rarely wrong. Was Maggie really Atoh Audril? "How . . . how do you know?" he tried.

"Hair fotter, de atoc . . . he has remembered."

"What," Dallin blurted, "her father? Atoc Jonathan? He's alive? You know where he is?"

"Yes, and he ees needin' our 'elp."

Dallin's heart sank. If Jonathan needed help, it could only mean one thing. "Darian has him?"

Without a word, the other three Shadow Dwellers raced off into the forest. The remaining Dweller looked around and explained, "No, Dallin Doone, eet ees Ryannon. Ryannon ees who has heem . . . and de zervahnt girl."

"Ryannon?" Dallin's confusion showed on his face. "Darian's son? Isn't that almost the same thing?"

"No, eet ees not de same. Ryannon ees fah worse den heez fotter. He ees de real enemy, Dallin Doone. He ees plotting tings . . . very bad tings."

"Like what? What bad things?"

"Maye friends 'ave gone to save de atoc, but eet ees de faya atoha dat he really wants. She ees de Child of Bahlance, afta all."

An expression of horror washed over Dallin's face. "Wh . . . what does he want with her?"

"He wants hair to zolve de Advantiere, so he can rule all de Lor Mandela, and den he ees goin' to destroy hair."

"Destroy her?" Dallin was panic-stricken. "What? Where is she? Is she safe? Where did Lortu take her?"

"Lortu ees watching ovah hair, but she could deesappeah at any moment."

"Yeah," Dallin shook his head and walked toward the forest, "she could." He seemed all at once quite determined. "Lortu can't stay with her if she transports. I know receptors have no effect on Dwellers, but I can stay with her. I can protect . . . ." his voice trailed off as he walked away.

Within a split second, the Shadow Dweller was standing in front of him. "We moust go to de palace, Dallin Doone. Lortu ees watching ovah hair," he repeated. "Yoah fate lies not by going to de atoha . . . Yoah fate lies at de palace."

"At the palace? Right," he snapped sarcastically, "and what if I refuse my fate?" he side-stepped around the Dweller and kept walking.

"Den," the Dweller didn't pursue. He didn't have to. "Der will be none to saev hair. De atoha ees as good as daed."

Dallin stopped in his tracks and slowly turned around. His own words ricocheted over and over in his mind. *Shadow Dwellers know things. They see everything.* He didn't say a word. He just stood in place staring at the once-again circling Dweller.

"Yoah fate lies at de palace, Dallin Doone . . . in de Advantiere Room."

CHAPTER XXXVI
THE MURDERER

"Lady . . . Lady!" Tabbit's voice squeaked from somewhere nearby. "Lady, wakes up!"

Maggie stirred a little; she rolled her head to one side and moaned.

"Ohhhhh. Wh . . . where am I," she asked groggily.

"Where am I," Tabbit's voice repeated. "Wakes up!" This time it was much louder than before. It startled Maggie wide awake.

"Who . . . who said that?" She sat up and glanced nervously around but couldn't see anyone.

The perky little voice echoed, "Who . . . who said that? Mees said that!" Just then, Maggie noticed that a nearby tree had developed a rather shocking characteristic. Two bulgy, brown eyes were blinking on its surface a few feet off the ground. She gasped and shut her eyes. After a couple of seconds, she slowly opened them again—first one, and then the other. No, she wasn't imagining it. The tree had eyes!

"Who are you?" she asked. "Where are the Shadow Dwellers?"

All at once, Tabbit's pudgy little shape emerged out of the side of the tree. "Where are the Shadow Dwellers," She repeated as her eyes darted side to side. "They is gones . . . all gones. I is Tabbit, goods Shadow Squanki . . . goods!" She brushed a flake of bark from her long, mossy green skirt—a skirt that just seconds before had been dark brown. In fact, her hair had been brown, and it was now white; her eyes had been brown, but were now baby blue. She rolled up and down on her bare toes, and sang, "Theys is chasing slarps in The Boggies."

Maggie's face bore an expression of both intrigue and alarm. She pointed at

Tabbit, and stuttered. "Y . . . you . . . you're my . . . my . . . my Hidey. It was you! You were the one in . . . in Pet Land!"

"You were the one in . . . in Pet Land," Tabbit echoed. "We has to goes, Lady. Big Shadow folks coming back soons. Times to go . . . go and get yous to safety!" Tabbit grinned from ear to ear. "Takes yous to the atoc . . . yeps, to the daddy atoc!"

"My daddy, um dad is not the . . . wait," she blurted, "you know where my dad is?"

"My . . . ." Tabbit's reply was interrupted by the not-so-distant whoops and yells of approaching Shadow Dwellers. "Oooo, times to go," she breathed.

Maggie sprung to her feet. She wasn't certain how she'd managed to escape the horrors that the Dwellers were sure to have planned for her thus far, but she wasn't about to stick around to find out. This little Tabbit was offering an escape, and she was going to take it.

"Come on," she commanded, thrusting her hand out toward Tabbit.

Tabbit grabbed it and smiled. "Come on," she repeated, and with a surprising amount of strength, tugged Maggie along behind her into the forest.

Before long, they were at the dark edge of the Bogs. Tabbit didn't slow; she zipped right into them, and all light disappeared.

Maggie closed her eyes, and tried to concentrate on the subtle twists and turns that Tabbit made as she pulled her through the dark. Suddenly, Maggie felt something yanking on her around the middle. Not thinking, she let go of Tabbit's hand.

"Lady! No! Don'ts let go!" The tiny voice seemed miles away. "Laaaaady!"

Suddenly, there was a muffled surging noise. Maggie stood still and waited. It wasn't long before a brilliant flash of blue blasted through the darkness. Even through her closed eyes, the bright light sent a sharp twinge through her forehead.

When the flash finally faded, Maggie blinked her eyes open. She was standing in a large, stone room—the same room she'd come to before—the room where Darian had killed General Linetal—but this time she was alone. She tiptoed over to the open door, and cautiously poked her head out into the hall.

"Ryannon," she whispered, "Ryannon? Are you here?" There was no response. She crept across the large marble hallway outside of the room, and peered through an open door—still no one in sight.

She was just turning back toward the room from which she'd come when a familiar voice echoed from down another hall.

" . . . And what makes you think that anyone in their right mind would believe it?" It was Ryannon and Maggie was thrilled to hear him. She raced out down the hall toward the sound of his voice, but quickly pulled back when she realized that he was walking toward her with his father.

"Because I am the one saying it," Darian answered. "If I say it, it is so."

Maggie ran back into the room with the wall of windows. "Not Darian," she panted. "This is bad . . . very bad!"

"But, she's fully ten years older than she was a year ago," Ryannon argued, his voice drawing nearer.

"And time on Drolana passes differently than it does here." Darian's usual silky tone held a hint of aggravation—and was also much closer. "You of all people should know that!"

Maggie heard their boots just outside the door.

There was nowhere for her to hide. The room was far too open. She rushed to the wall of windows, searching for some kind of escape, and much to her relief, the pair of windows in the center turned out to be a door. Without hesitation she flung them open and hurried out into the overgrown dried up courtyard outside. There wasn't even time for her to close the door again before Ryannon and his father appeared in the doorway. Maggie quickly darted behind the skeleton of a once-full evergreen tree, and listened.

"Time on Drolana is not the problem, father! You aren't listening to me! I refuse to be a part of your feeble plot!" Ryannon's voice was strong and unwavering.

Maggie smiled. She loved the way he was letting Darian have it. It was clear that Ryannon was looking out for her, and as intimidating as his father was, he wasn't afraid to stand up to him.

"How dare you," Darian seethed. "You will do what I tell you to do."

"Or what?" Ryannon sneered back.

Maggie cautiously peered around the tree. Ryannon and Darian were very close to each other, staring threateningly into one another's eyes.

"Don't anger me, boy."

Maggie could see the fires in Darian's eyes blazing.

Ryannon maintained eye contact with his father for several seconds, but then took a step back and sighed deeply. "You know what? This is pointless!" He threw his hands up in exasperation. "I don't want to fight anymore, father."

Darian smiled in victory. "Then I can count on you?" he sneered, and thrust out his hand toward Ryannon.

Ryannon looked at his outstretched hand and sighed. "Yes, father . . . fine." He reached out with his own gloved hand, and shook his father's. Darian chuckled and pulled him into a robust embrace.

"Oh great," Maggie whispered. "What are you doing? Don't give in to him!" She glanced at them again and noticed something glistening on the glove that Ryannon had on his father's shoulder. "Are those . . . ."

Ryannon raised his hand high in the air.

"...spikes?"

In one swift motion, he swung his arm down, plunging the long, thin spikes into Darian's back. Darian gasped and sputtered, and then crumpled into a lifeless heap at Ryannon's feet.

"I'm sorry, father," he hissed, "but it's like you've always taught me. Power is everything. And now, it's mine!" He laughed maniacally and pushed his father's dead body over with his foot. "Omer! Grayden! Get in here!" he bellowed.

Maggie shrunk back behind the tree. "Oh no, oh no, oh no," she repeated breathlessly. Within a few seconds, she heard the voices of two other men in the room.

"So, I guess we can assume he didn't listen," one of them observed, not sounding at all surprised by the murderous scene.

The other man's voice was a bit more timorous. "Wh . . . what are we going to do with him?"

Ryannon's gruesome reply only added to Maggie's current state of shock. "Oh, we'll just feed him to Syltar. I'll see to it. Don't worry your nervous little brain about it, Omer."

"So now what?" the first man asked. "Don't you think people will notice that he's not around anymore?"

Ryannon strolled over to the windows. Maggie caught sight of him out of the corner of her eye and retreated further around the tree. "Haven't you heard, Grayden? The atoc has returned."

"You mean the atoc imposter?" Grayden responded.

"No matter." Ryannon had been facing out into the courtyard, but turned and replied, "I'm sure we'll have no problem convincing everyone that he killed my father."

"What?" Maggie gasped.

"And what about the girl?" Omer asked. "Don't you need her for this to work?"

"Indeed I do," Ryannon oozed smugly, "but so far, my encounters with her have been quite pleasant. She's been very easy to draw in . . . just some flattery and a little passion . . . ."

"Must be difficult for you to sacrifice yourself like this," Grayden interrupted.

"Well," Ryannon chuckled sadistically, "I suppose if I must make sacrifices, playing love games with such a magnificent young thing is the way to go." He walked away from the window and continued, "Believe me, gentlemen; I won't have any problem getting her help."

"Wanna bet," Maggie seethed.

"Well then," Grayden replied, "if that's the case, why do you even need her father? Isn't he just in the way?"

"He was . . . both he and that Kahlie, the ex-ator's companion servant," Ryannon explained, "but I already took care of that. They can't be in the way if they're dead now, can they?"

"What? Nooooo!" Maggie wailed. She spun around the tree and looked directly at Ryannon. "You pig! You murdering cowardly swine!" she screamed.

Ryannon smiled. "Get her," he commanded calmly, and Grayden and Omer raced toward the open door.

Maggie didn't care. Let them come! She wanted to hurt them; she wanted to hurt Ryannon! If they happened to kill her, so what? It didn't matter now. She just stood there, with tears spilling down her cheeks—enraged—waiting to kill or be killed.

It was unclear what happened next. A huge gust of wind blew through the courtyard, enveloping it in a cloud of thick dust, and slamming the glass door shut just as Grayden and Omer reached it. Grayden struggled with the handle, but it wouldn't budge.

Maggie had gone numb. She was in shock and completely oblivious to anything going on around her. Only after several seconds did she realize that she was moving away—being pulled by the hand. Someone was leading her out of there. She looked down and saw Tabbit guiding her quickly along. She didn't feel Tabbit's hand. She didn't hear any sounds. She wasn't even sure if she was moving her legs on her own or not, but the desolate scenery around her was somehow floating by in a hazy, dismal blur.

At length, Tabbit stopped running and looked around to make sure they hadn't been followed.

Next to them was a big scraggly shrub that looked like unkempt chartreuse hair. Tabbit cautiously moved some of the shrub's chaotic branches to one side. Behind them, was a tiny sliver of blue light—a portal. She lifted one of her bare feet and pushed it against the thin beam. Instantly, it expanded. She stepped through with one leg, and then the other—all the while holding tightly to Maggie's hand. Maggie barely felt it as one of her own legs lifted and moved toward the blue light. It no sooner touched the portal, than the light stretched and surrounded her completely. She heard a strange popping sound, followed by a voice.

"Maggie!" Dallin rushed across the room and threw his arms around her shoulders.

Something about his embrace made her immediately dissolve. She leaned against his chest for support and sobbed uncontrollably.

"Maggie, what is it?" he asked. "What's the matter?"

She didn't answer for several minutes. Finally, she was able to gasp out a weak, "Dad."

Dallin looked pleadingly at Tabbit, who was sitting in a corner rocking back and forth on her backside and shaking her head sadly.

"Dad," she mumbled, "Ryannons, very bads."

CHAPTER XXXVII
ELAHK A BER LOR MANDELA

"You fools," Ryannon bellowed, "she's getting away!" He raced up behind Grayden and shoved him to the side. The door, which had been giving his two generals such a hard time, opened easily for him.

"Come on!" he commanded and the three of them burst out into the courtyard. The dust had settled, giving them a clear view of the area; Maggie was nowhere to be seen.

Ryannon pointed to the west. "You two, go that way!"

Grayden and Omer immediately sprinted off as Ryannon headed east. He reached the edge of the sprawling courtyard and let out a disgusted, "Aaaahhhhh!" while slicing and slashing angrily at the shrubs next to him with his spiked glove.

One of them, a wild looking chartreuse bush, literally crumbled after just two or three blows.

Ryannon stopped and kicked at the remaining stubs of the plants. In his mind, he was already formulating suitable punishments for his inept generals.

As he turned away he saw it out of the corner of his eye—a small glint of pale blue, flickering in the dark behind where the bushes had been.

"Of course," he breathed, "a Squanki."

He glanced around to ensure that he was alone and then touched his foot to the light. The portal expanded and his foot disappeared into it. A devious smile spread across his face as he slid the rest of the way into the portal, and was immediately engulfed in light. He moved rapidly down a long, brightly flashing corridor, but then suddenly jolted to a stop, and the radiant flashes around him faded.

"We need to get her to a doctor." Dallin's voice was the first Ryannon heard as he came out of the light.

He squinted and blinked to force his eyes to adjust, fully aware that as long as he wasn't seeing well he was at a disadvantage.

As his eyes cleared the forms of Dallin, Tabbit and Maggie rippled into focus. None of them were facing him at the moment so he seized the opportunity to duck behind a large pillar next to him.

"Need to get her to a doctor," Tabbit repeated mournfully, "Doctor Slades is best. Tabbits takes her rights away."

Dallin, whose arms were still around a softly sobbing Maggie, gently guided her out the door, followed closely behind by Tabbit.

Ryannon slid from behind the pillar with caution and looked around the room in which he was standing. It was large and lined on one side with a wall of windows. He started toward the door, but then stopped short and spun back around. "Wait a minute," he muttered as he realized that the room he was in was identical to the one he'd left only a few moments ago. He turned back toward the windows. Just outside, a thriving, green hedge sprawled across the back of a stunning marble courtyard.

"Mandela Palace?" he whispered, "how?" He started toward the window wall but then paused as he noticed yet another surprise. There, on one of the walls of the room, tiny sparks of red light flickered across the glittery words etched in its surface. Ryannon approached the wall and ran his hand over the glowing Advantiere.

"So this is what that stupid book is all about." Silently, he read through the glimmering lines. "Ahhh . . . so then she is the Child of Balance," he mumbled. "The Child of Balance can only restore . . . restore," he breathed. "Restore the dying planet? Make it . . . *new.*" He glanced at the flourishing, pristine courtyard once more. "Elahk A Ber Lor Mandela . . . Elahk A . . . Create a new . . . ?"

He didn't finish his thought. He spun around and, without hesitation, hurried back into the portal. The instant he popped out of it, he marched across the almost dead courtyard and back into the room where his father's body still lay sprawled on the floor.

As if on cue, Grayden and Omer burst in through the glass doors.

"Omer," Ryannon barked, "bring me Ator Gracielle's book . . . now!"

"Yes, sir," Omer replied, as he sped obediently from the room.

"Grayden, why do you think we conquered Mandela City and overthrew this palace so easily?"

"Your weapons were . . . ."

Ryannon didn't let Grayden finish his sentence. "It had nothing to do with my weapons," he snapped. "You were with me at the battle! You saw what happened!"

"You mean that thing the atoh did?" Grayden guessed. "She and that servant girl? You think some voodoo chant decided the outcome of a great battle?" He looked at Ryannon like he was insane. "I thought you were different from your father . . . that you had a brain in your head."

Just then, Omer burst back into the room. He ran to Ryannon and handed him Gracielle's little brown book.

"Come with me," Ryannon commanded, ripping the book out of Omer's hand and glaring angrily at Grayden.

He led them into the courtyard and toward the portal. "My father thought he needed the Child of Balance to restore this world," he explained, "but she's already done it!" He stopped and pointed to the sliver of light at the back of the hedge.

"A Squanki portal?" Grayden questioned. "Where does it lead?"

Ryannon glanced from Grayden to Omer. "It leads, gentlemen . . . to Mandela City . . . to the palace."

"What?" Omer sputtered. "But we're standing at Mandela Palace. Why would the Squanki need a portal to take them from the palace to . . . the palace?"

Ryannon pointed at a page in the brown leather book in his hand. "It's right here," he answered. "Elahk A Ber Lor Mandela. The ator wrote it right here." Grayden and Omer looked at the words scribbled to the side of the line from the Advantiere. 'Elahk / Create –Ber /new - create a new.'

"Create a new Lor Mandela?" Grayden asked skeptically. "What are you suggesting?"

A sly smile spread across Ryannon's lips. "I am not suggesting anything, General. I have proof." He thrust his hand out toward the portal and explained. "Beyond this portal is another Lor Mandela . . . not a dead and decaying one like this," He sliced forcefully at a dried up shrub near his side. "It's a living, breathing, thriving, and restored Lor Mandela."

Grayden eyed Ryannon with a look full of doubt.

"So what do we do?" Omer asked.

"We do what my father failed to do," Ryannon instructed. "You two go through the portal and find me that girl! She's been hiding it from me, but I know the truth! She *is* the atoh. Her mother's companion servant gave that away when I put what she thought was an inhibitor on the atoc. She knew then that he was Jonathan, and responded exactly how I wanted her to!"

Grayden glanced at Omer as Ryannon continued. "Wait for me at this new Mandela Palace. Make sure that portal *stays open* and don't let anyone into that room! I'll bring the troops through in the morning, and we will take what should have been ours in the first place."

"But why do we need *that* palace?" Omer questioned. "We already have this one."

"Let me speak plainly," Ryannon sneered, "then maybe your infinitesimal mind will be able to understand.

"This world has been dying, slowly and surely, for almost six years. I can only assume that it won't stop. Do you know what happens to the inhabitants of a dead planet?" He smacked Omer in a demeaning fashion upside the head. "They die, you fool!"

He glared at Omer and then at Grayden. "Audril created a new Lor Mandela with that 'voodoo chant', General. The Borlocs tricked us . . . fooled us into believing that we'd won the battle, but in reality, they sentenced us to slow, desolate death! The atoh has powers . . . powers given to her by Lor Mandela itself . . . powers that I need! I want her brought to me alive!" He pointed authoritatively toward the portal once more. "Now get in there and find her! Our battalions will join you in the morning, and," he continued in an eerily calm voice, "if you happen to find the Squanki Tabbit . . . I would like her head for my wall!"

Grayden and Omer nodded in acknowledgement and then stepped into the portal and vanished.

Ryannon turned on his heels, strutted back across the courtyard and disappeared inside.

The portal shrunk back to a small glint of pale blue. Right next to it, a large shrub, tattered by Ryannon's recent assaults, shuddered in a faint breeze that wafted through the courtyard. The shrub began to ripple and sway as a figure gradually materialized from its shadows.

"Captoor de atoha, you tink? Fooleesh," Lortu breathed, "Zo den, de Vritessa Ooltara ees once again maye best offer."

CHAPTER XXXVIII
HOLDEN (OF THE TRYSTAS?)

"**D**oot deebee scloot bippa boo googly doot." Tabbit attempted to cheer herself up by singing a song as she slowly sauntered up to the doors at Mandela Palace. "Doot deebee scloot deedle dee foom." Unfortunately, the song wasn't helping much. She wished there was a way she could just snap her little brown fingers and make Atoc Jonathan appear before her. "Thens atoh girl bees happy again," she breathed as she sent a short blast of wind from her fingertips toward the doors. They crept open with a pathetic *creeeaaak*.

She sulked her way up the steps and was almost to the top, when she noticed a big, fat greelan bug slithering along a leaf on one of the plants that lined the stairs. She stopped for a moment, watching it crawl around and around.

With a gurgling growl, her bulgy, bubble-like tummy rumbled loudly. "Ohhh," she moaned, placing her tiny hand on her stomach.

The bug started to scoot down the leaf toward the stem, when Tabbit—realizing that if she didn't act now, the opportunity would be gone—dove head first into the bush and disappeared. She landed on the ground inside the plant, clutching the wiggly bug in one hand and smiling triumphantly. She jiggled her wrist up and down a few times, raised her hand above her head, and dropped the bug right into her open mouth. "Mmmmm!" she sighed, as she swallowed the plump insect whole.

". . . And where, exactly does he expect us to look?"

A man's angry voice suddenly interrupted Tabbit's squirmy afternoon snack.

"This is plain stupidity!"

Tabbit peered out through the leaves, trying to make out who was there.

"Whether you like it or not, Omer," another man responded, "Ryannon's in charge now. We do what he says, unless of course, you want to go back to Koria, which is exactly where he'll send you if you cross him."

Tabbit recognized the men as the Brashnellan generals who had tried to capture Maggie earlier. She shrunk back and almost completely disappeared into the shadows of the shrub that surrounded her. Her big, bulgy, now-green eyes blinked across a clump of leaves.

Omer stopped on the steps and glared at Grayden. "Fine," he sneered, "let's just go find his precious atoh for him! The sooner we get this nonsense out of the way, the sooner we can attack this place and get it over with!" He stormed down the remainder of the stairs, followed by a snickering Grayden.

"We can attack this place and get it over with," Tabbit echoed quietly, "Oooo! Its is the times. Its is the times now!" She slipped silently out of the bush and kept an eye on the two generals until they vanished around the end of the palace. "Its is the times," she repeated. "The times to bring master Glarons backs from the dead!"

She tiptoed down the steps and then darted in a zigzag across the field between the palace and town. She moved very quickly; the long grasses, combined with her demure stature, made her nearly undetectable. She reached Mandela City, weaved through the gardens surrounding the pearly houses and scampered up and down a few of the streets. In a relatively short amount of time she arrived at the edge of the Sybran Forest.

The stately trees at its edge swished gracefully back and forth in the soft breeze. Tabbit ducked under the undulating branches and slid into the dark forest.

As she scurried along, she made a bizarre clicking noise with her tongue—a noise designed to imitate the mating clicks of a rynolt, the only creature Shadow Dwellers went to great lengths to avoid. She didn't want to be seen by anyone, but especially not by the Shadow Dwellers.

She moved deep into the forest, and was almost to its center, when she stopped. Just off to her left was a small cave almost completely camouflaged by jagged rocks and the shadows of the forest. She backed cautiously toward it, surveying the area with diligence, and making very certain that she hadn't been seen. Once she was confident that she was alone, she took a deep breath, and bounded into the cave.

There, glowing towards the back of it, a thin shard of blue light sparkled in the darkness. Tabbit took another quick glance around, and then leapt into the light and disappeared into the portal.

A moment later she reappeared just outside of Pet Land in the Glenhill Galleria. Still standing there were the blonde field reporter and Brody—the freckle-faced Pet Land employee.

Upon seeing Tabbit come through the wall, Brody jumped behind the reporter and shrieked, "There it is! I told you! There it is!"

The reporter let out a shocked squeal as Tabbit jumped up onto her perfectly styled blonde head and started yelling in a shrill, squeaky voice, "Glarons! Master Glarons of the Trystas!"

She sprang off of the startled woman's head and sprinted down the mall. "Master Glarons! Master Glarons," she squealed as she darted from store to store, running in, yelling for Glaron, and then running back out again. Occasionally, she would jump onto the head of an unsuspecting shopper to improve her vantage point. Before long, four security guards and several curious bystanders, all with camera phones in hand, were chasing her throughout the mall.

Outside, Bridgette and Holden hid behind the news van, fervently thanking the tech for throwing the police off their trail. The technician was nodding and waving them off, urging them to get themselves out of there, when all of a sudden, he stopped short. One of the monitors inside the van, which up to this point had been dark, had unexpectedly come to life.

"Are we on?" The blonde reporter, whose normally perfect coif was, at the moment, somewhat disheveled, appeared on the screen. "Michael, I am reporting from the Glenhill Galleria where a strange little creature seems to be running amok. We have reason to believe that this unusual child . . . or animal . . . or whatever it is, is responsible for thwarting the attempted robbery at Pet Land earlier today."

Slowly, Bridgette and Holden slid around to the side of the van where they could see the monitor.

The reporter continued, "Mall security is in pursuit, and management is asking shoppers to leave the mall."

Just then, a wide-eyed, wild-haired Tabbit jumped out of nowhere, landing once again atop the reporter's head, and screamed psychotically into the camera, "Glarons of the Trystas! Glarons of the Trystas! Where is you?"

The reporter yelped and the camera man practically dropped the camera.

"What was that?" the tech gasped.

Bridgette stared at the small monitor, gaping.

"I think we'd better get back inside," Holden calmly stated.

Bridgette started to nod, but then realized that Holden was already dashing for the mall doors. "W . . . wait!" she yelled and took off after him. She caught up to him just before he ripped the mall doors open. "What's going on?" she panted.

"I dunno," he replied. "Tabbit'd never risk being seen unless there's an emergency!" He sprinted into the mall and ran over to the reporter, who was sitting on the ground hyperventilating. "It jumped on me . . . again . . . why . . . why? Why . . . why me?" she whimpered mournfully.

"She isn't dangerous," Holden scolded as he helped her to her feet. "Where'd she go?"

The burly camera man, who had been awkwardly trying to calm the reporter down, glared at Holden, and barked, "Beat it, punk! Who do you think you are?"

Bridgette ran up behind Holden and put her hand on his shoulder. He looked back at her, and then at the camera man, "Well," he answered hesitantly, "My name is Glaron."

Bridgette's mouth dropped open.

"Glaron of the Trystas."

CHAPTER XXXIX
MALL MADNESS

A drizzling rain had started to fall as Dallin and Maggie skirted the east shore of Mystad Lake on their way back from visiting Dr. Slade. The lake's slate blue water rippled and danced as the warm droplets plopped against it.

"We should hurry," Dallin urged, "These storms . . . they move in kinda quick sometimes."

Maggie nodded her head but in no way accelerated her pace.

Dallin didn't push the issue. He didn't feel much like running himself.

Within a few moments, the slow sprinkling drizzles gave way to a substantial downpour. Maggie stopped walking and just let the rain drive down on her. She felt numb. She didn't care about the rain; she didn't care about Lor Mandela; she didn't care about Dallin, or the lake, or Darian's death or Ryannon. She wanted the rain to rinse it all away—to wash things back to the way they were before—she and her dad, quietly and inconspicuously living in Glenhill, Iowa. She longed for her dull life—for the uneventful, blasé simplicity of being nothing more than an ordinary teenager from a small Midwest town.

A bright flash lit up the afternoon sky followed by the rolling boom of thunder. Dallin gently took her hand and insisted, "We need to get inside. You'll make yourself sick."

It didn't matter if she did get sick; she didn't care if she died. She stared blankly at Dallin as he guided her along toward Mandela Palace.

They were thoroughly soaked when they reached the stone steps.

"I wanna go home," Maggie sighed. "I just want to get out of here."

Dallin tried to comfort her, but knew that no words would help. He felt pretty miserable himself. "I'm sorry. I wish there was somethin' I could do," he tried. "Kahlie and your dad were my best friends. I . . . ." He stopped short, knowing that he had just said exactly the wrong thing. "I . . . uh, what I meant to . . . um," he back-pedaled, wishing he could somehow erase his words.

"WHAT IS WRONG WITH YOU PEOPLE?" Maggie exploded. "I am not your stupid atoh! Why don't any of you listen! I've had it with this! I've had it with Lor Mandela and I've had it with you!" She turned on her heels and raced back down the side of the lake, wanting nothing more than to get out of Dallin's sight. In the distance were some tall evergreen trees; without a backward glance, she took off in a full run towards them.

The rain poured down on her, stinging her face and arms and hands as she ran, but camouflaging the proliferation of tears spilling down her cheeks.

After a minute or two, she reached the trees and slowed down a bit. She checked behind her to see if Dallin had pursued, but to her relief, he hadn't.

She stomped angrily further into the trees. "Get me out of here," she yelled at the cloudy sky.

She clenched both fists and pounded them hard against the trunk of a nearby tree. The rough bark scraped her hands, but she didn't care. She hit it again...and again...and again—pummeling it with all of her strength—sobbing bitterly, until the pain in her hands was too much to bear. The sight of her red, bleeding hands did nothing but make her even angrier. She kicked at the unaffected tree trunk, and stormed off deeper into the forest.

She was just beginning to maneuver her way around a large pine, when there was a rapid rustling, and Omer suddenly sprang out from behind it.

She opened her mouth to scream, but he grabbed her and slapped his hand over her mouth so fast that she wasn't able to get a sound out. Just then, Grayden also appeared from behind the tree.

Maggie kicked and squirmed, trying to escape, but Omer was too strong to wrestle away from. She shook her head from side to side which gave her enough of a change in the position of Omer's hand that she was able to open her mouth and bite down—hard.

"Ghandentel!" Omer bellowed. He turned away from her, but then, with his entire body, swung back around and slapped Maggie forcefully across the face, knocking her to the ground.

Her cheek burned and throbbed as amazing pressure built up behind it. It felt like it was going to explode. She hardly had enough time to cry out before Omer yanked her up from the ground by the arm and pinned her against a nearby tree.

"Not a sound," he growled, "or you'll be sorry."

He ran the back of his hand down her throbbing cheek and looked at her like she was an alluring prize he'd just won.

"Mmmmm! Not bad," he oozed. "Maybe I should teach you some manners."

He pushed his weight against her and moved his mouth toward hers.

Maggie cringed and turned her head in disgust.

Grayden stood behind Omer and chuckled.

Omer grabbed her face and turned it back toward him. "Come on, love . . . why don't the three of us have some . . . ."

"Get away from her!" Suddenly, Dallin burst onto the grove. "Get your filthy hands . . . ." He rushed toward Omer, but all at once stopped and let out a painful gasp.

Omer smirked at Maggie. He knew exactly what had just happened. He grinned and stepped to one side to give her a better look.

There, on the ground a few yards away, Dallin had crumpled to his knees. His eyes were wide, and he was holding his side and panting heavily. Maggie couldn't see what had happened at first, but then Grayden—who'd been facing Dallin the entire time—turned around, revealing the small, silver tube he held in his hand.

"Nooooo," Maggie screamed lunging toward him.

Omer grabbed her around the waist as she swung her fists wildly. She leaned forward and made contact, clobbering Grayden squarely in the jaw, before leaning back and stomping down as hard as she could on Omer's foot. She twisted her upper body around and bashed him in the nose with the heel of her palm, forcing him to double over, and allowing her to get away.

She raced toward Dallin who was strangely silent, and dropped to the ground in front of him, grabbing both of his arms and looking him helplessly in the eyes.

He held her gaze for a moment, and seemed to be using every ounce of strength he had to keep from crying out in agony. "I . . . I'm . . . sorry," he gasped, "I'm so . . . ."

Just then, Grayden grabbed Maggie from behind and yanked her to her feet. Both he and Omer took hold of her—Grayden on one arm, and Omer on the other.

"Let go of me," she screamed. "Let go!"

She fought with all of her might to break free as she watched Dallin slump over onto the rain-drenched, leaf-covered ground.

All at once, everything slipped into slow motion as the all too familiar *whoosh...whoosh...whoosh* surged behind her and an invisible force jerked her midsection backwards.

Grayden and Omer, who were holding her arms, gazed around with puzzled looks on their faces.

In an instant, a bright flash of blue light, mingled with distant thunder filled the murky gray sky. As the whooshing amplified into a roar, the soaking wet, battered and beaten trio was instantly transported off of Lor Mandela.

Ding dong.

Maggie, Grayden and Omer appeared in the entrance of the Fashion Forever store in the Glenhill Galleria, setting off the store door bell alert.

In their confusion, Grayden and Omer let go of Maggie, who took advantage of the situation and bolted away from them as fast as her shaky legs would allow.

She ran frantically down the mall yelling, "Help! Help me," but no one seemed to be listening. In fact, there were very few shoppers in the mall, and those that were left all appeared to be hurrying towards the exits.

Maggie kept running, heading toward an exit herself, when two security guards came out of a shop just a few stores away.

"Help! Help!" Maggie screamed again.

The guards looked up at her and sped in her direction.

"What is it," one of them yelled.

Maggie didn't have a chance to answer. She felt something rush past her head, and watched as a small red disk hit the guard nearest her squarely in the chest. He dropped to the floor and started shrieking as green goo oozed down the front of his shirt.

In the blink of an eye, the other guard fell to the ground wailing miserably as well.

Maggie heard a woman scream, "He has a gun!"

The exodus from the mall that, up to this point had been fairly calm, erupted into chaos as the remaining shoppers stampeded for the doors. People shouted, "gun!" and "There's a shooter!" and "Out . . . out . . . get out!"

In the commotion, Maggie slipped into a crowd of people, hiding herself from Grayden and Omer. She was almost to the mall doors, when much to her surprise, she heard her name being called from somewhere behind her.

"Maggie! Maggie!" She spun around to see Bridgette rushing toward her, looking rather frantic. "Maggie! Wait!"

"Bridgette, no!"

Bridgette shouted and waved as she ran through the mall. "Smaggs, I need to tell you something! Wait!"

Maggie watched in horror as her best friend stopped right next to Grayden.

At this point, Omer spied Maggie and realized that Bridgette was trying to get her attention. "Grayden!" he yelled and pointed at Bridgette, "Grab her!"

Grayden immediately responded by snaring Bridgette's arm. He yanked her to him and in one fluid motion, slid a dagger-like object from a sheath at his side and put it to her throat.

"Stop!" Maggie cried. The only people still remaining in the mall at this point were Grayden, Omer, Bridgette and her. "Let her go!" she insisted.

Omer responded and rushed to where she stood. He took her forcibly by the arm and escorted her back to Grayden.

"I don't believe you are in a position to be calling the shots, Atoh," Grayden sneered.

Bridgette looked questioningly at Maggie.

"Let her go," Maggie repeated. "She has nothing to do with Lor Mandela. I'm the one Ryannon's after, not her."

Grayden chuckled. "True, but I have a feeling you would do just about anything to keep her alive." He pulled the dagger tighter against Bridgette's neck; she whimpered and gasped in pain, as the dagger's razor sharp edge sliced into her skin. A crimson stream of blood trickled down her neck.

"Stop it! Please!" Maggie begged.

"Why should I?" Grayden scoffed.

"Because . . ." Holden's voice responded as he suddenly appeared from out of nowhere, "the lady said please."

In an amazingly fluid motion, he lunged at Grayden, yanked his arm away from Bridgette's throat and twisted it up behind him. Grayden flipped through the air, dropping the dagger and sending it sliding across the floor.

Omer charged, but before he'd gotten too far, Holden charged back.

"Get her out of here," he yelled to Bridgette, pointing at Maggie.

Grayden jumped to his feet and moved to assist Omer. From his pants pocket he pulled out the vystoran sleeve.

"Holden! Look out!" Maggie shrieked as Grayden took aim.

Omer threw a punch toward Holden's head, but Holden grabbed his fist mid-punch and held it in the air. He looked over and, upon noticing the weapon in Grayden's hand, wrenched Omer's arm to the side—a move that positioned Omer squarely in front of him. With a click and a swoosh, the vystoran sped from the sleeve and raced toward them.

Omer's eyes widened as he tried to dodge the disc, but he wasn't fast enough. It smacked into his upper arm and exploded into a green, slimy glob.

Holden pushed him to the ground and sped toward Grayden, who was quickly attempting to reload the sleeve.

Omer yelped and screeched miserably as he twitched on the hard tile floor.

Grayden, who realized he was not going to be able to get the sleeve reloaded before Holden reached him, threw it and the vystorans to the ground and dove toward the dagger.

In a flash, Holden changed course and raced for the vystoran sleeve instead.

Grayden scooped up the dagger and turned to face Holden.

Just as Holden clicked a vystoran into the sleeve, Grayden stumbled toward him and swung his arm, slicing a long gash into one of Holden's thighs. Holden's leg went out from under him and he landed on the floor with a thud.

Bridgette screamed as she watched him fall.

Suddenly, he rolled to the side, and raised the vystoran sleeve toward Grayden.

Grayden dove out of the way just as the vystoran whizzed past him.

Holden quickly popped another vystoran into the sleeve, but by the time it clicked into place, Grayden was already sprinting away at top speed. He raced down the mall, and within a few seconds, disappeared around a corner.

Maggie and Bridgette sped to Holden's side. He was lying on the floor in a puddle of deep red.

Bridgette gasped and pulled off the shrug she was wearing. She quickly tied it around the wound in his leg, but before she was even able to secure it, more blood was beginning to soak through. "We need to get him to a hospital," she cried.

She and Maggie struggled to help him to his feet, but as they raised him up, he moaned and his eyes rolled back in his head.

"Hurry," Maggie instructed, "drop him onto my back!" She hunched over as Bridgette fought to lift his now limp body.

"This isn't working, Mag," Bridgette yelped. "He's losing too much blood!" She mustered all of her strength, jerked him up a little higher and dropped him over Maggie's back. He stayed on for a second, but then slumped to one side. Bridgette quickly spun around and leaned backwards against Maggie's side to keep him from sliding off.

"Okay," Maggie instructed, "head for the door over by Burger Deluxe . . . ready . . . go!" They had no sooner taken their first awkward step, when the very thing Maggie was hoping wouldn't happen, did. The whooshing started again.

"Bridgette, move!" she wailed.

"He'll fall off!" Bridgette cried back.

The whooshing grew louder.

"Bridge, you have to get off me!"

"Wait for *mees!*" A squeaky voice reverberated through the empty mall. "Laaaaaady, *Wait* . . . Mees can help!"

Maggie looked up and saw Tabbit frantically bouncing toward them. Another whoosh sounded, and Tabbit dove through the air, landing clumsily on Bridgette's left shoulder, knocking her off balance and further back into Maggie.

"Whew!" The panting little Squanki looked into Bridgette's horrified brown eyes, and breathed a heavy sigh of relief, as the air around them exploded into a brilliant flash of blue.

CHAPTER XL

SHE IS THE DOOR

"**B**ridgette, move over," Maggie insisted, hardly waiting for the blue light to fade. "And Tabbit, you said you could help . . . how?"

Being transported in this manner was no longer a concern to her. Where she was and what was going on was far more important than how she got there.

Bridgette, however, was in a state of shock, but obeyed Maggie and took a step to the side.

Maggie twisted around and lowered Holden to the ground. He looked pale. The leg of his denim shorts and Bridgette's shrug were both soaked and deep burgundy.

"Please, how can you help him?" Maggie tried again, looking to Tabbit who was caressing Holden's hair.

"How can you help him? Mees takes him to Salera. Salera's bestest." Without hesitation, she turned around and raised one of her little arms in the air. She rolled her hand into a fist, and then opened and closed it repeatedly. As she did, a small dot of glowing blue light appeared. It hovered in the air for a moment, but then stretched down creating the same type of thin portal that she had used to pull Maggie away from Ryannon and his thugs. "Mees takes him quickly!" Tabbit smiled. She reached down and slid her scrawny arms under Holden's shoulders.

"Uh, can I help you?" Maggie asked, confused as to how this tiny creature was going to lift Holden's dead weight.

"Uh . . . can I help you?" Tabbit repeated. "Nopes." She raised her foot off the ground, and thrust it backward into the slit of light. In an instant, the light expanded and with a faint "pop," Tabbit and Holden disappeared.

"Is this . . . real?" Bridgette's voice was weak and shaky. "I . . . I was trying to believe you. I . . . I had no idea."

Maggie put her hand on Bridgette's shoulder. "Yeah, I know, Bubbles. Weird, huh?" She took a glance around to see if the scene was familiar—and much to her dismay—it was.

They were standing at the edge of the forest—not the one with the big swaying trees, but the one where she'd been chased by a rynolt—the one where she'd seen Ryannon for the first time—and it was no less creepy in the daylight.

Dead, mangled tree trunks and angry, leafless shrubs twisted around each other. A sickly gray, murky haze hung low to the ground surrounding the base of the dead vegetation. The jagged edges of the fog looked just like gnarled, bony fingers that seemed to have choked the life out of everything they had touched. Beneath the gloom, long, angled rips in the soil zigzagged like a hostile maze across the forest floor; and a dark, sharp, crooked mountain served as the appropriate backdrop to the disquieting scene.

"What is this place?" Bridgette breathed quietly.

"I dunno," Maggie answered, "but I think we better get outta here. Come on, Bubbles." She took Bridgette's arm and pulled her toward the half-dead grassy field.

They walked in relative silence. Maggie didn't speak because she was trying to be strong—forcing herself to not think about or believe that her dad was gone.

Bridgette didn't speak because she was trying to come to terms with the fact that she was traipsing around some foreign planet.

Suddenly, the stillness of the field was interrupted by the startling cracking of branches in the forest behind them. Maggie stopped in her tracks. Her breath caught in her chest as thoughts of a giant, two-headed animal sneaking up behind them flashed through her mind. Surely, this time she wouldn't be as lucky as she'd been the last.

She turned slowly as another cracking noise echoed out of the fog. Something was moving; she could see shadows of something through the haze.

"Bridge, if that's what I think it is . . . ." She didn't have a chance to finish her sentence. The shapes of two human-like figures came running out of the muck toward them.

She and Bridgette both jumped.

"Wait!" She squinted and blinked and then her mouth dropped open. It couldn't be. "*Dad?*" she whispered.

The figures moved closer they came clearer into focus.

"DAD!" she shrieked and started running back across the field.

"Angel!" he yelled and ran toward her as well.

Kahlie was with him, and upon seeing Maggie, she started laughing and galloping across the field behind him.

Maggie and her dad reached each other and Maggie dove into his arms.

He hugged her, lifted her in the air and swung her around. "Where've ya been?" he chuckled as he returned her to the ground.

"Oh, ya know," she replied, grinning ear to ear and crying at the same time, "only everywhere!" She embraced him tightly and sobbed. "Ryannon . . . he . . . he said you were dead! He said . . . he said . . . ."

"Hey, it's okay," he soothed, "we probably would've been, but we," he glanced over at Kahlie, "we escaped."

Kahlie gently placed her hand on his arm. "And, we probably shouldn't be standing out here in the open," she advised.

"Oh, of course not," he agreed. "Come on girls. Let's get outta . . . huh?" he paused and grimaced, "Uh, hello Bridgette." Apparently, he'd just noticed she was there.

He looked at Maggie questioningly, who shrugged her shoulders and then wrapped her arm lovingly around his, and leaned her head onto his shoulder. Words could not begin to describe her current state of happiness.

"Excuse me," Kahlie started, "I hate to bear bad news, Atoc, but I don't quite know where we should go. Everything is different here."

Maggie's happiness was suddenly obliterated by the sound of one word—atoc. She looked from her dad to Kahlie, unable to fathom what had just happened.

"Dad! Why are you letting her call you that? Why don't you tell her who you are? Wh . . . why are you playing along with their little game?"

"Angel . . . ."

"No!" Maggie shouted. "NO! Come on! You can't believe this! How can you possibly be this gullible?"

Jonathan's expression became contemplative. He acted like he hadn't heard a word his daughter had screamed at him. "Her father the key and . . . and she is the door." he breathed.

"WHAT!" she shouted. "What have they done to you?!" She turned on her heels and stomped away.

"WAIT!" His voice boomed with such authority that she didn't dare take another step. Bridgette and Kahlie watched as he marched up behind her, put his hands on her shoulders and turned her to face him.

"Listen to me," he began forcefully. "You have to remember! Everything . . . everything depends on it."

Maggie had never heard her father talk this way before. She couldn't pinpoint it. His tone, his expression, and the confidence he exuded—something was very different.

He continued, a bit more gently, but still with unwavering conviction, "Audril," he looked deep into her eyes, "Angel . . . remember."

All at once the field around her disappeared, and she stood alone in a large ivory room with lace curtains fluttering in a cool breeze. To one side, a tall pearly dollhouse sat in the corner—four little dolls were lying inside on the floor. She walked over to it, and ran her hand along the top of the roof.

Slowly, Kahlie—or an image of Kahlie—materialized next to her.

"Are you all right?" Kahlie asked. Her voice sounded like it was miles away.

Maggie turned to face her. She didn't know whether it was really her or not, but somehow, it wasn't important.

"You were over there," Maggie answered in a daze, pointing towards a green chair across the room. "I was playing with my dolls."

Kahlie nodded, but did not speak.

"You called me Buzzy . . . Buzzy Bug."

Again, Kahlie nodded, and in an instant the images around her changed.

Now, she was outside, standing at the edge of a large sparkling lake. "Mystad," she breathed.

Next to her, the tiny image of Tabbit took shape. Tabbit spoke, but her voice was wise and serious—not the odd, squeaky little voice Maggie was used to.

"You are the Child of Balance, Atoh." She rolled up and down on her toes as she spoke, and didn't look directly at Maggie; her words seemed to be intended for someone who wasn't there. "You know what it means . . . the Advantiere. Tell the ator. Tell her, Atoh. You know what you must do."

A faint rumbling sounded from the hills in the distance.

Once again, her surroundings changed. She was running down a big hallway—running and scared.

"Get in there!" It was her dad's voice, but she couldn't see him.

Her feet tangled, and she stumbled and fell, landing in a room that looked like. . . "The kitchen," she whispered, "the battle!" She didn't have to see it to know what was going to happen next.

Suddenly, there was a war all around her. She scrambled backwards across the floor and watched as, one by one, Kahlie, her father, and her mother all appeared in the room.

"Kahlie, go now!"

She watched as her mother pushed Kahlie toward the closet and a horde of warriors dressed in black burst in through the back door. She watched as her mother's bright blue eyes began to glow brilliantly, sending three of the warriors screaming to the ground in agony. She saw another warrior drop to the ground—a knife sticking out of the back of his neck. She watched as Kahlie grabbed his sword and started taking down more of the black warriors.

A nauseating, sick feeling twisted through her core. She knew what the next image would be. She didn't want to watch it again—it had been horrifying enough the first time.

"No," she breathed, "please . . . *not Momma.*"

She turned around just as one of Darian's soldiers thrust his sword downward toward her mother. At that very instant, however, everyone in the room—including Gracielle—suddenly disappeared. Everyone that is, except for Maggie and the warrior who took her mother's life. His sword continued downward, just as though Gracielle was still there.

All at once, he stopped, looked directly at Maggie, and smiled. It was a smile she'd seen before—a smile that had made her go weak in the knees. She rose to her feet, and looked at his eyes. As expected—black with flecks of glistening red.

"Ryannon!" she sneered.

"Atoh Audril." He bowed, still smiling, and then disappeared.

Now, she found herself in the room with the big wall of windows where Ryannon had killed his own father. Only this time, there was a plain wooden door standing in the middle of it. There was no wall, no frame, just a door.

She started toward it, not of her own will, but as though a giant magnet was pulling her—drawing her to the door.

She involuntarily raised her hand and pointed her index finger at the door's base, and a small yellow spark popped out of thin air where she was pointing. She lifted her arm and the spark followed as she traced up one side, across the top, and down the other side. Once the spark had reached the bottom, the door slowly creaked open.

From where she was standing, it didn't appear that the door went anywhere, except to the other side of the room, but once she stepped through the room instantly changed.

Instead of just being a gloomy, cold, window-lined room, it became a gloomy, cold, *utterly destroyed,* window-lined room. It was as if a bomb had gone off. Huge chunks of concrete and rubble and glass littered the floor. The windows were almost all blown out, and off to one side, a giant, black crater gaped where stone gray tile should have been.

Slowly, as though she was in a dream, she walked to the big pit. As she gazed down into it, a soft lavender glow rose from its depths.

The light grew brighter and brighter as a faint whisper—labored and strained—lifted from its depths.

"Vrrritessssse, Vrrritessssse."

As the light intensified, it started to take shape, twisting and churning, before finally condensing into the form of a tall, beautiful woman enveloped in a halo of purple light.

"Hello, Atoh." She bowed reverently. "I am Lantalia, Vritesse of the Trystas, Daughter of Satia, and mother . . . of Gracielle."

"Oh . . . um . . . well, I am Maggie . . . from Iowa . . . daughter of Nathan?" she tried.

Lantalia just smiled. "Your memories do not deceive you, my dear granddaughter. Why should you question them?"

"Because they're not real! They can't be," she insisted.

Lantalia pointed toward the other side of the room. There, glowing in bright red was the Advantiere, as though it had just been written there. "Only the Child of Balance can understand its meaning."

Together they crossed the room to the glistening message.

"What do you see?" Lantalia asked.

Maggie eyed Lantalia like she was crazy, but then reluctantly turned her attention to the glowing Advantiere.

Almost instantly, the bright red letters vanished and a face appeared on the wall.

"Darian," she whispered. "I see Darian!"

"And now?" Lantalia asked.

Almost as suddenly as the image of Darian had shown on the wall, another face emerged, one that was quite unexpected.

"Doctor Brockman? What could he possibly have to do with all of this?"

"Go on," Lantalia urged.

The next face to appear was Gracielle's, followed by a young girl's. Maggie vaguely remembered playing with this girl as a child.

"Nenia, right? She's Ultara's daughter." Lantalia smiled knowingly.

Ultara's face was next, followed by her dad's, and then Ryannon's, and then Kahlie's, and finally, her own face appeared on the wall—her reflection—like she was looking at herself in a mirror.

"You've seen it with your own eyes, daughter," Lantalia began. "Now do as your father commanded you . . . and remember!"

With that, images of Lantalia's eyes replaced Maggie's reflection on the wall. In each of them a glowing likeness of Lor Mandela materialized. The images were peaceful, active and alive. There were people, and animals, and plants and trees, all living and existing peacefully together.

Suddenly, tears welled in the corners of the eyes, and began dripping in rapid crimson streams down the wall like tears of blood. They flowed downward, almost reaching the floor, but then, all at once, reversed their course and crashed back into the images of Lor Mandela, drowning everything in their path in a sea of red. The flood was swift and terrible—nothing stood a chance. Finally, at last, the waves receded, and the images were peaceful once again.

But just when it appeared that the worst was over, a distant rumbling started to build. As the sound grew, the entire room began to tremble and roll. The noise grew louder and louder, sending chunks of plaster tumbling to the ground from the already unsound walls. Dust rose up from the floor, making the air thick and choking. The images of Lor Mandela shuddered violently as the rumble became a roar, which climaxed in a deafening explosion as both images of Lor Mandela disintegrated into a magenta dust. The force of the explosion lifted the entire room into the air and dropped it, knocking Maggie to the ground.

In an instant, the Advantiere reappeared on the wall, and Lantalia was gone.

Maggie looked toward the pit which, instead of glowing lavender, was now emanating a soft white light.

Again, a weak voice sounded from inside it and lulled Maggie slipped into a deep sleep.

"Find the twinssss. Find the twinsssss. Destruction from twins, and so it must end. Find the twinsssssss."

Maggie awoke to find herself lying in the half-dead field again, with Bridgette, Kahlie and her dad all huddled over her.

"Are you all right?" Kahlie asked—just as she'd done moments ago in her first vision.

"Maggie, can you hear me?" Bridgette asked.

She bolted upright and looked around at the three of them. "We've got to get out of here, *now!*"

She jumped to her feet and pulled Bridgette up from the ground. "Come on!" She commanded, and took off in a run across the field.

Jonathan, Kahlie and Bridgette followed.

"What is it?" Jonathan tried, "What's going on?"

"We need to find Tabbit . . . or another Squanki! We need portals! Lots of Portals!"

"What? Why?" he questioned.

She stopped running and turned back to face the three confused people following her. "Kahlie," she began urgently, "at the battle, you said something, remember?"

Kahlie just stared at her.

"I was saying the words, but they were coming from you?"

Kahlie gasped.

"Whaaaat," her dad breathed in surprise.

She continued, ignoring him and directing her attention to Kahlie. "We . . . you and I together . . . we created a clone of Lor Mandela."

"A clone?" Kahlie asked.

"Anika divided the soul of our world. The only way we could save it was to create another Lor Mandela so both parts of the soul could continue to exist, separate from each other."

"There are two?" Jonathan quizzed. "Of course! That makes sense! No wonder nothing here seems right!"

"Hold on a minute," Bridgette exclaimed; she had heard enough. This whole experience had just gone from unbelievable to impossible. "Maggie! What are you talking about? You're my best friend! I've known you since we were five! How can you be from this . . . this weird place, if you've been on Earth with me?"

"Bridgey," she began, "I know this seems crazy. *Believe me*, I know. But,

I'm not Maggie. I really am Audril Borloc. You've just got to trust me! I'll explain it all later. Right now, there's just not time."

She turned her attention from Bridgette to her dad. "This is the appointed time! Right now! We have to hurry, dad! We have to get everyone out of here and on to the *other* Lor Mandela."

"Um, even him?" Bridgette's eyes grew wide as she caught sight of someone moving near the forest.

There, hunched over, pacing side to side to side, and staring at them from across the field, was Lortu.

"What does he want now?" Kahlie asked. "Maybe he has more information about Ryannon."

"More information?" Audril questioned, "What do you mean?"

Jonathan was the one to answer. "He and his people rescued us from Ryannon. Lortu's the reason we're still alive."

"Hey," Bridgette exclaimed—shock evident in her tone, "where'd he go?" They all glanced toward the forest. Lortu was nowhere to be seen.

As they all glanced around, a dark form moved with great speed across the meadow. Bridgette jumped and let out a startled scream as Lortu again appeared, this time standing just a few feet in front of them. He began pacing again, and seemed to be contemplating what he should do next. He continued for a second or two, but then shook his head, looked at Jonathan and said, "Maye apologees, Atoc."

With lightning speed, he grabbed Audril, threw her over his shoulder and sped back across the field.

"No!" Jonathan, Kahlie and Bridgette all yelled in unison. They chased after them, but there was little point. Within seconds, the blur of Lortu and Audril disappeared into the dreary forest.

CHAPTER XLI
A PLEA FOR THE TRYSTAS

"**W**hy, thank you, Lortu. You may go. Your debt is paid."

Ultara's silky voice was the first thing Audril heard once she regained consciousness. She hadn't passed out from fear this time, but rather from her inability to get a full breath while being spirited through the Bogs by Lortu.

Audril felt him lower her to the ground as he whispered, "Zorry, Atoha."

When she looked up, she realized she was back in Ultara's throne room with Ultara sitting casually on the edge of the platform in front of her.

Behind her, she heard some commotion and glanced over her shoulder to see Tabbit attempting to grab Lortu by the hair. The little Squanki appeared very agitated as she kicked and swung her tiny fists at him. He, of course, didn't even flinch. He pushed her away, then leaned over and whispered something in her ear causing her to snarl and swing at him one more time before he faded away into the shadows.

As the last traces of Lortu vanishes, a Trysta guard came from behind the rock wall and took Tabbit by the hand. The strange Trysta stopped in his tracks when he saw Audril, and stared at her like he'd just seen a ghost.

"Lortu tells me that Darian is dead." It seemed an odd way for Ultara to start the conversation.

"Yes," Audril breathed, still trying to get her bearings straight. "Ry . . . Ryannon killed him."

"Ahhh, and now he is after you and your father? Seems to me that he has his priorities straight."

"What," Audril blurted, "his priorities straight? He's nothing but a devious, self-absorbed, murdering monster!"

Ultara didn't appear fazed. "Are you aware that he is going to be attacking Mandela City in the morning?"

"Yes, I am," she answered. She didn't know how, but at some point while watching the destruction of both Lor Mandelas in Lantalia's eyes, she'd realized that an attack was imminent. "I'm not sure how I am supposed to prepare for an attack, though, when you're holding me prisoner here," she snipped.

Ultara lowered herself down from the platform and walked over to where she stood. "Aren't you afraid of me, Atoh?" she asked, studying Audril's face.

"Should I be? I assume you're on my side. After all, you just tried to warn me that Mandela City is going to be attacked."

"I am on *my* side!" Ultara roared. Her reply was abrupt and charged with anger. "Your side wants me dead!"

She turned and glided back onto the platform and dropped into her tree throne." Give me one good reason why I shouldn't turn you over to Ryannon right now!"

Audril's confidence, which should've been deteriorating by the second, was doing exactly the opposite. She stared up at Ultara and calmly answered, "The Advantiere."

Ultara's interest was piqued. "The Advantiere? You've solved it?" She waved her hand dismissively in the air. "Impossible! You've only been here a short time."

Audril walked near to where Ultara sat and replied, "True, but I've been here long enough to know that the appointed time is upon us; I've been here long enough to know that there are two Lor Mandelas; I've also been here long enough to know that this one, and everyone on it, is on the verge of destruction." She paused and then added, "If you join us . . . ."

"Never!" Ultara snarled. "I will never fight alongside Atoc Jonathan!"

"What? Why?"

"He conspired with Darian to have me executed! He falsely accused me of a terrible crime, and his stubbornness is the reason your people were attacked in the first place!"

"What? What are you talking about? That's crazy!"

Ultara's expression turned to one of disgust. "Get her out of here," she commanded, motioning to the guard who had been standing quietly at the back of the room. He rushed across the bridge and grabbed Audril by the arm.

"Wait," she shrieked as she was being escorted somewhat forcefully out of the room. "Ultara! You have to get your people off this world! We need the Squanki to open portals! This Lor Mandela is going to be *destroyed*!"

Ultara turned away, ignoring Audril's plea.

Audril shifted her attention to the man who was pulling her along by the arm. "Please," she begged, "talk to her! You're all going to die unless . . . ."

"Shhhh! Not here," he insisted. He led her down a hall and into a small room at the end of one of the tree-lined corridors. He quickly checked over his shoulder to make sure they hadn't been followed, and then closed the door. "Don't worry," he started, "we'll get this figured out."

Audril eyed the oddly amenable guard and asked, "Why are you helping me? You're a Trysta, aren't you?"

The man signaled for her to take a seat on a small bench against a vine covered wall and explained, "Your mother was a dear friend of mine."

A knowing smile played across Audril's face, as she recalled a time when she'd heard her mother telling Kahlie about her Trysta friend who was helping her solve the Advantiere. "Glaron?" she guessed.

Glaron rushed over hugged her tightly—a move that was most unexpected. "Wow! I . . . I guess I was right?" she stammered.

"Only partially," he grinned, as he dropped down onto another bench on the opposite wall, cupped his hands behind his head and leaned casually back. "Dude! You're like gonna totally blow a fuse here, aren't ya Blue?"

"Holden?" She jumped to her feet in surprise. "You're Holden?"

He grinned ear to ear and stood back up; suddenly his expression became more serious. "So, what is all this talk about two Lor Mandelas, and this one being destroyed? And for Heaven's sake, Boo, have you finally figured out that sometimes boring is good?"

"Doc!" she squealed, "Oh good grief!" This time it was Audril doing the hugging. "That explains it! That's why I saw you in the Advantiere room! Of course . . . of course! One unknowing moves in haste. That was you! You sent us to Earth!"

"What?" he gasped. "Me? I just sent you there to keep you from getting killed. I . . . I was just trying to help." He couldn't comprehend that he, himself, had played a part in the Advantiere

"But by doing it, you fulfilled the second line of the Advantiere," she exclaimed, giving him another quick hug.

"Oh my gosh! All this time, you were Doc! Doc and then Holden?" she chuckled and added, "And you said you'd never keep secrets from me!"

Glaron smiled and nodded sheepishly. "Well it wasn't part of my original plan, but when I wound up on Earth with you and your dad, I had to figure out some way to keep you safe. The only thing I could come up with was blocking your memories and altering all three of us. I thought it would be best while I was figuring out how to get us back."

"Whoa, altering?" she gasped feeling all over her face. "So . . . so then I don't really look like this?"

Glaron smiled and tousled her curls, "I didn't change you that much, Boo. I couldn't bear to! You were so adorable! I just made you look a little older, that's all. In retrospect, that probably wasn't the best idea, since now you've aged like twelve years. I can change you back if you want, but trust me; you don't want to alter here! It's a lot easier to go through an altering on Earth." He rubbed his left arm like it was very sore and added, "Altering on Lor Mandela is an adventure!"

Audril smiled, but then suddenly remembered that there were more urgent matters at hand. "Listen, Glaron, we'll have to talk about this later. Right now we're running out of time. Do you know where Tabbit went?"

"Yeah," he replied, "Lortu told her to get all of the Squanki together and go find your dad."

"Lortu? Really," she gasped. The mysterious Shadow Dweller was becoming more of a contradiction to her by the minute. "Whose side is he on, anyway?"

Glaron's reply was all too familiar. "The one with the best offer," he answered.

Audril smiled and shook her head. "Well, then I guess all we need to do is find Tabbit and my dad. C'mon, let's go."

Glaron's eyes saddened. "I can't," he began. "I can't leave Ultara. She needs my help."

"What? I need your help!" Audril gasped.

"Listen," he explained, "Just transport to Mandela Palace. I'll stay here and convince Ultara that you're right, and then come and join you."

"But what if you can't?" she pleaded.

"I don't have a choice, Boo," he argued. "It's my duty. Now, get going! I'll catch up to you in a while. You should be able to transport once you clear the trees out back.

She grimaced and shrugged. "Transport?"

"Audril," he began, "Wow! That was weird to say. You're a Trysta heiress. All you have to do once you're outside get a good run going and shout out where you want to go. You'll be transported there instantly." He grinned and added, "And you thought you were the Mistress of Mediocre."

"But," She looked into the sparkling emerald green eyes of the person who'd protected her practically all of her life. "I don't want to leave you here!"

"You have to, Boodle. Don't worry; I'll take care of the Trystas. You just worry about everyone else." He walked to the back of the room and pushed against what seemed to be a tree trunk. It swung to the side, revealing that it was, in fact, a door to the outside.

Reluctantly, Audril dragged herself to the door and gazed pleadingly at him.

Once more, he wrapped his arms around her shoulders and held her tightly. "Here." He handed her a tiny black box. "If you want to stay, there are three of my receptors in there."

She opened the box and looked down at the three minute orange discs. "What reason do I have to go back?" she asked dropping the receptors into the palm of her hand. "I'm home. This is where I belong, Doc." She held her hand and showed Glaron as the tiny discs absorbed into her skin. "I guess I'm stuck here now."

"Be careful," he grinned, "I care about you guys! I just want you to be happy."

As he said the words, she mouthed them along with him." I will," she assured. "See you in Mandela City."

"You bet, Boo!" he smiled.

Audril turned from him and took off in a sprint. She headed toward a large iron gate that stood at the end of a massive lawn. It gave her some relief to see dozens of thin lines of blue hanging in the air in the far off distance. When she was a few yards away from the gate, she looked skyward and shouted, "New Mandela Palace!"

CHAPTER XLII
BRASHNELL ATTACKS

Audril reappeared outside of Mandela Palace on new Lor Mandela. She ran down the path that meandered from the front steps to the northern bank of Mystad Lake.

It was staggering how different these two clone worlds had become. Since she and Kahlie had created it, this world had revived, thrived and flourished, while it was clear that the old Lor Mandela had been—and continued to be—in a state of perpetual deterioration.

Lining the meadows around the lake, hundreds of people had assembled. Atoc Jonathan stood on a large rock outcropping addressing the congregation. "The Squanki have opened portal fields on the East side of Mystad, north of Koria, and in Westrim. Our generals have been assigned areas to evacuate. I assure you that they are thoroughly sweeping all of the populated areas remaining on the other world. We are expecting full evacuation no later than sundown. I ask that you all remain patient. You will be reunited with your families shortly!"

"Mag . . . uh, I mean, Audril!" Bridgette shouted from the meadow closest to where she stood.

Immediately, all eyes shifted from the atoc and locked onto her. There was a stunned hush throughout the crowd, but then the area exploded into cheers and applause.

Jonathan leapt down from the rock and ran around the side of the lake toward her. He rushed up and threw his arms around her. "I guess I can call off the hunting dogs!" he chuckled. "I don't know how you got back here, but I'm so glad you did!" He hugged her again, and kissed her on the top of her head.

After the accolades died down, Audril grabbed Jonathan by the arm, and pulled him back toward the palace. She wanted to make sure they were out of earshot of any of the Mandelans.

"Dad," she began, "we've got a major problem. How many soldiers do we still have?"

"Soldiers?"

She glanced over as a beaming Kahlie came running towards them. "How did you get away? We've been so worried about you," she shouted as she approached. It didn't take long for Kahlie to notice the concern on both of their faces. "What is it?"

"Ryannon . . . He's bringing his troops to attack in the morning," Audril answered.

"Impossible!" Jonathan replied. "How will he get here? All of the portals will be closed long before morning. He would need a couple hundred portals at least to get all of his troops through in any sort of time-effective manner."

"How many portals have the Squanki created?" Audril asked weakly.

Jonathan looked to Kahlie for the answer.

"Just under a thousand," she reported.

Audril sighed heavily. "Tell the Squanki to leave them open. This battle has to happen."

"What? Explain." Jonathan commanded.

"It's part of the Advantiere, Dad. If this battle doesn't take place, the Advantiere won't be fulfilled, and by this time tomorrow, *neither* of the Lor Mandelas will still exist."

"Wait . . . are you telling me that I have less than twelve hours to assemble hundreds of thousands of soldiers who have not been trained in over a year?" Jonathan was clearly troubled by the news.

"We need General Statlen," Kahlie interjected. "He's been working with the troops in your absence, sir."

Jonathan looked at her like she was the most wonderful person in the world. "M'lady, I could kiss you!" Both Kahlie and Audril blushed. "Find him right away!"

Kahlie cleared her throat nervously, and then turned and took off running.

Jonathan placed his hand on Audril's shoulder. "Don't worry. It'll be okay, Angel."

"But, Dad. There's something else."

"What?" he asked.

"The Trystas are all on the old Lor Mandela. Ultara wouldn't believe me when I tried to tell her that the world was coming to an end."

"You spoke to Ultara? Lortu took you to Ultara?" he fumed.

She waved him off, and explained what had happened and how Ultara refused to fight alongside him—and also about Glaron.

"He altered? But he's male? I've never heard of a Trysta male having altering abilities," Jonathan mumbled as he contemplated the things he'd been told.

Suddenly, General Statlen came running towards them, followed by Kahlie. "Atoc, we've got company! Your permission to mobilize the troops, sir? *Now!*"

Jonathan trusted Statlen implicitly. If he was asking to move the troops, there was reason for it. "Granted! Meet me at the palace in five minutes!" he yelled back. "Kahlie, what's going on?"

She took a deep breath and explained. "Ryannon . . . he found the portal field in Westrim. His armies are moving through right now!"

Jonathan sprinted back to the rock platform. "Mandelans," he boomed over the crowd. "The Brashnellan army is coming through the portals in Westrim. They're coming to attack! Any able-bodied of you are needed to *protect our home!* Those unable to fight are to get to safety immediately! Soldiers, report to the palace!"

Immediately, the assembled throng started to scurry.

Jonathan jumped from the rock and walked briskly back to Kahlie and Audril. He noticed Bridgette, hurrying a little boy along toward town and turned toward an elderly man who was shuffling quickly past him. "You there," he barked.

The man froze in place. "Yes, Atoc?"

"Go to that young lady over there," he commanded, pointing to Bridgette. "Tell her I need her at the palace and see that the child with her gets safely home."

"Yes, sir! Right away, Atoc!" The old man shuffled off to do as he was told.

"Dad, Bridgette!" Audril yelled as he approached.

"Don't worry, Angel. I've taken care of it. She'll be joining us shortly." He didn't break stride as he moved past her and Kahlie. They quickly followed behind him toward the palace.

"Dad, what about the Trystas?" Audril ran up alongside him and grabbed his arm. "What about Glaron?" she pleaded.

He stopped and turned to face her. "Listen, Sweetie, the Trystas are very clever, and Ultara is a survivor. They'll be fine. She'll work it out somehow. I know it." His eyes were not at all convincing. He was concerned, and it showed. He took a deep breath, gently lifted her hand off of his arm, and then marched off again.

General Statlen and three other officers—all in full battle armor—greeted them as they reached the stairs at the palace entrance.

"Report," Jonathan commanded as he continued up the stairs past the general.

"Units one through seven have secured a perimeter around the palace. Eight through twenty are awaiting orders, sire. Approximately sixty percent of troops have reported and messengers have been dispatched to notify the remaining forty."

"Impressive, general! Thank you."

Jonathan stopped at the top of the stairs and waited as two of the other officers raced to open the door. "Move eight through twenty to the portal field at the east side of the lake and tell three through seven to join them there." He looked toward one of the officers who had opened the door—a tall, rugged, battle-scarred, middle-aged man. "Commander, go to the portals. I need the Squanki, Tabbit. I believe she's still down there. Bring her back to the palace. If you can't find her, just bring another Squanki . . . go!"

The commander bowed and sped away.

General Statlen remained, staring at Jonathan in disbelief.

"Yes, General? You have something to say?" Jonathan pressed.

Audril couldn't help but marvel at how quickly he had resumed his role as ruler.

"With due respect, Atoc," the general began, "shouldn't we be moving toward Westrim . . . to stop them? The last time we were attacked here it was a blood bath."

"General, there are roughly fifteen million people on Old Lor Mandela who haven't come through those portals yet." Jonathan hesitated and put his arm around Audril. "The atoh—who as you know is referred to in the Advantiere as the Child of Balance—has seen in a vision that the destruction of Old Lor Mandela is imminent. If my daughter had the power at the last battle to actually create a planet, I am not going to question her, and neither should you. When Tabbit arrives, I am going to instruct her to destroy the portals near Koria. You will send units one and two to Old Lor Mandela to complete the evacuation. Tell them it doesn't have to be neat, just fast! All other units will join us at the portal field."

"We're going to bring millions of people in through one portal field?" This time it was Kahlie who was questioning his plan.

"If we keep the Koria portals open, at least half of our units would have to be sent there to protect the people coming through. Ryannon's army is bigger than ours, I'm sure of it."

He looked to General Statlen, who nodded in agreement.

"If we divide, we won't survive." He paused as if planning his next words carefully.

"Statlen, we have to stand strong as a people, we'll need *anyone* who can to fight. Send those who are unable back to town and equip the rest with weapons. Keep your troops on the south end of the lake, between Westrim and the east fields. Our priority is to guard those portals and get our people through safely!"

Just then, Bridgette burst into the room. "They're coming," she blurted. "We can see them on the hills!"

"General! *Go!*" Jonathan commanded.

Bridgette huffed and panted. "There . . . there's so many of them," she sputtered.

"Follow me, girls," Jonathan instructed, leading them out of the foyer and to a room that was full of weapons and armor in all shapes and sizes.

Bridgette and Kahlie each were given a sleek, dark charcoal grey suit that looked like smooth stone, but weighed next to nothing.

Bridgette picked up a weapon that resembled a bow and arrow. "I did take first in archery at Camp Hideaway," she smiled.

Kahlie, of course, reached for a sword.

"Audril, here." Jonathan handed his daughter a suit similar to the others, but with some very distinct differences. A bright silver, ornate metal work scrolled intricately around the neckline, forming a plate of hard steel that wrapped around the mid-section; the sleeves extended into mesh gloves at the end. In the center of the abdominal shield, was an etching—a picture of a beautiful, glorious angel. "This was your mother's," he sighed, "it will protect you."

Audril took the suit and climbed into it. She grabbed a sword and looked to Jonathan who had just clicked the last buckle into place on his armor.

"Get to the portals," he ordered, hugging her tightly. "Bring our people home safely, Atoh."

Audril smiled, but worry was present in her eyes.

Jonathan turned his attention to Kahlie. "Don't let anything happen to her, Kahlie," he pleaded. Kahlie gasped as he spoke the exact words that Gracielle had just before the last battle. "Don't worry. I . . . I won't," she stammered.

Without another word, Jonathan grabbed her by the arms, pulled her to him, and kissed her squarely on the lips. "Don't let anything happen to you, either," he grinned, as he ran the back of his gloved hand gently down her cheek.

Bridgette giggled, and Audril smiled.

"Now, go on girls!" He took a deep breath, and then added, "I'll join you after I speak to Tabbit."

CHAPTER XLIII
THE BATTLE OF LOR MANDELA

The fighting was already in full swing when Jonathan appeared at the northeast side of Mystad Lake. With him was a full contingent of soldiers. The Mandelan Army had lined up a barricade at the west end of the lake, but the Brashnellans were slowly breaking through.

Audril, Kahlie and Bridgette were hurriedly pulling people through the portals. Those who were willing and able to fight were sent immediately to the Fifth Unit to receive armor and weapons. Those who weren't able were quickly escorted out of the meadows and back to Mandela City.

Audril had just looked up and realized Jonathan was approaching, when suddenly, all hell broke loose. The Brashnellan Army made an aggressive push forward, broke through the line, and burst out onto the field. Ryannon's soldiers, as though trained to do it, immediately headed for anyone who wasn't armed. Every Mandelan who had weapons was forced to come to the aid of those who couldn't defend themselves. Audril, Bridgette and Kahlie rushed to the other side of the field, leaving the people at the portals to come through into the chaos of a full-fledged war.

Adding to the tumult, the people coming through the portals began screaming and yelling. Those who had already come through the portals were frantically reaching back, yanking others from the old world as fast as they could.

"What is it?" Bridgette shouted. "What's going on?"

"I'll find out!" Audril responded, as she stabbed a Black Warrior. She pushed him to the ground and sped across the field.

Jonathan and his soldiers reached the portals just a moment before she did. "It's flooding!" he yelled. "They say there's a huge wave!"

At that moment, she realized that the vision she'd been shown by Lantalia wasn't symbolic or a warning. It was an actual, literal fate. The water was streaming into Old Lor Mandela and it was minutes away from *real* destruction. "Dad," she shrieked, "we have to get them through!"

As the battle raged on behind them the Brashnellans began to cheer and point at the sky. There, about twenty feet in the air, perched on the massive pewter back of Syltar, was Ryannon. He flew overhead, raining vystorans down on the Mandelans below. They dropped to the ground in droves writhing in agony before dying.

"Stop him!" Jonathan yelled toward his troops. "Take him down!"

The words had no sooner left his lips than an arrow swooshed through the sky and pierced into Syltar's side. Jonathan glanced toward the direction from which the arrow had come, and saw Bridgette holding her bow up high. She quickly reloaded, and launched another arrow, this time narrowly missing Ryannon's head.

"Ugh," she sighed and stomped her foot, "how'd I miss that?"

Syltar shrieked out in pain and squirmed and twitched. The giant creature's cloak-like black wings slashed through the air as it twisted suddenly to the side with such force that Ryannon slid off and fell hard to the ground. Syltar plummeted to the ground landing in a loud thud just a few feet away from Ryannon.

This would have been the opportune moment for the Mandelan soldiers to capture Ryannon, had something completely unexpected not happened. The very second his body hit the ground there was a brilliant blast of light, and Old Lor Mandela flashed into view—suddenly visible—floating alongside East Mystad Field, right where the portals had been. It was as though the hundreds of small portals suddenly combined into one enormous planet-sized portal—one that didn't expand or collapse, but stayed constant and wide open. Hundreds of thousands of shocked people stood at the edge of Old Lor Mandela staring at the near mirror-image that had appeared before them. Hundreds of thousands of shocked people stood on the battlefield of New Lor Mandela staring back.

Audril looked toward the distant hills and mountains of Old Lor Mandela. There, swelling behind them was a colossal, thundering wave.

"*Run!*" A general aiding in the evacuation on Old Lor Mandela bellowed with all his might.

Everyone on the old planet broke into a full run, barreling through to New Lor Mandela in an attempt to flee the giant wave that was now cascading over the hilltops, and crashing into the valley below.

Several people fell and were trampled by the stampeding mob. Others were washed away as the relentless wave swept over them. The flood waters rushed across the fields and lake on Old Lor Mandela, colliding with a bang into an invisible barrier that now seemed to be separating the two worlds.

The distraction had given Ryannon the time he needed to recover from his fall. He rose to his feet, and in an unnaturally amplified voice, roared, "KILLLLL THEMMMMM!"

The Black Warriors descended on the unarmed Mandelans like wolves, obeying Ryannon's command and killing whoever they could. Men, women, children, crippled and elderly; it didn't seem to matter to the ruthless Brashnellan Army.

Panic consumed Audril as she watched the horrible scene unfolding on the battlefield, combined with the mountain of water pounding the invisible wall, washing away the hundreds of people who had not been fortunate enough to have made it through.

Just as panic threatened to render her immobile, someone ran behind her, bumping her on the shoulder as they went by.

"Look out, Blue!"

She spun around to see Glaron engaged in a duel with a Brashnellan soldier.

"Where'd you come from?" she shouted as she moved toward another Black Warrior. "Where are the Trystas?"

Glaron spun around and thrust his sword backwards. It plunged directly into its intended target's chest. "I don't know! But don't worry, they'll be all right! They can breathe under water for a while."

He spun to the side to face another attacker and added, "Ultara found out I let you go! I'm in serious . . . *Whoa . . . dude!*"

A Brashnellan jumped out in front of him with a vystoran sleeve. He dropped to the ground and rolled out of the way, just as the Sleeve discharged. The vystoran splattered against the back of the warrior Audril had been fighting, and he collapsed in a shrieking heap.

Glaron wasted no time in dropping both the Warrior he'd been fighting, and the one who had shot the vystoran.

"Glaron! You don't understand," Audril shrieked. "It's about to blow!"

"What? What do you mean?" They were only a few feet apart, but had to yell loudly to be heard over the din.

"Old Lor Mandela!" Audril pointed toward the old planet which was now engulfed in water; a giant liquid wall stretched from the ground to the sky. The invisible barrier, which had been keeping the huge wave from dropping down on top of them, now seemed to be deteriorating, as streams of water began to trickle through the weak spots. The impending annihilation via tidal wave seemed to be having little or no effect on the Brashnellan Army, however. They fought like machines seemingly spurred on by the gloominess of the situation.

Audril glanced over her shoulder to where she'd left Kahlie and Bridgette. They were both battling ferociously—as was her dad. As she watched them, she, herself, was met by an attacker. She fought him off with relative ease and then, seeing that her dad was dueling two Brashnellans at once, took off across the field to help him.

Suddenly, the roar of the water dropped in volume almost down to nothing. Audril stopped running and looked nervously toward Old Lor Mandela. The wall of water was shrinking. The flood was starting to recede!

As the massive wave retreated she noticed that—miraculously—there were still hundreds of people standing where it had just been. They banged and kicked against the barrier, which was all it took. Within just a few seconds, the weakened barrier completely gave way and the frightened crowd moved in a collective run toward New Lor Mandela.

A low rumble sounded in the distance.

"Get off! NOW!" Audril shrieked and bolted toward them. "MOVE! MOVE! GET OUT OF THERE! HURRY!"

Glaron ran up behind her and caught her by the shoulders. "Boo, what's going on?" he bellowed. "What's that noise?"

The rumbling amplified.

Audril struggled loose from him and took off running again. "We've got to get them out of there! It's gonna blow! THE PLANET'S GOING TO EXPLODE!"

"WHAT?" Glaron gasped. "NO! THE TRYSTAS!" He broke into a frantic run, speeding right past her.

"GLARON! NO! GET BACK HERE!"

The rumbling grew louder and louder and was now shaking the ground like a powerful earthquake. The battle had virtually stopped, as no one could move from the careening spots on which they stood.

The group of soaked Mandelans had made it through, but several of them were now just inches inside and unable to go any further. Glaron fought to get past them but was held back by the swaying planet and the mob of people.

The rumbling became a growl; the growl became a roar; the roar escalated to a ghastly shriek; and then suddenly, in a cloud of choking magenta dust, there was a massive catastrophic explosion.

Glaron dropped to his knees. "NOOOOOO!" His anguished cry was the last thing Audril heard before a forceful shock wave ripped through the field and sent everyone flying.

Audril barely noticed she'd been thrown. The moment she was able to move again, she pulled herself back to her feet.

"Ahhgghh!" she cried, as a jolt of pain surged through her right leg. It buckled at the knee, and she almost lost her balance and fell over again. She tried to survey the damage, but the air was still clouded with thick dust. What she could see were the dark forms of bodies lying motionless everywhere around her.

As the air finally began to clear, the horrific scene became even more terrifying.

The Brashnellan Warriors were almost all back on their feet, moving together toward one side of the field.

Very few of the Mandelans had regained consciousness.

Audril tried to take advantage of the dust that was still settling by crouching down behind it and moving from body to body, shaking the crumpled forms in an effort to revive them. The pain in her leg was searing and her hunched over posture made it all the worse. It stabbed in throbbing rhythm with each step she took.

"Come on, wake up," she whispered as she shook a lifeless Mandelan soldier.

"Hey," came the welcome sound of Bridgette's louder than necessary whisper. "Are you okay?"

"Yeah," she fibbed, "my leg's a little messed up but I'm okay." She shook another body and asked, "Have you seen my dad?"

"Your dad and Kahlie are all right," Bridgette assured. "They're doing the same thing you are right now."

"What about Ryannon?" Audril kept her voice low as she and Bridgette continued their attempts to rouse the Mandelans.

Bridgette opened her mouth to respond just as a sinister, gravelly, angry sound permeated the dusty air. "Where is she?" It was a strange, unworldly voice.

Audril turned and saw Ryannon standing amongst the Brashnellan soldiers at the other side of the field. There was something very different about him now; he had become dark—almost like a shadow—a change that was noticeable even through the clouded air.

"Where is she?" he hissed again, and started in a stagger across the field.

She could only assume he was looking for her.

He lumbered toward her, sword drawn and stabbing everyone with whom he came in contact—including the occasional Brashnellan that got in his way.

"Where is she?" he bellowed a third time.

Just then, there was another commotion near where Ryannon had been standing moments before. Several Brashnellan soldiers were falling to the ground—one by one—victims of a single warrior.

That warrior was Kahlie. She was unbelievable in her skill—twisting and turning—spinning her sword one way and then reversing and flipping it around in another direction. Every move was intentional and purposeful; every thrust of her sword was deadly accurate.

The dark Shadow of Ryannon, which had been moving nearer and nearer to Audril, suddenly stopped his advance. "*There!*" he shrieked, spinning around and pointing at Kahlie who was systematically slaying his warriors—despite the increasing number of them moving to challenge her.

He stumbled back toward her. "It is my turn," he sneered. "*My* turn to kill!"

By now, the air had cleared enough for Audril to realize the full bleakness of the situation. There were possibly a hundred Mandelans left standing amongst what seemed to be ten thousand Brashnellans—and the battle was resuming.

And the hopeless scenario was about to get much worse. A strange sloshing noise echoed through the air echoing from somewhere deep within the lake. The water in the Mystad shuddered and shook and tiny circles rippled across its entire surface. The sloshing became louder and louder and then erupted, as thousands of forceful jets of crystal water streaked skyward.

Inside each jet, a human form was visible. The jets ascended high above the peaks of the surrounding hills and then dropped suddenly, leaving multitudes of Trysta soldiers hovering in the sky where they had been. As the water splashed back onto the surface of the lake, one very large jet shot up from the center and disintegrated in a flash of gold. There, hovering in the air was Ultara, there to lead her Trysta army into battle. The Trystas levitated above Mystad for a moment, and then Ultara shouted, "Lortu! Now!"

On her command, the shadows in Mandela City started to wriggle and move as hundreds of thousands of Dwellers materialized out of the shadows, and slinked slowly and deliberately towards the few remaining Mandelans.

"Oh no," Audril gasped.

She looked towards Ultara, trying to prepare for what was going to happen next, when Glaron appeared in front of her.

"What's she doing?" she asked, hoping he would somehow know Ultara's intentions.

"No idea," he answered, seeming a little uneasy that the Trystas were there, albeit relieved that they had actually survived.

What Audril saw next made her heart sink.

She just happened to glance over at the dark form of Ryannon who was smiling victoriously. "Yessss," he hissed, "I was beginning to wonder what was taking you so long, Mother!"

Ultara gazed down at him with a stone-cold expression, but then smiled at Ryannon. She turned to Branlor, who was hovering at her right.

He made a nodding gesture and all of the Trystas, with the exception of Ultara, lowered down to the field.

"Use your eyes!" Ultara commanded so loudly that it reverberated off the mountains in the distance. "Finish them!"

"Oh no, oh no, oh no!" Audril repeated.

All at once, a buzzing permeated the air. The sound was similar to the buzzing that Audril had heard in Iowa, back when the Trystas had placed receptors on her.

She watched in horror as the Trysta army fanned out across the field. In colorful intense waves, their eyes started to glow and surge.

Suddenly, hundreds of Brashnellan soldiers collapsed to the ground in pain. The lights in the Trystas' eyes intensified and the field was filled with the agonizing shrieks of the Brashnellan Army. Any of the Black Warriors who were not being electrocuted by the Trystas were being attacked by the remaining

Mandelans…or the nearly invisible Shadow Dwellers.

Ryannon continued to move toward Kahlie. The Trysta assault seemed to have no effect on him.

"*How dare she*," he seethed. "No matter! I will kill *her* still!" It sounded as though he was talking to himself. He looked over to a group of his Warriors who had managed to break away from the Shadow Dwellers and commanded, "Get the atoh! I will take care of her!"

In the blink of an eye, Ultara appeared at Audril's side.

"Atoh," she nodded. "Let's get this over with, shall we?"

A Brashnellan soldier charged toward them. Ultara raised her hand and he flew backward easily fifty feet through the air.

"I can't even tell you how happy I am to see you, Vritesse," Audril beamed. "And, I'm certainly glad you're on our side now!" She watched the warrior that Ultara had just repelled land in a thud on the ground.

"I've always been on your side, Atoh. I told your mother I would watch out for you and protect you, and that is precisely what I have done."

Four more Brashnellans came running up behind them. "Look out!" Audril warned. "Oh, so I suppose that having Lortu kidnap me was for my protection then?"

She took on one of the soldiers, while Ultara handled the other three.

"Of course it was." Ultara flicked her wrist and one of the Brashnell Warriors stiffened like stone and dropped over backward. "You would have been safe in Koria. But Glaron here kind of threw off my plans a bit." She leaned her head back towards Glaron who was fighting off Brashnellans behind her and added, ". . . yet again."

Glaron smiled sheepishly. He kicked his foe in the stomach, causing the warrior to double over and drop to the ground. He leaned back and playfully gave Ultara a quick peck on the cheek. "Sorry, Vritesse," he chuckled, "I was only trying to help!"

She shook her head and continued to toy with the one Brashnellan soldier of the three that was still left standing.

As she sent him zooming through the air, at least twenty more raced toward Audril.

"Lortu! Time for you to have some fun," Ultara yelled loudly.

In a flash Lortu was with them, fading in and out of shadow, confusing and tormenting the Brashnellans.

"'Ello, Atoha," he hummed, bowing as he passed in front of Audril. "You zee?" He grabbed a warrior from behind and hurled him through the air right into another one. "De Vritessa is steel maye best offer."

Before long the Brashnellan Army was on the run. They were clearly no match for the Trystas, the Shadow Dwellers and the remaining Mandelans, many of whom had regained consciousness and had gotten back into the battle. Furthermore, several of the Shadow Squanki, including Tabbit, had come to fight for Mandela.

But now, a new problem was developing. Water—and not just a little of it—was seeping up through the ground, rising rapidly, and washing in strong waves over the bodies that remained on the ground—carrying them away toward Mystad Lake. New Lor Mandela was beginning to flood.

Ultara floated into the air, along with many of the Trystas, and began pulling people up onto rocks and into trees. Everyone left on the ground struggled to keep their footing, lest they be swept away in the growing current.

"What's going on?" she asked, looking directly at Audril.

"It's the Advantiere," Audril replied. "Give me a second!" She clambered her way up onto a rock that was jutting up out of the water.

"I don't believe we have a second, Atoh," Ultara replied.

"Glaron!" she yelled. "Get over here! I need your help."

The water continued to rise as Glaron waded to her side.

"I'm going to have to create a bolder chamber!" she yelled, pulling a green pebble from a small bag that hung at her side and tossing it onto the ground.

"What?" Glaron blurted. "You can't! It's suicide!"

"Just cover me," she insisted. "Make sure no one interrupts the process, and I'll be fine!"

Ultara stepped onto the pebble and raised her arm skyward, and a sheet of water obediently rose into the air. It swirled around her in a wide, twisting, transparent whirlpool, as a giant sheet of a crystalline, glass-like material started to form across the floor of the field.

The water that had been steadily rising was forced out and around the barrier.

Once the glassy floor of the bolder chamber completely covered the field and areas around it, jagged crystal walls started to inch up from it, gradually encasing Mandela Palace and all of the surrounding territories and pushing the water further away from the hundreds of thousands of people who had been in danger of being swept away just moments ago.

Audril was intrigued by what Ultara was doing, but forced herself to focus on the Advantiere. It was up to her to save New Lor Mandela from the same fate that had just obliterated its clone.

"One comes swiftly in the morning," she began. "One comes swiftly in the morning." She thought hard, frantically searching her mind for any clue to the mysterious prophecy. As she repeated the line a third time, it hit her. "Of course! The pictures!"

She looked at Glaron whose horrified eyes were locked on Ultara. "One comes swiftly in the morning!" she yelled, "The first picture was Darian! It matches! He attacked Mandela City in the morning!"

The water continued to rise outside the bolder chamber.

"Okay," she continued, "One unknowing moves in haste."

In her head, the image of Darian was slowly replaced.

"Next was Doctor Brockman," she spoke loudly and quickly, as if she were explaining the Advantiere to Ultara, who was, in fact, listening intently from inside the cyclone.

"One beloved though mighty fallen." Again the image changed. "That's momma . . . at the battle, and One is chosen to forget her place."

She struggled to remember who'd been next. "Nenia?" she questioned, "Yes! The next picture was Nenia!"

Ultara's eyes grew wide. "What?" she gasped. Her voice was strangely distorted by the water in the funnel around her.

Audril shrugged her shoulders. "I don't know . . . I saw Nenia . . . it was her!" she explained loudly. "Chosen to forget her place?"

She tried to figure out what that could have possibly meant.

She looked across the field and noticed that Ryannon and Kahlie were isolated in an area near the Anaria, locked in a violent battle. Kahlie was amazing, the way she bashed her sword so forcefully against Ryannon's that he was having a hard time keeping his balance.

Kahlie took two or three more swings, and then spun around to give her next blow added momentum. As she stepped out of the spin, she lost her footing and tripped on a large jagged rock that was sticking up out of the floor of the bolder chamber. She fell hard onto the pointy rock, which ripped through the leg of her armor.

Jonathan saw it too, and raced to help her.

Ryannon lifted his gloved arm into the air and aimed it at Jonathan. Several long thin spikes glinted in the few rays of sun that had pushed through the predominantly cloudy sky.

Jonathan grabbed for Ryannon's arm, but narrowly missed as he jerked it back. The black form of Ryannon leered at Jonathan and took aim.

"Dad! Look out!" Audril screamed. She jumped down from the rock and raced across the field, knowing there was no way she would make it to her dad in time.

Ultara was also watching the scenario play out from inside a clear cyclone of water. The walls of the bolder chamber were just starting to curve over at the top in the beginnings of a ceiling.

Glaron could see what was happening as well. He jumped in front of Ultara, hoping to distract her from what he knew she was about to do.

"Audril! Transport," he screamed.

She didn't hear him, though. The sound of the water funnel drowned out his voice.

Just as Ryannon was about to unload his spike darts into the atoc, Ultara lowered her arm and flung it forcefully toward Ryannon. A golden beam of light ripped through the meadow, hitting Ryannon in the chest and sending him hurling violently through the air.

An enormous jolt of energy surged down through Ultara. She jerked ferociously and then collapsed into a gasping heap onto the ground.

Glaron dropped down next to her. "Oh, Vritesse! What have you done?" he breathed.

Kahlie, Jonathan, Audril and Bridgette all saw Ultara fall wasted no time rushing across the field to her aid.

"What happened? What's going on?" Kahlie asked, gaping at the panic-stricken Glaron.

"You can't stop a bolder chamber once you start! It has to be finished or all of the power it takes to create it flows back through the creator!"

He lifted Ultara into his arms, and blurted, "She stopped it; she stopped it to save the atoc."

"What?" Jonathan gasped, dropping to his knees at Ultara's side, and looking pleadingly at Glaron, "What can we do?"

Ultara sputtered and coughed. "Don't trouble yourself, Jonathan. You've done all you can. You need to know though; I didn't kill them . . . your parents . . . it was Darian."

His eyes saddened. "I'm sorry, Ultara," he breathed. "I should have trusted you. You saved us. None of us . . ." He took her by the hand. "*None of us* would have survived this had it not been for you."

With his words, the water that had been steadily rising around the bolder chamber started to slip quickly back into the ground.

"Dad . . . I think it's finished," Audril muttered with a somewhat surprised expression on her face. "That was the final thing that had to happen." She stood silently for a moment, and then breathed, "His hatred die for love to grow."

Glaron looked up at her questioningly.

The water continued to soak back into the soil as Audril surveyed the bleak scene.

The fields, once green and lush, had been reduced to mud and rocks. All of the bushes and shrubs that had lined the lake were ripped out and lying in tangled masses around its banks. Several people, who had been carried away, were swimming back to the shores of Mystad—some of them dragging with them the bodies of those who had not made it.

Kahlie, Glaron, Jonathan and Bridgette all tried to help Ultara, who was coughing and gasping for breath.

And then, it started.

At first, it was nothing more than a low hum, but it didn't take long for the hum to turn into a dull rumbling.

Audril looked skyward and shouted, "WHAT? No! It's done! It's over!"

She began replaying the Advantiere again in her mind. "One comes swiftly, Darian! One unknowing, Glaron!"

The rumbling amplified.

"One beloved, Gracielle! One chosen to forget, Nenia! One though strong must fall forbidden."

She couldn't remember right away whose face had appeared on the wall after Nenia's? Who was it? She closed her eyes, and the elusive image came sharply into focus. "Ultara," she breathed. She looked over where Ultara lay, and sighed sadly, "Ultara."

The rumbling grew, and seemed to be moving closer.

Audril continued through the Advantiere. "One made low shall rise again."

She didn't have to try to remember who the next picture had been; as she glanced at her dad she witnessed first hand the fulfillment of that line. A humble accountant from the Midwestern United States, restored to his rightful place as the High Ruler of an entire world.

"One must be as these words written."

She thought for a moment. The next picture had been Ryannon's. Her immediate assumption was that by attacking, Ryannon had satisfied his part of the Advantiere but then she gasped, "No, wait a minute!"

She scanned the field for any sign of the dark form that Ryannon had become. "Where is he?" she cried.

But it wasn't Audril who spotted him first. Kahlie had already sprung to her feet and was racing back across the field toward a slightly hunched, heaving, shadowy figure that was staggering back toward them.

The moment he saw Kahlie, he too started running.

They raced toward each other. Kahlie drew a sword, and Ryannon produced one as well.

The rumbling of the planet was growing more and more deafening by the second.

"THAT'S IT!" Audril screamed, "That's what's missing!" She looked back across the field. Kahlie and Ryannon were still charging at each other, and only a few yards away from colliding. "It wasn't Ryannon! It was Ryannon and Kahlie! ONE MUST BE AS THESE WORDS WRITTEN!"

Ultara bolted to sitting and looked at her wide-eyed.

The rumbling was shaking everything, and was getting closer . . . and closer!

Audril kept her gaze locked on Ryannon and Kahlie. Their swords crashed together, and as they did, Kahlie started to glow white. It was exactly what Audril was waiting for.

The whole world was reeling. Again, everyone was being held in place by the movements of the gyrating ground. Everyone it seemed, except Kahlie and Ryannon who were dueling ferociously as though nothing else was happening around them—Ryannon, an evil, dark, corrupt monster, and Kahlie a good, strong, noble, pillar of light.

"Destruction from twins, and so it must end," Audril mouthed.

She knew what had to happen. Lor Mandela had to be restored; it had to be made whole again—and the process was almost identical to the way it had been divided. She started in an awkward gallop towards Ryannon and Kahlie. The movements of the planet made it very difficult to move—but she had to! She had to get to Kahlie and Ryannon.

She gritted her teeth in determination, and forced herself to go faster.

Suddenly, she remembered the power she possessed. "The Anaria!" she shouted loudly, and in an instant appeared within just a few feet of the duel.

Ryannon took a step backward, and thrust his sword in toward Kahlie's stomach. Kahlie—who had been momentarily distracted by Audril's sudden appearance—wasn't ready for it. His weapon was less than an inch away from plunging into her midsection, when Audril thrust her arm into the air.

As she did, both Ryannon and Kahlie's arms that had been holding their swords flew upward. Audril could feel the resistance from both of them, as they fought to regain control of their arms—but she kept her elbow locked and her arm extended.

They both looked at her with shocked expressions.

"What are you doing?" Kahlie yelled.

Ryannon just growled.

"Destruction from twins, and so it must end!" she repeated, and then…despite the fact that she was the one moving her lips, no sound came from her. Instead, the words exploded from the mouths of Ryannon and Kahlie. "ELAHK A BER LOR MANDELAAAAAAAAA!"

Suddenly, the black shadow that possessed Ryannon shot into the sky. The white light that enveloped Kahlie also raced into the air. They twisted around each other, each seeking to devour its opposite.

The white light wrapped steadily around the black until it had almost completely choked it out.

All at once, however, the blackness expanded and in a crackling roar, overtook the white. A heavy darkness blanketed the planet. There was a brief pause in the rumbling, and then, a monstrous explosion rocked through the atmosphere—and everything disintegrated into magenta dust.

CHAPTER XLIV
FROM THE END TO THE BEGINNING

C ountless tiny specks of brilliant white light flickered and floated through the charged air. Where there had been seemingly unending chaos just moments before, there was now a pervasive silence, peace and calm. The sparkling particles descended, drifting down onto the battle ravaged landscape, falling like glistening, rejuvenating raindrops—and rejuvenate they did. No sooner had the miniscule flecks landed, than thin shoots of green grass sprouted up in the muddy fields. Shrubs and trees that had been ripped from the ground in the flood were replaced as new ones wriggled and stretched up toward the light.

Audril was stunned to find that she was still standing—still alive. She quickly patted herself all over to make sure everything was intact, and then glanced around and saw many of the people in the field doing the same. In the city, people crept out of their houses, looking about in surprise. Occasional whispers permeated the shocked silence. The whispers were replaced by excited chatter, and then, one by one, everyone started to cheer. Whoops of delight and thunderous applause piled on top of the cheers, creating quite a commotion throughout Mandela City and the fields surrounding Mystad Lake.

"Magiiiieeee!" Bridgette squealed from a few feet away, running over and wrapping her arms around Audril. "Sorry! I mean Atoh Audril," she giggled playfully and bowed. "You did it! You *really* did it!"

Audril couldn't speak. She was so relieved that Bridgette was alive, and she was alive, and her dad and Kahlie, and Glaron—they were all alive! Even Ultara seemed to be doing better. She was sitting up on her own, and smiling warmly at Glaron who was doing a goofy little dance.

Jonathan slowly walked to where his daughter stood. Tears streamed down his dusty cheeks. He didn't say a word; he just grabbed her and pulled her into a tight hug. Emotion overcame them both as they cried together, and then started laughing.

They were just moving back from their embrace when Glaron tapped Jonathan on the shoulder. "Atoc, the vritesse would like to speak with you." His expression was uncharacteristically solemn.

Audril glanced over to where Kahlie was sitting, holding Ultara, who was again sputtering for air. "Oh, no!" she breathed as she followed her dad to the vritesse's side.

"Ultara," he began, but she stopped him before he could say anything else.

"I don't want . . ." she coughed a few times, "your sympathy, Atoc." She drew in a sharp breath and continued. "I have lived the life I was born to live, and now, I just ask that you let me have an honorable death."

Jonathan struggled to remove any sign of emotion from his face. "What do you want me to do?" he asked soberly.

Ultara leaned forward, wincing in pain as she moved. "Just make sure I get away," she instructed. "Don't let me die here."

With great strain, she rose to her feet, took in a deep breath. She pulled her shoulders back and lifted her head. "I, Ultara, Daughter of Anika and Vritesse of the Trysta People, call you," she looked directly at Kahlie who slowly rose to her feet as well. "Nenia," Ultara continued in a much softer tone, "as my wise and able successor." She reached into her cloak, pulled out the little silver box, and placed it in Kahlie's hand. "Rule the Trystas well, my daughter." She bowed humbly and then turned, as if nothing were wrong, and sprinted off. "THE DEPTHS OF THE CAVERNS!" she yelled loudly as she ran, but then collapsed into a heap on the ground. Suddenly, there was a loud pop, and Ultara vanished.

Kahlie stood staring at the little box in her hand. Jonathan walked up behind her and placed his arm lovingly around her shoulder. She spun into his chest, and he wrapped his other arm around her. He was still holding her when

General Statlen ran up behind them.

"Sir," he interrupted.

"Yes, General?"

He moved Kahlie back gently from the embrace.

"Forgive me, Atoc. It's, um . . . it's about Ryannon."

"What about him, Statlen?"

The general explained, "Captain Morringe and several of his men took him into custody shortly after the explosion."

"Excellent," Jonathan replied, "congratulate Morringe for me!"

General Statlen paused for a moment.

"Morringe is dead, sir. Ryannon killed him. He caught them off guard . . . killed them all, and then ran off, sir. He ran into the Sybran."

Jonathan wasted no time. "Trystas and Dwellers! To the forest! Squanki! Destroy all of the portals! Find Ryannon! NOW!"

His command boomed through the valley, as the Trystas shot into the sky, and the Dwellers faded into the shadows.

Audril stood off to the side, watching the search commence, but then felt something sharp press into her back.

"Shhh, not a sound," Ryannon's voice whispered behind her.

He pulled her backward—back toward the forest.

"How do you feel about dying, Atoh?" The bleak indifference in the tone of his question sent icy chills racing through her. "You're about to find out," he hissed.

"Dad!" she screamed. Everyone in the meadow spun around.

"Ryannon! *No!*" Jonathan cried and raced toward them.

Ryannon watched at the frantic atoc, and laughed. He spun himself in front of Audril and plunged a long dagger straight into her chest.

Jonathan gasped and dropped to his knees.

No one moved. All eyes locked on Audril.

Ryannon took a step back and stared at her with both intrigue and shock in his eyes.

Jonathan slowly rose back to his feet. His mouth was gaping open. "What the devil?" he breathed.

There, with the sleek black dagger handle protruding out of her chest, Audril stood, completely unaffected.

Audril was every bit as shocked as her dad, but at the moment, her surprise was greatly overshadowed by a sense of rage. She glared at Ryannon in contempt and disgust. "How dare you," she seethed. "Haven't you done enough?"

She reached down and grabbed a hold of the dagger handle. Slowly, and with her eyes fixed on Ryannon's, she slid the dagger out of her chest.

Ryannon watched with a sick aroused fascination.

"How do *you* feel about dying, Ryannon?" she sneered as the tip of the dagger's blade appeared at her sternum. She took a step toward him. "*You're about to find out!*" In a fluid twist, she flipped the dagger around and placed it at his throat.

An evil smirk spread across his handsome face. There was no fear in his eyes—only the hint of an obsessive enthrallment with Audril's apparent immortality.

"Not yet, love," he hissed, and flung his arm upward—knocking the dagger away from his neck and out of Audril's hand. He grabbed her and kissed her hard on the lips, "I'll be back for more of that later," he sneered, and then turned and disappeared into the darkness of the Sybran.

"After him!" Jonathan commanded. "Now!" He watched his remaining soldiers charge into the forest, and then rushed to Audril's side.

CHAPTER XLV
THEN WILL ONE FOREVER REIGN

The Council Hall at Trysta Palace buzzed with excitement. For the first time in more than six years the Council was convening. Delegates, who thought they would never see another gathering, were, at long last, reunited. Among them were representatives from lands once deserted, (now in various stages of renewal); representatives for the Trystas, and the delegates of Mandela City. There were also three newly-appointed delegates; Lortu of the Shadow Dwellers; Tabbit, of the Shadow Squanki; and Bridgette Lawson, of Glenhill, Iowa.

As the council members settled into their blue satin chairs the platforms rose to the appropriate levels. The motion and staggered heights of the platforms added to the overall sense of activity and exhilaration in the room. The radiant sun streamed through the crystal ceiling above, sending a flood of energizing warmth, and ribbons of vibrant color dancing across the rich brown walls.

When the majority of the delegates had settled in, the three large doors at the back of the hall swung open with a *clunk*. The delegates rose to their feet and started applauding.

Kahlie entered through the door on the left. She was dressed in a long, stunning black gown encrusted about the bodice with hundreds of tiny sapphires. Around her neck was a delicate, cascading necklace that shimmered and sparkled in the rays of light and color. Her long wavy, now black, hair was also dotted with small sapphires that matched her deep blue eyes perfectly. She bowed to the delegates, and lowered to one knee.

The applause exploded into cheers and whistles as Jonathan entered from the door on the right. He was in a black tuxedo with a bright cobalt sash. He placed his gloved hand on top of Kahlie's and also lowered to his knee.

Suddenly, the roaring applause literally doubled in volume as Audril— dressed in a beautiful, vivid blue, floor length gown—appeared through the door in the center. She glanced uncomfortably at her dad and Kahlie, who were bowing to her, and motioned nervously for them to get up. They chuckled, and rose to their feet, and together with Audril, strolled past the cheering council members to the red velvet chairs on the platforms at the center of the room.

After the lengthy ovation, a hush fell over the crowd.

"Council members of New Lor Mandela," a voice echoed out from the top of the room, "prepare for the reading of the lineage!"

"Our highest ruler, Jonathan Borloc . . . Atoc of Lor Mandela."

Jonathan stepped on to his platform, and it rose almost to the ceiling.

"His entrusted, Kahlie Nenia Borloc . . . by marriage, Ator of Lor Mandela . . . by birth, Nenia tu Sybran of the Trystas . . . Daughter of Ultara, and as called, Vritesse of the Trysta People."

Kahlie moved on to her platform which ascended until it was next to Jonathan's on the left.

"And in conclusion of our noble and great succession, Atoh Audril Borloc, daughter of Atoc Jonathan Borloc and our beloved departed Ator Gracielle tu Morning of the Trystas and in the ancient language of our Derite ancestors, Clest Anaria . . . The Child of Balance."

Again the room was filled with raucous cheers and applause.

She mounted her platform, and it rose to just below her dad's and Kahlie's.

After the resurgence of applause faded, Jonathan lowered to his seat, followed by the rest of the council. He leaned forward and pressed a small green button on the arm of his chair. The room darkened and his platform glowed in the signature Borloc blue.

"My friends," he began, "it's good to be together again." He turned his eyes to Kahlie, who nodded in agreement. "First of all, Ator Kahlie, my daughter and I wish to express our thanks to you and your communities for your support and faith on our behalf. Many marvelous things have taken place on Lor Mandela." He waited for the clapping that followed to die down before adding, "As you are all aware, I have recently taken Kahlie as my entrusted. With the passing of Ultara, she was also called as the Trysta vritesse."

He looked lovingly at Kahlie. He could have never imagined that the gawky girl who used to daydream and flit around Mandela Palace would one day hold such an honored position . . . or his heart. Admittedly, at first, his feelings for her had frightened him a bit; he didn't want to forget Gracielle, but it was Kahlie's own love for Gracielle that finally assured him that she would never be forgotten; she would always be a part of them all. After staring at Kahlie for several seconds, he cleared his throat and continued. "I believe that this symbolizes a new era on Lor Mandela . . . a new beginning. It has been more than a thousand years since the ator has also been the vritesse. It speaks to us of unity and peace . . . of oneness."

Oneness, Audril repeated in her mind. She marveled at the power of the word "one." It had been the recurring theme in the Advantiere. One planet divided had to become one again to survive. Twins had to be one to restore the decay and deterioration of one soul. Two races that had ruled side by side for generations were now a single ruling body—one. The final line of the Advantiere, *Then will ONE forever reign*, echoed over and over again in her head.

Suddenly, a sobering realization swept through her mind. The pictures— the faces she'd seen on the wall—until this very moment, she'd forgotten the last one. It hadn't been Kahlie's like she'd remembered at the time of the battle. The last face she saw that day in the Advantiere Room had been her own. The line that she'd assumed referred to Ryannon—*One must be as these words written,*—was actually fulfilled by *both* Ryannon and Kahlie. Twins had to act as one, and speak the words that were written—together. Only after they did, would the destruction caused by twins be undone. Only then would ONE forever reign.

It was her! The last line of the Advantiere—it was to be fulfilled by her.

Then will one forever reign. *Forever. . .forever.* Was that why Ryannon hadn't been able to kill her?

She sat in a contemplative daze on her platform for the rest of the meeting. Even after the majority of the delegates were gone, she remained deep in thought, sitting on her burgundy velvet chair, staring into space.

It was Kahlie who first noticed how distracted she was.

"Audril? Hey Buzz, what is it?" At this point, both Bridgette and Jonathan had joined Kahlie and were looking with concern at Audril.

"Angel," Jonathan tried, "are you all right?"

Audril's eyes were glassy and distant.

"Dad, I think I know why the dagger didn't kill me." As she said it, her expression changed from dazed to terrified. "It didn't kill me . . . because I don't think I can be killed."

"What?" Jonathan chuckled, "Yeah, well that would be wonderful, sweetheart, but . . . ."

"No, Atoc." A familiar voice oozed from a wall a few feet behind them. "Ze atoha ees correct."

A dark wave rippled across the wall as Lortu slinked out of the shadows.

"De Child of Bahlanz. De Clest Anaria, she ees now eemortal."

He glided across the room and looked Audril in the eyes. "Aye was wondereeng how long eet would take for hair to feegure eet out."

"What," Audril whispered, "how?"

Lortu paced around for a moment. "Dis beezness of doeeng tings just to be nice ees not profitting de Noble Lortu."

"You were given a spot on the council, Lortu. What more do you want?" Jonathan retorted.

"Aye am requiring a portal, Atoc, in De Bogs . . . only one portal. If you would arrange eet weeth your friend, Tabbeet . . . ?"

"Out of the question!" Jonathan snapped. "So you can what? Transport Ryannon off of Lor Mandela? How much has he paid you, Lortu?"

Lortu growled at him as though he was thoroughly disgusted. "Ryannon of

Brashnell does not have anyting dat Lortu desires," he seethed. "He ees de enemy. He will never be maye best offer!" He turned and in a huff moved back toward the wall.

"No, wait!" Audril blurted. "Please, Lortu . . . don't go!"

Lortu looked into her pleading blue eyes and sighed. He walked back to Jonathan, and explained, "Dis portal . . . It weel benefit de both of us zomeday zoon, Atoc."

The anger was visibly slipping from his face as he went on. "But, eef you say no, for de good of your people, aye weel not put de Lor Mandela een danger. Aye weel steel tell you what leetle aye know about de atoha."

Jonathan studied Lortu's face. There was nothing there but sincerity— something that was not commonly found in a Shadow Dweller's countenance.

"I'm sorry Lortu," he apologized, "I shouldn't have been so quick to judge." He thought for a moment and then added, "You and I will discuss this portal. If I can see the benefit, and you can assure me that it will be very well hidden, I'll have Tabbit accompany you to The Bogs."

"Ahhh, tank you, Atoc." Lortu bowed. "De atoha," he explained, "she was geeven a gift in exchange for saveeng de Lor Mandela. She ees geeven great powah, and all eternity to use eet."

"Wait! How? I mean, what power?" Audril stammered. "I don't understand. You're saying that I'm . . . *immortal?*" It was difficult for her to even say the word. "How? I mean, how is that even possible?"

Lortu paced along the back wall. As he did, he ran his thin hand slowly along its rich brown surface. It was odd to watch his hand disappear and reappear as it slid in and out of shadow. "De Shadow Dwellers know many tings, but we do not know all," he explained. "What we do know, Atoha, ees dat de answers you seek . . . de answers only you can find . . . day are steel hidden from you." He leaned against the wall and slowly faded into it. His final words resonated from a dark corner after he vanished from sight. "Day are steel hidden in de Advantiere."

Epilogue

"You know . . . you're gonna have to speak to him eventually." Audril leaned playfully against Bridgette and made a pouty face. "Look at him," she continued, "he looks so sad!"

She was referring to Glaron, who was standing across the ballroom from them, looking very handsome, but also very gloomy.

It had been three weeks since the battle, and since Bridgette had realized that the guy she thought she was in love with was actually someone else. There was something about the fact that he was a twenty-six year old magical alien that made her feel sort of violated. She'd been doing a masterful job of avoiding him—until now.

"I don't even know him," she responded defensively, but then turned to the side a little and pretended to be fidgeting with her dress so that Audril couldn't see her glance in his direction.

"You thought I was someone different too, Bridge," Audril scolded, "and you still speak to me."

"That's different," she replied. She spun to face Audril and raised her head like she was snubbing Glaron. "You didn't know you were someone else. *He* did!" She smoothed the skirt of her pale pink gown and continued, "It makes me mad, ya know? It makes me so mad, I just wanna, I dunno . . . I just wanna," She rolled her hand into a fist. "punch him right in the nose!"

Audril grinned and her eyes widened. "Well," she smirked, "here's your chance." She looked past Bridgette, to Glaron, who had come over and was now standing right behind her.

"Mmm hmmm," he cleared his throat, "may I have this dance?" He bowed humbly, and then added, "Please, Bridge, don't say no."

Bridgette slowly turned to face him. She had to admit that he did look stunning in his dress uniform. "Oh, all right," she agreed, "just one dance, though!"

He smiled and playfully asked, "You're not going to punch me in the nose, are you?"

"I might," she snipped. She took his arm, and walked with him to the dance floor.

Audril was left alone with her thoughts. What a ride this had been! She couldn't believe all that had happened in such a short time. She looked out over the festive celebration before her; everyone seemed so happy. The ladies were beautiful in their many colored gowns, and the men were dashing in their suits and uniforms. Couples danced, friends visited and laughed. It was truly a glorious scene.

What she couldn't understand, however, was why—in the midst of all this contentment—she felt so uneasy and so miserable. Maybe it was because she didn't have someone special in her life. It seemed like everyone else did. Bridgette, her dad, and Kahlie—they'd all found love. All she'd found was some lunatic murderer who cared little about anyone but himself.

The song that had been playing ended, but Bridgette and Glaron stayed on the floor. "*Just one dance, though!*" Audril mocked Bridgette. "Yeah, like I didn't see that one coming!"

Just then, there was a tap on her shoulder. It was so light that at first she almost didn't feel it. She turned around to see a tiny little creature bouncing up and down behind her. "Oh . . . hello, Tabbit!" she grinned. "Don't you look lovely this evening?"

Tabbit twirled around in her shimmery peach dress, giggled and repeated, "Don't you look lovely this evening?" She reached up for Audril's hand and whispered, "Times to dances, Atoh Lady!" She winked and then started pulling Audril along toward the dance floor.

Audril was a little embarrassed that she was being asked to dance by Tabbit. *Oh well*, she thought, *I guess it's better than nothing!* When they reached the edge of the floor, Tabbit bobbed up and down on her toes a couple of times, and then skipped merrily off.

"Okay," she sighed, "maybe it's not better."

"What's not?" She spun around—shocked by the voice she'd just heard.

There, clean-shaven, neatly groomed, and dressed to the nines was Dallin Doone—holding a pale purple rose—very much alive!

"Here, this is for you." He gestured toward Tabbit who was nodding and beaming from ear to ear. He leaned over and whispered, "She said you wouldn't dance with me unless I gave you a flower."

Audril was speechless. She took the rose from his hands and just stared at him.

"What?" he chuckled nervously. "You don't want to? Ugh! You don't want to!" He grunted disgustedly. "I knew it! I look stupid, huh?"

Audril gasped and coughed. "Uh . . . no . . . no! You don't look stupid. You look just . . . ."

He raised his hands into dance position. "Shall we?" he smiled.

She smiled back and took his hands.

The rest of the evening flew by as she and Dallin danced and talked the whole night away. When the celebration ended, he didn't want to leave her.

"You wanna take a walk?" he asked.

"As a matter of fact, I do," she answered. "There's somewhere I've been dying to see."

"Really, where?"

She smiled and took him by the arm. "The Ator's Anaria."

He escorted her away from the ballroom and out toward the main palace doors.

"Wait, not this way." She pulled him toward a corridor at the far side of the entrance foyer. "Come on!"

"Where are we going?" he asked as they made their way down the dim hallway.

"You'll see." Audril stopped outside a wooden door and motioned for Dallin to go in first.

He pushed the door open. "A kitchen?" he asked.

"Yeah, a kitchen," she breathed. "This is where . . ." she took a couple of steps into the room, "where my mother was killed." She touched a small crystal on the wall, and a faint light flickered on. "I just wanna see if this memory . . . ."

She didn't finish her thought. She grabbed Dallin by the hand and led him to the closet at the back of the room.

"In the floor, under the shelves that line the back wall," she breathed.

Dallin opened the closet door and peered inside. "What are we looking for?" he asked.

Audril slid past him, and walked around to the back of the shelves. "That!" she answered, pointing. There, in the floor, was a large dark tunnel. "Come on!" She sat down on the edge and lowered herself in.

"Are you sure this is safe?" he chuckled as he dropped down into the hole.

What had been the floor seemed to magically twist, and was now the ceiling.

"Whoa," Audril giggled, "that was weird."

"Yeah," Dallin agreed, "which way?"

She shrugged her shoulders, but then pointed down a long tunnel and they started off. It wasn't long before the smooth, muddy stone walls were replaced by twisting, vining tree roots.

"Wow! I can't believe this is all down here," Audril mused. "It's awesome!"

Dallin looked at her and smiled. "How did you know about this? Did your mother tell you?"

"I overheard her talking about it," she answered.

They rounded a corner and came to a place where several tunnels all merged together.

"Which way?" he questioned.

"Let's try over here."

He took her by the hand and they continued on. After a few moments of silence, Audril stopped and turned to Dallin. Something had been weighing heavily on her mind.

"Dallin," she tried, "I hope you don't mind me asking, but how did you survive that vystoran? I saw it hit you!"

Audril cringed as his face dropped.

"Oh, uh . . . if you don't want to tell me," she stammered.

"No, it's all right," he assured. "You saw it hit someone, but it wasn't me."

"What? I don't understand."

Dallin continued, "It was raining and cloudy." He paused, then added, "And there were a lotta shadows."

"Wait! A dweller?" Audril gasped.

Dallin nodded. "He saw the vystoran comin' and sorta blended in to me. I didn't even realize he was there. He actually stabbed me in the side so I'd look like I was in pain. He knew that they'd shoot me again if I didn't go down."

"What happened to the Dweller?" she asked, hoping that Dallin would tell her how Dwellers aren't affected by vystorans, and how he just ran off into the forest afterwards.

He shook his head sadly.

"But, that doesn't make sense," she argued. "Why would he sacrifice himself like that? Aren't Dwellers profiteers?"

"Well, yeah . . . they are, but as a group. They consider it honorable to sacrifice themselves to profit a bigger cause."

"What bigger cause?"

Dallin looked down at his toes and seemed to blush. "Lortu said that it's my destiny to protect you from Ryannon. He told me that as long as Ryannon is alive, I have to stick around and keep you safe."

"Keep me safe?" she giggled nervously. "Well . . . I, um . . . how flattering, sir!"

Suddenly, her eyes and Dallin's met. She found herself locked in his gaze as she stared deeply into his soulful brown eyes. She couldn't break eye contact and she really didn't want to.

Slowly, he leaned closer to her; slowly, she leaned closer to him. He moved his hands onto her waist and slid them around and up her back.

"I'm glad you came back," he whispered.

"I'm glad you did too."

She tilted her head slightly and closed her eyes in anticipation. A flood of heat and emotion welled inside of her as his arms wrapped around her, and he pulled her tightly to him. She felt his warm breath on her cheek, when suddenly. . . .

"Ahhhh! NOOOO!" A scratchy, squeaky, blood-curdling scream echoed through the tunnels, followed by a loud crash.

"Tabbit!" Audril gasped.

"Tabbit? Come On!" Dallin grabbed her by the hand and they sped off toward the direction of Tabbit's voice.

Audril's eyes darted around frantically. "Tabbit," she called out, "Tabbit! Where are you?"

There was no answer.

"Over here!" Dallin instructed. "I think I saw something." He pulled Audril toward what looked like a beam of light on the floor, which seemed to be coming from a source around a corner. No sooner had they run across the light, when it expanded, and there was a loud pop.

"A portal?" Dallin yelped as they emerged. "I thought the Squanki were s'posed to destroy 'em all!" He glanced over at Audril who was staring out at the scene before her in horror. All of the color had drained from her face, and she was barely breathing.

He turned to see what had caused such a reaction, and what he observed was unlike anything he had ever witnessed before. Piles that looked like they had recently been buildings lay smoldering across the landscape. Trees and shrubs were blackened and smoking. There was no movement at all—no activity and no life whatsoever—for as far as the eye could see.

"Oh, no." Audril's nearly inaudible voice trembled. "Dallin, we're in Glenhill."

Out of the corner of his eye, Dallin caught sight of the one thing in town that still remained standing. Now, his face too, bore a look of terror. He reached out and tugged on the waist of Audril's dress. She turned her head towards him. He was looking straight ahead and pointing. She followed the direction of his finger and there, where Glenhill High School had been before, a single structure stood intact. It was the school's marquee. Across it in black plastic letters were the words,

"WELCOME BACK, ATOH AUDRIL BORLOC".

LOR MANDELAN TERMS TRANSLATED FOR READERS FROM DROLANA (EARTH)

Terms with identical spelling as Earth words have also been added, due to slight variations of meaning.

A

ad•van•tiere \ad-van-'tir\ **General Term** : an inspired utterance or prediction

Al•ter•ing \'ôl-tər-ēŋ\ n. **Event** : a Trysta ritual of change in which an invoker with altering abilities harnesses power from glow stones to transform into another being of the same gender

A•nar•i•a \ə-'när-ē-ə\ **Place** : **1:** large tree **2:** the place of respite and retreat for the ator and her guests

A•ni•si•a Mys•tad Re•gion \ə-'ni-sē-ə 'mis-tad 'rē-jən\ **Place** : the most prominent and wealthy region of Mandela City. Considered the city center, as all council members reside in Anisia Mystad. Translated from ancient Trysta, Anisia means "overlooking". The region gets its name from its location overlooking Mystad Lake

a•toc \'ā-tôk\ **Hierarchy** : **1:** the male High Ruler of Lor Mandela **2:** a male sovereign

a•toh \'ā-tō\ **Hierarchy** : female member of the Noble family, usually the daughter of the atoc

a•ton \'ā-tôn\ **Hierarchy** : male member of the Noble family, usually the son of the atoc

a•tor \'ā-tôr\ **Hierarchy** : **1:** the entrusted or widow of the atoc **2:** female member of the Noble family equal in rank to the Trysta Vritesse

B

Bogs \'bôgz\ **Place** : **1:** area of the Sybran Forest that is completely devoid of light **2:** home of the Shadow Dwellers

bol•der cham•ber \'bôl-dər 'chām-bər\ **Weapons & Defense** : a room that can only be created by the vritesse to provide an impenetrable
barrier against enemies and the elements. (halting creation of a bolder chamber before completion is usually fatal for the vritesse)

Brash•nell \brash-'nel\ **Place** : geographically the largest area of Lor Mandela, situated north of the Mandela mountain range, bordering Westrim to the east and the Delovic Region of Mandela City to the west

C

cal•an•dry \'kôl-ən-drē\ **Animal** : large, flying beast of burden from the Northern High Forests. Rarely seen outside of wooded areas. Related to the rynolt of the Sybran, distinguishing features include: one crested head, three curved razor-sharp claws on each foot and black uneven wings. Calandry are shy creatures, but deadly when provoked. The largest known calandry on record measured thirty-six hands high at the shoulder

C (cont.)

Cal•ling \\'kôl-ēŋ\\ **Event** : momentous occasion when a new vritesse is appointed by her predecessor

Cas•tine Re•gion \\kas-'tēn 'rē-jən\\ **Place** : (also known as the hills) the Castine Region is inhabited primarily by soldiers, hunters, fishers and their families. Comprised of the Foothills of the South and the Sybran Forest

Cel•e•bra•tion of Light \\sel-ə-'brā-shən 'əv 'līt\\ **Event** : the annual social gathering of the heads-of-state and members of the Council, held in the Terrace Ballroom at Mandela Palace

Chief Ad•vi•sor \\'chēf ad-'vī-zər\\ **Hierarchy** : the high-councilor of the Trysta Empire. Second-in-command to the vritesse and appointed by her, the chief advisor can be male if deemed worthy by the vritesse

Com•pan•ion Ser•vant \\kəm-'pan-yən 'sər-vənt\\ **Hierarchy** : the head servant at Mandela Palace and lady maid of the ator

D

Del•o•vic Re•gion \\'del-ō-vik 'rē-jən\\ **Place** : the most populous area of Mandela City, located east of East Mystad Field and north of the Lodi Region

Der•ite \\'der-īt\\ **Race** : an ancient people who inhabited Koria prior to the rule of Vritesse Kamalee. The Derite language is composed primarily of words, combined with gestures and magic. Creators of the Koria Caverns, the race was all but wiped out by a supposed volcanic event in the Caverns in the second year of Kamalee's rule

de•rox•is \\dē-'roks-is\\ **Nature** : carnivorous plant species that grows in the Eternity Pools west of Koria. Deroxis appears liquid in its resting state, but produces large leaf-like appendages as it captures its prey. Deroxis devours its prey slowly, sometimes over a period of centuries

Dro•la•na \\drō-'lô-nə\\ **Place** : planet in the Drol system located approximately 92.9 million miles from its solar body. Known by its inhabitants as Earth

E

East Mys•tad Field \\'ēst 'mis-tad 'fēld\\ **Place** : the large meadow bordering Mandela Palace on the East side

en•trust•ed \\en-'trust-ed\\ **General Term** : life companion

Ex•alt•ing \\eg-'zôlt-ēŋ\\ **Event** : the process in which an entrusted of a member of the noble Borloc Family takes on the Borloc traits of black hair and blue eyes

F

frol•nisk \\'frōl-nisk\\ **Animal** : small, furry creature of the Sybran. Frolnisk are very common, due to the large number of pups born in each litter. Some frolnisk litters can have as many as 200 pups. Domesticated frolnisk have become common pets particularly in the areas surrounding the Sybran.

G

ghan•den•tel \gan-'den-tel\ **General Term : 1:** term used to swear a curse on someone. **2:** the ultimate insult

glow stone \'glō 'stōn\ **Nature :** stones found in the area surrounding the Koria Caverns that have a natural luminescence. Glow stones are one of the required elements for a Trysta altering

gra•zixs \grô-'zēks\ **Nature :** valuable gem stone found in the mines in the Lodi Region

gree•lan bark \'grē-lən 'bärk\ **Nature :** the bark from the Swinging Trees in the Sybran Forest. Greelan bark is a required element for a Trysta altering, and has calming and pain relieving properties

I

in•hib•it•or \in-'hib-it-ər\ **Weapons & Defense :** object used to reverse the effects of a receptor

K

Kor•i•a \'kōr-ē-ə\ **Place :** located south of Westrim and the Castine and Lodi regions, Koria is home to the Trysta Empire. Koria encompasses the Bogs of the Sybran Forest, Trysta Palace, the Eternity Pools, Koria Major and the Koria Caverns. The region is said to have mystical properties, but this may be attributed to the powers possessed by the Trystas

L

Lo•di Re•gion \'lō-dī 'rē-jən\ **Place :** geographically the smallest area of Mandela City. The Lodi Region is primarily farmland and was established after the farms of Anisia Mystad were abandoned

Lor Man•del•a \'lôr man-'del-ə\ **Place :** planet in the Lorma system located approximately 90.6 million miles from its solar body. The planet on which we live

M

Man•del•a Ci•ty \man-'del-ə 'si-tē\ **Place :** first city of Lor Mandela encompassing Mandela Palace, East Mystad Field, the Anisia Mystad Region, the Delovic Region, the Castine Region, the Lodi Region and Mystad Lake and surrounding meadows. The Lor Mandela world governmental center

Man•del•a Pal•ace \ man-'del-ə 'pal- əs\ **Place :** home of the ruling Borloc family and the High Ruler, ator and all atons and atohs.

Mys•tad Lake \'mis-tad 'lāk\ **Place :** the lake adjacent to Mandela Palace

O

O•bee•o, o•bee•o, \'ō-bē- ō\ **1 : Game :** game where two or more opponents attempt to catch a free-flying crystal encrusted disk while it is glowing **2 : General Term :** the crystal-encrusted disc used for the Obeeo game. This disk flies on its own in unpredictable patterns

P

por•tal \\'pôr-təl\\ **Weapons & Defense :** doorway to another world. Can only be created by a Shadow Squanki

R

re•cep•tor \\rē-'sep-tər\\ **Weapons & Defense :** Trysta object used to transport non-Travelers between worlds. The number of receptors needed to transport varies depending upon distance between worlds. All Trystas receive a supply of receptors at age seven

ry•nolt \\'rī-nōlt\\ **Animal :** large predatory animal primarily found in the Sybran Forest, but also in other forested regions. Distinguishing features include two serpent-like heads atop elongated necks; thick, muscular equine body; and long razor-sharp teeth. Rynolts have innate senses of smell and hearing. They are related to the calandry of the Northern High Forests

S

Sha•dow Dwell•er \\'sha-dō 'dwel-ər\\ **Race :** race descended from the Shadow Squanki (also referred to as Dwellers). Dwellers can fade in and out of shadows, have extra-sensory abilities, and can move at extraordinary speeds

Sha•dow Squan•ki \\'sha-dō 'skwôn-kē\\ **Race :** race of demure, magical creatures who can camouflage into their surroundings, create portals and, to a certain extent, control nature

slarp \\'slärp\\ **Animal :** fast-moving, worm-bodied brachycephalic (flat-faced) creature with mangy brown fur, excessive saliva and pungent breath. Highly adaptable, can be found in many regions of Lor Mandela. As slarps are herbivores, they are not considered dangerous, but can be highly offensive

spike dart \\'spīk 'därt\\ **Weapons & Defense :** weapon consisting of a glove holding thirty thin, yet strong, spikes
The spikes can be launched from the glove at a rapid rate of speed, or the weapon can be used in close range hand to hand combat. A fatal dose of poison is held in each spike and is released upon penetration into the target

Sum•mon•ing \\'sum-ən-ēŋ\\ **Event:** performed by a Trysta Heiress, the Summoning calls or summons the spirit of a living being. The summoning chant is "stoi cantara"

Sy•bran For•est \\'sī-bran 'fôr-əst\\ **Place :** the densely forested area to the west of the Anisia Mystad Region. The Sybran is abundant in wildlife and can be treacherous. The Bogs are located in the northwest quadrant of the Sybran

T

tran•sen•dar \\tran-'sen-där\\ **Place :** buildings that house the records, books and reference materials of Lor Mandela. Transendars for each region are controlled by the regional governments

trans•port \\'tran-spôrt\\ **Event :** when a Trysta heiress transfers herself from one place to another instantaneously. A transport is achieved by the heiress running and announcing the location in which she would like to go

T (cont.)

Tra•vel•er \\'tra-vəl-ər\ **Race** : sub-race of the Trystas, Travelers can travel between worlds unaided

Try•sta \\'tri-stə\ **Race** : **1.** The highly-magical race that occupies Koria. **2.** A matriarchal people, led by the vritesse

tur \\'tər\ **General Term** : teacher or instructor of royal persons

V

vri•tesse \vri-'tes\ **Hierarchy** : The matriarchal leader of the Trysta race, who holds all of the powers available to a Trysta. The vritesse is equal in rank to the ator

vys•tor•an \vis-'tôr-an\ **Weapons & Defense** : small disk containing a combination of chemical poisons that are fatal on contact. The red vystoran covering acts as a protective barrier, but once the barrier is compromised and the poisons
are released, death is almost immediate. Developed by Ryannon of Brashnell for law enforcement officials

vys•tor•an sleeve \ vis-'tôr-an 'slēv\ **Weapons & Defense** : long, metal, tube-like weapon in which vystorans are loaded and shot at the velocity necessary to rupture their protective covering on impact. Developed by Ryannon of Brashnell for law enforcement officials

W

West•rim \\'west-rim\ **Place** : Territory west of the North Mountains. Although Westrim is primarily a farming community, its location between Brashnell to the north and Koria to the south make it a strategic military location in times of war